Junkyard Dog

A Hellhounds Novel

Katja Desjarlais

TULE
PUBLISHING

Dedication

For my mom,
who encourages me
every step of the way.

And for my dad,
who will receive
a G-rated version of this book.

Acknowledgments

I would be remiss if I didn't open with an enormous thank-you to my agent, Sharon Belcastro, for yanking me from the slush pile, pushing me into the publishing world, and instructing me to write more books.

Alongside her is my husband, Mark, for providing me with nouns when my brain was unable, and for siding with Sharon when my procrastination attempts become excessive. You've been my rock and partner for close to twenty years, and there's no one on earth or in the underworld I would rather stand back-to-back with.

I would like to thank my children, for attending to my health by ensuring I never sit down to write long enough to develop circulation issues. And Marbles, our cat, who is never on the right side of any door.

I'd also like to give a huge thank-you to my editor, Lee Hyat, who was wonderfully supportive with her encouragement and suggestions, to the amazing team at Tule Publishing for shining up *Junkyard Dog*, and to Ravven for the incredible cover art.

And, of course, my friends. My bestest bud Jennifer for being my cheerleader, my beta readers Rheyna and Colleen for texting me at all hours with their reactions, and the wonderful Guthrie staff who fed me treats and fresh bread while cheering me on.

If you meet the Black Dog once, it shall be for joy; if twice, it shall be for sorrow; and the third time shall bring death.

—W.H.C. Pynchon

Chapter One

ALEX ECHIDNA GLANCED down at his speedometer as he hit the highway, his foot heavy on the gas pedal. "I've picked up stale scents at every tourist trap in the region, so the guy's definitely not a local."

"Perhaps narrowing your search to the temporary accommodations in the area would be a better use of time," Ryan suggested, his voice crackling through the phone's speaker as Alex drew closer to the north entrance of Joshua Tree National Park. "The territory is too large to effectively patrol alone."

Rolling his eyes at his older brother's recommendation, he slowed his approach to the park and scanned the darkness for signs of life. "If that's your subtle way of saying Bo should join me out here, no. I have enough on my plate without adding his drunken ass into the mix."

Ryan's resigned sigh told Alex all he needed to know about his twin's current condition. The eldest of the trio by a decade, Ryan usually took the reins whenever Bo's impulsiveness took a dangerous turn, Ryan's levelheadedness a good counterbalance to the wilder twin's inclinations. "Call

1

me if you manage to find the guy."

The phone went black and he pulled over onto a gravel road, killing the engine before tucking his cell and wallet into the glove box and getting out, stretching his arms over his head and rolling out his neck.

The hunt for the cursed Pirithous bloodline was taking its toll on all of them, centuries of tracking down the descendants of Hades's enemy culminating in what they hoped would be the final quest, the last task for Cerberus before they could return to the underworld and resume their place at the heels of their master and mistress.

At least, that was what drove Ryan, the oldest of the brothers and the one most bonded to their master.

Alex tugged his black shirt over his head and tossed it onto the front seat of his SUV, shaking his blond hair out of his eyes as he undid the fly of his shredded jeans.

Alex was decidedly less determined to return to the banks of the Styx to continue his centuries of subservience at the whim of a god and his overly indulged wife. He tracked the Pirithous because it was his job, a curse spat in a moment of anger by a vengeful god with impulse control issues.

Yeah, he was bitter.

Glancing around once more before kicking his boxers off, he nudged the door shut and dropped to his knees, the transformation of his body into that of a hellhound complete within seconds.

The wind whipped up, sending a flurry of sand and

odors across his muzzle, his ears zeroing in on the gentle movements of a rabbit nearby. Filtering through the stench of gasoline and rotting animal carcasses, he lowered his nose to the ground and set off across the park, dodging the chollas with their prickly spines that were a bitch to remove.

Tracking his late-night snack, he darted along the sand, wholly engulfed in the hunt for the elusive rabbit that had gone still among the brush. The scent grew stronger while he crept eastward, the heart rate of the animal thumping in his ears as it grew brave enough to dart out of the safety of its hiding place, kicking up dust when it tore across the paved road to the rockier terrain on the other side.

The predator in him went into full gear and he took off after the rabbit, completely oblivious to everything but his meal until the glare of headlights blinded him, the screech of brakes ringing in his ears as the car barreled into him and knocked him off his feet.

Ignoring the burst of pain in his ribs, he scrambled up, rabbit long forgotten when the driver flung his door open and the stench of the bloodline assaulted his senses.

Pirithous.

Staggering across the terrain, Alex doubled back to the north entrance to call it in.

✕

CHARLOTTE ROSE TO her feet, brushing the fine sand from

her pants. "And which way did you say this dog was heading?"

The shaken man leaned against his shredded tire and looked to the north. "That way," he muttered, flexing his bruised hands. "I've never seen a dog that big. Or that fast."

The crunch of stones alerted her to her coworker's approach, the lights of the truck coming into view around the bend. "I'll be right back with some water," she assured the injured tourist, bending to pat his knee. "And we'll get a tow truck out here as quick as we can."

She jogged over to the white truck and yanked the passenger door open. Max, her partner on the graveyard shifts, leaned his head back against his seat. "High or drunk?" He sighed, his mirrored sunglasses hiding his dark eyes.

"Neither," she hissed, climbing across the passenger seat to reach the water bottles in the back. "Another black dog sighting. Same as the last two." She pulled a bottle from the floor triumphantly. "Straighten your hat and come sit with the poor guy while I check for prints. And take off those stupid sunglasses. It's pitch black outside."

Although he muttered incoherently for a moment, Max slammed the truck door and made his way to her side, his brimmed ranger hat neatly leveled. "So a big black dog, eh? You sure it wasn't a cougar or a bear? We get the odd one around here."

The man's head shook slowly, his eyes fixed on the ground. "Definitely a dog." He swiveled his head toward the beam of her flashlight. "You're not going out there, are you?"

"Chuck's just checking for prints," Max answered, kicking gently at the crumpled front end of the man's car. "You really did a number on this."

"Yeah," the man murmured, taking a long sip of water. "I clipped the dog before I bottomed out on the ridge."

She turned her flashlight toward the front of the vehicle. "A hit?" she called out as she closed in on her target. "Max, I'm going to take a few pictures while you call in a tow truck."

"Yes, ma'am," Max replied, tapping the tip of his hat before he returned to his truck to call in the accident.

Focusing on the misshapen indent, she balanced her flashlight between her knees and began snapping pictures of the small tufts of black fur embedded in the cracks of the plastic grill. She reached out, pulling a few of the long hairs out and running them lightly between her fingers.

"Definitely not a bear," she muttered, bringing the beam of the light closer to the vehicle to assess for blood. "How far back down the path were you when you hit it?"

"Right there," the tourist replied, pointing a few feet away. "It didn't even hesitate, just got up and kept running." He looked back out into the darkness. "Hope it's not too badly hurt."

She glanced over the terrain and smiled at the man. "You probably just spooked it. How about we get you into Max's truck to relax until the tow arrives?"

✕

MAX PASSED A sandwich over to Charlotte, the corners squished flat in his large hands. "Why do you always put them in *my* truck? Why can't they wait it out in yours?"

"Because you need to work on your people skills, and a captive audience is better than nothing." She grinned, biting into the offering and grimacing. "Ew. Mustard."

"Gimme that," he grumbled, snatching the sandwich from her hands and passing over another. "Ham and cheese, no mayo, no mustard, no butter, no taste. Just like you prefer, your highness."

Reclining her seat a fraction, she peered into the blackened landscape of Joshua Tree. "You'd think if someone's dog got loose, they'd have notified the station or something," she mused. "Or someone would have seen it during daylight. If it's covering this much ground, how has no one gotten a good look at it?"

"Because it's a cougar," he replied, his mouth full. "Like you."

"I'm not a cougar," she protested, whacking his arm with her hat. "I'm barely thirty. And it's not a cougar. The fur on that grille was consistent with dog fur. Same coarseness."

"Then it's a dog."

She crumpled the sandwich wrapping in her hand. "I'm coming back tomorrow to check out the area in daylight."

Easing his sunglasses back on, he grinned over at her and

started the truck. "Okay there, super ranger. I'm spending my first day off in bed, out of the sand, and out of the heat. But you do you and give me the CliffsNotes version on Wednesday."

"I don't even know why you wear those at night," she grumbled, straightening her bun and setting her hat to rights. "You look silly."

"I look badass. Like the Terminator."

✕

ALEX MUTED THE television and groaned as he rolled over to find his ringing phone, his broken ribs protesting every move. "Hey."

"How bad is it on your end?"

He rolled his eyes at his brother's barked question. "It's all good," he reassured Ryan, balancing his phone on his shoulder while he inched off his bed to recheck his injuries over in the small bathroom. "You getting much of an echo?"

Ryan muttered under his breath for a moment. "Bo's too wasted to feel much of anything. I caught the initial impact, but not much outside of a dull ache now."

Skimming his fingers over his skin, he angled his side toward the mirror. "Two broken, a bit of bruising, and a bonus grille imprint as a souvenir."

"And a second sighting," Ryan pointed out, the frustration in his voice coming through loud and clear.

"I'm on it," he said, gingerly tapping at one rib that didn't look properly aligned. "I'll walk the trail tomorrow to clear anything questionable, then head back after work to pick up the scent. Brace yourself."

Ryan let out a sigh of exasperation, speaking through gritted teeth in anticipation of the discomfort that was about to blast through the bodies of the Cerberus brothers. "We can be out there within the week if you need us."

Pressing against the misplaced rib, he pushed it into place with a grunt, Ryan echoing him through the speaker. "Until I find his base, there's no point."

"And now we're up against a second sighting," Ryan reminded him.

"Whatever," he muttered, rifling through his medicine cabinet for a bandage and coming up empty-handed. "Fucking sedans." He eased his shirt back down. "If the guy stays local, I'll track him, okay? You know that. Tell Bo to call me sometime this week."

"Will do. Touch base tomorrow night."

He fumbled the phone, cursing as it hit the floor of his trailer.

He had a few hours of darkness left. Enough time to return to the scene and establish the exit route the man had taken.

Few campers noticed him as he walked through the grounds to the gates and crossed the highway. He took his time climbing the small ridge at the perimeter of the park, listening in the stillness for intruders before he stripped down and stood naked in the faint wind until the transformation dropped him to all fours.

He arched his head up to scent the air.

Diesel.

Gasoline.

Chuffing in disgust, he began his leisurely descent into the park to hunt. The cooler nighttime temperatures brought out the wildlife of the desert, the skittish rabbits and the lone coyotes being his favorites. He crossed the rough terrain slowly, his ribs protesting as his paws navigated the brush. The vastness of the barren land made hunting more difficult than in the forested regions of the northern states, but the challenge of stalking prey without natural cover appealed to him.

As did the distance from his brothers.

Picking up the scent of another rabbit, he made his way across the uneven ground, taking special care to avoid the chollas that were interspersed with the less problematic plant life. The path of his prey was fresh, the tracks in the sand clean and unblemished. The sedan temporarily forgotten in favor of a fresh meal, he sped up his pace, his predatory side taking hold as he closed in on the small animal.

"You promised me an hour. It's only been twenty minutes."

Alex flattened himself to the ground as a woman's voice carried on the wind, mentally cursing the spines of a cholla digging into his belly.

"Fine, fine," a surly male voice relented, pulling Alex's attention to a truck parked in the distance, its lights and engine off. "You've got forty minutes until sunrise, and then you're buying me breakfast. Anything I want. Now get those damn binoculars off me."

Keeping his attention on the white truck, Alex inched across the landscape and listened in on the pair, squinting in the dim light of the quarter moon to read the decal plastered on the body of the vehicle.

US Park Ranger.

He cringed, flattening down a little further.

Of course the hit had drawn their attention.

His work was about to become much more difficult.

"It has to be out here," the woman muttered. "The damage to that guy's car was too great for an animal to escape unscathed. Whatever it was could be injured. Hurt." Her voice rose as the man grumbled something unintelligible. "Yeah, well, if it does make it to one of the campsites and attacks someone, you're doing the paperwork."

Alex bowed his head, keeping the glint of his eyes hidden from the prying gaze of the binocular-wielding park ranger. The slope of the stretch of land he was on was wide open for observation from the truck's vantage point, his movements easily visible if he was too quick or rose from the minimal camouflage of the brush.

A stalemate, with the sun's appearance threatening on

the horizon.

As the first illumination of the desert approached, the truck's engine revved to life.

"What the hell, Max?" the woman hissed, her window rolling up.

"We have drive time and clocking out to account for," the man explained, the red lights of the truck's brakes lighting up the sand. "And you owe me a shit-ton of bacon and eggs, Chuck."

The truck rocked as it pulled off the slope and onto the gravel route used by the more adventurous drivers. The voices disappeared with the rumble of the engine until neither the truck nor the lights were visible in the slow arrival of the morning sun.

Rising carefully, he backed up over the slope and eased his way toward the more inhospitable territory. He skirted the low ridge, ignoring the prickly stems embedded in his fur while he made his way to his backpack, the scrawny rabbit meal long forgotten while he put as much distance between the humans and himself as he could.

Chapter Two

CHARLOTTE TUGGED AT the hem of her gray shorts as she made her way alongside the large tracks still visible on the sandy plateau. She paused to photograph a print next to her hiking boot before kneeling and pushing her hands into the ground to mark the length of the animal's stride.

"Is there something interesting down there, or do you need to be airlifted out of here?"

Falling gracelessly onto her elbows, she scrambled to right herself. "Interesting. No." She shook her head, brushing the sand from her auburn ponytail and glancing up. "No, I'm fine. Just looking."

The tall backpacker grinned down at her from a small incline in the brush a dozen meters away. "Wanted to make sure," he called, maneuvering his way across the terrain. "Watching out for my fellow hiker and all that."

"Appreciate it." She smiled, tightening the straps on her backpack and putting her phone into the pocket of her shorts. "You doing the Lost Horse Mine trail?"

"That's the goal," the man replied, shaking his long blond hair out before feeding it through the opening of his ball cap and readjusting his sunglasses. "Are you heading that way, too?"

Only if I can walk behind you and stare at that ass.

Her cheeks reddened at the invasive thought that had sprinted through her head. "No. Just checking out this stretch today," she lied, averting her eyes and taking a long sip of water to distract herself from the visible cut of the hiker's abs under his shirt.

The man pursed his lips and shrugged. "Damn. I could've used the company." He stepped closer to her, his hand extended. "Alex. You know, if they need to identify my body at any point."

And lucky for you, I've got that body memorized from top to bottom already. All six-foot-six of it.

"Charlotte," she mumbled, looking past his shoulder as her traitorous mind flipped through a barrage of flirty and filthy replies. "Watch your footing in the third mile and stay away from the chollas."

Chollas? Really?

A look of amusement crossed Alex's face, as though he had heard the smut her head was spinning. He gave a quick nod and turned toward the mine, his long legs clearing ground at an enviable speed. "Nice to meet you, Charlotte," he called over his shoulder. "Good luck with your photography."

Rolling her eyes at her own awkwardness, she crossed her arms and watched as the man effortlessly made his way over the harsh landscape, his blond hair disappearing around the bend.

"Damn," she whispered under her breath, shaking the image of the hiker's smirking lips from her head. "Damn, damn, damn."

She waited until he was out of sight before she looked back down at the sand to resume her research, the massive paw prints scuffed out by large hiking boots.

"Damn," she whispered.

✖

ALEX ADJUSTED HIS pack, easing it to the left to relieve the growing discomfort of his broken right ribs. He leaned against the fence surrounding the mine shaft entrance and glanced around at the barren terrain.

"Fuck," he muttered, groaning at the realization he still had to make his way back. Wiping the sweat from his brow with the bottom of his shirt, he rolled his aching shoulders out and scanned the area for the quickest route back to his car.

Doubling back it is.

Keeping his eyes on the ground, he made his way through the winding trail, scuffing the sand as he passed the more ingrained paw prints he'd missed on his initial trek. With a water bottle in each hand, the pressure of his back-pack was reduced to a manageable, almost ignorable, pain.

Fucking sedans.

The imprint of the mesh grille was still visible on his skin, a carryover from his miscalculation the night before. Even the minor movement of his shirt while he walked was irritating, the fabric catching on his fresh wounds.

Determined to be out of the park before dusk, he kept his focus on eliminating the trail he'd left, erasing the prints one Miss Charlotte had found so fascinating.

Miss Charlotte with the short shorts and long auburn ponytail flecked with sand.

Yeah, that Miss Charlotte.

Miss Charlotte with the voice he had instantly recognized.

Scuffing out another print with his boot, he took a long sip of water.

Miss Charlotte was way too interested in sitting in trucks with binoculars and in photographing animal prints for Alex's comfort.

With a grunt, he hefted his pack back onto his shoulder and made his way to his SUV.

✕

MAX WAVED OFF the wad of bills Charlotte set on the bar. "No way, Chuck." He snorted, running a hand through his spiked brown hair. "I'm paying, so I'm picking."

She groaned and flopped forward dramatically. "Be

kind," she pleaded. "I've been up for twenty-four hours. I shouldn't even be here tonight."

"Two tequila," he called out as he nudged her knee with his own. "The others will be here after shift," he said, the nudging becoming more insistent the longer Charlotte ignored him. "Sit up and take the damn shot."

She lifted her head reluctantly, freezing as the bartender came into focus.

"Well, hey there, Miss Charlotte." The bartender grinned, tossing a cloth over his shoulder and sliding two shots of tequila across the bar. "Taking a break after a long day of just looking?"

A blush rose in her cheeks as her hands instinctively smoothed down her ponytail. "Oh, uh, hi. Alex, right?" she asked, straightening her back and looking up at the towering beast of a man. "How was the mine trail?"

Alex slipped Max's money into the till and smoothly slid the change toward him, his attention wholly on her. "Long and hard," he replied, tucking a stray strand of his blond hair behind his ear.

"That's what she said," Max whispered beside her, further firing her cheeks.

Amusement danced across Alex's face before his attention was caught by another customer.

"What the hell, Max?" she muttered, gripping the small glass of tequila. "Maybe you should be drinking a shot of shut-the-hell-up."

He snorted, lifting his glass toward her. "Oh, uh, hi, uh, Alex, uh," he mimicked. "I think I know why you can't get a date, Chuck."

She tossed her drink back, wincing as the alcohol burned down her throat and into her empty stomach. "Don't want to get a date," she corrected as a shiver ran through her. "I hate tequila every time I have it."

Slamming his empty shot glass on the counter, he looked pointedly at the hot bartender. "Yes?"

"That," she muttered, nodding toward Alex, "has fuckboy stamped on his forehead with another warning label on his ass. No."

Max rubbed his own forehead and grinned. "You know, just because guys like us are genetically blessed doesn't automatically make us cheating dogs."

Turning her back to Alex, she nodded toward the empty tables at the back of the lounge. "I've bought into that lie enough times, thanks. Let's go sit."

As their coworkers filtered into the bar and the music began to get louder, she kept her attention on the animated conversations surrounding her while her fellow rangers compared horror stories of past assignments. The women in their group had spotted Alex the moment they filed into the tavern, their conversations peppered with sly comments regarding the size of his hands and the fit of his jeans whenever he bent down to grab a beer from the bar coolers.

Not that she noticed.

She was busy keeping her back to the bar and, more importantly, to the bartender. Her weakness for dangerously pretty packages had given her enough emotional battle scars to last a lifetime.

She definitely hadn't noticed the way his shirt rode up when he reached for a wineglass.

Hadn't seen him playfully flex his arm for a group of elderly women at the back table, showing off the expanse of tattoos that disappeared under his sleeve.

And she definitely hadn't noticed how he leaned across her every time he brought another round of drinks to the table, inundating her with the scent of his intoxicating cologne.

"Chuck!" Max yelled over the din of music and conversation. "What do you want?"

She blinked a few times, her mind desperately sorting through the last remnants of discussion around the table.

"Yeah, *Chuck*," Alex's amused voice echoed behind her, "what do you want?"

"Uhhh…" She trailed off for a moment as her cheeks reddened again. "Nachos. No tomatoes, no chives, no sour cream, no—"

"Nachos, just cheese?" Alex offered as Max's barking laugh crossed the table.

"Yes, please," she confirmed, narrowing her eyes at Max in a death glare.

"My pleasure, Miss Charlotte."

✕

ALEX COULD HEAR the squeals of the women as he pushed through the kitchen doors and passed the food order over to the unimpressed cook and owner.

"Food cutoff's in ten minutes." The stocky man snatched the bill out of his hand and read it over. "Just cheese?"

"Picky eater," he replied, pulling a fry from a greasy bowl. "How long have these been sitting here, Thomas?"

"Two hours."

With a shrug, he scooped up the rest and gnawed through them. "That group of rangers come in here often?"

Thomas glanced back at the order. "Ah. The nachos are for Chuck. She likes the cheese layered. Max must be the steak sandwich, double garlic toast. Next time just note who it's for at the top of the bill."

"They a thing?" he asked, cracking the door open a sliver to scan the lounge. And to get a quick glimpse of Miss Charlotte. "Max and Charlotte?"

Thomas's eyes narrowed as he appraised Alex. "No. Why?"

"Just getting to know the locals." He grinned, pushing the door fully open.

Charlotte's back remained to him, just as it had all evening. The tantalizing blush of her cheeks had disappeared, her profile animated while she spoke rapidly with one of the younger women in the group. Leaning against the bar, he crossed his arms over his aching ribs and watched as she stood for a moment to adjust her low-slung jeans. Seemingly oblivious to the attention her movements were getting from several men in the lounge, she proceeded to fix the hem of her shirt before hooking her thumbs behind her and inelegantly tugging the band of her bra down. Apparently comfortable again, she flopped into her chair and smoothed her hair back.

"Alex!" Thomas yelled from the kitchen. "Order up."

THOMAS DOWNED A glass of water and joined Alex in his monitoring of the dance floor.

"Not a thing?" Alex reiterated wryly, nodding toward Max and Charlotte as they screamed and emoted their way through a Meatloaf song.

"Nah," Thomas replied, refilling his cup. "Stay on here for a few months and you'll see Max swing through with a new woman every two weeks. Chuck's been his best friend since she was transferred to the park last year." He side-eyed Alex. "She's a nice girl."

"I'm a nice guy," he muttered.

Thomas looked pointedly toward a table of return customers, college women impeccably dressed and manicured. The redhead had tracked him all evening, her knowing smirk giving away the night he'd spent with her.

"I'm still a nice guy," he insisted, tearing his eyes off the pair to settle a tab at the register. Flashing the women a smile, he pocketed the substantial tip, phone numbers, and rejoined Thomas. "Why haven't I seen the rangers in here before?"

Thomas hefted himself onto the counter. "Depends on shift schedules. Max and Chuck are on nights right now, so we'll be seeing them only on nights off until that changes."

Alex turned away from the dance floor and focused on preparing the bar for closing.

He had no interest in dating. Definitely no interest in dating a nice girl. Flings, one-night stands, booty calls—those were more his thing. Answering to someone else, being responsible for someone else—definitely not his thing. The idea of tying himself down to someone when he could be gone at any moment held no appeal, no matter how hot that someone looked when she was concentrating on loading a nacho chip with the perfect amount of cheese.

"Excuse me?"

He glanced up from the beer fridge. "Hey, Miss Charlotte. What can I do for you?"

Her cheeks flushed instantly, her dark brown eyes narrowing as she studied him. "I just want to settle up my tab." She glanced back for a moment, scanning the room. "And Max's, before he gets back to the table."

As he rose to his feet, she held out two bills and a wad of cash. "You're about five minutes too late." He grinned.

"That sneaky bastard," she muttered, shoving the money into her back pocket. "Now I'll be stuck making lunches for the next week." She smoothed her ponytail and tilted her head back, drawing his attention to the smooth skin of her neck. "I hate cooking."

"You know," he said, leaning on the bar to get just a little closer, "you could always swing by here on your way to work and pick up some of Thomas's sandwiches."

And maybe keep me company at the bar while you wait.

He straightened, pushing the thought to the back of his head.

Keeping company outside the bedroom was definitely not his thing.

Stepping back, she tugged at her shirt. "Yeah, maybe. Have a good night."

She walked back to the table, beelining straight for Max and wagging a stern finger. Alex knelt back down, his ribs protesting when he twisted around to grab a case of beer.

Yeah, he definitely didn't need to be keeping company with Miss Charlotte.

Chapter Three

MAX CLIMBED INTO Charlotte's truck, his mirrored sunglasses sitting on the brim of his hat and giving her a rare glimpse of his hazel eyes. "Slow night."

She passed him a peanut butter sandwich and nodded. "I only counted four tents on the west side. Two less than yesterday."

"I'm not eating that again," Max stated, tossing the sandwich onto the dash. "Gimme your radio."

Giving him the handheld, she snatched the sandwich and tucked it back into her bag. "You say I'm picky? Three nights of the same thing won't kill you, you know." She narrowed her eyes. "Who are you calling at two a.m.?"

Putting the call on speaker, he grinned. "The station," he proclaimed, shushing her with the wave of his hand. "Yeah, James? Can you patch me through to the tavern?"

She frowned before her mind connected the dots. "No! No way! Hang up!"

"Too late," he sang as the telltale ring of a phone echoed in the cab. "I overheard Alex's suggestion Monday night and figured you were probably too chickenshit to go in there and feed us properly."

She lunged at the handpiece, his long arm holding her back as the dial tone ended and a familiar voice came over the speaker.

"Tom's Tavern."

With a Cheshire cat smile on his face, he angled his head away from her. "Hi, Alex. It's Max from the other night."

"Hey, man," Alex replied, a touch of confusion in his tone. "What can I do for you?"

"Not for me," Max said, placing his body between her and the radio. "Chuck has something she wants to ask you."

She dropped her face into her hands, shaking her head frantically.

"Charlotte? Yeah, of course." The music of the lounge drifted through the truck. "Fire away."

Swatting blindly at Max, she lifted her head. "Uh, yeah. Um, I, well, we—"

Max rolled his eyes. "Do you guys do delivery?" he called out. "I'm in the mood for a hoagie and Chuck needs a lot of meat...*ouch*...a grilled cheese sandwich like only Thomas can do." He glared at her. "Stop pinching me."

The low laugh that came through the speaker caught her attention and she froze, midpinch. "I'm off in ten. How far into the park are you?"

Max went on the defensive, sticking his elbow out to block her attack.

"We're fifteen minutes north of the south entrance," she

panted, breathless from the effort it took to pay Max back.

"Be there within the hour." Alex chuckled before the line disconnected.

"Oh, my god," Max howled, throwing his head back. "That was so painful! Uh, um, uh, um. Damn, Chuck."

She fixed her hat in the mirror, running her fingers across the brim. "I hate you," she stated clearly. "I hate you with every ounce of my being."

"No stammering through that statement, huh?" he teased. "Seriously, though, any guy willing to drive food out here in the middle of the night can't be too bad. Think of it as a test."

With her lips tight, she glared out the window. "This isn't a test. This is a pity-feed." She refused to look at her best friend. Her traitor of a best friend. "I can't believe you're making him do this."

"Oh, Chucky. I'm not making him. You heard him. He was game right out of the box."

RECON.

Nothing more than a little recon work.

Alex glanced over at the Styrofoam containers on the passenger seat of his SUV.

Recon work, a hoagie, and a grilled cheese sandwich with double cheese, fries, and seven packets of vinegar.

He turned off the highway onto the narrow road of the park and slowed his speed.

Four nights.

He'd even taken an extra shift for Thomas on his Wednesday off in case Charlotte decided to make good on his suggestion.

Yeah. Recon.

His headlights illuminated the road, providing just enough light to avoid veering off into the soft sand. For a brief moment, he contemplated covering the remaining ground on foot.

Cholla in the underbelly.

Scratching at his stomach, he tossed the idea out of his head. The hassle of stripping down, packing, transforming, and going through it all in reverse while staying out of sight of Miss Charlotte and her binoculars wasn't worth the ten minutes he'd save.

Besides, his ribs were still hurting like a bitch.

The lights of the national park ranger truck blared across his retinas as he rounded a bend in the road. Pulling off to the side, he slid the carefully packed meals into his backpack and got out.

"My savior!" Max yelled out to him, jumping out of the passenger side and breaking into a jog. "She tried to feed me knockoff peanut butter on stale bread again." He began rifling through Alex's bag, pulling out two large trays. "I'll eat these on the way. Duty calls."

As Max ran off toward a truck in the distance, he made his way over to the white truck and rapped his knuckles on the passenger window. "Delivery for Miss Charlotte," he called, opening the door and setting his bag on the seat. "Thomas sent extra vinegar and…and…"

And…

He could feel the precise moment his brain short-circuited.

It was the moment the scrutinizing dark eyes lit up at the words *extra vinegar*.

He cleared his throat. "Extra vinegar and napkins."

Charlotte's cheeks flushed as she pulled the Styrofoam tray onto her lap. "You really didn't have to do this," she said, reaching into the back seat. "But thank you."

Gripping the roof of the truck, he leaned in and looked around. "Anytime. Mind if I get in or is there some park ranger law I don't know about?"

"Probably," she muttered. "Yeah, you can get in. I'm due to be written up soon anyway." She opened her wallet and began pulling bills out.

"Put that away," he barked, reaching under his seat to adjust the leg room. "My treat for our local heroes in, what is that, gray and khaki?"

With her eyes still frustratingly averted, she scrunched her nose. "Not my best colors, but yeah. Brown hikers, too." She lifted her foot to reveal the practical, unappealing footwear.

"But you have a badge and that's pretty cool," he pointed out. "So what's on the docket for tonight? High-speed desert chases? Tracking poachers?"

She swallowed and laughed, her eyes meeting his for a millisecond before they dropped again. "I'm pretty much doing it right now. Once I finish eating, I'll drive the main pathways, check on the campers in the west grounds, and then loop back to the station in time to clock out."

Remembering his internal rationale for contacting the woman again, he looked out into the blackened desert. "What about animals? Any of those out here?"

With her attention on carefully opening the small packet of vinegar, her dark brows knotted. "Other than the coyotes and jackrabbits, we have a good amount of bighorns around here. The odd cougar." She glanced out the window. "A stray dog here and there."

Stray.

Whatthefuckever.

Ignoring the unintentional slight to his ego, he pressed for more. "Bet you get a few owners out here up in arms about their missing poodles and cockapoos."

"Hmm." She hummed, drenching one fry in vinegar at a time before lifting it to her mouth. "I'm heading up the search for one out there right now. Big guy. Probably a Great Dane or a mastiff, though we've had no reports of missing pets," she mused, licking her lips and testing his resolve to remain on total recon when the simple movement amped his heart rate. "A tourist clipped the poor thing with his car last week, so who knows where the pup holed up."

On my lumpy mattress with a bottle of Tylenol and a World War II documentary.

"What do you do in cases like that? Injured animals, I mean."

She smirked, a slightly guilty look crossing her face. "We send the wild ones to a rehabilitation center, but if a pet owner doesn't come forward, we're supposed to hand them over to an animal rescue."

Catching the slight hitch in her words, he cocked a brow and reached over to snatch a fry. "Supposed to?"

"We're legally obligated to place the animal with the proper agencies. So the last cat I found may or may not live with me now." She grinned, examining her fries. "Her name may or may not be Marbles. And if I find that poor dog, I may or may not bring him home, too."

CHARLOTTE WATCHED IN her peripheral vision as Alex bent forward slightly and rested his elbows on his knees. "I don't think it's something I'd be fired for," she quickly added, fighting the urge to watch his biceps as they tightened. "Not like drawing a weapon without just cause or anything."

His jaw flexed in the dim light of the cab as he pursed his lips. "No, of course not." He finally chuckled. "I have a lot of respect for animal rescue." He smirked and tilted his head, his blond hair falling into his eyes. "So, you like dogs?"

"Doesn't everyone?" she countered, passing what was left of her meal his way.

"You'd be surprised," he muttered, accepting the container and diving into the vinegar-soaked fries. "How the hell do you have any taste buds left after eating this? I mean, damn, girl. What the—"

Blinding headlights appeared suddenly as a vehicle spun around the bend and barreled straight toward them, braking into a cloud of dust. An unnatural snarl echoed in her ears, her own voice catching in her throat for a moment before her brain caught up with the gait of the driver while he strode through the beams. Throwing her door open, she jumped out of the truck and leapt onto the man, yanking his arm roughly behind him and flipping him onto his back as Alex appeared at her side.

"Dammit, Chuck." Max coughed, struggling to get back up and glaring at her when she slammed her shoulder into his to keep him down. He arched his head back to grin at Alex. "You two behaving yourselves?"

Alex shook his head in disbelief, his eyes flicking between Charlotte and Max. "I don't know if I should be impressed or terrified."

Her chest heaving from the exertion, she gave one final smack to Max's ribs and rose off him, dusting the sand from her clothes. "Sorry," she panted, kicking a little extra dirt onto her partner as he got to his feet. "Max thinks he's funny."

"I'm a fucking riot." Max coughed again, untucking his shirt to check for damage. "You've gotten faster." He turned to Alex. "Figured you could use a little demonstration of what Chuck can do to you if you try anything funny."

Her cheeks flamed as her lips tightened into a thin line.

"Message received," Alex replied, stepping closer to her. "On that note, I think I better get my ass home. Swing by the tavern before work tomorrow if you have time."

"Thanks for dinner," she ground out, her muscles still tense from the adrenaline rush. She continued to glare at Max while Alex disappeared down the dark road to his SUV. "I'm going to kill you."

Max gave a friendly wave to Alex as he flipped around and disappeared down the road. "I know guys like him. Young. Hot. Completely on their game," he said cheerfully, shaking the sand from his hair and pulling his hat back on. "I am guys like him." He bent to scoop her hat from the ground and handed it to her.

"That was so embarrassing," she seethed, smacking her dusty hat against her leg. "Why would you do that?"

He tossed his arm over her shoulder. "To throw the player off his game, of course. Make sure he knows messing with you isn't a good idea." He paused. "And it was funny."

✕

ALEX PULLED INTO his parking stall, killed the engine, pulled his phone from his pocket, and dialed his brother.

"Bo, honey," a woman mumbled sleepily, "phone's for you."

"'Sup?" Bo's gravelly voice was heavy with exhaustion or booze.

Probably both.

"Hey," he said quietly. "You talk to Ryan this week?"

Bo yawned loudly, the rustling of sheets transmitting through the phone. "Yeah, yeah. Midsized white guy with a goatee and a sedan. You good?"

"Just a few broken ribs," he replied, pressing on them to assess the healing. "I've got a question for you."

"Fire away," Bo grumbled.

"You ever date a woman who's tougher than you?"

Chapter Four

"CAN'T HIDE IN there forever!"

Charlotte tossed her TV remote onto the sofa and stomped to her door, flinging it open with a lethal combination of annoyance and exhaustion. "Do you mind?" she hissed, glancing down the halls in anticipation of irate neighbors.

"Good morning, Sleeping Beauty." Max smiled, pushing his way into the small apartment and flopping into the recliner.

"Get out."

He flipped the chair open, crossing his arms behind his head. "I will. Once you're dressed and beautified and, ugh, showered." He made a production of looking her up and down, his nose wrinkled in disdain. "You look like you got off work and fell facedown in a plate of toast."

Dropping onto the sofa, she grabbed the remote and turned up the volume. "I did just get off work and now I get two Max-free nights before I have to be civil to you again." She locked a dead glare on him. "Don't you have a date?"

"That's tomorrow. Tonight you're coming out with us

for some wings, beer, and more rambling stories from what's-her-face. You know who. The new one from Montana." He shuddered. "I need you to cockblock that one for me."

She snorted, keeping her eyes glued to the television until Max stood up and placed himself directly in her line of sight.

"Come on, Chuck," he warned. "We're heading over to the Washout, so there's no excuse for you to ditch out. Get. Up."

Sighing in defeat, she rolled off the sofa and hoisted herself to her feet. "I still hate you."

He snatched the remote and hip-checked her down the hall before he settled in to wait. His laughter carried over the rush of the shower water, earning a stern shushing from her and a thumping foot from the apartment above. By the time she was ready to go, she was certain she'd be coming home to an eviction notice.

Giving her an exaggerated once-over, he stalked around her. "Cougar on the prowl," he purred, checking out the black leather pants she'd paired with an off-the-shoulder pewter crop top. "I'd consider doing you."

"Ha!" she scoffed, tugging her heeled sandals on. "Because that's why I'm dressed up. To become a consideration for your man-whore self."

He passed over her purse as they walked out of the apartment, adjusting the collar of his black button-down and smoothing it over his chest. "Just saying you look kick-ass.

Much better than the glaring psychopath you turn into every time a certain bartender is in the area."

Her eyes narrowed. "Well, you sure did your best to make sure that'll never happen again," she muttered, swinging the door to Max's truck open.

"Can you blame me?" He laughed. "It's weird seeing you crushing on a guy."

Buckling her seat belt, she leaned back and groaned. "I know, I know." She rolled her head to the side and looked at her best friend. "He's just so damn pretty, my brain kind of zaps whenever he looks at me with those weird eyes. He's one of those guys who's going to snag a rich sugar momma and jet-set around the world until she up and dies and leaves him with all her money and a Pomeranian." With the wrinkling of her nose, she played with the electric locks of the truck. "Add that to the fact he's gotta be a good five years younger than me, and I'm definitely meant to admire his ass from afar."

Max's barking laughter filled the cab. "I'll be your wingman tonight at the Washout if you block the Montana mumbler from me. We'll find you a good, not-as-pretty boy to get your mind off Alex's ass."

The Washout was packed for a Thursday, the college kids still on leave from school. Max pushed his way through the crowd with Charlotte in tow until they spotted their coworkers. Annexing two chairs from a neighboring table, she and Max joined the group and flagged the waitress over.

"See the group of guys on the far left of the dance floor?" he muttered into her ear. "What do you think of the tall one in the Blue Jays hat?"

She scanned the men over. "I like the one in the Spider-Man shirt," she whispered back, pulling her chair forward slightly to block the Montana mumbler from making eye contact with Max. "Tall, dark, and sober. Blue Jays guy looks sloshed already."

The pair made casual chatter with their group before hitting the dance floor, Max angling his back to Spider-Man to give her the opportunity to better check the guy out over his shoulder. By the third dance, Spider-Man was watching with subtle interest.

"We're hitting 'couple' territory here," he said, leaning in to avoid being overheard. "Follow me."

He walked to the edge of the dance floor, placed himself beside Spider-Man and the waitress taking orders, and pulled out his wallet. "Could I please get a Bud for me and a vodka Coke for my cousin?" he asked, slipping two twenties onto the woman's tray and looking her over in appreciation. "And three shots. Your choice." When the waitress smirked at him and nodded, he tilted his head toward her, his voice loud enough to be overheard by their target. "I have such a weakness for blondes."

"I can't believe there's one in the county you haven't scored yet." She grinned, catching Spider-Man's interest in their conversation. "When she comes back, I'll make myself scarce."

He frowned. "I'm not leaving you to sit alone."

Their target leaned in, his hands shoved deep into the pockets of his jeans. "Your cousin can sit with us," he offered, smiling over at her. "I'm Chris."

✕

CHARLOTTE PUSHED HER chair back and crossed her legs, laughing as Chris pushed his phone in front her to show off pictures of his iguana. "She's very pretty." When he launched into an excited recount of the lizard's latest escapades, she took a moment to look him over.

He was cute.

Sweet.

Dark eyes. Straight teeth.

Funny.

Passionate about lizards.

Logically, he was a good match for her.

Maybe the whole butterflies-in-the-stomach thing is overrated.

"You like this song?" he asked, motioning toward the dance floor.

She nodded, accepting his hand as he led her to join the mass of people bouncing and grinding to the music. She checked the bar for Max, laughing when he caught her eye and gave her a thumbs-up.

"So you and your cousin hang out here a lot?" Chris asked, stepping closer to her without missing a beat.

"Not really," she replied, forcing a smile when he turned an accidental brushing into a full-on hold on her hip. "We usually hit another place."

He smirked at her, pulling her a little closer. "Then I'm glad you came here tonight."

The butterflies finally appeared when she caught sight of a tall blond making his way across the dance floor.

✕

ALEX COULD DEFINITELY appreciate the gorgeous woman shimmying in front of him as the music pumped through the bar. Melanie, his date for the evening, was stunning. Perfectly polished and expensively dressed, she was everything Bo had recommended. And she'd placed herself directly in his line of sight at the tavern two nights prior, a welcome distraction from the woman he was forbidding himself to think about.

As Melanie turned around and backed up against him, her hips swaying against his, he dutifully placed his hands on her waist. The club was the last place he had wanted to end up that night. Spending his time off in the same environment he spent his working hours wasn't his idea of a break, but she had been adamant they head to the Washout after their dinner.

And he was nothing if not an accommodating date.

He glanced toward the bar, frowning as he recognized Max leaning against the counter, his attention on a busty blonde waitress. His eyes instinctively scanned the room for Max's partner, squinting in the low light for any sign of an auburn ponytail.

"Want to grab one more drink?"

His attention snapped back to his date, her heavily lined blue eyes looking up at him with suspicion. "Lead the way," he said, intertwining his fingers with hers to make up for his moment of distraction.

Melanie slithered in front of him, holding her hand out behind her as she ordered for both of them. He pulled a twenty out of his wallet and gave it to her, keeping his head turned slightly to avoid being recognized by Max.

Not that it mattered.

Drinks in hand, Melanie leaned against the counter and smiled up at him. "How about we head back to my place for a movie after this?" she suggested, wrapping her painted lips around her straw.

"Sounds good," he replied, knowing damn well where a movie would lead and finding himself surprisingly ambivalent to the idea.

"Good." She smirked. "Watch my drink. I'll be right back."

He stepped aside to let her pass and halfheartedly admired her ass as she walked away.

"What kind of cologne do you wear that makes this so easy for you?"

Cocking a brow, he turned toward Max. "What?"

Max nodded toward Melanie's retreating form. "I've been wheeling a waitress for the better part of the past two hours, and I'm pretty sure I'm going home empty again." He pointed his drink toward a table of women. "Every chick in that group is ogling you and would replace Miss Hotpants in a heartbeat. Now spill."

He took a swig of his beer. "Animal magnetism?"

"Where do I get my hands on some of that?" Max grumbled, looking at the dance floor. "So, Chuck's here."

His jaw tensed as he resisted the overwhelming urge to scan the club. "Oh, yeah?"

Max gestured to the dance floor. "Over there with Spider-Man."

Feigning disinterest, he tracked Max's arm and spotted the guy immediately. "I better find Melanie before she changes her mind," he muttered. "Good luck tonight."

His date's drink long forgotten, he wound his way through the crowd until he had a good view of Spider-Man.

And Charlotte.

The ponytail and T-shirt were gone, replaced by sleek auburn waves, tight leather pants, and a neckline that draped off her shoulder, the fabric clinging to her figure.

He took another long drink as he watched her chatter with the asshole in the Spider-Man shirt, her animated movements giving tantalizing flashes of her stomach before she paused and tugged the hem of her top down. When the guy put his hands on Charlotte's hips and pulled her closer to him, he took an involuntary step forward.

"Where's my drink?"

"Shit, sorry," he muttered, reaching for his wallet as Melanie crossed her arms and lifted a perfectly plucked brow. "I'll get you another."

"Never mind." She sighed in exasperation, wrapping her arm around his. "Let's just go."

THE LIGHT OF the fuller moon illuminated the desert floor, allowing Alex to easily maneuver through the brush as he tore across the sand.

Bo was an idiot.

Get over one woman by getting on top of another.

Dumbass advice from a dumbass.

As a hound, his sense of smell was unmatched. Even against the multitude of scents kicked up as he ripped over the hills, Melanie's expensive lotions and perfume clung to his skin. The chemical taste of her lipstick was still on his tongue.

The assaulting odor of latex intermingled with the unmistakable smell of sex.

So, this is what regret smells like.

He slowed to a trot as the sun peeked over the horizon. He lifted his nose to the sky and howled, mildly pleased when coyotes across the land joined in.

I could just stay out here for a decade or two. No women. No work. Just rabbits and beetles.

The idea was almost appealing, the thought of staying topside to avoid the servitude dealt to him through his birthright a harmless fantasy as he pawed over to his backpack and scanned the area for intruders before transforming. Focusing on imagining an existence untethered to the politics and games of the underworld pushed out the less pleasant images of a certain park ranger cozying up to some random guy.

A random guy that wasn't him.

Not that it mattered in the long run. Once he tracked the Pirithous and Cerberus dragged the bloodline down, he'd be right back to guarding Hades's realm, patrolling the banks of the Styx for another dozen centuries or so until his boss decided to send his junkyard dogs topside again to clean up another mess.

Shaking the thoughts from his mind, he tossed his backpack onto the passenger seat and started the engine. What little freedom he had up here was an illusion, and pretending it was anything else was a dangerous game.

Chapter Five

CHARLOTTE TURNED HER phone facedown and pushed her unfinished breakfast toward Max.

"Aren't you gonna answer that?" Max asked, shoveling a forkful of eggs into his mouth. "Might be your boyfriend."

"He's not my boyfriend," she muttered. "We went out for coffee once. Hardly even a date."

"So now you've had your fill?" he snorted. "What was wrong with the guy?"

She sat back against the fake leather of the booth. "Nothing. He's nice." She tore a piece off her napkin and rolled it into a ball. "He has an iguana named Stuart. It's a girl. She likes oranges."

He dropped his fork to his plate with a clank. "But?"

But he's vanilla.

With a shrug, she changed topics. "You heading out with the waitress tonight?" she asked.

"Yup. Days of phone tag and I'm finally in the zone," he stated triumphantly. "I'll swing her by the tavern after dinner."

She rolled her eyes and pulled her wallet out of her purse.

"Have fun with that. Call me later."

Unable to protest with his mouth full, Max waved her off and returned his attention to the cold scrambled eggs.

She climbed into her car and drove the winding streets back to her apartment. With Chris's missed calls piling up, she'd have to deal with it sooner rather than later.

She just wasn't good at the intricacies of dating.

Rather, she didn't care much for them.

At the age of thirty, she was well versed in the danger of falling for the smooth tongues of gorgeous men who caught the eye of every woman in the vicinity. Men who drew smiles and collected phone numbers while they shopped for groceries. Men who were passed drinks with whispered offers in the bars.

Men who stared down temptation day in and day out until they finally relented.

She didn't need to relive those experiences again. It had taken a few tries, but she'd learned her lesson. One year here, two years there, so much time and heartache wasted on bad boys who inevitably lived up to their reputations, their red flags waving in the breeze as they ripped out of her life, leaving her heart and bank account drained.

Her phone pinged loudly, earning a muffled moan as she fell onto her bed and checked the message. *"I'll consider it a personal favor if you size my date up tonight."*

Pursing her lips, she glared at Max's text before responding. *"We'll see."*

✕

"ALEX, MY MAN! Two tequilas, one Bud, and a paralyzer, please."

Alex glanced up at Max and grinned when he saw the blonde waitress tight to his side. "I'll bring it right out to you."

Max motioned for the woman to head over to the table of rangers that had been filtering into the tavern over the past hour. "Chuck here?"

"Is she supposed to be?" Alex asked, keeping his voice disinterested.

With a frown, Max looked around the room. "Yeah. Like, an hour ago. Well, I better get over there. If Chuck comes in, send her my way." He leaned in closer. "I need a woman's opinion on Steph."

Alex gave Max a quick salute and got to work on the drink order, refusing to look toward the door where Charlotte should be entering any moment.

Probably on the arm of the Spider-Man jerk.

His mood appropriately soured, he began loading a tray.

"You can take off after you run those out," Thomas barked out from the kitchen door. "It's slow enough for me to be up front and your overtime this week is going to put me out of business."

Nodding, he made his way to the table and began handing out drinks.

"I hate it when she does this," Max muttered absently, staring at his phone as he handed Alex a twenty. "Hey, Jerry. Who's on shift tonight?"

A short man across the table leaned forward. "Becky and Jonas. Why?"

Alex gave Max his change and began collecting the empty glasses from the table.

"What are the chances they're still in the station?" Max asked, rising from his seat.

Jerry took a sip of his beer. "Probably nil. Why?"

With his phone to his ear, Max walked toward the exit. Alex poked his head into the kitchen. "I'm out!" he called to Thomas, collecting his keys and wallet from under the till as he left.

Max stood outside, a lit cigarette hanging from his lip and his phone tight to his ear. "I don't know," he snarled. "Maybe start with the place of the sighting and go from th— Yeah, I get that you have to cover the west, but... Well, you're the asshole who told her about them, so yeah, you're the asshole who's going to go look. Yeah, I've had a few. Call me every time you hit the station." He looked over at him. "Aren't you working?"

"Thomas gave me the rest of the night off," he replied, refusing the offered cigarette. "There a problem?"

"Probably not," Max grumbled, taking a long drag. "Jonas let it slip that there've been a few more dog sightings this week, and now Chuck's gone off on one of her save-the-animals quests." He looked at his phone. "At midnight. Alone." He ran a hand through his hair and dropped his cigarette to the ground, crushing it with the toe of his shoe. "She's probably fine."

Alex's stomach knotted.

Dog sightings.

"Want me to take a quick tour through the east end?" he offered, his feet already moving him toward his SUV. "I know the area pretty well."

Max followed him as he opened the contacts list on his phone. "She'll stick to the paved roads in her coupe," he said, passing the phone to Alex. "Put your number in and I'll text you so you have mine. Phones don't work in the park, but if you loop around and see her...or don't...I'd appreciate a call once you hit the highway."

Alex entered his number quickly and leaned into the SUV to start it. "Last dog sighting?"

"Lower southeast quadrant," Max answered, firing off a text to him. "Probably eleven miles from here as the crow flies."

CHARLOTTE SCOOTED HIGHER onto the trunk of her car and leaned against the windshield, carefully setting her flashlight down. "Here, puppy, puppy, puppy," she cooed into the darkness, closing her eyes to give them a break.

"Come on, boy. If I don't catch you, someone else will. And they might not be as nice as I'm gonna be."

Her stomach was the only growling response.

Popping another saltine into her mouth, she sat back up and resumed scanning the moonlit desert with her binoculars.

She'd been at it for hours, sitting atop her car and calling into the night for a dog that was probably miles away by now.

But it was better than sitting in a lounge watching her crush play tonsil hockey with the stunning woman she'd seen clinging to Alex's arm at the Washout. The woman was supermodel-gorgeous and looked expensive.

"Show yourself, you damn dog," she muttered, her mood souring again as she used her flashlight to scan the immediate perimeter for snakes and other nocturnal creepy-crawlies.

Popping another cracker into her mouth, she froze when her ears picked up the yipping of a coyote to the south. Sliding the rustling saltine package away, she cocked her head as other coyotes joined the chatter from all directions.

The southern yipping stopped abruptly, replaced by a long, low howl. Every coyote in hearing distance joined in, their voices spreading through the park. She eased herself onto the roof of her car and slowly scanned the peaks and valleys of the terrain as the southern howl morphed into a territorial growl, silencing the others instantly. Lifting her binoculars back up, she zeroed in on a movement over the ridge three hundred yards southeast.

Rabbit.

A fast rabbit.

"Dammit," she whispered, fumbling her binoculars and cursing when they hit the ground.

✕

ONE BRAVE, OR stupid, coyote let loose another call into the night air and Alex lifted his nose to the sky to snarl a warning until quiet returned to the park.

He'd run the terrain for well over an hour, his SUV, clothes, and cell phone a good thirty miles away by now. With no sign of Charlotte near the Lost Horse Mine trail, he had ventured farther east toward the Keys, sticking as close to the paved roads as he could without being seen by a wayward tourist or determined hiker.

"Dammit."

His ears perked up when Charlotte's familiar voice carried on the breeze, stilling and listening as something thumped to the ground eight hundred yards to the north. The rockier terrain slowed his progress as he maneuvered toward the sound, his nose finally picking up her scent when he reached the apex of a ridge.

He sat and watched, unnoticed, as she slid off the hood of her small car and bent over to retrieve something. Cocking his head, he let out a snort of appreciation for the view, raising his ears when she jumped in surprise and spun toward him.

"Oh, my g—" she breathed, taking a step forward and zeroing in on him. "Woah. You are a big boy, aren't you?"

When she took another step off the road, he rose up and flattened his ears back.

"Okay, okay," she cooed, backing up and lifting an open palm. "You come to me, boy."

A slew of dirty dog jokes ricocheted through his head as he padded down the rocky incline, his ears instinctively tracking the movements of the rabbit to his left. When he was just over a hundred yards away from the road, he sat back on his haunches.

She knelt, extending her hand out farther and rubbing her fingers together. "It's all right, boy. Come on. I'm not going to hurt you."

Bullshit.

He chuffed and lifted his front paw. When she inched forward, he dropped his head and growled low.

"Fine." She laughed. "You come to me. Let me make sure you aren't injured. I... Wait."

He tilted his head as she rose to her feet slowly and opened the trunk of her car. She hefted a green bag onto her hip and resumed her position beside the car. "I brought something for you."

The bag crinkled as she opened it, releasing an unpleasant scent into the air.

Dog food.

He recoiled slightly and pointed his nose to the hare that had gone motionless under a cactus.

"You leave that poor little bunny alone," she chastised, dipping her hand in the foul-smelling bag and holding a pile out to him. "C'mon, boy."

He let out a whimper and lowered his nose to the ground, his ears dropping.

"It's not that bad," she cajoled, shaking the food pellets in her hand and sending the atrocious stench across the desert. "How about I put it in a bowl? Hmm?" She leaned back and opened her car door, reaching across the console to the passenger side. "Still a few crumbs in here from dinner, but it'll work."

Rising to his full height, he closed the gap between them by a few more yards and stopped.

Walk away.

Now.

Walk. Away.

His hackles rose as Charlotte got to her feet and took a slow step his way, Styrofoam container of dog food in hand.

"I'm just putting this out here," she purred quietly, her steps hesitant. "And when you're hungry, you can come get it. Okay, boy?" When he snorted in response and began pacing back and forth, she lowered the food to the sand and began to retreat to the car. "Kind of a beast, aren't you, boy?" She laughed, a hint of nervousness in her voice as she sat in the driver's seat and leaned forward to rest her elbows on her knees.

He watched her watching him as he continued to pace across the sand.

Get closer.

Run.

Closer.

Run.

✕

CHARLOTTE GLANCED BACK toward the ridge and sighed.

One hour.

She'd been so certain the lure of food would bring the enormous dog close enough for her to assess, so certain his stomach would win out over his wariness. When his pacing had stopped and he'd torn back over the hill he'd initially appeared on, she had slumped back in her seat in defeat.

Finally resigned to the fact the dog wouldn't be returning anytime soon, she sealed the bag of food, tossed it into the back seat, and started the car. She eased her way through the curved paths, continuing to scan the dark plateau for any sign of the animal until the bright lights of an approaching vehicle temporarily blinded her. As it came to an almost complete stop beside her, the driver's hand shot out, almost grazing her car.

"What the hell!" She gasped, hitting her brakes and

checking her rearview mirror. She squinted as the other vehicle's door opened, her foot ready to hit the gas.

"Charlotte?"

"Alex?"

His large hands gripped the top frame of her car as he leaned over her window. "Fancy meeting you here," he stated, one brow lifting.

"I…" She looked down at the time. "What are you doing out here?"

"Looking for you," he said flatly as he looked around. "Am I good to text Max and tell him you're fine?"

Dammit. Max.

"Oh," she mumbled, dropping her gaze from the biceps twitching in her peripheral vision. "Right. Max. Yeah. I'll text him when I hit the highway. Did he send you out looking for me?"

He hummed in response, his lips drawn tight. "I got off early and volunteered." He pushed off the car and began walking away. "I'm following you back to town. Don't speed. Last thing I need tonight is a ticket."

Chapter Six

ALEX STOOD AT the bar, his back to the door while he carefully removed each bottle of alcohol from the top shelf and wiped it down before replacing it in perfect alignment. A slice of sunlight pierced the lounge when the heavy door opened and the first patrons of the afternoon entered. "Be with you in a moment," he called over his shoulder, finishing up the row and inching the final bottle into place.

"Take your time, Alexandros."

His hand froze midair as the familiar voice slithered across his spine. He turned to Hades, giving Persephone a tight smile. "Hey."

Seph hopped up onto a stool and reached across the bar to push Alex's hair behind his ear. "Hey yourself, boy." She glanced around the empty lounge before giving him a bright smile. "Keeping busy?"

Nodding absently, he dropped his head a fraction in deference to his master. "Been a long time since I've seen you venture topside."

Hades's black eyes flicked to his wife, her pointed look urging him to pull up a chair beside her. "Someone's becoming anxious to have her boys back home," he stated, sitting down and placing one hand on Persephone's knee. "How's the hunt going?"

"Slow and steady," he replied, grabbing two chilled mugs from the cooler and holding them up for Hades's approval. "It's a big area to cover, but I'm making my way through it." He fought the desire to roll his eyes as Seph reached over again and rolled down the wayward hem of his shirt sleeve. "Are you here for business or pleasure?"

Hades waved off Alex's gesture toward the beer taps. "I'm here to find out why my tracker hasn't locked on to the Pirithous scent in this region despite a second sighting."

Glancing around the empty room, he set Persephone's perfectly poured beer in front of her, slipping a napkin under the glass and turning his attention back to his boss. "I'm doing what I can between shifts here," he stated, instinctively clasping his hands behind his back. "I'll find him. I always do."

Seph took a sip of her drink and set it down, smiling politely. "I know you do, boy," she cooed, subtly pushing the beer away. "But if there's an issue we can help with, you really need to let us know. We miss you boys back home."

"Nothing more than a rough start." He gave his mistress a smile and a wink to reassure her he was fine. "These jaunts topside every decade or so always take a few months of readjustment." Sliding his phone across the counter to her, he smirked. "Check out what these can do."

His bosses had yet to fully grasp that the topside world didn't work on the same barter system used in the underworld, an issue that frequently left the brothers scrambling with every venture.

Hades rose to his feet and held his arm out for Seph, peeking over her shoulder as she swiped the phone to life and delicately tapped on the music app, smiling as she squealed in pleasure when a song came through the cell's speaker. "Fascinating as this is"—he chuckled, pushing the phone back toward Alex—"we need to return home. Stay the course and bring the line down swiftly, Cerberus. We miss our guard dog."

✕

CHARLOTTE TOOK A deep breath and pulled the tavern's door open, carefully balancing the box of baking on her hip. The bar was almost empty, the lunch crowd gone and the first of the after-work crowd still an hour away from trickling in.

"Alex?" she called over, smiling at the stunning strawberry-blonde woman skipping past her on the arm of an immense man with jet-black hair and a deep set scowl.

"Hey, Miss Charlotte. What can I get you?"

Glancing quickly at the baking, she gave him a nervous smile. "After a very long lecture from Max, I figured I'd bring you something to say thanks. For checking on me. On your night off."

His closed expression, the same one he'd worn the night before, morphed into mild interest as he flipped the lid of the box open and cocked a brow. "You baked for me?"

She pulled her hands from her pockets and tugged at the cuffs of her sleeves. "I picked them up from the grocery store." She grinned. "But I chose the box."

His lips pursed, his strong jawline flexing as he visibly fought to keep a straight face. "So, basically, thank-you Oreos?" He finally smirked, plucking a cookie from the pile and examining it before taking a bite. "You buy good cookies."

"I try."

He swallowed and gave an exaggerated moan of approval that sent a flush straight to her cheeks. "Damn good. You work tonight?"

She shook her head, doing her best to hide the rush of excitement that ran through her every time he spoke. "Not until tomorrow."

He crossed his arms and leaned against the back counter. "Big plans for the evening then? Date? Dog-hunting?"

"Oh." She laughed nervously. "No. No, no. No date. No."

"Really."

"Really," she echoed, biting her lip. "What about you? Are you working all night?"

Cocking his head, he smirked. "Just so happens I'm off

in twenty."

✕

LET SLEEPING DOGS lie, you fucking moron.

The mantra had been looping in his mind the whole drive to the bistro, becoming more insistent as he pulled up beside Charlotte's little coupe and offered her his arm. By the time they were seated on the intimate patio, the chant was clanging through his skull.

"I love this place," she murmured, poking at the flower arrangement on their table. "It was one of my first discoveries when I moved here."

Looking over the coffee menu, he adjusted his position on the small iron chair. "Where did you move from? Thomas mentioned you were transferred here a year ago?"

Her cheeks pinked up and she brought her menu up a little closer. "I'm originally from Ohio, but I've spent most of the past seven years bouncing from state to state as promotions came up." She looked up at him and his heart damn near stopped. "How about you?"

"Three months," he replied, pausing to listen to their server describe the specials before placing his order and biting back a grin as Charlotte placed her very specific request. "The heat's a little intense, isn't it?"

"The worst," she groaned and flopped back in her seat. "Everyone says I'll get used to it, but I think they're lying at this point. Where are you from?"

"Everywhere." He chuckled. "I'm a bit of a nomad."

"Why here?"

The hunt.

"The terrain." He sat back, trying to keep his voice casual. "I'm surprised you're free this evening. Is your date from the other night working or something?"

Subtle.

"No. I don't know. We didn't really hit it off."

That's a damn shame.

She took a sip from her latte and looked out toward the fields of date trees surrounding them. "And your girlfriend? She's okay with you hanging out?"

He winced inwardly, thinking back to the night he'd spent with Melanie. "We didn't really hit it off either." *For more than three hours.* He scooted his chair a little closer to her.

She rolled her eyes, her cheeks flushing as she bit back a smile. "Sorry to hear that."

"I'm not." He grinned, following her gaze as her dark brown eyes narrowed and she tilted her head to get a good look at his arm. "You into tattoos?"

Nodding, she played with her napkin. "Any meaning behind them?"

Nothing I'm gonna share.

Rolling his shirt up to his shoulder, he angled his right side toward her. "It's one continuous piece across my back that stretches down my arms. A work in progress." He straightened his sleeve. "I'll show you the whole thing sometime. This probably isn't the most appropriate place to show you that or the one on my chest. But enough about my ink. What I want to know is how someone your size is strong enough to take on someone Max's size."

The blush returned, leaving him little choice but to lean forward and hope his shirt hid his physical reaction to it.

"Peace officer training," she said, taking a sip of the coffee. "Everyone finds their niche, and mine happened to be channeling pent-up rage into flattening bad guys." She smirked. "Or flattening Max."

"Speaking of Max, have you two ever been a thing?"

She hesitated just long enough for him to conjure up a whole lot of visions he didn't want to think about.

"Well, we did kiss once," she said slowly.

Fucking kill him.

"But it was just for a picture to send to his mother so she'd think he was dating a nice girl."

He cocked a brow. "Did she buy it?"

"She said we looked like an old married couple who should have divorced a decade ago but were attempting to put up a good front for the sake of the children."

Blinking a few times as he processed her words, he dropped his hand to his knee, his knuckles grazing her thigh as all memory of Hades, his mission, and his brothers slunk to the recesses of his mind. "And since then?"

"Oh, yuck. Ew."

✕

THE COOLING MISTERS lining the patio powered down as the sun began to sink on the horizon and Charlotte glanced down at the tab, nudging Alex gently in the ribs when he snatched it from view and placed it facedown with a stack of bills. "I won't fight you this time, but next time is definitely on me," she stated with feigned sternness, catching the implication of her words a fraction too late.

A strange look flashed across his face before he smirked and tucked his hair behind his ear. "If I knew you were game for a next time, I wouldn't have talked so fast this time."

Biting her lip, she hooked her purse onto her shoulder and stood. "So, do you see colors differently out of each eye?" she wondered aloud as he downed the last of his fourth coffee. "Like, are things bluer with your right?" When he looked over at her, brows raised, she grinned. "I've been trying to figure it out since I saw you without your sunglasses."

"Never thought about it." He chuckled and straightened to his full height. He covered his blue eye first, then the hazel one. "No difference. Is that why you always look at me like I'm a specimen under a microscope?"

You're a specimen, all right.

"I've been wanting to poke at your eyes since I saw

them," she replied.

Grabbing his wallet and keys from the table, he offered her his hand. "Not gonna lie. That's a little freaky."

He escorted her out of the bistro, slowing their speed as they approached their vehicles. "So, I have Max's number," he stated, leaning against his SUV and gently tugging her close to him. "But I'd rather not go through him to set up another date with you."

She took a subconscious step back, untangling her fingers from his as she pulled her phone out and handed it to him. "I don't really date," she blurted out as he used her phone to fire off a text to his own.

"I don't either," he muttered, giving her cell back and grinning with his perfect teeth. "So neither of us will be shocked when this goes to hell. I'll call you tomorrow."

Chapter Seven

ALEX PACED THE small hall of his trailer, his phone tight to his ear. "Yeah, I'm still on the hunt," he growled. "I've been out four times this week alone."

Ryan switched his tone. "Look, I'm sorry, man," he grumbled. "I'm just a little on edge, and Bo's going off the rails again. The sooner we track down the final descendants, the sooner—"

"Yeah, yeah," he interrupted. "We all want to wrap this mission up. But it's a big area with a lot of ground to cover." He ran his hand down his healing ribs. "There's been nothing in the news about any murders in the region, but usually there's a break between the second sighting and the first kills."

"Maybe Bo and I should relocate."

He stopped pacing and ran a hand through his hair. "Give me a little more time to scout the smaller towns, and I'll call you the moment I pinpoint our target. It would be a big help if you scan the news, though."

Ryan went quiet. "Bo said you called him about a girl. That wouldn't have anything to do with your inability to track down the bloodline, right?"

With a snort, he pulled his phone away from his ear and looked down at it. "You're kidding, right?" He flopped onto his sofa. "So has Hades checked in with you lately?"

"Why the hell would he?" Ryan asked, his voice cutting in and out. "He hates coming topside."

He leaned his head back and scratched the stubble on his chin. "Just curious. I'll call in a few days with an update."

He had to get back to work.

Bouncing between the underworld and topside life was taking its toll on all of them, the last remnants of the elusive Pirithous line forcing them back up every few decades, forcing them to settle back into an ever-changing human world while they followed scents and leads throughout the continents.

Every time, it became harder. Technology eliminated the freedom they once had to roam and settle at will. Computerized identification that hadn't existed thirty years prior, smartphones, even the existence of the internet had been in its infancy the last time the brothers had ventured into the human world.

Hunts that once took days or weeks topside now took months or years, the diluted line in its final death throes.

It had been the hunt for this particularly evasive Pirithous descendant that brought Alex to the Coachella Valley. *The last of the male line*, Hades's seer had hissed hours before the brothers found themselves in a Colorado field less than a year ago, wearing clothes that had gone out of style in 1989.

Shoving his keys into his back pocket and tossing his backpack over his shoulder, he strode out the door to make the most of the remaining night hours.

CHARLOTTE HAULED THE dog food out of her work truck and dumped some into the new bowl she'd picked up on her way to the park. With her offering in hand, she slipped a large black collar over her wrist and walked cautiously through the brush and set the food in a clear patch. "Dinner's served," she called into the dawn light, disappointment settling in when not even the howl of a coyote answered back.

Her radio buzzed to life, Max's voice crackled with the poor reception. "Clocked you out, Chuck. Location?"

She jogged back to the truck and lifted the handpiece. "The Keys," she said, her eyes on the ridge to her left. "I'll head out of here in an hour or so."

"Text me when you get home," he replied before the line went silent.

Crawling onto the hood of the vehicle, she took off her hat and badge, undid the top three buttons of her work shirt, and hiked the neckline of her tank top up as she reclined back against the windshield. "Here, puppy, puppy, puppy," she called out halfheartedly, loosening the laces of her boots and freezing when a soft bark answered her.

She sat up and watched as the huge beast descended the ridge toward her, his head low and ears alert. In the sunlight, the deep blackness of his long fur was amplified against the beige of the landscape, his immense size more pronounced when he wasn't blending into the night sky. "Hey, boy," she whispered, easing her legs over the side of the truck. "Hungry?"

He stopped a good fifty yards away and sat, turning his nose up at the bowl.

"What?" she asked with feigned offense. "You don't like my cooking?"

The animal huffed and rose to his feet, his hackles rising as he approached the food. He sniffed the bowl, blowing out what she could only think of as a resigned breath.

"Go on," she encouraged. "I know it's not a fuzzy little bunny, but it's good for you."

She leaned forward in anticipation as the dog's huge head dropped and he buried his nose into the bowl.

"Awwww, you're such a good boy."

ALEX FOUGHT BACK against his gag reflex, forcing the last of the kibble down.

Fucking. Humiliating.

He sat back and used his paw to brush the crumbs from

his snout.

Bo can never know about this. Ever.

He'd lasted two nights without seeing Charlotte, work obligations for both of them demanding he remain content with intermittent texts and quick phone calls.

It wasn't enough.

"Still hungry?" she called over to him, waving the nasty green bag his way.

He chuffed, shaking his head and batting the bowl away. Taking the hint, she slipped off her work truck and crouched, one arm tucked awkwardly behind her back.

"Come on, boy," she cooed, then frowned. "Girl? Awww, maybe you're a girl!"

His mind whirring with comebacks, he padded cautiously toward her, his head down to keep his fur over his distinctive eyes. When she lost her balance and moved suddenly, he jumped back instinctively, his ears flattening.

"Oh, honey!" she murmured. "I didn't mean to scare you. Come here. C'mon!"

Wondering how many dates it would take to hear her call him honey in human form, he inched forward until he was just out of reach. From his angle, he had a good view of her cleavage as she leaned toward him, her shirt gaping open.

He dropped his head.

No looking. That is so not right.

Stretching his snout into her open palm, he began warring internally about the morality of what he was doing. She was completely oblivious that the dog she was petting so gently was the man she'd be dining with in two nights.

"Such a good boy," she murmured as something slipped over his muzzle, her free hand sliding it over his ears and releasing it as it hung loose around his neck.

Collar.

With a low growl, he pulled his head out of her hand and backed up before turning tail and barreling away.

✕

CHARLOTTE GROANED IN protest as her phone buzzed again, waking her from a heavy sleep. She smacked around her nightstand until her fingers found the cell.

"I'm going for groceries in twenty. Care to join me?"

She squinted and looked at the sender's name.

Alex.

Flinging her blanket off, she scrambled to the bathroom to shower, racing back to her room to reply. *"Sounds good. Meet you at the tavern."*

She blasted through her routine, forgoing a ponytail when her wet hair refused to comply and tossing her work clothes into a bag. With a final look in the mirror to ensure her jean shorts weren't too short and her black peasant shirt was the appropriate level of casual, she slipped on her sandals and jogged down the stairs to her apartment parking lot, gasping when she got into her car and the heat of the seat belt brushed her thigh.

Alex was leaning against his SUV when she arrived, sunglasses on and long hair pulled through the back of his ball cap. "Hey, Miss Charlotte," he greeted, not even trying to hide his perusal of her. "Hop in."

She climbed into the passenger side and looked around. "This is way cleaner than my car."

Revving the engine, he backed up and turned onto the road. "I cleaned it out today so you wouldn't see what a slob I actually am." He grinned. "Don't feel around under your seat. I ran out of time."

As they walked into the grocery store, he reached down and scooped her hand into his. She looked down at the giant mitt encasing her fingers. "Worried you'll get lost?" she teased, hoping her voice didn't reveal the thrill that ran through her with the casual contact.

"Worried you'll find some hot guy in the freezer section and leave me stranded with a single tomato and a can of tuna." He smirked, tightening his grip a fraction.

Picking up a basket, he gestured toward the produce. "I just need a few things," he said as they made their way to the fruit. "And I figured this was as good an excuse as any to see you before tomorrow."

He led her through the store, weaving in and out of the aisles while they chatted about work and bosses. When they hit the pet aisle, he slowed. "So you said that dog from the park didn't seem too thrilled with the food you put out for him. Maybe it's the type."

She frowned and scanned the shelves. "He's probably just used to hunting, but there's no way an animal that size is finding enough prey to keep him healthy." She plucked a bag off the shelf and scanned the ingredients.

"Maybe he's more of a raw-meat dog," he suggested, leaning over her shoulder and wrinkling his nose. "That smells like rotting pig's feet."

"It does not." Elbowing him lightly in the ribs, she sniffed at the bag. "Oh. Yeah, it kind of does." She placed it back and sniffed at another brand. "Yuck."

"Tell you what," he said, tugging at her hand and leading her toward the back of the store. "I'll grab a few cheap steaks and you can try it tonight."

He spent an inordinate amount of time selecting the meat, finally adding three steaks and a pound of raw hamburger to his basket. Once they reached the till, she pulled her wallet from her purse to cover the dog meat.

"Put that away," he stated, putting his large form between her and the cashier. "This is my annual contribution to animal welfare in the greater Coachella Valley."

✕

MAX GLARED AT the bowl as Charlotte opened her small cooler and pulled out a steak. "You aren't seriously doing this, are you? That stupid mutt'll be eating better than you."

"You're just mad I didn't bring one for you," Charlotte retorted. "The poor thing is probably starving out here."

Rising to his feet, he rolled his eyes. "If this dog is as big as you say, something's keeping him here. Maybe he's picking off the coyotes."

"I got a collar around him last time, so I'm hoping to leash him and bring him in next time I get close enough." She shone her flashlight toward the ridge before she headed back to the truck. "We should probably hit the north quadrant now. Becky mentioned the campground was packed by seven."

He followed her through the park, flashing his brights at her periodically to signal he was veering off the road to check the various gravel paths that wound into the desert. As they approached the campground, they were met by a large group of people waving frantically.

She pulled up to the group, rolling down her window. "Everything okay over here?"

One man stepped up to the truck, pointing toward the moonlit plateau. "The guys over there found two bodies near the dam trails," he said breathlessly. "My wife and son just took off toward the visitor center to find help."

Chapter Eight

ALEX TURNED THE music down and paced the bar with his phone tight to his ear, oblivious to the ire of his customers. "Yeah, I get it's your job, but get someone to cover for you tonight. You sound exhausted."

He could hear Charlotte moving around her apartment as she sighed. "It's fine," she answered, her voice tired. "I've showered, eaten, and downed a pot of coffee. One more night won't kill me."

"Yeah, right," he muttered. "Will you at least stay tight to Max? You shouldn't be working alone until whoever killed those people is caught."

"Max is guiding the investigators through the trails. I'll be fine. I have a gun and the CB with me in the truck at all times."

He stormed behind the bar, cranking the music back up to appease his snarky clientele. "Will you at least promise not to leave your truck?" he asked, almost yelling to be heard over the din of the room. "No dog-feeding, no animal rescue?"

"Sure," she replied distractedly, her voice muffled.

"Look, I better run. But I'll text you when I'm off."

He leaned against the counter and dropped his head. "Please do," he muttered. "It's not easy to find a dinner date on short notice."

Her laugh rang through the phone before it went dead. He ran his hand through his hair, grabbed a pen and paper, and hit the floor.

CHARLOTTE TURNED ON her high beams as she flipped around at the north entrance and made her way back down the deserted road. The campgrounds had emptied out quickly after the bodies were discovered, the tourists in no rush to be the next victim.

Max had radioed updates in intermittently throughout the early evening. Both men had been found a good trek off the beaten path, their bodies hidden among the rocks and out of view from the walkways and roads. Homicide believed one body was fresh, dumped within the past forty-eight hours. The other was weeks old and, according to Max, in bad shape. The park had been crawling with police all day, keeping her and Max on shift well into the early afternoon, giving them a few hours of rest before their scheduled shifts.

She turned off the pavement onto a gravel road that looped for several miles. A flash of movement ahead of her headlight beams caught her eye and she hit the brakes, her hand hovering over her gun. The movement drew nearer until it stood directly in the light.

"Damn dog," she exclaimed in relief, putting her hands on her pounding heart. She unrolled her window and reached out. "Come here!"

The dog stalked toward her, his ears and nose twitching. When he reached her hand, he ducked his enormous head and nuzzled it briefly before he continued on.

"Where're you going, boy?" she asked, leaning out her window as the beast gracefully leapt into the back of her truck. The entire vehicle rocked back under his weight while the dog circled around and sat, his ears alert.

Stretching across the cab, she reached over and opened the small back window, wiggling her fingers toward her new travel companion. "I don't think you're going to like this," she warned as the dog ducked down and gave her hand a lick. "It's going to be bumpy ride back there."

She rolled up her window and eased onto the gas, adjusting her rearview mirror. "You going to keep me safe? Or is it the other way around?" she asked, rounding a narrow bend slowly and chuckling when the regal-looking dog flashed its paws out to balance himself. He gave a low snort. "We've got a stab-happy psycho on the loose," she continued, her shoulders relaxing slightly with the animal's presence. "If you see him, you bark. Got it?"

The dog growled in response, his long fur blowing back as she picked up speed.

She nattered away to replace the silence of the cab, keeping one eye on the road and one on the dog.

"I can't keep calling you 'boy,' can I?" she asked as she pulled back onto the pavement. "How about Rex?"

He snorted.

"Okay, then what do you think of Fido? Spot? Phil? Any of those make you happy?"

Each suggestion was met with obvious disdain.

She turned toward a quiet campground and stopped. "I just need to do a quick walk-around and we'll head back to the station," she said, slipping a new leash into her pocket and turning on her flashlight. "Coming, boy?"

The dog jumped down from the truck and began pacing the perimeter, his nose lifted into the air. When she began her walk toward the tents, he appeared at her side, the top of his head almost to her shoulder. She rested her hand on his back, running her fingers through the long fur and slipping them under the huge leather collar hanging loose along his throat, doing her best to clip the leash on without startling the beast.

When the clasp closed with a *snick*, she could almost swear the dog's shoulders hunched.

"Nothing exciting," she whispered, scanning the last of the tents with her light as the leash remained slack in her hand. "Let's get back to the truck. You can ride up front."

✕

ALEX LAID HIS head on the armrest and closed his eyes.

Riding up front had been abandoned the moment he crawled into the passenger side and realized it was about half as big as he needed, so he was relegated to the back seat.

Charlotte's fingers gently played with his ears, lulling him into a daze as he stared out the window and relished in the scent of her skin. Every so often, her hand would still until he nudged her, reminding her he was there.

It was a small reprieve from the humiliation of the leash and collar.

"Okay, boy, I'm going to need to head inside and sign out," she said, unbuckling her seat belt. "You stay here and I'll be right back."

She unrolled the windows, slammed the door, and locked him in.

He sat up and scanned the area, the morning sun providing enough light for him to make out the small lizards scurrying across the sand. He strained his neck back in the cramped space and watched Charlotte through the window as she chatted with her coworker. Lifting his ears, he could make out most of the casual conversation. Updates about the road conditions. Annoyance with the litter outside the west campground. Gossip about Becky and one of the cops that had been on duty the day before.

No leads on the murders.

Charlotte walked out, her hat under her arm as she pulled the elastic from her ponytail. She opened the back door and stepped aside. "All right, boy. You're coming home with me."

He lowered himself out of the truck, his haunches aching from the tight fit. When she bent to scoop up the leash, he ducked out of her reach and took off into the desert.

He had a date in seven hours.

CHARLOTTE SWATTED HER fork at Alex's, effectively ending his foraging of her precious lava cake. "We all have lines in the sand," she warned, pulling the plate closer. "This is mine."

He sat back in the booth and grinned, sliding his fork across the table in defeat. "All right, all right. I give."

Eying him suspiciously, she lifted another bite to her lips. "How long have you bartended?"

She tried to focus on his answer and not fall into the distraction of his soothing baritone or the way his blue button-down shirt clung to his muscles and amplified the different colors of his eyes.

Heavens help her, she was failing miserably.

From the moment she opened her door to see him standing there, daffodils in hand and black jeans that rode sinfully low, her mind had gone on the defensive. He was pretty. Too pretty.

Harmless fling. Just a harmless, flirty fling.

The stress of the past forty-eight hours had dissipated as Alex kept her entertained with tales from the bartending front and gossip about the locals. He prodded her about her police training, musing aloud about the best gym in the region for her to show him her moves.

"That's it," he announced, flagging the server over. "You're exhausted, and I'm taking you home before you're facedown in that cake."

She blinked, shaking her head. "No, no. Sorry. I'm good."

He handed a stack of bills to the woman, ignoring her obvious flirting for the umpteenth time that evening. "I'll give you three choices," he said, counting them down on his fingers. "One, we go to my place and watch a movie. Two, we go to your place and watch a movie. Three, I take you home, I go home, and I call you tomorrow for a lunch date. Which'll it be?"

She swallowed the last of the lava cake, thinking over her options and debating just how far she was willing to let this date go. She *was* exhausted. And her brain wasn't firing on all cylinders.

Sensing her hesitation, he leaned across the table. "When I say watch a movie, I mean we're watching a movie."

Hoping her relief wasn't too evident on her face, she nodded. "How about my place? Max rigged my computer up to my TV so I can pretty much get anything on there."

He stood up, holding his hand out for her. "You pick the

genre, I pick the flick?"

✕

ALEX STRETCHED HIS arms across the back of Charlotte's sofa and looked around the apartment as she cranked up the air-conditioning. "There's a lot more pink in here than I expected."

"I like pink," she huffed, firing the computer screen to life and handing him the controls. "Pick something from the thrillers or horrors."

He arched his neck back to watch her walk toward her bedroom before he began flipping through his options. Finding an old favorite, he paused the movie titles and continued to peruse the decor as a wary gray cat stared at him from the kitchen table. "I don't think Marbles likes me," he called out, narrowing his eyes at the old cat.

"I don't think Marbles likes *me*," she replied, her bedroom door opening. "She's an angry ol' girl. Want a beer?"

"Water's good," he muttered, refusing to look away from the cat until she finally blinked slowly and turned her head away.

Charlotte handed him a glass, crossing in front of him to sit at the far end of the sofa.

Damn.

Date-Charlotte had been smoking hot in her knee-high boots and black baby doll dress.

Post-Date-Charlotte was smoking hot in a well-worn oversized academy shirt and basketball shorts.

Watch the movie, horndog.

Forcing his attention to the screen, he ignored the view to his right, the sight of her legs drawn up onto the couch, exposing most of her thighs.

"What is it with you guys?" she suddenly grumbled, her feet pushing against his knee. "Spreading across the whole sofa like you're establishing dominance."

Pushing back against her, he grinned. "That's precisely what we're doing. Making ourselves as big as possible so no one messes with us." He glanced over at the cat, who looked away instantly. "It's a territorial thing."

"Like pissing on a tree," she muttered, tossing her legs onto his and returning her attention to the movie.

Tired Charlotte was apparently cranky Charlotte.

Halfway through the film, he refilled their waters and returned to see her sitting up, smiling at the television.

"I figured out the ending," she proclaimed. "It's all in his head."

"Does this mean you want me to turn it off?" He laughed, setting the cups down and flopping back in his seat.

"Of course not. Now I get to see that I'm right. And I like to be right."

His intentions had been so good. Had he been hooked to a lie detector back at the restaurant, he would have passed with flying colors. But those intentions were disappearing rapidly as he watched her lips turn up in a satisfied smirk.

"Hey," he said, shifting in place to face her. "What are the chances of you booting my ass out of here if I said I wanted to kiss you?"

Her eyes locked on the television, she licked her lips. "I dunno," she muttered. "I really like seeing how right I am, so if you interrupt that, you better be very, very good at it."

Definitely a risk worth taking.

He leaned across the sofa, his hand brushing her hair back. "How about a compromise?" he offered, bringing his lips to her neck. When she kept her attention on the screen but tilted her head to give him better access, he ran his tongue lightly across her skin to her earlobe.

She drew in a deep breath as he tangled his fingers into her hair and trailed kisses down her throat to her collarbone. His other hand inched onto her thigh, pulling her closer to him as he worked his lips to her jaw. "Can you still see?" he muttered into her neck, his senses going into overload from the intoxicating combination of the taste of her skin and the scent of her perfume.

"Uh-huh," she replied, shifting slightly but refusing to look away from the screen.

He sat back and gripped her hips, pulling her slowly across the sofa and rolling his eyes when she lay back and pointed to the TV.

"The clues are so obvious once you know the outcome."

He pushed her oversized shirt up to expose her stomach

and ran his fingers over the smooth skin. "Want me to stop?" he asked as he bent down to run his tongue across the band of her shorts.

Her fingers ran through his hair. "No. You seem pretty content. Just stay above C-level."

He looked up at her. "Sea level?"

"C-level," she repeated. "The center line. Keep your paws off my drawers."

"I…" He glanced down, lifting his hands off her hips and sliding them up her ribs, stretching her arms above her head. "Better?"

"Much."

Recognizing that his powers of seduction were no match for Charlotte's desire to see her plot predictions proved correct, he straddled her, wedging his knee into the back of the couch and ignoring the discomfort the wooden frame provided as it dug into the bone. He grazed his hands along her stomach, her sides, and her arms, noting her responses and stashing them in his head for another time when he wasn't competing against a well-spun story line.

"Knew it!" she called out, clapping her hands together once and gesturing to the screen. "Can I call a twist, or can I call a twist?"

He leaned over her, his hair falling forward to block her view of the television. "I'm impressed. Kiss me."

Her scrutinizing dark eyes narrowed as she looked at him.

"Please?" he added, cocking a brow.

She lifted her head up, her soft lips brushing against his.

So. Fucking. Done.

Chapter Nine

"GET YOUR LAZY a—Whoa, boy."

Max flung Charlotte's apartment door open with a bang as he announced his presence, his jaw dropping open as he took in the sight of her bedhead and Alex still crashed out on the floor at her feet.

"Shush!" she hissed, easing her legs out from under Alex's arm and tiptoeing past him. She grabbed Max's shoulders and spun him around forcefully, walking him to her room.

"I spent yesterday evening overseeing an FBI rock climb and you got laid? How is that even fair?" he grumbled, sitting on the edge of her bed and glaring. "We've been called in early for a briefing before we head out for the night. So hurry the heck up."

"I did *not* get laid." She gasped, glancing behind her to ensure Alex hadn't woken and followed them. "Just give me ten and I'll be ready to go."

She snatched clean work clothes from her drawers and rushed off to shower, her mind still foggy from the sudden waking. The water took forever to warm, leaving her slightly chilled by the time she dried, dressed, and began brushing her hair out to the sound of Max grilling a groggy Alex about the evening's events.

"Leave him alone!" she called out, wrapping an elastic around her wet hair before she attempted to rescue Alex from Max's interrogation. She was still carefully tucking in her beige work shirt as she entered the living room to see Max standing in the middle, his arms crossed, and Alex still leaning against the sofa. He looked up at her and grinned lazily, licking his lips and giving her a reminder of just how skilled those lips were.

"You here to rescue me?" he teased as he pushed himself to his feet.

She rolled her eyes and picked up her hat from the kitchen table. "Yeah, yeah, pretty boy. I have to head in early tonight, so…" She paused.

What am I even supposed to say right now? Get out? Call me? Thanks for the make-out session, you've obviously had a lot of practice?

Alex pulled his boots on, staying well out of Max's reach. "Call me when you're off in the morning." He smiled, backing out the door. "Maybe we can grab breakfast before you head home."

Grateful for the graceful exit, she waved quickly and let the door close before laying into Max. "Give me my key," she seethed, extending her hand.

Max's shoulders slumped a fraction. "Aw, come on. How was I supposed to know you had a guy over? You've never had a guy over. Ever."

She laced her boots and shook her head. "You are so damn lucky Alex didn't flatten you. So damn lucky I didn't flatten you. You could've called. Knocked. Buzzed in." She thought back to how long Max had been marching into her suite. "Have you ever knocked?"

"Yeah. Like, five times." He grinned, holding his hand out to help her to her feet. "I'm driving. And I picked up a whole lot of pizza, so you have to forgive me."

She followed him to his truck, scanning the lot for Alex's SUV before getting in. The pizza boxes were still hot, the late summer heat keeping both the food and the cab uncomfortably warm. "So anything come out of the climb?"

He snorted, his mouth full. "'Course not."

"Did you see Butch anywhere?" she asked, carefully peeling the mushrooms off her slice of pizza.

"Who's Butch?"

"The dog." She grinned as he picked up the discarded mushrooms and added them to his own slice. "I have to call him something. So I'm naming him after my grandma's evil old cat. Damn dog took off on me yesterday, leash and all. I'm worried he'll catch it on something."

"Sorry. No Butch and no killer. But I have a date next week with one of the cops from the hike, so it wasn't a total write-off."

She snorted. "What happened to Stephanie?"

"Ex-boyfriend was a little less ex and a little more boyfriend than I can handle," he grunted. "That's a minefield I ain't touching with a ten foot pole." Smirking at her, he turned onto the main road. "What's going on with Alex?"

"Nothing," she muttered, wrinkling her nose at a wayward mushroom. "We went on one official date."

He grinned wide. "That ended at your place with plans for another? Yeah. That sounds like a whole lot of nothing in the making."

"Shut up and drive."

Cranking the music, he drove them down the busy highway and onto the deserted roads of the park. Out of habit, he lowered the volume and hovered his foot on the brake once they breached the entrance, the light of dusk a prime time for the wildlife to begin making themselves known. "All right," he announced as they pulled up to the station. "Let's get this meeting over with so we can go veg out on the trails for the night."

ALEX PULLED INTO the tavern parking lot, his phone tight to his ear. "What else am I supposed to be doing?" he growled at Ryan, throwing the SUV into park. "You know as well as I do that a single scent could take months to locate again in a place like this."

"Maybe Bo and I should join you," Ryan offered, his voice slightly muffled. "We could split up, take shifts. I can wrap stuff up here and Bo isn't working right now."

"Big surprise," he muttered. "No, I'm in no position to put anyone up right now. And the snowbirds'll be making their way down here soon, so there's no room at the inn. And with the FBI crawling all over this place, my movements are limited around the scene. If I can't find the line within a couple weeks, I'll call you two in. Deal?"

Ryan went silent for a moment. "Deal."

Killing the engine, he strode into the tavern to find Thomas swamped with customers, his surly expression etched deep on his face. Without hesitating, Alex began taking orders from the crowded tables, shooing Thomas to the sanctity of his kitchen with a stack of appetizer requests and a glass of ice water.

The rush was finally waning when Hades and Seph strode back in, Hades's towering presence parting the crowd for the diminutive goddess skipping alongside him, her hands wrapped around his forearm. She waved at Alex as they made their way to a booth at the back of the bar, Hades scanning the room's patrons with mild disdain.

Ringing through a tab, he pocketed the customer's phone number and smiled absently as she rose up on her toes to whisper a reminder of their meet-up after his first shift at the tavern.

Hades watched the exchange with interest.

Nodding the woman off, Alex grabbed a tray, collecting abandoned glasses as he strode over to his master. "Two visits in one week. No pressure, right?"

While Hades's black eyes narrowed, Persephone patted Alex's thigh and looked up at him. "Alexandros, honey. Please don't start. You know I dislike unpleasantness."

He glanced at a table of drunken women flagging him over for another round. "Aw, hell, sorry," he muttered, bowing his head a fraction. "Things are just a little hectic around here right now. Let me get caught up and I'll have a few minutes to update you."

"Add a platter of whatever passes for food here," Hades grumbled, his ire dissipating as Seph squeezed his knee. "And two glasses of wine."

Nodding and flustered, Alex returned to his duties, his back prickling with the vigilant gaze of Hades.

He knew better than to blatantly disrespect his master.

Knew better but was too caught up in his own head to stop himself.

He was done for. And he knew it.

He'd screwed up orders all evening, his mind still clinging to the brief make-out session the night prior.

The way her knees tightened across his hips when he kissed her.

The gentle circling of her fingers through his hair.

Her pathetic attempt to cover up the yawn that ended things and placed him contentedly on the floor, Charlotte's hand tucked into his as she crashed hard.

"Who is she?"

His gaze snapped up from the cooler and he rose, bowing his head in deference to Seph. "Who's who?"

Seph tossed Hades a smile across the room before leaning closer to Alex. "Miss Charlotte? The woman we saw here the other day?"

Placing the beer bottles onto a tray, he bit his lip in feigned concentration. "I have a lot of women in here," he stated, pulling a wad of papers from his back pocket and tossing them onto the counter. "See if you can find her in these."

A perfectly manicured brow lifted. "Gravitating more toward Bo's habits than Ryan's, I see." She opened each paper and meticulously folded them into a neat pile. "You look tired, honey. Hades and I are concerned."

Printing off a tab for a table, he shrugged. "Maybe I'm getting too old to be pulling double-duty." He grinned, hefting a full tray in his hand. "Go get comfortable and I'll follow you with the wine."

Seph returned to her booth, she and Hades quietly discussing him as he dropped off their glasses and circled the rest of the bar.

Tired didn't begin to describe how exhausted he was. Between work, the hunt, dating Charlotte, and guarding Charlotte, he was lucky to pull two hours of rest a day. He was running on autopilot, collecting meals and dropping them off while his mind sluggishly ricocheted between Charlotte's lips and the unexplored park terrain he'd yet to cover.

Seph and Hades left with nothing more than a wave, the plates untouched save for a half-eaten chicken wing. By the time he rang out the last tab, he was a few hundred dollars richer and ready to be facedown on his bed. He drove home as the sun rose and walked straight into his tiny shower to rinse the odor of stale booze from his skin before he collapsed onto his mattress and glanced at his cell for any word from Charlotte.

He picked up his phone and fired off a quick text to her, knowing she wouldn't receive it until she was out of the park in two hours.

"If you're up for breakfast after work, call me."

With a killer on the loose in the Tree, a two-hour nap was all he had time for.

✕

ALEX FLEXED HIS hands under the table as Charlotte hung up her phone and dug back into her chicken strips. "So they're pairing you with a cop tonight?"

She nodded, rolling her eyes. "Yeah. The guy wasn't at the briefing last night, but Max met him a few days ago and says he's a total douchebag man-whore." She grabbed the salt and poured an impressive amount on her fries. "Some Kevin guy. I'd call out sick if I wasn't due back in an hour."

Keeping his face expressionless, he poked at his own

meal, his appetite gone once irrational jealousy set in. "Maybe it won't be too bad," he said, forcing himself to believe the platitude. "But, in case it is, maybe you should chow down on a ton of garlic and onions."

She grinned. "If I'd known about this before we ordered, I'd definitely be on board for that." She pushed what was left of her meal toward him. "You look way less tired tonight."

"Yeah, well, the chick who was supposed to call me and wake me up for breakfast forgot, so I slept all damn day." He smirked. "I don't think she realized I was counting on her to be my rooster."

Charlotte's dark eyes narrowed. "Chick."

"Woman," Alex corrected, raising his hands in surrender. "Lady. Female." He paused. "Hottie."

"I'm armed, you know," she warned, patting her hip. "And this *woman* was on autopilot for the last three hours of her shift. You need a less overworked rooster."

He flagged down the server, motioning for the bill. "I like the rooster I have, even if it is defective," he replied, tapping her calf with his foot. "You better run. I'll grab the tab and call you tomorrow, okay?"

"Thanks," she said, hesitating as she walked past him. When she bent down to kiss him, the knot that had been forming in his stomach released slightly, his pulse speeding up with her proximity. "Have a fun night off!"

Taking his time to finish the last of her meal and his, he laid a wad of cash on the table and headed out to his SUV.

He hit the highway, making his way to the western entrance of the park and pulling into a small turnout just outside the perimeter.

The moment he heard playboy Max had deemed Charlotte's impromptu truck mate a horndog, the hunt for the Pirithous scent moved from the north quadrant to Charlotte's route.

She can handle it herself.

The mantra had been playing softly in the back of his head since he'd left the restaurant. And, logically, he knew she would probably be fine.

Unfortunately, logic was in short supply in his brain when it came to her.

He knew it and he didn't care.

He stripped down and shoved his clothes into the crevices of a large rock pile, doubling back to the SUV to grab the collar in his glovebox before he dropped down to all fours and his body morphed, the sounds and scents of the landscape temporarily assaulting him as his snout elongated and his ears perked up. Charlotte had a good two hours on him by now, her typical route placing her closer to the Keys. He took off across the desert, his ears and eyes alert to any sign of humans in the darkness. When he passed the Keys with no sign of her, he continued to press eastward, his nose scouring the air for her scent until he caught it.

Sheep's Pass.

Padding across the smooth stones carefully, he made his

way over the hills until he saw her truck parked among the small collection of campers unbothered by the prospect of a murderer on the loose. He lowered his head while he approached the vehicle, a low growl emitting from deep in his throat as a man spoke.

"We don't have to call it a date," the guy said, his elbow resting on the open sill of the truck window. "Just dinner and drinks between colleagues."

Before Alex could nip at the protruding arm, Charlotte replied, her voice cold. "Call it whatever you want. I'm busy."

"How about another night then?" the agent pressed. "You seem tense. You could probably use a night of loosening up."

He bared his teeth and closed in on the truck, crouching to slink along the side until he was flush with the grille.

"I'm busy every night you aren't," she bit back. "And I'm tense because I'm stuck in here with a handsy jerk with an inflated sense of self-worth and a juvenile vocabulary."

Handsy?

Raising up on his hind legs, he let out a snarl and placed his paws on the hood of the truck. The guy jumped, a string of curses flying from his mouth as Charlotte gasped in surprise before she recognized him.

"Awwww, come here, Butch!" she called, rolling down her window and extending her hand out. With his eyes on the douchebag, Alex nuzzled her hand. Noticing his attention was focused on her companion, Charlotte cupped his snout in her hands. "Butch, meet Kevin. Kevin, Butch."

Kevin relaxed slightly into his seat. "Big-ass dog," he muttered, extending his hand toward Alex and conveniently brushing it against Charlotte's shoulder. Alex snapped at him, grazing the fingers with his teeth and growling. "Not well trained either, huh?"

"He's very well trained. I don't think he likes you," she murmured, her dark eyes amused. "You are trained, aren't you, boy? Can you sit?"

Keeping his attention on Kevin, Alex sat.

"Such a good boy," Charlotte purred. "Shake?"

Lifting his paw to demonstrate just how trained he was, he shoved aside the slight to his ego for the greater good. Namely, to avoid the tranquilizer darts he was pretty certain were stored somewhere in the truck.

"Animals have a very keen sense of who they do and don't like." Without waiting for Kevin to respond, she nudged her door open and got out of the truck. "Here, boy. Let's get you in the back and I'll see what I have in the cooler for you. You and I need to have a little talk about where you put your leash."

Chapter Ten

ALEX GRINNED AS Max and Charlotte pushed their way through the lunch crowds of the tavern, holding their arms up in victory. "All hail the afternoon shift!" Max announced, earning a round of applause from his fellow rangers. "It was a long haul, but we made it. We survived." He draped himself backward over the bar counter dramatically, pulling Charlotte along with him. "Barkeep, a celebration tequila if you will."

Leaning over Charlotte, Alex took the opportunity to kiss her forehead. "So you survived your night with the douchebag cop?"

She closed her eyes and smiled. "I did. Help me up?"

He gently lifted her shoulders from the counter, ignoring the whoops and whispers that rose from the table of rangers as she pulled up a stool and poked Max in the ribs. Alex poured a round of tequila shots for the group, punching them into the till as a promotional tab before setting the tray beside Max. "On the house," he said, laughing when Max leapt up and began running the shot glasses over to his colleagues.

"You shouldn't encourage him," she chastised, her eyes lighting up when he placed a cup of coffee in front her. "No one needs tequila before noon."

"I'd have a celebratory shot myself if I wasn't working." He smiled. "So how bad was it last night?"

He knew damn well how bad it had been. He'd spent most of the night riding around in the back of her work truck listening to Kevin spew story after story about how successful he was, how athletic he was, how important he was, and how much all his ex-girlfriends still desired him.

But at least the jerk kept his hands to himself.

She groaned and rolled her head back. "Well, Becky isn't speaking to me now because apparently Kevin decided to go around the station and ask about me." She leaned forward and lowered her voice. "He's the guy Becky was caught with in the break room." She shuddered. "Guys like that are just so ew." Her gaze shifted to the table of women watching Alex with obvious interest and her smile fell slightly.

He pushed back the urge to abandon his post and head out into town to hunt down Kevin. "You know, you could have just told him you have a boyfriend."

Her dark eyes dropped to her coffee, her cheeks lifting as she fought back a smile. "Boyfriend, eh?"

Catching his own words too late, he crossed his arms and took a slight step away. "Yeah, well, isn't that what women say when guys don't take the hint?"

Dammit.

Dating was casual. Relaxed.

The boyfriend label held a lot more expectations. Expectations he couldn't fulfill.

As though sensing his unease, she shook her head and looked up at him. "Me saying no to one guy shouldn't need to be justified by the existence of another guy. If I say no, that should be good enough. I won't back myself up with some fictional boyfriend to have my decision validated." She smirked at him and picked up her coffee. "You really do suck at dating."

He watched her as she joined the other rangers, pulling a chair up beside Max and holding up a lemon slice for him.

You're a moron.

Every day that passed was another day Alex was digging himself into a hole. The more he talked with Charlotte, the more he wanted her. The more he wanted her, the more he thought about her. And the more he thought about her, the more his time and energy was divided.

Personal history taught him the sooner he slept with her, the sooner she'd be out of his system and out of his head. It was a foolproof system that had served him well in the past.

But this…

He walked into the back room to grab a few cases of beer, calling over to Thomas as he passed by. "I promoed a round of tequila for the rangers," he said, hefting two cases up. "Max and Charlotte finished night shift."

Thomas grunted. "I'll write off their meals, too." He

picked up the last case of beer and followed Alex. "I don't like that girl working nights. Especially with some psycho on the loose."

"Me either," he muttered, opening the beer cooler as he glanced back at the loud group.

Thomas passed him a few bottles. "What's going on between you two?"

"Just hanging out."

Setting the rest of the case at Alex's feet, Thomas snorted. "I'm old. Not stupid. Who's keeping who at arm's length?"

✕

CHARLOTTE HUFFED AND finished off the rest of her coffee. "We're just friends."

The women at the table leveled her with a flat stare. "Really," Becky stated, apparently prepared to forgo the silent treatment in exchange for gossip. "Let's put that to the test."

She stood up and sashayed over to the bar, leaning far over the counter to give Alex a view of her cleavage. Charlotte feigned disinterest as Alex smiled at Becky and poured her a drink, nodding at something she said. When Becky tilted her head to the side and pushed a small piece of paper across the bar, he took a step back and leaned on the counter until she walked away.

Becky set her drink down on the table and looked

around at the expectant women. "I gave him my number and a good view of the twins," she announced, giving her breasts a quick tap and lifting her brows. "He didn't look at either one, told me I was sweet, and said he's taken. Who's he taken by, Chuck?"

Flashing back to Alex's obvious panic over his use of the term *boyfriend*, she shrugged as her phone buzzed. Grateful for the interruption, she looked down at the message. *"More coffee?"*

She typed in her affirmation quickly, biting back a smile.

"Here he comes," Becky sang, sitting back and crossing her arms under her bust.

The coffeepot appeared in her peripheral vision as Alex topped up her cup and addressed the group. "Anyone hungry?"

He took the orders of the others, leaving her for last. "Miss Charlotte?"

"Steak sandwich, well done, no mushrooms, no onions, garlic toast on the side, please," she said, smacking Max as he mimicked her.

His hand grazed her shoulder as he walked away, her phone buzzing moments later.

"Meet me in the kitchen?"

Ignoring Becky's loud postulating about Alex, she rose to her feet and walked through the heavy kitchen doors, waving at Thomas as she passed through and met up with Alex at the back exit. "What's up?"

"Your coworker Becky is exactly my type," he stated, scooping her hand into his as she lifted an unimpressed brow. "Melanie, too. That's the woman I was with the night you were out with that Spider-Man guy. Same with over a dozen women scattered through the lounge right now, all of which I've been with. But you? You are really, *really* not my type." He released her hand when she yanked her fingers from his grip and crossed her arms. "That was a really bad opener," he muttered.

She pursed her lips, refusing to show any disappointment or anger despite the growing hurt rising in her chest. "That was a really clear opener," she corrected, turning away and walking back through the kitchen. "I'm going back to wait for my food."

Her group had become exponentially noisier when she got back to the table, amplifying the thoughts going through her head. Forcing a smile, she ignored Becky and joined in Max's conversation with Andy, tossing in a few opinions about underinflated footballs for good measure. When Alex arrived at the table and began passing out plates, she kept her attention on Max, ignoring the gentle nudging of her elbow until he walked away, and her phone buzzed.

"Let me finish?"

She glared at the message. *"I'm eating."*

Thomas had prepared her meal exactly as she liked it, the steak and fries not touching, no veggies, and a small plate for her garlic toast. But despite the perfect presentation of her lunch, she found it unappealing, finally succumbing to Max's insistent attempts to snag her steak. She pushed her plate toward him while she stood and walked over to the bar. "Finish," she said, placing her hands on the counter.

Alex shifted his stance and shoved his hands into his pockets. "My type knows I'm out the door after I get laid, and they're cool with it. My type has five others like me waiting in the wings," he replied, his strange eyes flicking over the lounge. "My type doesn't even get saved into my phone because there'll be another one within the week." He pulled his phone from his pocket and pushed it across the counter toward her. "I have eight numbers in my contacts. Two are my brothers, one is Thomas, one is my RV park office, and the other four are you, Max, the park station, and the national parks emergency line."

"So you're a man-whore," she muttered, refusing to touch his phone. "That's appealing."

"Yeah, well, I come from a long line of them," he retorted under his breath before clearing his throat. "What are you doing tonight?"

She looked over her shoulder, glaring at Becky briefly. "We're heading to the Washout for a night of debauchery. If you want to meet up, we'll be there around nine." She turned and walked back to her table. "And don't freak out. It's definitely not a date."

✕

ALEX SHRUGGED AN unwanted hand from his arm and craned his neck toward the dance floor, scanning the hordes of people until he caught sight of Charlotte. Weaving through the crowd, he made his way toward the group, stopping at the perimeter so he could watch her for a few moments.

He'd screwed up, and he knew it.

His pathetic attempt to meander his way to admitting how much he actually liked her had backfired horribly. The hardening of her dark eyes had been instantaneous, hitting him in the gut with more force than he ever thought a simple look could give. And the speed with which she had frozen him out still had his head spinning.

The logical side of him recognized it as a good thing, the universe reminding him he wasn't meant for the topside world.

His less rational side, the one that reared up every time he was around her, disagreed.

Becky caught sight of him first, leaning toward Charlotte and pointing. Charlotte gave him a brief smile and a wave before returning her attention to Max and his over-the-top emoting of the dirty lyrics blaring over the sound system. Alex crossed the floor and joined them, risking a harsh rejection as he came up behind her and placed his hands on her hips. When she didn't miss a beat, he relaxed a fraction and leaned toward her ear. "You look incredible."

And she did.

Hot damn did she ever.

Black miniskirt, high black boots, and a tight black button down? Yes, please.

She arched her head back to look at him. "We just got here," she called out over the music, her hips swaying as she reached back and wrapped one arm around his neck.

"Want one?" Max yelled over, passing a beer toward him.

"I'm driving," he replied, gritting his teeth when Charlotte's ass pressed against him.

Noticing his problem, Max grinned as he exited the dance floor. "Good luck there, Romeo."

The song switched to one he had heard a hundred times, and he braced himself for the inevitable squeal of the women in the crowd. Even Charlotte joined in, stepping away from him to join Becky and the others in something he had always deemed the mating call of the clubbers.

But as Charlotte ran her hands down her body and flung her hair back, he felt the full-blown effects of the beat for the first time.

Hot. Damn.

He backed up until he hit the railings surrounding the floor and watched shamelessly. Every so often, another woman would interrupt his view and he'd switch positions, his attention locked on Charlotte and her slithering movements.

"You're in the doghouse," Max's voice called out, pulling him back to reality. "She's *mad* mad. What the hell'd you do?"

He tore his eyes off Charlotte. "I tried to tell her I like her by bringing up other women," he grumbled. "Rookie mistake, right?"

Max looked thoughtful for a moment. "Dunno. I never told a woman I liked her before. At least, not since sixth grade." He pointed his beer at the women. "That's her hunting outfit. You better not stray too far from her view tonight or you'll be out for good."

"Dammit," he muttered, running his hand through his hair. "Did she say anything?"

"Not a word. Which should terrify you."

Dammit.

The music turned to something heavier and the dance floor emptied, Charlotte trailing the others as they headed back to their table. With Max's warning hanging in his head, Alex cut her off from the group. "Could I get you a drink?"

She shook her head. "You could actually get me out of here." Pausing, she looked up at him, her big brown eyes uncertain. "Unless you're scoping out the place for your next conquest."

He reached down to tuck a strand of hair behind her ear. "One more chance," he said, ignoring the well-deserved jibe. "I promise not to freak out about the word *boyfriend* if you promise to be okay with me calling you my girlfriend." He paused. "And if you're cool with me using you as chick-repellent. Women are as pushy as men, you know. I've never said 'I have a girlfriend' before. I'm curious to see if it works."

There was a small shift in her expression as she processed his words. "So ginormous you wants me to protect you from big, bad Becky?"

"Pretty much." He wrapped his hand around hers and led her through the crowd toward the doors. "So, Max mentioned that's your hunting gear. What exactly are you hunting tonight?"

"Pretty bartenders who notch their bedposts until they fall apart." She smirked, wrinkling her nose. "Dating them never ends well, but they're perfect for a fling, wouldn't you say?"

Holding the door open, he bit back the blast of disappointment that passed through him. "Then how about we forget the dating idea and just call it exclusively hanging out in our downtime?"

She nodded and tucked in tight to him as they walked to his SUV. "You did say you were taken. And we wouldn't want to make a liar out of you."

He grinned. "I am taken. Even if you walk away from me right now, I'm taken."

Chapter Eleven

CHARLOTTE STRETCHED OUT in her bed, keeping her eyes shut tight as she smiled into the empty room, her mind winding through her evening with Alex, lying on the hood of his SUV and watching the Perseid meteor shower.

"I'm related to the guy this is named after, you know," Alex stated, grinning when she elbowed him lightly in the ribs. "What? Distant relative, but still."

"You are not." She laughed, inching closer to him and pointing at another meteor flashing across the clear sky. "I, however, am a descendant of the illustrious Scarlotti line, of Dayton, Ohio. You may have heard of us. We're known in most circles as the noisy neighbors with those damn dogs."

He worked his arm under her shoulders. "Come from a long line of animal lovers then?"

"It's in our blood." She smiled. "My dad's a farm vet and my mom runs a rodent and bird rescue. My brother followed Dad's footsteps, but I couldn't handle the whole sick-animal thing, so I went a different route."

"Yeah," he scoffed. "Stalking wild dogs and trying to domesticate them."

She paused to listen in the still night for Butch. "He's already domesticated. Shaking a paw, slack leash…someone trained him well. I think he just needs a little TLC."

Alex had hummed in agreement and gone silent after that, his arm tightening around her until the first light of dawn faded the stars.

It was exactly what she didn't know she needed when she'd shown up at the bar, half of her hoping he'd stand her up and prove her right, the other half scared he would.

Even if you walk away from me right now, I'm taken.

Silver tongues had ensnared her before, pretty promises from handsome men who operated on a different level than she did. The sting of his "type" speech remained a small warning in the back of her mind that he was a different breed than she was, a breed she knew well.

But this was different.

She was walking in with her eyes open and expectations low.

He was a fling. And flings weren't messy.

They were on the same page.

And that would keep everything in line.

"I'M COMING TO you. Address?"

Alex reread the text and slowly scanned his trailer.

Whoa.

He fired off his address to Charlotte and got to work straightening up the neglected RV, filling his trash can quickly as he frantically sprayed down and wiped off every surface he passed until the place looked better than it had since he moved in. Calculating out the time he had remaining, he jumped into the shower without waiting for the water to warm.

Every hour that had passed as they lay on the hood of his car, he'd sworn to himself time was up, that he was going to take her home and head back out on the hunt.

And every hour, he'd pulled her in a little tighter.

Rinsing the shampoo from his hair, he shoved aside the guilt seeping into his head. Guilt over lost hours he should have been tracking the Pirithous. Guilt over the halfhearted trot he'd taken through the western rim of the park in the early morning hours after he'd walked a groggy Charlotte to her door.

And the guilt over not regretting a moment of it.

Bang her tonight and it'll be over.

Even the most alluring goddesses lost their appeal for him after a roll in the sheets. The sooner he bedded Charlotte, the sooner she'd be out of his system. The chase would be over, and he could get his head back to the hunt he should be focusing on.

Almost believing his own lie, he turned off the water, wrapped a towel around his hips, and scooped up a pair of shredded jeans he was ninety-nine percent certain were clean.

Her little coupe pulled up as he yanked his shirt over his head, his wet hair already dampening his collar while he opened his door. "I know what you did there," he said, lifting the bags of takeout from her arms. "And I'll have you know, I had this place cleaned with ten minutes to spare."

She laughed, her sunglasses hiding her eyes as she entered the trailer. "I'm impressed. More impressed a guy your size even fits in here. Show me around."

Smirking, he pointed out the grand tour. "You're standing in the living room, kitchen, and dining room. Bathroom's through that door, and you can see the bed from here. I... Damn. I forgot to make the bed."

"I like it," she said, passing him a box of Caesar salad. "If I wasn't so averse to bugs, I'd definitely live in something like this. Apartments suck. And you can just pick up and go anywhere whenever you want."

He nudged her hip to the side to open his cutlery drawer and handed her a fork as she sat. "How the hell do you work in a desert if you hate insects?"

"Easy," she mumbled, swallowing a bite of spaghetti. "Bugs outside, no problem. That's their house. But in my home? No way. I'll blast those little bastards with all the hellfire I can rain down on them." She looked around. "Where's the TV?"

"Uh," he stammered, tilting his head. "That way."

"The bedroom."

He grinned. "Yup."

She stood and wandered down the short hall, peering into his messy room. "I'm not sitting on that bed."

"You should," he insisted, refilling his plate. "You'll be the first woman to step foot in there. Think of it as a mission to Mars. Boldly go where no woman has gone before." His jaw flexed as he realized the truth to that statement.

He'd been in thousands of beds, but very few had ever been in his. And even then, the sporadic few that had breached his sanctuary had done so only out of necessity.

He looked up to find her watching him, her eyes thoughtful. "You really do have issues with any kind of relationships, don't you?"

"My job keeps me pretty opposed to it," he muttered, holding out a slice of garlic toast to her.

She accepted it and sat down beside him. "Meh." She shrugged. "You're young. Maybe the nomadic bartender lifestyle will lose its appeal at some point."

With a grunt, he leaned back against the sofa, stretching his arm across her shoulder. She settled into him and began asking a litany of questions about RV living as he tangled his fingers in her hair. Once she was satisfied with his responses, she stood up and opened her purse, popping a mint. "Movie?"

He hesitated.

He definitely didn't want the evening to end. But he wasn't an ass either. "Let me tell you a few things first, and if you're still into a movie after that, I'll pick up my dirty socks and put one on."

Charlotte eyed him warily and sat just out of reach, her sudden closed position momentarily throwing him. "Okay," she said slowly. "Go."

Flipping through everything he wanted to say, and matching it up to everything he could say, he took a deep breath. "Bartending is kind of a secondary job," he began, studying her reactions intently. "My brothers and I work for another business that sends us all over the world, and right now, Coachella Valley is it."

Her expression changed, her dark eyes widening slightly in interest. "That's pretty cool!" she exclaimed. "What do you do?"

Hitman.

Killer.

"Bounty hunter."

She froze, her brows shooting up. "What?"

"We track down bad guys for payment," he continued, his fingers itching to reach for her. "My brothers are pretty heavy into it. Definitely more invested in it than I am. We're tracking one now with a pretty important payout for us. If we catch the guy, I'll be moving on to the next job." He ran his hand through his hair. "So this," he said, gesturing between them, "has a time limit."

She sat back against the far side of the sofa, her arms wrapping around herself. "You kill people for money."

"Catch," he corrected, thinking about the loophole he

was currently exploiting. "I catch them, alongside my brothers. I'm better at picking up the trail than they are, so I'm more on the recon side."

Bullshit.

Her dark eyes narrowed. "How bad are these bad guys?"

Poisoned bloodline.

"All I can say is that for each one we eliminate, we save dozens of lives."

She looked away, her lips pursing. "So this killer in the park, is he one of your hunts?"

He shrugged. "Won't know until I track him down. The guy I'm after now was in this area six months ago, so it's definitely possible. The kills are consistent with his profile."

She regarded him for a few agonizing moments. "And I take it fraternizing with the locals is frowned on?"

He ran his hands through his hair and leaned forward onto his elbows. "Yeah, that's the problem. I've been putting my brothers off for a month now, and there's a really good chance one or both of them will be coming here any day. And my boss probably wouldn't be too pleased to find out I was spending any hours off the clock or extending my time here for even a day."

"Why are you?"

He gave her a pointed look. "Why do you think? Because the tips at Tom's Tavern are too good to pass up? I'm hanging around in the hopes I can, I don't know, have a half-assed normal relationship before I'm shipped off to hell."

Literally.

"Hence why you're spilling all this now," she stated, crossing her arms.

"No," he argued. "Well, yes. I'm spilling it because I really, really want to kiss you again and it doesn't feel right to do it unless you know where things stand. And because, yeah, I have an older brother who's kind of controlling and a twin with more issues than *Vogue* who could show up tomorrow and screw me over in any way they deem appropriate."

She went silent again until her lips turned up slightly. "A twin?"

He glared at her. "Seriously?"

"I'm sorry." She laughed, tugging at her shirt hem. "It's just a lot to take in and I have no idea how I'm supposed to react." She adjusted her position to face him. "You track down killers, pass them to your brothers who, what, dispose of them? And then you leave. Oh, and you're currently lying about your work to your family, who may or may not show up here and be really pissed. Did I miss anything?"

He leaned his head back. "Aside from the kissing you part and the fact I'm lying to my brothers about the kissing you part, no."

"You're trusting I won't go to the cops with this," she said, ignoring his sarcastic response.

"I don't exist in any database."

She licked her lips, her eyes narrowing. "What would

your boss do if he knew you were telling me this?"

Shoving the memories of chains and muzzles from his mind, he shrugged. "I'd rather not think about it."

She whistled low. "You're in a bad situation."

"No," he replied, reaching over to grab her hand. "I'm in a good situation that's going to go bad eventually. Big difference."

CHARLOTTE LOOKED DOWN at the large mitt completely enveloping her hand.

Of course he was a bounty hunter. Why wouldn't he be?

"This is a lot heavier than you being a man-whore," she said, her eyes still locked on their joined hands.

Alex snorted. "It kind of ties into it."

"So what do you want from me?"

He mulled over the question, his blue and hazel eyes darkening and lightening as thoughts passed through his head. "You," he finally settled on.

She rolled her eyes. "And if you get me, you'll leave. Why bother?"

"It's worth it for me," he muttered, turning her hand over in his and examining her palm. "You'll eventually get the total shit end of the stick, if you don't get fed up with me before that. But if you know we have an end…" He sighed and leaned back. "This is a stupid idea."

She cocked her head and looked at him long and hard.

Morally questionable.

Ethical issues through the roof.

Nothing more than a dangerous little fling with a guarantee of no strings.

She leaned across him and brought her lips to his, kissing him softly until his head caught up with what she was doing.

She smiled against his mouth. "I'm not sleeping with you, since your shelf-life is limited. This is purely a meet-and-greet."

"I think I can be okay with that," he murmured, pulling her to him. One large hand wound into her hair at the nape of her neck, sending a little thrill buzz through her body as she crawled onto his lap and straddled him. "I'm totally okay with that, too." He moaned, trailing his lips down her throat and shifting his hips beneath her.

She could do this. Live on the edge a little. Add a dash of limited risk to her life until he poofed away and she could return to her happy, safe existence with her cat, her badge, and her grilled cheese sandwiches in a quiet apartment.

Sitting back in his lap, she hesitated. "We agree this is just temporary then, right? No expectations."

"No expectations," he echoed, his eyes flicking between her lips and her eyes. "Friends with benefits."

"Perfect." She swatted a rogue hand as it moved toward her breast. "No way, killer," she warned, whimpering when he ground against her center.

"Hunter," he corrected, slipping the chastised hand under her shirt and skimming his fingers lightly along her ribs. He brought his lips back up again, his tongue sliding into her mouth and dancing with hers leisurely as she traced her fingers down his arms, circling the muscles there before venturing to the abs she'd been drooling over for weeks.

"Keep it above C-level," he teased, pushing her back and gently tugging at the hem of her shirt. "Yes?"

She took a deep breath and pulled the fabric over her head, dropping the tee beside them as he gripped her hands and placed them on his shoulders.

"Damn," he muttered, his hips jerking up involuntarily. "I... Damn. I promised no sex, right?"

"Not in so many words, but yes." She grinned, her confidence spiking as he ran his hands over her bare skin and licked his lips.

"I'm an idiot."

Chapter Twelve

ALEX PADDED THROUGH the back streets of a small town north of Joshua Tree, making use of the first few hours of moonlight before Charlotte got off work. She had assured him that she and Max would be traveling together for the first few afternoon shifts as they acclimated to the different procedures and responsibilities that day shifts provided. He'd swung by for a quick belly rub before heading north, taking the rare opportunity to nip at Max's hand when it got too close.

The guy did kiss her once, after all.

And man or beast, he definitely owned up to his jealous streak when it came to that woman. Even if they were officially nothing more than make-out buddies.

He was nose-deep in a discarded burger when he caught it.

Pirithous.

He lifted his snout, turning slowly to pinpoint the direction of the scent. Once he zeroed in on it, he maneuvered through the streets, keeping tight to the dark corners to avoid detection as the bloodline grew stronger. Stopping at the entrance of a small apartment complex, he inched across the tiny parking lot, following the smell until he hit the jackpot.

Fucking. Sedans.

Memorizing the address and license plate, he tore off toward the highway where his SUV sat abandoned on a side road. He morphed quickly, yanking his jeans over his hips and pulling his cell phone out of the glove box.

His thumb hovered over the phone icon.

One more night.

He glanced at the time. Charlotte would be off in an hour, and it would take him that long to circle the park and meet her at the station.

He'd found his prey. One more night wouldn't be the end of the world.

Shoving his phone into his pocket, he started the engine and pulled onto the highway.

"DUDE," MAX SAID, gesturing wildly. "The thing is, like, this tall. Huge. You need to tell your woman to keep her distance from that animal. If it turns, it'll kill her in a heartbeat."

Alex lifted a brow and leaned against the counter of the ranger station, watching Charlotte as she trailed her finger along a map to show a pair of hikers their path. "Tell my woman?" He laughed. "How about you tell your partner. See how well that goes over."

"I did. She yelled at me."

He smirked and turned his attention back to Charlotte, listening in to her enthusiastic description of Skull Rock, her dark eyes lighting up as she spoke. "Damn," he muttered, taking a long drink from his water bottle. "So, is the dog aggressive?"

Max snorted. "Rolls over like a fucking kitten for Chuck. Tried to take my hand off, though." He leaned in and flexed his hand in front of Alex's face. "Almost lost those three fingers."

Other hand.

"I wouldn't be too worried," he mused. "If the animal's loyal to her, then he's probably a good guard dog. And since no one seems able to track down whoever left those bodies in the park, a guard dog is a pretty appealing idea right about now."

Grumbling a reluctant agreement, Max leaned back in his chair and kicked his feet onto the counter Alex was using to remain upright, his entire body aching from lack of rest and the hours he'd spent monitoring Charlotte's route and tracking his target.

But it was a small price to pay to have one last uninterrupted evening with her. One more night before he called in Bo and Ryan.

No harm, no foul.

Charlotte dropped into the chair beside Max, her face

flushed from the intense heat of the summer that battled valiantly against the station's air conditioner. "That's it. I'm done. Want to head back to my place for a bit?"

Max slammed his hands on his knees. "Yes, yes I do." When she leveled him with a glare, he grinned. "See you tomorrow. Leave your car and I'll pick you up at eight."

Alex extended his hand to help Charlotte up. "Have a good night, Max," he called over his shoulder as he led her to his SUV and opened her door. "Hungry?"

"Tired." She sighed, slumping back in the passenger seat and smiling at him lazily. "I'm getting too damn old to work in this heat."

Creeping through the park until he hit the highway, he looked over at her. "Any chance you'll be transferred out?"

"I keep one eye on the job postings," she said, turning the music up a fraction. "My degree is in animal science with a few extra courses in environmental conservation, so between that and the police training, I'm hoping to move up the ladder pretty quick."

He turned into the residential area and wound through the side streets to her apartment. "So the whole white-picket-fence-settling-down thing isn't in the cards anytime soon then?"

"Not really. You and I are in kind of the same fenceless boat, I guess." She chuckled, shaking her head. "Both of us have careers keeping us from putting down roots. Except your job has less paperwork." She led him to her door, fumbling in her purse for her keys. "We should hit the twenty-four-hour gym sometime. I haven't stayed on top of my training as much as should." She pushed her door open. "Besides, I want to see if I can knock you on your ass."

Every time you fucking look at me.

He turned on the TV and got comfortable. "And I'll enjoy you trying." He flicked through the channels. "Documentary or corny B-horror?"

"Horror," she called from her room before she joined him on the sofa, her beige and khaki uniform traded in for an oversized shirt and gray cotton shorts. She relaxed against him, curling up under his arm. "I've seen this."

Flashing to their last movie on her couch, he smirked. "I was kind of hoping you had."

He could feel the upturn of her cheek against his healing ribs.

He held off twenty minutes before making his move.

"Smooth." She giggled when he wedged his hand underneath her ass and unceremoniously lifted her to straddle his lap.

"I try," he muttered, dropping his head into the crook of her neck and nipping at the soft skin. When her breath hitched, he trailed his tongue to her earlobe. "Are we still operating in the no-sex zone? The whole friends-with-benefits thing?" he whispered, inching his hands up the back of her shirt.

"We are," she breathed, her thighs tightening against his

hips. "So behave, friend-with-limited-benefits."

With the practiced flick of his fingers, he unhooked her bra and smiled triumphantly. "I will."

✗

ALEX SAT IN his SUV and stared absently at Charlotte's window, watching as her shadow moved through the rooms and turned off the lights.

Drive away, dumbass.

He thumbed his phone in one hand, the Pirithous bloodline's address fisted in the other.

It was too late to call Ryan or Bo. Ryan would be sleeping. Bo would be drunk.

He could do it in the morning.

Slipping the crumpled paper underneath his phone case, he pulled out of the lot and headed north. The streets were busy, the bars closing down and unleashing their clientele into the world again. He hit the highway, blasting his music to drown out the thoughts rampaging through his head.

Every night he put off reporting the bloodline's whereabouts was another night Ryan went without closure. It was another night Bo spent hunting for the ultimate high. Another night Charlotte slipped deeper into his mind.

He circled the run-down apartment block slowly, scanning the windows for signs of movement. The sedan remained untouched, the scent of the driver fading. Parking beside the vehicle, he left the SUV running and got out, kneeling in front of the grille to remove the fur still hooked along the metal.

Two dead already.

He rose to his feet and ran his hand over his knotted shoulders. It was only a matter of time before the line struck again.

His hesitation would be the unofficial cause of death of the next victim.

He climbed back into his SUV and backed in tight to the shadows of the apartment block, locking his tired eyes on the sedan and forcing himself to remain focused and alert. If he could wait out the last hours of night, he could call Ryan on his way back to the park. Catch him before he left for work. Run Charlotte's route ahead of her to ensure the Pirithous hadn't passed through.

Maybe talk to Bo before he cracked his morning beer.

Hear Charlotte's voice before heading to his shift at the tavern.

He ran his hands through his hair, his fingers flexing as they continued to hold the sensation of her skin, the heaviness of her breasts in his palms. Leaning back in his seat, he rolled down his window and allowed the faint warm breeze to hold him in the moment, to force his focus to his mission and away from the siren luring him from it.

Chapter Thirteen

CHARLOTTE BIT HER lip and took a step back as Alex closed in on her, his long hair tied back in a low ponytail he had instructed her very sternly not to pull. He assessed her stance, choosing to go with a frontal attack this time and regretting it as his back bounced off the gym mat.

He rose up on his elbows, his healing ribs protesting loudly. "I give," he announced, dropping back down and closing his eyes. "I'm man enough to know when I'm outclassed."

"You lasted longer than Max," she offered, kneeling at his side and placing her hand on his stomach. "You're all sweaty and gross. You slid right over me."

His arms shot up and wrapped around her, pulling her on top of him and holding her tight to him, sore ribs be damned. "It's not gross," he countered, tightening his hold when she screeched and attempted to squirm away from him. "It's manly."

"It's icky." She laughed, pushing off his chest and holding her palms out to him. "*Eeeewwwwwwww.*"

He reached up, ran his hand along the back of her neck,

and looked at her with amusement.

"I'm glowing," she retorted, rising to her feet and snatching a towel from the bench. "I'm glowing like a stuck pig but glowing nonetheless." She tossed the towel at him. "Go shower up. I'll meet you in the lobby."

He grunted as he got to his feet, admiring the view while she walked away from him, her shirt clinging to her glowing form. Keeping the water barely tepid to cool his amping libido, he showered quickly and dressed, running his fingers through his hair as he pulled his ball cap on.

She was leaning against the door when he exited the showers, her gym bag slung over her shoulder and her wet hair dripping down the back of her shirt.

Damn.

"How's the ego?" she inquired with a grin, glancing down when he grabbed her hand.

"Nothing a raw steak can't heal up." He tossed his bag into his SUV. "You're going to have to teach me that shoulder move so I can kick some ass on the job." He smiled at her. "You coming over?"

She hesitated.

He tilted his head and watched while her expression grew thoughtful, her eyes hardening slightly as she tugged her hand out of his.

"I think I'm going to head home," she finally said, unlocking her car and throwing her bag in. She bent to get in before pausing and straightening, crossing over to kiss him quickly. "I'll text you later this week, okay?"

He leaned against his SUV until she was out of sight, knowing it was time to make the call he should have made two mornings ago.

CHARLOTTE EASED OFF the gas as she rounded a bend in the road, cracking a smile as Butch jogged up alongside the truck, his leash dangling from his jaws. "Hey, boy!" she called, draping her arm out the window for a quick ear scratch. "You riding in or out this evening?"

Butch butted the door with his head, his preference clear. She unfastened her seat belt and got out, opening the back door for the beast and waiting until he'd settled before she tucked the leash tight to him and slammed the door closed. "I've got nothing but kibble today," she warned, laughing when the immense animal snorted and turned his head away from her. "What do you say to a tour of Sheep's Pass?"

The dog laid his head on her armrest as she drove, chuffing in protest every time she stopped the soothing petting of his ears. "Demanding thing, aren't you?" she muttered, turning onto the narrow road that led to the pass. "We've got an hour of daylight left. Let's walk it."

Butch jumped from the truck and padded alongside her, his ears twitching with every bristle of the browning foliage. She kept one hand on the beast's back as they made their way up the path, her steps slowing as the climb became steeper. "This isn't so bad," she panted, balancing on the poor dog more than she should. "No men. No moral conundrums. No weird rules. Just you, me, and the red coachwhip over there."

The dog placed himself between her and the snake, adapting his speed until she was out of striking distance.

"You probably have another eight or ten years left in you," she continued, bending down to pick up a discarded coffee cup and shoving it into her back pocket. "Better odds than wasting time on some random guy with a short shelf life."

Butch's head turned up to her for a moment, his long fur flopping into his eyes.

She wrinkled her nose at him. "You get it. Come on. Top of the pass and we'll head back." Looping the leash around her wrist, she continued the climb. "You know, it would be so much easier to just wham-bam-thank-you-sir that guy if he wasn't so damn sweet. And funny. Super-hot guys are so rarely funny." Butch chuffed and shook his head. "But there he is, being all chivalrous with opening doors and asking permission to kiss me. Who does that? None of the guys I date, that's who."

Scooping a nasty cigarette butt off the sand, she shoved it into the crushed cup in her pocket. "And a bounty hunter? What the hell, right?" When Butch responded with a snort, she patted his head. "That's one of those things that could put me on a daytime talk show." Her hand tightened on the leash as her heart tightened in her chest. "Though I suppose Alex is the perfect final fling before I enter the career-spinster years Max keeps warning me about."

✕

ALEX DROPPED HIS snout to the sand and froze.

Pirithous.

"Fifteen more feet," Charlotte cooed, her fingers massaging his shoulders as she attempted to encourage him forward. She took another step, cursing in surprise when he snatched his leash from her hand and bounded ahead of her to block the way, his head lowered and ears flattened back.

She eyed him warily. "Move, boy. I'm just going to peek over the ridge and we can go."

He growled low, his nose picking up the scent of his target among the large rocks to his right.

"Butch," she said, her voice stern. "Move."

When she took another step toward him, he bared his teeth and crouched, his hackles rising. The scent was dissipating on the faint breeze, intertwining with the odor of death.

"What's your problem, boy?" she grumbled, continuing her climb with deliberate movements intended to avoid spooking the dog in her way. "Come show me."

He backed up the over the rocks, his options limited.

Biting Charlotte would be bad.

Herding her could be worse, her footing on the stones already tenuous.

Transforming would result in questions he didn't want to answer. Probably more screaming than he liked, too.

With his head swinging from side to side and ears tuned in to every rustle in the area, he monitored her as she progressed to the apex of the pass and looked around, her attention zooming in on a crevice.

"See boy?" she whispered, beginning a descent down the other side and reaching into her back pocket. "Nothing to growl about." She lifted small binoculars up as he nipped her shirt, tugging her back lightly. "I… Oh." Her hand flew to her mouth. "Oh, my god."

Kill number three.

He spread his paws across the stone as her balance wavered and she gripped his neck. He scanned the area for signs of movement, any indication the Pirithous line was still on-site. Satisfied that the scene was abandoned, he nudged her back to the peak, staying tight to her as she skidded down the rocks and took off toward her truck.

MAX CROUCHED BESIDE Charlotte, refilling her mug with another cup of burnt coffee. "It's midnight," he barked to the FBI agent sitting across from them. "I'm taking her home and you can continue this after she's had some rest."

She looked to Kevin, who'd been interrogating her relentlessly for four hours. "I don't know what else I can tell you."

All business, the FBI agent nodded stiffly. "Fine. Be back on-site for noon and we can review anything else we've found at the scene."

Max extended his hand and helped her to her feet, setting the bitter coffee to the side. "You're riding with me tonight. You can get your car when we come back in the morning, okay?"

She nodded as they made their way outside. "Wait! Butch is out there. What if they mistake him for something and shoot him?"

Max doubled back into the station and spoke quietly with Kevin for a moment before returning to her. "They'll be on the lookout. Let's go."

The drive to town was silent, Max periodically checking his phone once they hit the highway and Charlotte staring out the window.

A foot. A foot with a sneaker on it.

The FBI had located the other one shoved deep inside another crevice, following the trail of dismembered limbs, one arm still affixed to a backpack.

She shuddered as Max looked down at his phone.

"Everyone's at the tavern," he said quietly. "Why don't we stop by there for a few minutes? Get a shot or two to calm your nerves?"

She stared out the window. "I'm not sure I want to see Alex tonight."

Max sighed and slowed as he turned off the highway. "Everyone's worried about you. If Alex is working, I'll talk to him, okay?" When she refused to reply, he pressed on. "Unless something bad went down between you two."

She shook her head, forcibly ignoring the rising urge to jump out of the car and run to the tavern on foot, the sudden need to be wrapped tight in Alex's arms entering a dangerous territory she didn't want to deal with that night. "No. Nothing. One drink and we're out."

✕

ALEX KEPT HIS head down, meticulously drying the same glass for five minutes as he followed through on his promise to Max.

Give her space.

His hair fell forward, shielding his eyes as he watched Charlotte sit tight beside Max, her legs drawn up onto the chair, her face completely devoid of expression. Her fellow rangers had greeted her with hugs and reassurances when she and Max walked into the lounge an hour earlier, Max breaking off from the group to halt his beeline toward Charlotte.

She needs us tonight, man. Not you. Not anything compli-

cated.

He ran his hand through his hair and shelved the glass, grabbing another from the dishwasher.

Complicated.

There was nothing complicated between them. Unless he counted every half-truth and omission on his end. Or Charlotte's sudden freeze-out earlier that day.

She'd given him little more than a tight-lipped smile when she came in with Max, her arms tight around herself when he jumped the bar counter in his need to ensure she was still unhurt.

And it stung.

He risked a glance over at her, his stomach turning when she laid her head on Max's shoulder and he muttered something into her hair.

Cute couple.

"Can't believe they allowed that girl to patrol the area by herself with everything going on," Thomas grumbled, setting down a case of beer. "Poor thing, on her own seeing that."

He knelt to stock the fridge, unable to formulate a response outside a grunt of agreement.

Had he picked up the scent earlier, been less distracted by her proximity and her words, Charlotte would never have made it to the peak. Never would have seen the dismembered body tucked unceremoniously into the crevices of the stones, the hiker's shoes and backpack still affixed to his severed limbs. He would have fought her back to her truck on flat ground, feigning feral if he had to.

If only he'd been more alert.

More awake.

If only he'd sent out the SOS to his brothers the night he'd found their prey.

But he'd screwed up.

He'd been so desperate to steal a few more precious hours of normalcy with her, he'd selfishly shoved aside his mission, his brothers, and her safety.

The looping thoughts in his head turned his stomach as he shoved the last of the bottles into the fridge and stood, shaking his hair out of his eyes and crossing his arms as Max approached him.

"I'll settle the tab."

"Thomas took care of it," he said, leaning against the counter. "She okay?"

Max glanced back at the table. "What went on with you two? Anything I need to beat your ass for?"

He looked down at Max, lifting a brow. "I think she's bothered by our different life paths."

"That's stupid," Max replied, shoving a wad of bills into the tip jar beside the till. "They all lead to death, am I right?"

MAX SNATCHED A pillow off Charlotte's bed and sat. "Set your alarm so we don't both get written up for being late."

She nodded and rolled onto her side to check her clock. "So was he mad?"

"Who? Alex?"

She lay back and tossed her arm over her eyes. "Of course Alex. What did he say before we left?"

Max hummed for a moment, annoying her with his false contemplation. "First tell me what the deal is between you two and then I'll tell you what he said."

"Friends with limited benefits," she muttered, booting her leg out when Max laughed. "Shut it. That's as close as I'm getting to the hunk of beautiful man-whore." When Max continued to snicker, she lifted her arm off her face. "I froze him out earlier because he suggested we head back to his place and it just seemed like too much and too often for what we're supposed to be. And I may have wanted to go with him so bad I could taste it." She groaned. "Why is something that's supposed to be uncomplicated and uninvolved so damn involved and complicated?"

He shook his head and patted her leg in the most condescending way he could muster without her smacking him. "I've obviously failed to teach you proper booty-call protocol. The key to keeping it casual is to, I don't know, go with the flow *casually*. Don't want to hang out? Hit him with a 'sorry, babe, I've got plans.' He doesn't need to know your plans involve dying alone surrounded by your horde of cats."

She rolled her eyes. "I have one cat, Max. One."

"It's a start." He adjusted his position as his expression

morphed into total seriousness. "Freezing a guy out implies you're attached in some way. And that, Chuck, ain't casual. You've seen how players play up close and personal. Channel that and you'll be good to go."

"So I should bang some guy against Alex's SUV to show him just how casual we are?" she grumbled, cringing when the memory of her last breakup zipped across her mind.

He shrugged. "Maybe don't take it that far. Start with responding to his texts a few hours after he sends them and build up."

With a huff, she tucked her blanket tight under her chin. "Games are just cruel. And he's a smart guy. No way he'd put up with that kind of crap." She wrinkled her nose. "And he's too hot to have to put up with it."

"Yeah, well, so are you," he stated. "But there's a big difference between dating and a fling when it comes to boundaries, Chuck. You need to change how you think and act around Alex if you want to keep it chill."

Burrowing her head under the comforter, she groaned. "What if my heart doesn't want to keep it chill?"

"Hearts have no business in the fling game, Chuck. Remember that, and you'll be golden."

Chapter Fourteen

CHARLOTTE STARED AT the lone SUV in the tavern lot.
Drive away. Get another cat.

She smiled despite herself, Max's ridiculous, and unsolicited, relationship advice ringing in her ears.

It's okay to test-drive a Ferrari, Chuck. Even if you know you won't be buying it, you can enjoy the ride until the salesman tackles you, rips the keys from your hand, and calls the cops.

Killing the engine, she exited her car and walked into the deserted lounge.

"Alex?" she called, her eyes struggling to adapt to the dark interior after a long afternoon in the bright sun guiding FBI agents through Sheep's Pass.

He rose up from behind the bar, a pen between his teeth. "Ch…" He spat the pen into his hand. "Hey, Miss Charlotte."

She pulled up a stool and folded her hands on the counter, rehearsing the first line from her apology speech in her head before she spoke. "So, I'm kind of new to this friends-with-limited-benefits thing."

He eyed her warily, keeping his distance. "Same here."

He tossed the pen onto the counter and washed his hands out in the sink. "Was it the friends or the benefits that sent you running?"

"I don't even know," she huffed, her practiced speech no longer sounding right in the moment. She took a deep breath. "I freaked out, and I'm sorry."

"No," he replied slowly, easing his hands into his back pockets and scrutinizing her. "Freaking out usually involves yelling. And gives a lot more info about the reason. You froze." He slid his phone toward her, his messenger app open. "If you're second-guessing this, I get it. If it's too much, I get it. But this radio silence..."

She looked down at the unanswered texts sent to her and breathed out. "I'm sorry," she muttered. "You're right. Wow, this is dumb. You're going to be leaving. Which is good."

Scooping his phone back up, he retreated to the back of the bar again. "I will be, yeah."

"Soon?"

His jaw tensed as his gaze moved past her face to the door opening behind her. "Probably."

She rose up on her seat, tucking her foot under her while she debated the stupidity of her next question. "Logically, friends with benefits sh—"

"Friends with *limited* benefits," he interjected under his breath, his eyes tracking the new customer.

"Friends with *limited* benefits..." she hushed, glancing back to ensure she wasn't being overheard. "Should have pretty clear lines between the friends and the benefits, *limited* as they may be." She hunched over her coffee, her throat tightening in anticipation of her next statement. "Maybe we should keep this more in booty-call territory. If you're okay with it."

His eyes widened for a moment before they darkened, his lips drawing tight. "Booty-call territory."

Keeping her attention on her mug, she nodded. "Yeah, well, you're leaving soon. I could transfer out whenever something comes up. Neither of us are in a position to actually have a relationship, whether we want one or not."

Ignoring the immense man with the long black hair sitting at the end of the bar, he spread his hands on the counter and narrowed his eyes. "You want this to be nothing more than a hookup?"

"No. Yes. No," she stammered, flustered. "I'm trying to be realistic."

"Realistic," he echoed.

Looking up at him, she shrugged. "What do I say? Yeah, I want more than a hookup, but I'm not dumb enough to think it can be anything else."

"You've had a brutal twenty-four hours. You've probably slept, what, two or three of those? I'm going to hazard a guess based on your ponytail that you were at work this morning." He ran his hands over his face. "I'm not sure you saying this now isn't some knee-jerk reaction to the stuff you're dealing with."

"I freaked out before I found the…" She paused as the visual flashed across her mind and set her coffee down. "I'm almost as bad at this as you are. And you, Alex, are really, really bad." When he pursed his lips to keep from smiling, she leaned across the bar and stretched one hand toward him. "I forgave you for your 'Becky's my type' speech, so you kind of owe me a mulligan. Think about it and text me when you decide what you want."

His strange eyes narrowed at her, his hand inching across the bar toward hers before he adjusted his stance, blocking her view of the large man behind him. "Are we negotiating the benefits, too?" he asked quietly, giving her fingers a quick squeeze and releasing them.

"Ha! Maybe."

✕

HADES REMAINED IN place until the door closed behind Charlotte. "You heed her call."

Twisting the cap off a bottle of beer, Alex slid it across the bar and knelt to resume counting inventory. "Guy's gotta get laid, right?"

"You've yet to bed her," Hades stated as he took a sip of the drink and thumped it down. "She still watches you with uncertainty and curiosity."

Jotting down the final tally, he tossed his notepad beside the till. "Just chasing rabbits. It's always about the hunt, isn't it?"

His master rose to his feet slowly, his immense height dominating even Alex's considerable size. Hades sauntered around the bar until he stood toe-to-toe with him. "Ryan will always return to me willingly," he said, crossing his arms. "It's in his nature to obey, to carry out my commands. He has always derived satisfaction from a mission well done." When Alex looked away, he sighed. "And Bo? Bo follows Dionysus in all his incarnations, be it up here or back home. He's easily leashed. Easily subdued with the right persuasions. But you, Alexandros." He chuckled. "You obey out of obligation, an internal sense of duty. And I suspect my orders will not always take precedence."

Ducking out of Hades's intense stare, he took a step back. "I've given you no reason to question the depth of my loyalty."

His boss glanced over his shoulder. "It's not the depth I question."

Without another word, Hades strode past him and out the door, leaving him alone in the dimly lit lounge.

He eased his cell from his pocket and tapped the phone to life. "Hey. Can I come over?"

ALEX SNORTED AS Charlotte's front door was flung open, Max stomping through her kitchen.

"Does he ever knock?" he whispered, tightening his arms around her when she moved to stand.

Max poked his head around the corner, a slice of cold pizza in hand. "I've knocked. Chuck and I figured I've knocked five times since we met. And I have a key because I'm her favorite." He crossed the room and wedged himself between the pair, forcing Alex to release Charlotte before she was crushed. "What are we watching?"

Charlotte booted Max's foot off her coffee table. "Alex and I are watching an old Kevin Smith. You, however, are leaving."

Max glanced over at him. "You hear how she treats me? Mean, mean, mean." He stuffed the last of the pizza in his mouth. "We've been put on mornings for the next two weeks to aid in the sweep of the park."

"And you couldn't text me?" Charlotte snarled, looking over to Alex apologetically. "I'm sorry my baggage has such poor manners and smells like teriyaki chicken."

"Mean, I tell you," Max reiterated as he stood. "Lost my phone somewhere on the trail. It must've flown off the dash on a corner." He strode toward the open door. "If you plan on scoring tonight, do it quick. None of that drawn-out tantric bullshit. I'm picking you up in seven hours."

She flopped back against the sofa and restarted the movie. "This is why I suggested we go to your place. A Max-free evening never happens around here."

He pulled her back to him, happy when she grabbed a pillow and lay her head across his lap. "I'll risk a run-in with

Max if it means hanging out on your couch over mine." He grinned, easing the elastic from her ponytail. "Comfort trumps convenience."

She hummed in agreement, reaching behind them to grab a blanket. He tossed it over her and zoned out to the familiar soundtrack of one of his favorite films.

Their first attempt at a booty call was failing miserably.

The call had been placed, but it wasn't the booty he needed.

He watched her in his peripheral vision as her nose wrinkled and she rolled her eyes at a crude line, echoing it under her breath subconsciously.

It was so normal.

As long as the voice mails he'd left for his brothers remained unreturned, he could almost pretend the two of them were a regular couple hanging out on the sofa after a long day.

Circumstances aside, she liked him. And that knowledge almost eliminated the sting of her words in the park earlier.

Some random guy with a short shelf life.

He didn't want to be some random guy. But he was. And he could live with that as long as she continued to slap his knee every time a good scene came on screen.

Adding the booty to the call would rip this away.

Unwilling to end the hunt yet, he settled into the sofa and got comfortable, feigning sleep until the credits rolled and Charlotte sighed, covering him with a blanket before she disappeared into her bedroom.

Chapter Fifteen

THE TAVERN DOOR opened, a pair of gorgeous women stepping out into the heat of the late afternoon. Charlotte smiled at them, listening in as the women grumbled about the hot bartender who had shot down their offers for a night out.

Loosening her ponytail, she made her way into the lounge, rubbing her eyes when they refused to adapt quickly to the dim surroundings.

"Hey!" Alex called over, abandoning a tray of empty glasses on the counter.

She smirked as he sauntered across the floor to her. "Hey yourself, hunter," she teased, a small jolt running through her when his large hand wrapped around hers. "You almost done?"

He led her through the kitchen doors. "Thomas wants to feed you while I finish up." He gave her hand a quick squeeze before he disappeared back into the lounge.

"So this is why my bartender's been watching the clock all afternoon." Thomas grinned over the grill, pushing a stool toward her with one hand as he flipped a steak with the other. "Better order fast. I don't think that boy wants his date held up by a burger patty."

"I'll just take a grilled cheese, please," she requested, snagging a fry from a bowl. "Max stuffed me with microwaved bagels and eggs earlier."

Sneering in exaggerated disgust, Thomas pulled a bag of bread off the shelf. "He was in last night with some new arm candy. Rude little thing. I can't remember the last time Max ended a date before midnight."

"I heard all about it." She laughed, rolling her eyes. "Someday, Thomas. Someday, Max will find a good woman and settle down."

Thomas glanced up from his careful cheese layering. "Alex did, so there's hope for them all, I suppose."

She snorted inelegantly. "Don't get sappy," she chastised, her eyes widening in appreciation as the elderly bar owner added an extra cheese slice. "We're just having a little fun until Mr. Nomad gets antsy and hops a plane out of here."

Thomas eased the sandwich onto the grill and flattened it with his spatula. "Sometimes even the most restless animals can be calmed with the right touch." When she wrinkled her nose, he changed the topic. "Any leads on those deaths?"

"Nothing," she said, snatching another fry. "Max and I have been pulling double shifts for three days, tromping around the western ridge, and all we have to show for it is sand-blasted boots and ugly tan lines." She leaned forward to watch her sandwich. "I've barely had time to eat."

Thomas shook his head, muttering under his breath as he walked into the large cooler at the back of the kitchen.

The past three days had been little more than a blur of sand, stones, and snubbed kibble, punctuated by late-night texts with Alex and early morning calls from Max. Her long days had been made bearable by her beast of a companion that tracked her down every shift for a quick petting before he made his way to the highest point of the terrain and stood watch. When the FBI joined her and Max on the ground, Butch remained tight to her side, his slack leash providing a modicum of comfort for the wary agents.

Alex poked his head into the kitchen. "Any chance you can throw a burger on for me?" he asked, smiling when Thomas grunted and tossed two patties on the grill.

"Go keep that boy company," the older man ordered, pointing his spatula at her. "I'll bring these out when they're ready."

She grabbed a handful of fries and hopped off her stool, saluting Thomas on her way through the door.

The lounge was quiet, three groups huddled around their tables talking quietly and drinking slowly. Alex rounded the bar, grabbing the pot of coffee and a mug. "Thomas chase you out here?"

She pulled up a stool and sat at the bar, a small jolt running through her body when he set a mug of coffee down for her and kissed her forehead. "Tossed me out here on my tail." She smiled. "So I was thinking we could drive through the park quick and then head back to your place. Since I haven't seen it when you haven't had time to straighten up first."

"You like to live dangerously." He chuckled, leaving her to deliver a tray of drinks and returning with a credit card. "I could be up for that. Why the park?"

"I didn't see Butch this morning. I want to check in on him and make sure he eats," she replied as he ran the card and slipped the paid receipt into a cashier clip, tossing a pen on top. "Besides, I think you should meet him. He reads people well and I'm curious how he'll react to you."

✕

ALEX SLOWED THE SUV as he took the corner of the narrow path. "He's probably holed up somewhere for the night," he suggested, unsure how much longer the hunt for Butch was going to last.

Not that he was complaining.

The hour they'd spent looping the park was the longest he'd spoken with Charlotte all week, and he wasn't anxious for it to come to an end.

She sighed and sat back in her seat, rolling up her window. "You're right. Damn." She smiled up at him lazily. "I was kind of hoping he'd nip at you like he has every other guy he's met."

"Every guy you've introduced him to is a dick," he muttered, wrinkling his nose as he recalled the obnoxious cologne of the last two agents she had been assigned to assist. "Dogs love me. They recognize that I'm an alpha and they respect that."

She elbowed him in the ribs before settling against his arm. "All right, Alpha-Man. Let's head back to your place before someone recognizes me out here and they put me back to work."

He sped up a fraction.

No way in hell was he going to risk losing one of her two days off. Not when he had company arriving any day.

He made it back to his place in record time, mentally running through the mess in his trailer and determining which areas needed to be dealt with.

All of it.

"That bad?"

He snapped out of his head. "What?"

She opened her door, grinning. "You've been staring at your front door for a minute with the most serious look on your face. Is it that bad?"

Surrendering his key to her, he got out of the SUV and followed her in. "It's probably worse than I remember."

He had barely had time to do more than strip down and shower for weeks. If he wasn't working, he was monitoring the Pirithous or watching over Charlotte as she worked, keeping enough distance to remain out of the way of the stalled investigation, but close enough should anything be uncovered.

He was exhausted.

"This isn't so bad," she called over her shoulder, disappearing into his trailer. "A laundry hamper would do wonders for this place, though." He pulled the door closed and locked it, cocking a brow as she tiptoed through the piles of discarded socks and jeans and began carefully lifting shirts off his bed. "I need to know something."

He crossed his arms, his head dropping slightly in defense as a litany of potential questions flew through his mind. "What?"

"Before I even consider sleeping here tonight, when was the last time you washed these sheets?"

CHARLOTTE BIT HER lip at Alex's hesitation, his eyes darting to a small cabinet to the left of his bed. "I don't want to know, do I?"

He shook his head and licked his lips. "I have another set, though."

She plucked a T-shirt up and placed it in the makeshift pile beside her. "You're probably going to want to find it," she said casually, purposely ignoring the flash of hunger in his eyes. "I'll trade you places."

He stalked toward her, holding her hips as he brushed past her in the narrow hall. She sat on the sofa, crossing her legs and watching with amusement as he tore his bed apart, replacing the blue sheets with a set of black ones. She extended a hand. "Pass me the pillows and pillowcases."

He lobbed them toward her before returning his attention to wrestling with his comforter. "What movie do you want tonight?" he called over his shoulder, snapping the blanket smooth.

Something boring that neither of us will be into.

"Pick some blockbuster moneymaker sequel," she replied, tucking one pillow into its case and fluffing it. "One where none of the original cast returned."

He laughed and flopped onto his bed, stretching over to reach his remote and giving her a good, long look at the abs she hadn't seen in ages.

Damn, he was hot.

Her fingers were still aching from the grip she'd maintained on her purse to keep her hands from drifting down to his muscled thighs as he stretched his arm behind her headrest and grazed his thumb along the nape of her neck while they traveled the park.

She loaded her arms with the pillows, adding the small throw cushions from the sofa, and joined him. His eyes were fixated on the television, scanning the descriptions of each movie before making his selection triumphantly and sliding the remote back onto the ledge beside him. "This work?"

"Perfect."

She waited patiently as he tucked his arms behind his

head and got comfortable, his long legs crossed at the ankles and hanging over the edge of the bed. Once he stopped shifting, she tucked a pillow up beside him and snuggled up nice and tight, tossing one arm over his chest.

"You're off tonight," she murmured, tentatively broaching the somber undertone their evening had held. "Are you okay?"

He nodded and sat up, folding his pillow in half before lying back on it again. "All good."

Unwilling to rock the boat on one of their first nights as a not-a-couple-but-not-a-booty-call relationship, she resettled, changing the subject. "You're really warm."

He looked down at her. "I tend to run hot. Probably why I keep the air conditioner blasting in here constantly."

She'd noticed it weeks ago, how his skin was always warm to the touch whether they were out in the blistering heat or holed up in the sweet coolness of the lounge. She had even taken to cranking her own air conditioner up when he was at her place, his natural heat battling alongside the desert temperatures.

Without the slightest effort to watch the movie Alex had selected, she began drawing loops on his black shirt. Her fingers grazed along his body, the slight quickening of his breathing merely encouraging her as he kept his eyes on the small screen. She trailed her hand as far up his biceps as she could reach before doubling back and skimming the neckline of his shirt, smiling when he held his breath a fraction longer. Growing bolder, she dipped down to the hem and inched her fingers underneath. "I'm not bothering you, am I?"

She glanced up as he swallowed, his eyes still locked on the movie. "Nope. I'm good."

Fascinated by the amount of heat he was giving off, she continued her exploration slowly, skipping her fingertips over his ribs and skirting his abs. He shifted his hips, drawing her attention to the growing issue he was dealing with as he uncrossed his ankles and bent one knee. She dragged her pinky along the inside band of his jeans, impressed when his only reaction was to dig his heel further into the mattress.

She tilted her head up to him. "Want me to stop?"

"Nope," he muttered, his jaw muscles flexed. "I'm good."

That makes two of us, big boy.

She glanced down and bit her cheek.

Big, big boy.

Resuming her exploration, she snuggled her pillow further down to increase her scope. She ran her hand down one of his thighs then ventured back up the other one, her arm grazing the bulge in his jeans and earning a sharp exhale from him. Rising up onto her elbow, she hooked her thumb into the waistband of his jeans. "Can I?"

His unique eyes had moved from the television to her fingers, his hands clasped behind his head and biceps tight. "That depends. Booty calls redraw the limited benefits guidelines, right?"

"I'm not up for the booty part of the call tonight," she replied, smirking at him. "You, however, have a loophole."

"I fucking love loopholes."

She popped the button and eased the zipper down, taking care to avoid making contact with the beast she was unleashing. Keeping one eye on his reactions, she hooked her fingers into his belt loops and rose to her knees, tugging the stubborn jeans off his hips and pushing them down until he was able to kick them onto the floor.

"You really need a laundry hamper," she said, thumbing the hem of his black boxers.

"I'll pick one up tomorrow."

"I can come with you," she offered before she could stop herself.

He pushed himself up onto his elbows, his hair falling forward as he watched her intently. "We'll go after breakfast."

Deciding to deal with their unintentional plans later, she tossed one leg over his and straddled him, tracing his mouthwatering V-cut and stopping just short of the very prominent promised land. As he reached toward her, she sat back and crossed her arms. "Uh-uh. Keep those paws to yourself."

"Seriously?" His eyes flickered between her face and her hands that had dropped back to his boxers, her fingers finally touching his length.

"Seriously," she stated. "Though if you want to be helpful, you could take off your shirt." He sat up slowly, glancing behind her as if expecting a filming crew before he yanked his shirt over his head. She sat back on her heels, biting her lip as she took in the smooth expanse of his chest and studied a black symbol tattooed over his heart, tracing the thick C shape and arrow with her thumb. "Any meaning behind this?"

He leaned back on his elbows again, his attention locked on her every move while she resumed her exploration of his body. "Um, yeah. Probably." With each grazing of his member, he held his breath a fraction longer. With every trailing along his inner thighs, his hips shifted slightly.

And when she finally inched her hand under his boxers and gripped him, his head dropped back, and a low moan escaped him.

The power rush alone was enough to encourage her further, his heavy breathing merely a bonus as she stroked him slowly. His fingers stretched toward her periodically before he'd remember her instructions and they would snap back down to the mattress, tangling in his sheets.

"Damn," he muttered, making a valiant effort to sit up enough to watch her as she worked him. With the quick twist of her hand and a tightening of her grip, he dropped back onto his pillow with a grunt. "Hot damn, baby. Let me...lemme return the favor?"

"Nah," she replied, smirking when his eyelids fluttered.

"I kind of like calling the shots right now. I'm good at it."

"Very." He moaned, digging his heel into the mattress. "And I'm definitely not complaining."

She was fascinated.

Fascinated with the goosebumps that had risen on his hot skin when she loosened her hold on him and ran her thumb over the tip of his length.

Fascinated with the string of curses he let out when she gripped him at the base with one hand while she pumped him slowly with the other.

Fascinated by how she turned him into a hot mess with nothing but her hands.

"Charlotte. Honey?" He growled, breaking her no-touching rule to still her movements. "I'm really, really close right now."

Swatting his arm away, she ignored the endearment, tightened her grip with one hand, and placed the other on his stomach, digging her nails into his taut abs. "Close isn't what I'm after."

ALEX LEANED AGAINST his cluttered kitchen counter and ran a hand through his hair, keeping one eye on Charlotte's sleeping form while his phone continued to buzz in his hand.

Bo had been calling relentlessly for twenty minutes, yanking him out of a deep post-orgasmic sleep and hurling him straight into his messed-up reality.

Every day he spent with her, he was falling harder.

And after last night, he was pretty sure he didn't want to examine just how deep that fall had taken him.

They were slipping into an accidental relationship easier than either of them wanted to admit out loud, and he wasn't anywhere near ready to put the brakes on.

A text pinged in.

"Answer, you hideous fuckwad."

With a final check that Charlotte was still out cold, he eased the front door open, sat on the metal step of his trailer, and tapped Bo's number. "What's the plan?"

"About fucking time," Bo grumbled, his voice rough and words slurred. "Get your couch ready, brother. I'm on my way."

He rubbed the back of his neck and closed his eyes. "Why don't you call me in the morning and I'll see if I can hook you up with a room around here," he suggested. "This place is too small for both of us."

"Fuck that." Bo snorted. "I'm tying up a few ends here and I'll be bussing in." A loud clatter echoed through the speaker, followed by muffled swearing. "Goddammit. I just replaced the glass on this thing last month."

"Bus?" he asked, sitting up. "Where's your truck?"

Another *thunk*. Another curse. "Impounded. I'll text you when I'm getting close, probably Tuesday."

"Why not drive down with Ryan?" he asked, caught between relief knowing his brothers were closing in and a strange pressure in his chest at the thought of what that meant for Charlotte.

"I'm not spending hours locked in a vehicle with him. I'll kill him." Bo laughed. "Holy shit, Lex. He just doesn't fucking ease up, does he? See you on the flip, numbnuts."

A cold emptiness settled into his limbs despite the intense heat of the desert night. He took a deep breath as the line went dead and rose to his feet, slipping back into the trailer and checking on Charlotte before he turned his phone off and slid into bed beside her.

Bo.

Charlotte.

Even without Ryan's presence, Bo's arrival would put a definitive stop to everything he wanted to have with her.

At max, he had thirty-six hours left.

Knowing sleep would evade him, he rolled onto his side, wrapped his arm around her, and pulled her tight against him while he still could.

Chapter Sixteen

CHARLOTTE SCHOOLED HER face as she marched into Tom's Tavern, her phone in hand. She spotted Alex immediately in the crowded lounge, his hulking form towering over the crowd as he made his way back to the bar. Setting her cell on the counter, she pushed it toward him and crossed her arms. "And what exactly is this?"

He smirked, glancing down at the open messages that had whizzed through her phone once she had hit the highway after work. "That would be me providing you with the details necessary for you to make an informed decision regarding your calling of the shots."

"This," she said, leaning forward to give him a view of her cleavage, "is borderline pornographic."

"That," he countered, his eyes drifting toward her intended target, "is all I've been able to concentrate on all day."

She pulled up a stool and sat, slipping her phone into her back pocket. "You made a few valid points. How long until you're off?"

"Forty-five minutes."

She glanced around the full bar. "If you start the caffeine

drip on me, I'll wait for you."

He poured her a coffee, lifting her hand to his lips before he turned his attention to the customers swarming the bar. She pulled out her phone and began absently flipping through celebrity gossip until a hand tapped her back.

"This seat taken?"

"Nope," she replied, eyes on her cell and coffee in her fist. "Go ahead."

The guy pulled up uncomfortably tight to her, his leg resting against her bare thigh. She glanced at the offending appendage for a moment before she angled her body farther away and tucked her skirt tighter underneath her.

"Could I buy you a drink?"

Keeping her phone in her hand, she gave the guy a tight smile. "No thanks." She lifted her mug in his direction. "I'm on the caffeine tonight."

The man tipped his beer bottle at her. "A shot then. Your choice."

Realizing she wasn't going to easily shake him, she crossed her legs away from the guy and hunched forward. "I'm good, but no thanks. I'm waiting for someone."

"One of your little girlfriends?"

An arm draped across her back, sending a cold chill through her. She shrugged it off roughly, her polite smile replaced by a look of pure annoyance. "The bartender." She turned her back to him completely, scanning the crowded room for Alex and running her best angles of takedown should the guy push her further.

The man stayed beside her for a few moments, taking a long swig of his beer before he rose to his feet and strode in front of her, his chest puffed up and face contorted. "Just going to ignore me, bitch?" he snarled. "Fucking slu—"

His feet left the ground before he could finish his insult, Alex's long arms yanking the guy back from her and pinning him against the counter. The guy sputtered, cursing in enraged surprise.

Alex's face was stoic as he bent the man's arms behind his back and marched him toward the exit. "Next time you walk in here, I'll remove both kneecaps with a bat. We clear?" Several patrons cleared a path, one young guy holding the door open for Alex as he hefted the man out into the parking lot. With a quick roll of his shoulders, he scooped up the man's discarded beer bottle and stalked back to the bar, his stoicism morphing into concern. "You okay?"

She side-eyed the curious crowd until they turned away from them. "Been called worse." She let out a breath. "I was handling it, you know."

He cocked a brow. "I've had issues with that asshole before. I didn't do anything more than I would have done if he'd behaved that way to any other woman in here." He paused. "Except maybe the threat. And I might have given him a little nudge onto the cement out front."

She grunted, partially appeased that he hadn't gone full caveman. "I could've kicked his ass myself."

"And I saved you from an assault charge." He grinned tersely, pulling a stool behind the bar. "I'm doing last call now. Sit here and stay out of trouble for thirty more minutes." When her eyes narrowed, he reached over and pushed a strand of hair behind her ear. "I'm really trying to keep the whole jealous boyfriend thing under wraps, but I'm about ten seconds from tracking that fucker down and beating the shit outta him. Just let me pretend I can protect you, okay?"

ALEX WAVED AT the last of his customers as they hooted and hollered their way out the tavern door, slamming it shut behind them. He sprayed down their abandoned table, wiping it clean with the last of his fresh towels before he sauntered over to Charlotte and set his chin onto her head. "Ten more minutes and we can go."

He returned to the lounge floor and attempted to cool his temper with the monotonous task of straightening chairs.

It wasn't working.

The moment his back was to her, the image of that guy towering over her flashed into the forefront of his thoughts, his stance an unmistakable display of intimidation.

He glanced at the beer bottle tucked right against the till.

He could track the bastard in hound form.

Corner him.

Take him down.

Transform in front of the prick before he bleeds out so he would see my face during his final seconds on earth.

"How do I turn this up?"

Snapped from his increasingly violent thoughts, he looked over to Charlotte as she bent over the tavern's sound system. "The dial on the bottom right." When the bar filled with a grinding bass beat, he rolled his eyes. "What is it with women and this song?"

"It makes us feel sexy."

"Whatever," he called out, tucking the last of the stools against the back wall. "You're always sexy." He turned toward the bar, freezing in spot when he caught sight of her, her hips swaying to the beat as she ran her hands up her body, lifting her shirt over her head.

She trailed the red fabric across her chest and tossed it at his feet. "Maybe to you, but sometimes I actually feel it." With a slow spin, she turned her back to him and reached behind her, unhooking her bra. "Like when this song is on."

Fuck. Me.

Please.

She dropped her bra beside her and looked over her shoulder at him, a smug smirk on her lips when he loped across the bar, stopping just short of tackling her to the filthy bar floor. She backed up against him, the rhythmic movement of her hips providing a torturous friction that had his brain firing on way more cylinders than he could handle at the end of a long day. He ran his hands up her ribs and cupped her breasts as she reached back to wrap her arms around his neck. "Behave," she warned, grinding against his erection. "I really like this song."

He nuzzled the back of her head, inhaling the scent of her shampoo. "Trust me, baby, this is me behaving right now."

He tracked the crescendo of the music, counting down the beats until the final note rang out before he spun her around and kissed her hard, his arms pulling her as tight to him as he could without crushing her. He walked backward without breaking the kiss, leading her slowly to the padded booths lining the side wall and stopping when his thighs hit a table. She tugged roughly on his shirt, leaning back just enough to allow him to yank it off before she kissed him again, her fingers working on the button of his jeans.

"I was thinking," she panted as he ran his tongue down her neck and wormed his hands under her skirt to cup her ass. "We kind of screwed up the booty call thing by not actually following through on the booty part of the call, right?"

"Right," he muttered, running his thumbs along the band of her panties and easing them down, waiting for any sign from her that he'd crossed a line. When she stepped out of them and pushed his own jeans off his hips, he tossed his wallet on the bench within reach, spun her around, and lifted her onto the table, shuddering when her small hand gripped him through his boxers.

"And you did make a few good points in those texts," she murmured, her head dropping back as he tentatively reached between her thighs and ran his fingers through her slick folds. She whimpered when his touch whispered over her sensitive nub, her nails digging into his shoulder. "I...you...I—"

"Just a few?" he breathed, circling a dark pink nipple with his tongue and grunting when she tangled her fingers in his hair.

He slipped one finger inside her, his dick twitching in anticipation when she ground against his hand and she kissed him roughly. As her body began to tighten, he eased another finger into her and increased the speed of his thumb on her nub, the soft chanting of his name on her lips testing his control while he released his erection from his boxers. He led Charlotte's hand to it, clenching his teeth when she pumped him. Grabbing his wallet, he fumbled a condom from the packed leather and ripped the package with his teeth before he reached between them and slid it on, grimacing at the tightness. "Yes?" he asked, dropping his head into the crook of her neck as her wet center touched the tip.

"Lex...oh, god...I...yeah...yes...Lex..."

With the first fluttering of her core around his fingers, he pushed into her, the combined slickness and heat almost doing him in instantly. As the first wave of her orgasm hit her, her back arched off the table, her legs wrapping around his hips and holding him still inside her. He tore his eyes off her flushed skin while her body gripped him, his determination to last more than fifteen seconds deteriorating with every moan coming from the woman beneath him. The vise grip her legs had on his hips lessened and he grabbed her thighs to anchor her as he rocked inside her, the gentle ghosting of her fingertips on his chest sending his senses into overdrive.

Longer than two minutes. Just make it longer than two minutes.

He braced the edge of the table, caught between the primal urge to plow into her like an animal and his desire to slow his movements to hold on to the sensation as long as he could.

She breathed out his name again, effectively removing the decision from him as he dropped to his elbow, his building release well past the point of no return. Her legs crossed behind him, her heels digging into his ass rhythmically to spur him on.

"Holy *fuck*!" He grunted, losing his tempo and slamming into her as he came hard, his knees almost giving out on him. He vaguely registered her fingers trailing up and down his spine, her breathing slowing while he struggled to hold most of his weight off her. The fog finally clearing, he pushed himself up, tucked his hair behind his ear, and glanced around the empty bar. "I wasn't expecting that."

She smiled up at him lazily. "Neither was I. But then you

went all caveman-alpha and it may have been kind of hot. In a small, case-specific dose."

Dropping his head into the crook of her neck, he waited for the post-orgasmic high to shift, propelling his feet out of the building with a halfhearted promise to call, just as it had been for centuries.

But it wasn't the urge to leave that settled into his mind.

Chapter Seventeen

A LEX LOOKED OVER at Charlotte as he wound through the dark streets. Her hair still held that freshly fucked look he had been aching to see since the first day he'd seen her on the trails. He drew in a deep breath, the words sour on his tongue. "So, we have a problem. *I* have a problem."

She had seemed to take on an unspoken commitment to avoid all discussion of his other job, which suited him just fine. As long as she didn't bring it up, he could avoid the figurative elephant between them and continue to hide from the impending reality of his situation. Aside from calling him "killer" or "hunter" when she was in one of her more playful moods, she had avoided all talk of his secondary job, treating it as a forgotten minor inconvenience.

Of course, he had left out the whole hellhound thing.

And Hades.

Maybe omitted the entire section about returning to hell once the last of the line was tracked and eliminated.

"You're zoning out on me again." She nudged, her hand finding its way to his thigh. "Spill it."

"Bo's on his way here," he muttered. "Tomorrow. Ryan's

wrapping up some work with a few clients, so I'll be babysitting Bo's sorry ass on my own for a few days."

Her fingers clenched on his leg a fraction. "Ah. So that means…"

"Yeah." He sighed, pulling into the parking lot of her apartment block. "I found him."

She unbuckled her seat belt and turned to him, her face showing nothing more than mild interest. "And Bo is?"

"Twin."

"Nice."

He elbowed her. "Stop that. This is kind of a problem."

She unlocked her door and pushed it open, swinging her legs out of the SUV. "A problem that isn't happening tonight," she stated, standing up and leaning into the open door. "I assume tracking down and taking out bad guys takes a few days at least. A little planning, maybe a map or two. And unless you're going to vanish the moment the guy is dealt with, I figure there's at least a week or two before we actually have to deal with anything. Besides, if I think about it, I'll cry, and I'm not ruining our night with that mess."

She leaned over to give him a toe-curling kiss, disappearing into the entrance of her building without another glance his way. He watched her windows until the lights of her apartment came on.

It took another twenty minutes before the tightness in his throat cleared enough for him to drive away.

✕

CHARLOTTE PEERED THROUGH the corner of her curtains as the SUV's lights finally pulled out of the parking lot, her towel wrapped tight around her body and her hair dripping down her back.

I found him.

She slumped onto her bed, running her hands over her face.

There had been a morality battle warring in her head since Alex exposed the real reason he was in the valley. Part of her was appalled that guys like him existed, working under the radar and outside the laws she was bound to uphold.

The other part of her had been glad to have a built-in reason they would never be more than what they were. Because as long as they could never be more, she could continue to rationalize away the attachment that crept into her thoughts more and more frequently.

Their time was limited, and she was a little more than a blip on his radar until he moved away, resettling in another city or country while he moved on to the next target.

It was a harmless fling, her first experiment in a growing hookup culture.

He was a pretty package. The fact that he was intelligent and funny and compassionate was merely a bonus to his hotness during those times they weren't locking lips.

And now the countdown was on.

She was prepared.

Mentally, at least.

Her heart was struggling to understand the concept.

✖

ALEX RAN HIS hand through his hair before he crossed his arms and leaned back against his SUV, his sunglasses hiding his eyes as he scanned the lot for Bo. His phone buzzed and he glanced down at it, smiling while he read over Charlotte's rambling text about who would be at the Washout that evening, who Alex was supposed to bite his tongue around, and who he could pull alpha on.

"If you and your twin have nothing better to do."

He and his twin had a lot to do. But he couldn't think of anything better than seeing Charlotte again.

And it scared the hell out of him.

Responding with a quick hint at which outfit he was hoping she'd wear, he slipped his phone onto the front seat and continued to watch the lot.

Three women exited the bus depot, two of them tight to Bo's sides and the third a step behind the group, her expression hard and angry.

"Alex," Bo called out, disentangling himself from the women and sauntering across the pavement. "Do we have room to drop these lovely ladies at their hotel?"

He shoved his hands into his back pockets as the group

approached. "In a bit of a hurry, man," he replied tersely. "Maybe another time."

"Sorry, ladies, the boss has spoken." Bo snorted, opening the hatch and tossing his bag in. He turned to nuzzle the neck of one of the women, holding out his hand as she whispered something into his ear and passed him her phone.

He looked away while Bo added a fake number to the woman's cell, a move he himself was well rehearsed in. He flung his door open and got in. "All right. Let's get going."

With a feigned apologetic shrug, Bo strode around the SUV and got in, shaking his hair out as they pulled onto the street. "Holy fuck, Alex," he groaned, snatching Alex's ball cap from the dash and covering his face with it. "The redhead gave me the most painful, chafing hand job I've ever had just outside of Sacramento." He adjusted himself and flopped back again. "Where're we heading?"

"You're crashing on my couch for a few days until the long weekend crowds leave," he said, turning onto his street and slowing down.

Bo turned his head to the side and scanned the trailer park. "Any good meat around here?"

"The fridge's full," he muttered, pulling into his site and turning off the engine.

"Women, you fucking dumbass," Bo grunted, swinging his legs out of the SUV and leaning forward on his knees for a moment. "Any doors I can go knocking on once my dick heals up?"

Alex gritted his teeth, unlocking his front door and flicking the air conditioner on. "Not around here," he replied, his voice low. "It's a quiet park. Got it?"

Bo pushed himself to his feet and slammed the SUV door, opening the hatch to grab his bag. "Yeah, yeah. No pissing in your own yard." He looked across the chain link fence toward the road. "I need a run."

Checking the time on his phone, he calculated Charlotte's likely location in the park. "Fine. Toss your stuff here and we'll drive over."

BO STOOD ON the top of the ridge and scanned the terrain, the heaviness in his face lifted with the promise of a run. Alex tugged his socks off and shoved them into his backpack, watching while his brother pulled his shirt over his head and tossed it onto the rocks behind him, scratching at Hades's marker embedded into the chest of each of the hellhounds. He frowned as he took in the numerous bruises and gashes peppering Bo's skin.

"What the hell happened to you?" he asked, stripping his own shirt off and balling it up.

"Just a little problem with debt repayment," Bo called over. "I was so drunk I didn't feel a thing. So you probably didn't either." He shoved his jeans down in one smooth movement, his transformation complete before his paws hit the ground.

Alex climbed the ridge and collected the discarded clothes, tossing them into his bag and adding the rest of his own. He dropped to all fours, his nose wrinkling as his enhanced senses were assaulted with the stench of diesel and coyote excrement. Bo padded over to him, nipping his shoulder and tearing across the stony landscape. Alex took off after him, steering his brother away from the more popular roads of the park as they chased each other through the sand and chollas.

I miss this.

The thought flashed through his head as Bo gained ground on him and leapt onto his back, sending both of them muzzle-down into the sand. While Bo shook the dirt from his fur, Alex scented the air and growled low, his head cocked toward a small cluster of bushes. Bo's ears flattened down, his jowls holding a hint of a grin as he stalked toward the rabbit cowering under the brush. Alex took a wider arc around the animal, intent on blocking the creature's escape should it notice Bo's smooth approach.

As he reached striking distance, Bo froze, his ears lifting and head swinging toward a narrow path beneath the ridge. Alex crouched down, ignoring the rabbit as it ripped past his tail and beelined it over the horizon. A small ATV rounded the bend, its riders stopping abruptly as they caught sight of them. Bo rose up, the tilt of his head mimicking the cockiness he held in human form. When the riders doubled back down the path, he snorted and broke into a jog toward the path, ignoring Alex's growled warnings. Deciding that staying tight to his brother was infinitely better than allowing him free rein in the park, he followed Bo, catching up and steering them away from the road that led to the Keys.

And Charlotte.

The slow descent of the sun cooled the desert sand a fraction, easing the discomfort on his paws while he and Bo explored the clusters of rocks and boulders that were scattered throughout the terrain. One run-in with a small rattlesnake under a pile of stones had tempered Bo's curiosity, allowing Alex to guide their explorations through the areas he was most familiar with. As the sun began to turn the sky a soft orange, he nudged Bo back toward the ridge where their clothes were tucked away from view.

He really did miss it. Running alongside Bo and Ryan, completely unencumbered by everything that weighed heavily on their minds day in and day out.

Work and money.

Pirithous.

Home.

Charlotte.

Turning his nose toward the setting sun, he let out a long, low howl. Bo circled him, purposely flicking his snout with his tail before he joined in, his distinctive gravelly barks drawing the attention of the coyotes and setting off a chorus of yelps that echoed through the park until the sun finally disappeared.

✕

CHARLOTTE SPUN FOR Max, nervously anticipating his response.

"Keep the bustier and go back to the jeans," he finally stated. "The skirt gives a trashy vibe, and the leather pants are more dominatrix than you can pull off." He sprawled out on her sofa and dug back into a bag of popcorn. "And hurry the hell up."

Returning to her bedroom, she pulled her jeans on and grabbed a pair of heels from her closet. She stood in front of the mirror, scanning herself from every angle while she ran her fingers through her hair to loosen the few renegade curls that were holding their bounce more than she wanted.

"Come *on*!" Max hollered, smacking her door. "Alex has seen you in your work uniform. Trust me when I say anything else is a step up."

With a huff, she joined her partner and followed him to his truck, climbing in and pushing a pile of takeout bags to the floor. "You're disgusting."

He grinned, slipping his sunglasses on and revving the engine. "But I'm hot, so women overlook it."

Thinking back to Alex's trailer, she hummed in agreement.

Max tore onto the highway, blasting the music and air-conditioning as he flew down the road toward the Washout, oblivious to her increasing nerves.

What if Alex's brother didn't like her?

What if she didn't like him?

Did any of it really matter since everything they had was temporary?

"You aren't going to wear that jacket all night, are you?" he asked, pulling into a tight spot. "It's ugly and makes your boobs look small."

Fixing him with a dead stare, she pushed the offending clothing off her shoulders and tossed it into the back of his truck. "I don't know why I even talk to you anymore."

"Because I tolerate you." He elbowed her in the ribs before stopping to flip one of her straps. "Let's go get me laid."

The Washout was packed, forcing them to jostle through the crowd to find the rest of the rangers and agents. As they closed in on their table, she caught sight of Alex crouched beside a stunning redhead, his arm resting on her chair and his eyes locked on her plunging neckline. When he trailed one finger along her thigh and wedged his hand between her knees, her stomach plummeted and she took a step backward.

"Before you walk out of here or slash any tires, that's not me. And you look incredible."

She jumped as Alex's voice murmured in her ear from behind, swinging around to see him standing there, a carbon copy of the man across the table. She looked back for a moment. "Wow. That's actually kind of creepy."

An odd look flashed across his face. "Why don't we go grab a drink? Maybe delay the inevitable introduction to my asshole of a brother?"

She laughed in relief, taking his arm and resting her forehead on his biceps, inhaling the familiar scent of his cologne. "He can't be that bad."

He gave her a tight smile as they squeezed through group after group of partiers. "Bo's a lot to take if you aren't prepared," he said slowly, waving the bartender over and ordering two beers. "So just be ready for anything and don't let anything he says or does get to you, okay?" He waved off the change when the bartender returned and handed over her drink, putting his arm around her waist and taking a breath. "Let's do this."

Chapter Eighteen

CHARLOTTE'S EYES WIDENED as Bo began to expand on his suggestion. "Excuse me?"

"Ignore him," Alex snarled, pulling his chair tighter to her and staring his brother down, the tendons in his neck straining.

Bo leaned back and downed the last of his whiskey. "All I'm saying is Alex and I have had a lot of practice and we have a pretty tight system. I think you might get a kick out of it." He met Alex's glare, rolled his eyes, and stood. "Or not."

She watched Bo weave toward the bar, stopping intermittently to flirt with the women who approached him every few steps, and looked at Alex. "What's tag-tea—"

"Nothing," he growled, tracking his brother. "This was a mistake."

She put her hand on his arm and rested her head on his shoulder, pulling her phone out of her purse. "It's fine," she countered. "He's nothing I can't handle."

"Yeah, well, he's still mildly sober," he muttered, absently spinning the base of his beer on the table. "This is Bo on his best behavior."

She finished reading the definition of *tag-teaming* on her phone and sat up, slipping her cell back into her purse.

Whoa.

Alex ran his hand through his hair, plastering a fake smile on his face when Max approached them. "How's the hunt tonight?"

"Two shutdowns and a find-me-later," Max reported. "I'm stealing your chick for a few dances."

She pursed her lips.

"She's going to kill you one of these nights." Alex laughed, shifting his legs so she could stand up. "I'll get Bo to back off a bit and I'll be in a better mood when you return, okay?"

Biting back a comment about her newly acquired tag-team knowledge, she joined Max and the others on the dance floor, refusing to allow her imagination to ruin her night out.

ALEX STOOD BESIDE Bo, his gaze drifting to Charlotte while she danced with Max and the rest of her coworkers.

So damn gorgeous.

"Some chick you're just hooking up with?" Bo sneered, yanking Alex's attention back to his increasingly drunk brother. "That," he slurred, pointing his shot of tequila at the dance floor, "isn't one of your hookups."

"Friends with benefits," he murmured, tearing his eyes off Charlotte. "She's a nice girl. Anyone else in here is fair game." He scanned the bar. "Just ease off her, okay? She isn't like us."

Bo eyed him with suspicion. "This isn't the piece of ass you were asking me about a few weeks ago, right?"

"The hell? No," he scoffed, passing the bartender a twenty and handing Bo another beer to chase the shot in his other hand. "Charlotte's just a regular at the lounge with the rest of the rangers."

"Good," Bo replied, slamming back the tequila and sliding the glass across the counter. "Because Ryan thinks you're holding out down here, and he thinks that's the reason why." He cocked his head toward the dance floor, his normally gravelly voice growing hoarser the more he drank. "Your friend-with-benefits has no ass but great tits."

Alex took a long swig of his beer.

He should have ended it weeks ago. Before there was any chance Charlotte would find her way into Bo's sights, and before he could become irreparably tarnished in her eyes.

Before you slept with her, you bastard.

And therein lay the problem. Sleeping with her should have ended the chase.

It had, for lack of a better word, not.

He set his empty beer bottle on the counter, shaking his head when the bartender offered another. "See the blonde over there?" he asked Bo, motioning toward a group of women standing beside the dance floor. "Yeah?"

Bo smirked, finally tearing his eyes off Charlotte to scan the women over. "I'm in a brunette mood tonight." With a grin, he pushed away from the bar counter and led Alex across the room.

He pulled his phone from his pocket and fired off a quick text to Charlotte before he followed his brother through the crowds.

✕

CHARLOTTE'S EYES SNAPPED open to the obnoxious buzz of her apartment bell. She rolled onto her side and picked up her phone to check the time.

6:02.

And over a dozen missed texts, all from Alex.

She got to her feet, wrapping her blanket around herself as she walked to intercom. "Who is it?"

The speaker crackled. "Alex. Can I come up?"

Pressing the entrance button, she unlocked her door and opened it, listening as uneven footsteps thumped up the stairwell. Alex's hulking form appeared at the end of the hall, his shoulders hunched as he used the wall to balance himself. She backed into her apartment and held the door open while he stumbled in, his head bowed and eyes on the floor.

"I thought you were going to be right behind me," she stated, closing and locking her door as he leaned against the wall and bent down to pull off his shoes, tipping to the side twice before he succeeded.

"I tried," he muttered, standing up and reaching for her fingers. "Don't be mad, okay?"

She pursed her lips, allowing him to wrap his hand around hers but making no move toward him. "If you wanted to spend the rest of the night with your brother, you just had to say so," she said, leading him into her living room. "I waited up for over an hour, and I work today."

He slumped onto her sofa, his elbows on his knees and head dropped. "I'm sorry. I didn't want to go there, but Bo…those chicks… So I walked… It was a lot farther than I thought." He looked up at her, his eyes glassy and bloodshot. "I just wanted to come home."

She turned to the kitchen and filled a glass of water, kneeling in front of him when she handed it to him. "You were nowhere near drunk when I left the Washout."

With his gaze still unfocused on the floor, he set the cup down and lifted his hand to hers, grasping it tight. "I just wanna go to bed," he slurred. "Here. With you."

She sighed and stood, helping him to his feet the best she could. "Let's go."

She led him to her bed, running her hands over her face when he collapsed on the mattress fully clothed, the stench of stale beer and rye permeating the room.

She had questions. Questions he was obviously too drunk to answer.

He closed his hazel eye and tracked her as she crawled into bed beside him, annoyed enough to keep her distance but not enough to banish him to her couch. When she was settled in, he lay back. "You have a great ass."

She rolled onto her side and leveled him with a dead glare. "Thanks. Go to sleep."

She turned away from him, caught between feeling comforted and angered when one heavy arm was flung over her hips and he pulled her to him.

✕

ALEX SHOVED THE pink comforter off his face and swung his legs over the edge of the bed, groaning as his pounding head protested the sudden shift in position. He pushed himself to his feet and stumbled out of Charlotte's room, scanning the small apartment and finding it empty.

Right. Work.

He returned to the bedroom, rummaging around for his phone and coming up empty-handed. Straightening the bedding, he began hunting the rest of the rooms, pausing when a faint buzz came from the entranceway. He followed the sound, kneeling beside his shoes and finding his phone tucked neatly between them. Swiping the screen with his thumb, he sank back against the wall and ran his hand through his hair.

A number he didn't recognize had sent him a series of

photos interspersed with flirtatious commentary. One picture of him and Bo, plastered out of their heads and sprawled across unfamiliar couches, surrounded by women he could vaguely recognize from the Washout. Another of him alone, hunched over his phone with an empty shot glass at his feet. A selfie of the blonde. A shot of him and Bo licking salt out of the hands of an attractive brunette, tequila at the ready.

Fuck. Fuck. Fuck!

The texts were worse.

Exaggerated disappointment that he'd left early.

That whoever the sender was had gone to bed alone. And that one was accompanied by a photo.

Promises to stop by his work.

His stomach knotted, the blood draining from his face as he checked the time stamps of the messages.

There was no way Charlotte hadn't seen at least one of them.

He tapped her name and listened as her number went straight to voice mail, her phone unreachable until she left work at the end of her shift.

Rising to his feet, he did a final walk-though of the apartment, scanning for a note that might clue him in to how deep he'd dug himself.

Nothing.

Flipping the lock on her door, he began the long walk home, his wallet tucked safely between the seats of an SUV that was parked at some woman's apartment complex. Patting his pockets, he looked up and cursed into the bright sunlight.

Wherever his SUV was parked, his keys were located somewhere in that building.

He dialed Bo's number, dodging a blue car as he crossed the street. When Bo answered, his words still heavily slurred, he sighed. "Where the hell are you?"

"Lemme find out," Bo replied, yelling into the faint din coming through the speaker. He parroted the address, correcting himself twice before getting it right.

"I'll be there in twenty," he said, flashing back to the hundreds of times he and Bo had done this dance. "Find my keys and meet me downstairs."

"Will do." Bo laughed at something murmured in the background. "Allison wants you to come up."

He closed his eyes and took a deep breath. "Just meet me downstairs in twenty, okay?"

CHARLOTTE GLARED AT Max, wanting nothing more than to knock his stupid sunglasses off his face. "You guys seem to have it all worked out, don't you?" She slumped back in the passenger seat and looked out at the empty campground.

"Alex played wingman for me before and it didn't bother you. So what's the problem now?" Max asked, stuffing a piece of beef jerky into his mouth. "He's really good at the whole wingman gig."

Because you and Alex don't have a tag-team routine down pat?

Because I know now why he's so good at it?

"I'm just annoyed," she grumbled. "When Alex is with you, you guys are right there in front of me, not drinking your faces off at some chick's place until six a.m."

Max nodded. "Fair enough. *If* you two were an actual couple. But you're not. Sorry, Chuck, but you don't get a say in this." He examined another piece of jerky before shoving it in his mouth and wove them through the park, stopping periodically to check in with a tourist or pick up a stray plastic bag until they reached headquarters and she jumped into her own truck, eager to spend some quiet time alone.

Max was half right. She had no business being angry about what had gone down after Alex left the Washout. But she was. She was angry and hurt and no rational explanation of their quasi-relationship was going to erase it.

Alex's phone had pinged all morning while she got ready for work, lodged between her bed frame and mattress.

She hadn't intentionally looked at the screen as she dropped it between his sneakers.

But even now, the image of Alex's tongue running across the outstretched hand of some strange woman was crystal clear.

Shaking the vision from her head, she made her way to

the Keys and got out, scanning the area for hikers until a familiar form breached the horizon.

"Hey, Butch!" she called out, crouching down and extending her hand for him to examine. The beast padded through the sand toward her, circling her before he backed away and cocked his head. "Where've you been, huh, boy? And where's that collar and leash? You know you'll be taken in as a stray if you don't keep that on," she cooed, rising up and leaning through her truck window to grab something for him to eat. "It's not steak, but you might like it anyway."

Butch approached the beef jerky, his nose twitching before he drew his lips back and plucked the offering from her hand. She bit back a smile as the dog began chewing the tough meat, his concentration wholly focused on shredding the jerky enough to swallow it.

"You coming with me for a bit?" she asked, opening the back door of the truck. "I could use the company today."

The beast's head tilted as he regarded the open door. He padded closer to her, nudging her hand with his enormous head and chuffing when she scratched his ears. She knelt beside him and buried her face in the soft fur at his neck. "In you go, boy."

Butch licked her hand, his ears perking up and tracking a sound she couldn't hear. Turning tail, he bounded out of her reach and tore across the sand, disappearing over the ridge.

Chapter Nineteen

A LEX LOOKED UP from his beer inventory, giving Thomas a quick wave.

"I'm old," the man stated, setting his glass of water beside the grill. "When I see you back here, and then I see you walk in the front door seconds later, I question my mental competency."

"Oh, right," Alex exclaimed, rising to his feet. "Yeah, my brother's in town for a while. He at the bar?"

Thomas nodded, pulling a pile of patties from the freezer. "Scared the hell out of me." He laughed. "I mean, there's twins, and then there's twins." He shook his head and pried a few patties apart. "Two of you. What does Charlotte think of that?"

He shoved the last of the beer cases against the wall and wiped his hands on his jeans. "Probably not too happy today," he muttered, glancing over at Thomas. "Bo and I tied one on last night."

"I figured that out hours ago." Thomas grinned. "You're sweating the booze out in buckets."

He pushed through the doors, scooping a beer from the

cooler and handing it to Bo without thinking. "I'm off in two hours," he said, pouring a glass of water for himself.

Bo drained half the bottle and set it down with a *thunk*. "Good. We're going tracking when you're done." He eyed Alex suspiciously. "You do know where the Pirithous is holed up, right?"

Busying himself with realigning the bottles on the back shelf, he shook his head. "Been sitting on his location for a few nights. No movement."

Finishing his first beer and tapping the bottle impatiently on the counter, Bo leaned forward. "None? This late in the second sighting? You aren't saying that because you've been slacking on the job?"

Fixing his twin with a glare, he tapped Bo's empty bottle. "I'm slacking?"

Bo licked his lips. "Know what I think? I think Ryan's right about your little fuck buddy. I think there's more to it and you're screwing the rest of us over so you can play white-picket-fence."

He tossed the cap of the second beer in the trash, his expression locked down. "What gave it away? The constant texts I got from that Allison woman this morning? The two women crawling all over me at that dirty apartment? Or is that the only reason you can think of for me not getting laid in the bathroom of some random woman's apartment?"

Bo leaned back and guzzled the second beer, slamming the empty down. "I'll be waiting for you back at the trailer," he said, standing up and walking toward the door, pausing before he opened it. "Your girlfriend gives decent rubdowns, *Butch*. I see why you keep her around."

✕

ALEX CRANKED THE SUV's air conditioner, waiting for Charlotte to answer.

"Hello?"

He leaned back in his seat and closed his eyes. "Hey. How was work?"

"Fine."

He flinched at her cold tone. "I just got off, and I need to get some stuff done with Bo, but could I maybe come by later?" He rubbed his jaw, trying fruitlessly to release the tension when her silence stretched out. "I have some groveling to do."

Charlotte sighed. "No, you don't. We aren't actually dating, so groveling isn't necessary."

His head dropped forward. "Please? I want to make things right with my girlfriend."

She went quiet again for a moment. "I'll be up."

He revved the engine and tore out of the lot, speeding through the side streets until he hit his trailer park. Creeping through the narrow paths, he parked and got out, flexing his hands at his side and opening his front door.

Bo was crashed out on the small sofa, his legs dangling

over the edge into the dining room bench. He slipped past him and opened the bathroom door, sealing the shower off from the rest of the trailer and stepping under the cool spray.

Your girlfriend gives decent rubdowns, Butch.

The rush of fury that had overtaken him hours earlier returned with a vengeance. He turned off the water and snatched a towel from the floor, wrapping it around his hips and slamming the bathroom door closed.

"You're a real prick," he snarled, booting Bo's leg and jostling him from his drunken sleep.

Bo's eyes fluttered open and he squinted up at him. "The hell's your problem?"

Alex stormed into his bedroom and yanked his closet open, tossing clean clothes onto his bed. "Stay away from Charlotte. Fuck whoever you want around here, drink yourself stupid as much as you want until we're done here, but stay. The fuck. Away from her." He tugged his shorts over his hips and turned to his brother. "And if I catch you anywhere near her in hound form again, I swear I'll kill you."

Bo snorted, rising up onto his elbows and arching his neck back to look at him. "You know how this ends."

"Yeah, I know how this ends."

Groaning as he sat up, Bo stood and stretched, scratching at the healing wounds covering his torso. "Okay then. You show me where the Pirithous is holed up, and I'll buy you a few days to nest with your little girlfriend before Ryan arrives." He narrowed his eyes at Alex, using the tiny counter for support. "You know he's going to kill again soon. No pussy is worth what that bloodline is going to do."

"Don't use that word when you're talking about her," he snarled, shoving Bo's shoulders back against the sofa.

He stepped past Bo and watched his brother disappear behind the bathroom door, the shower turning on. Going outside to wait, he pulled out his phone and called Charlotte. "Hey."

"Hey."

Exhaling loudly, he sat on the step. "I should probably start the groveling early." She remained silent. "This is all kinds of screwed up," he mumbled, trying to formulate his thoughts into something that sounded less caveman than the mess running through his head. "I didn't cheat on you," he opened. "I drank a ton of tequila, and I'm pretty sure I threw half of it up in an alley north of you, but I swear I didn't cheat."

She was quiet for a moment. "It's so weird how often I've heard that exact line."

He ran his hand through his hair, digging his fingers into the back of his skull. "I'm sorry, baby. I swear I'm not that guy," he said weakly as he listened for Bo, relieved to hear the shower still running. "I blocked the girl this morning, if that counts for anything. I'm pretty sure I wasn't the one who gave her my number."

She hummed, whether in agreement or disbelief, he couldn't tell. He waved at his neighbor as she walked by with her dog. "I know I messed up," he said quietly, giving the woman a thumbs-up when she passed, politely inquiring about his evening. "The only thing that really stands out from last night is how bad I wanted to see you."

"You said as much when you got here," she replied, the resignation in her voice slicing him. "Look, I'm just on my way out to grab a coffee with Max. Are you coming by later or can we just count this call as the discussion you wanted to have?"

He gritted his teeth. "I'm coming by."

The shower turned off as she disconnected the call, leaving him to stare absently toward Joshua Tree until Bo joined him, his long hair dripping down his black shirt.

"All right, troll, show me where this asshole is staying," he called to Alex, getting into the SUV and grabbing Alex's sunglasses from the dash.

He rolled his eyes and got in, pulling onto the highway. "How's Ryan doing anyway?"

"Working too much, fucking too little." Bo grinned, aiming the air vents at his face and scanning his phone. "This won't take long, will it? Allison and Carrie want to meet up at that bar again."

Hiding the swell of relief that washed over him, he shook his head. "It's a twenty-minute drive." He ventured a glance at Bo. "I'll drop you at the bar before I head out."

Bo sneered, his mouth opening for a moment, then snapping shut. He cranked the music up, staring out the window until Alex pulled into the small parking lot where the sedan sat. The pair got out of the SUV and circled the car, Bo crouching down to examine what was left of the damage. "He clipped you pretty good. Amazed I didn't feel that one."

He rubbed his ribs and snorted, ignoring the obvious. "Whatever shop he had do the repair did a poor job. I'm guessing the rental company doesn't even know."

Bo wedged his finger into the grille and pulled out a small tuft of fur. He blew it in Alex's direction. "Soft like a little bunny."

"Whatever," he grunted, leading Bo around the complex and pointing to a window. "Far as I can tell, that's his suite."

Bo flicked his phone on and snapped a picture of the window, the complex, and the street signs. "I got all I need for now. I'll report back to Ryan that we caught the scent in the next town over." He got back in the SUV and cranked the air-conditioning up. "You aren't serious-serious about this chick, are you?"

He shrugged, locking his eyes on the road.

"And how much does she know?"

Turning back onto the highway, he sped up. "I told her we were bounty hunters."

Bo settled back in his seat, his attention wholly on reading Alex's every involuntary reaction. "How long has this been going on?" When he hesitated before opening his mouth, Bo grunted. "Your nose twitched, man. Don't lie."

"We met around two months ago."

Whistling low, Bo cocked a brow. "So this is the chick you asked about."

"Yeah."

"You falling for her?"

"Can we drop it for tonight?"

Bo leaned back and closed his eyes. "Sure. But if you don't end it soon, I'll be taking care of it myself. Happy endings with white fences and green grass only exist in fairy tales, brother."

CHARLOTTE OPENED HER door and stepped aside to allow Alex in. "You're early." Without a word, he extended his arms, a bag of takeout in one and three orange lilies in the other. She accepted the peace offerings, setting the food on the counter and rummaging through her cupboards for a vase. "Completely unnecessary, but thank you."

He came up behind her, his arms wrapping around her waist as he dropped his head onto her shoulder. "Consider it part of my penance," he mumbled into her skin, his lips grazing her throat.

Arching her head away from him, she opened a drawer and pulled out a pair of scissors, snipping the stems of the lilies and placing them in a vase. "Were you high last night?"

Alex's arms tensed around her. "No."

"You sure?" she asked, turning in place and looking up at him. "Max was just saying Bo was pounding the whiskey back like a pro and he thought maybe—"

"My brother's a heavy drinker," he growled, his eyes narrowing as he released her and crossed his arms. "Maybe Max should mind his business once in a while."

Her brows shot up. "Don't try and turn this onto him," she snarled.

"Maybe if Max wasn't always in bed with us, I wouldn't." He backed away from her, his shoulders rising a fraction. "Forget it. You're right." His eyes darted around the room, as though hunting for the exit. "Bo's my brother. I know what he is and what he does. I don't need anyone pointing it out, and I don't need anyone discussing it."

She took a step toward him, a pang of sorrow rippling through her. "I'm sorry," she said softly, reaching out to him. "I've been bit by this kind of thing before and I'm not handling it right, am I?"

"Yeah, well, you haven't kneed me in the balls yet, so we're doing okay," he grumbled, reluctantly taking her hand. "What else do you want to know about last night?"

A litany of questions flew through her mind. "Did you sleep with any of them?"

"No."

"Kiss?"

"No."

"Touch?"

"Yes."

She narrowed her eyes, dropping his hand.

He looked down for a moment. "You saw the pictures, I'm sure. I sucked lemon wedges from between some chick's teeth. Licked a lot of salt off a lot of wrists attached to a lot of women." When she opened her mouth to press for more, he continued. "Two of them tried to sit on my lap. Allison sent that picture, too."

"Allison," she repeated, wrapping her arms around herself.

He flipped out his phone and swiped the screen, angling it toward her. "Look through these."

She accepted the phone and began scanning the texts and pictures, a tightness forming in her throat. "She's pretty."

"She's nothing."

He took his phone back, pulling up the photo of him sitting alone, hunched over his cell. Using his fingers to enlarge the picture, he zoomed in on it. "This is what I remember most about the entire night after I left you at the bar. Texting you and hoping you'd let me come home." He cleared his throat. "Here. Come here."

She stared at the picture for a minute, blinking to keep herself from crying in frustration over the sense of betrayal that had settled in her stomach over the random guy she knew was going to be leaving any day.

"Don't do this," he said quietly. "You can yell or scream or kick me, but you aren't a crier, and if I make you cry..."

He trailed off, stepping closer to her and caging her in his arms. "I'm sorry."

Steadying her breathing, she rested her forehead on Alex's chest. "I'm mad that I'm mad."

His arms wrapped around her and he laid his chin on her head. "If this was reversed, I'd be kicking in some asshole's door, beating him to a pulp, and snapping your phone in half."

She took a deep breath. "We both know this is temporary. I guess I'm just not sure exactly what we expect or want here."

"Yeah, well, I didn't want any of that. I wanted this."

ALEX NUZZLED CHARLOTTE'S hair, trying to erase the image of her tearing eyes from his mind. Her hold on him had changed, the hesitant grip she initially had on him tightening, her thumbs brushing against his shirt in a soothing, rhythmic motion. He ran his lips along her forehead, bringing his hand under her chin so he could kiss her properly.

"I'm sorry," he whispered against her lips, pushing her hair behind her ear and closing his eyes when she drew in a shuddered breath.

Killing me.

When she didn't resist his initial advances, he trailed his

tongue across her lips, tangling it with hers when her mouth parted and gave him entry. Her chest was still rising in short bursts against his, a constant reminder of his screw-up despite the fingers trailing softly up his spine, sending jolts of lust through him as he kissed her leisurely.

He ducked his head into the crook of her neck, running his tongue up to her earlobe and pulling her against him when he breathed into her ear and she shivered, her nails digging into his back. "Are we making up?" he asked, dragging his tongue down her neck and kneeling in front of her, pushing her shirt up to kiss the soft skin of her stomach.

Her hands tangled in his hair, her breath hitching when he began easing her shorts off her hips. "Do kind-of couples do that?" she whispered, stepping out of the shorts and whimpering as he rose up, pulling her shirt over her head and cupping one lace-covered breast.

"Damn right we do. I'm sorry," he reiterated against her lips, kissing her deeply while he backed her slowly toward her bedroom, unhooking her bra and dropping it on the floor. He lay her on the bed, taking off his own shirt and fumbling with the buttons of his shorts before he kicked them off and crawled on top of her, desperate to be as close to her as he could. Hooking his thumbs in her panties, he pulled them off and sat back on his haunches to admire the view.

Her knees drew together, her arms crossing over her breasts. "Stop looking at me like that."

"Like what?" he asked, nudging her knees apart and

wedging his hips in between them. He grabbed her wrists and unfolded her arms from her body, flicking his tongue over one nipple as he ran his thumb over the other.

"Like you're going to eat me. It's unnerving," she huffed, her back arching toward his lips and canceling out her feigned indignation.

He pushed himself up onto one elbow and reached between her thighs. "Would you let me?" he asked, glancing down at his hand and smirking when she blushed and shook her head. "You might like it. I sure as hell would."

When her knees began to tighten around his hips defensively, he let her off the hook, kissing her softly. "Another night?" She looked away, ignoring his request. He trailed his lips to her ear, sliding his fingers through her wetness and groaning as her hips lifted to his hand. "I have an embarrassingly low amount of self-control with you," he murmured, circling her nub with his thumb and ignoring his demanding hard-on while he began describing just how hot she was making him. He listened for the telltale changes in her breathing as he worked her, getting even more turned on when he realized her strongest responses came with every thought he whispered into her ear.

Charlotte reached between them and wrapped her hand around his length, running him through her slick folds and sending his eyes rolling back. When her hips lifted to him impatiently, he stilled her hand. "I'm probably going to last thirty seconds if you do that," he warned, slipping two fingers inside her and covering her body with his, nibbling on her ear. "Want to know what did me in last time?"

Her breathing grew shorter, her thighs tightening at his hips. "What?"

"The way you said my name when you came," he breathed, the memory alone nearly setting him off. He adjusted the pressure of his thumb and was rewarded with a soft gasp. "The way your nails dug into my back like they are right now," he continued, easing his fingers out of her and lining his erection up with her entrance, lolling his head back when she wound one hand into his hair and tugged. "And that." He groaned, pushing inside her as her body began to tighten around him.

He thrust into her heat slowly as she began to gasp, her nails scratching down his back and his name finally on her lips. He swallowed and gritted his teeth, amping up his speed. "Come on, baby." He moaned, pushing up so he could watch her face as she came undone, her back arching off the bed and her grip on his hair becoming deliciously painful.

"Lex..." She dug her heels into his ass. "Harder?"

He lost his rhythm for a moment with the request, dropping back to his elbows and biting down on his tongue hard enough to draw blood. He gripped her hip with one hand and plowed into her, his body taking over the instinctual act as she fell over the edge, dragging him along with her. He snarled out a slew of curses as he released inside her, the euphoria taking over his entire mind and body until he collapsed onto her, his toes still curled with the aftershocks.

Chapter Twenty

CHARLOTTE TRACED THE defined lines of Alex's chest with her fingers, marveling at the amount of heat he was still giving off despite the amped-up air conditioner blowing across them. "I'm not answering that."

He rolled her onto her back and straddled her, his long hair falling forward. "Fair's fair," he stated, sitting back and running his hands up her body. "How many?"

"Hardly fair," she complained. "'More than I want to admit' is not an answer."

He looked down at her, closing one eye, then the other. "I honestly lost count. Is it more than five?"

"Yes."

He frowned and sat up straighter. "More than ten?"

"Seven, including you," she rattled off, her eyes narrowing as his jaw flexed. "You can't seriously be annoyed, Mr. Lost Count," she chastised.

He rolled his eyes and lay back down beside her, pulling the blanket around her shoulders. "That's like, six more than I like to think about."

Her post-sex panic over their lack of a condom had

evolved into a discussion she wasn't sure she wanted to continue. Between her birth control and Alex's insistence he was infertile, the completely unsexy talk about STDs had started, with her nervousness over his extensive experience taking front and center stage.

"Next question," he stated, folding his arms behind his head.

Thinking about the best way to ask, she pursed her lips. "The, um, tag-teaming thing. I googled it and…" She trailed off, not sure what she was asking or if she wanted to know.

He stared up at the ceiling, his brows knotted until he cleared his throat. "You could probably look up most things, and I've done it," he said slowly. "Usually when Bo and I are in the same area, things get a little out of control since the opportunities just kind of present themselves and…" He paused, tilting his head and locking his eyes on a small flaw in the ceiling paint. "And there's no way for me to continue talking without burying myself, so I'm going to shut up."

She swatted him. "I get it. You've been there, done them all, got all the T-shirts."

"Pretty much."

"You're such an ass," she muttered, tossing up a wall to block the creeping feelings of jealousy from permeating the reality of their situation.

He glanced over at her. "Know what I haven't done?"

She braced herself for an answer she definitely didn't want to hear. "What?"

"Slept with the same woman more than three times," he said casually, as though it was completely normal. "Three's the cutoff. Any more than that, and it's bordering on relationship territory."

She sat up and looked down at him, the blanket held tight to her chest. "You're an idiot."

He licked his lips and pulled at her comforter. "The bar," he stated, tugging the blanket down and exposing her breasts to the cold air. "A quickie in the SUV after the bar, which counts as number two even if it was the same night because we switched locations." He wedged one leg between hers, then the other. "And one official groveling." He grinned up at her, shifting his hips to punctuate his point. "That's three. Want to cross over into number four?"

She rolled her eyes, refusing to allow the glimmer of expectation that had risen in her head to take root. "We haven't switched locations. So technically, this would still be number three by your messed-up logic." She cleared her throat as it tightened. "Looks like this train's pulled into the station and you need to get off."

"Damn," he grumbled, biting his lip until he broke into a smile. "Want to have a dress rehearsal for number four then?"

THE INCESSANT BUZZING of his phone pulled Alex from a

deep sleep, his hand slapping around the edge of the bed for his cell until his fingers found it. He rolled onto his back, glancing over at Charlotte's empty side of the bed.

Her side of the bed.

Shaking off the rush of contentment the thought gave him, he scanned the litany of incoming texts, jumping out of bed and scrambling for his clothes.

Another dead hiker, and a hell-storm of agents descending on the park.

He pulled up Charlotte's number as he dressed, putting her on speaker so he could get ready. When his call switched to voice mail, he dialed Bo.

"What are you hearing?" he barked, glancing in the mirror and running his fingers through his hair.

Bo yawned loudly, the sound of rap music playing behind him. "Single male, dismembered, several body parts still missing. Let me get out on the balcony." The music faded, the noise of traffic taking over. "If the Pirithous is going feral after a handful of kills, we need to call in Ryan. Now."

He dropped his head. "I'll do it on my way over. Where are you?"

Bo snorted. "Fuck if I know. I'll start walking and call you when I hit a street sign."

Taking the stairs two at a time, he tried Charlotte's cell again, swearing under his breath when her voice mail greeted him cheerfully. He ran her schedule in his head, calculating her approximate whereabouts if she was sticking to her routine.

Sheep's Pass.

He hit the highway, Bo texting his location within minutes. Doubling back, he pulled up alongside his brother and stopped. "I work in two hours," he said. "We'll scout out the guy's apartment and phone it in to Ryan."

Bo was surprisingly quiet on the drive, the jump from routine kills to total dismemberment an unexpected breach of the standard route the males of the Pirithous bloodline followed. The amped-up timeline didn't bode well with Ryan several states away.

And Charlotte working the Pirithous's hunting grounds.

When a fifth unmarked police car whizzed past them, Bo shook his head. "This is bad."

"We know where he is," he stated, his voice tight. "We'll track him in shifts until Ryan arrives, take him out, and spend happily ever after in hell."

"If he's the last," Bo countered. "We need a name. Something Ryan can run. If this guy got laid even once, we need to know about it."

He glanced over at his brother. "You still think that Pirithous line in Albany managed to spawn a kid before we got to him, don't you?"

Bo shrugged. "Your little girlfriend have anything to report?"

Pulling into the Pirithous line's parking lot, he shook his head and ignored the girlfriend remark. "I can't get a hold of her until she's outside the park," he said, stopping tight beside the freshly washed sedan. "No cell service there." Nudging Bo, he pointed out a woman walking toward the apartment complex. "Go."

Bo hopped out of the SUV and sauntered across the lot, flashing a smile at the woman as he approached her. She looked over his shoulder at Alex before nodding and leading Bo to the door, opening it and smiling as Bo held the door for her. The pair disappeared into the building, Bo finally returning ten minutes later.

"Suite twenty-two," he reported. "Name on the mailbox is Joshua Hornsby."

He fired off the info to Ryan, his thumb hesitating over the phone icon.

"The Pirithous slipped out a back way," Bo stated. "That's all he needs to know for now."

Nodding, he pressed the green phone and listened for the ring.

✕

CHARLOTTE PICKED UP the headquarters landline and turned to Max. "How long did they say we'd have to stay?"

"Four more hours," Max grumbled, glaring at the cold burger in his hands. "Think this is okay to eat? It's been sitting here since we got on shift."

Shaking her head, she smiled for the first time all day

KATJA DESJARLAIS

when Alex's voice came on the line. "Why do you sound so panicked?" She laughed, Alex's frantic greeting mildly amusing.

"You never call from this line," he yelled over the tavern's music. "Jeez, Charlotte. You scared the hell out of me. I thought something had happened."

"Sorry." She grinned, waving at the group of agents walking in the door as she dropped the volume of her voice. "Just wanted to let you know the place is crawling with FBI."

"Noted," he called, the clinking of glasses almost drowning him out. "I don't care what time it is, promise you'll call when you're off. And be careful."

"Will do. Butch has been hanging out here most of the evening, so I'm definitely well guarded. Though someone seems to have lost his collar, didn't you, boy?" she cooed.

He went dead silent for a moment. "Good. Talk to you in a bit."

She grabbed her hat off the counter and tossed Max the truck keys, calling over two of the men assigned to them. They piled into the vehicle, Charlotte climbing into the back where she could stroke Butch's ears as they drove, the enormous dog on a makeshift rope leash and collar putting the new agents on edge.

They stuck to the western loops and scanned the area for any movement, the park having been closed to visitors with the recent gruesome discovery. As they closed in on Lost Horse Mine, she tapped Max on the shoulder. "We should do a quick walk-around here before we start heading back. Butch needs to stretch and I have a bottle of water for him."

Max rolled his eyes with exaggerated annoyance, pulling off the main road and parking in a small inlet. "I'll give you ten minutes." He sighed, turning to the two agents. "You guys keep an eye on her out there and don't let her follow that stupid mutt into the brush."

The men exchanged a look but obeyed, dutifully following her out of the truck and stepping aside as she reached into the front seat and grabbed a Tupperware bowl. Filling it with water, she placed it down for Butch and sat cross-legged in the sand, giving him a vigorous rubdown. She smiled up at the agents. "He doesn't like men, so you'll probably want to take a step back."

When the agents didn't budge, Butch lifted his huge head from the bowl and swung it in their direction, his ears flattening as he bared his enormous teeth.

The agents took several steps back.

Smirking, she buried her head in the animal's neck. "Good boy."

"Charlotte."

She looked over at Max, shielding her eyes from the truck's headlights. "What?"

"Get up."

Scrambling to her feet, she heard the cocking of three guns, Max and the agents aiming through the twin beams at a dark shadow approaching the vehicle. Butch's ears lifted for a moment before he broke into a slow trot toward the intruder, his head slightly bowed.

"Don't shoot Butch," she warned, stepping farther from the truck to the sound of Max's angered orders and the clipped demands of the agents behind her. "I'm not going out there," she hissed, watching as the creature came into view. "Oh, wow."

"You've got to be kidding me," Max groaned as Butch doubled back toward them, an identical dog hot on his heels. He dropped his gun to his side, de-cocking it and slipping it back into his holster. "This is the exact definition of bullshit, Chuck."

The agents held position, the younger one shifting nervously as the newcomer circled him, butting his head against the man's holster until he lowered his weapon.

She tracked the animal's movements for any sign of aggression, holding her hand out for the new one to scent her. He padded over to her and nuzzled her fingers, flashing his teeth at Butch when he sidled up to her. Noting the familiar black collar on the newcomer, she crossed her arms. "Butch?"

Butch barked in response, then turned to growl at his companion. The second dog chuffed and paced in a circle before he stopped and responded, his bark coarser, less crisp. She put her hands on her hips. "You're an imposter, aren't you?" she scolded, flipping Max off when he began going off about hordes of wild dogs taking over the park. "Where did you two come from?" she muttered.

Butch rose up, nudging the other dog toward the brush. When the animal finally broke into a trot toward the ridge,

Butch circled her once, sniffed her hand, and tore off after his companion.

ALEX WAITED UNTIL Bo was dressed and untangled from the rope collar before he threw the first punch, gritting his teeth as the echo of his hit rumbled through his own jaw. "Stay away from her," he growled. "One easy request."

Bo's head snapped back, his cheekbone bruising up instantly. He doubled back on Alex, catching him with one hit to the ribs and another to the gut. "I was doing you a fucking favor," he yelled back, dodging another fist and hitting the ground when Alex booted his leg out from under him. "Holy *fuck*! The hell's your problem?"

"It's sick," he snarled, jumping onto Bo in time for Bo's knee to catch him in the kidney. They rolled across the sand as they struggled to catch their breath. "It's not that hard, Bo," he grunted, heaving his brother off him. "Get your twisted kicks out of someone else." He rose to his feet only to get knocked back down as his fist made contact with Bo's jaw, sending him stumbling backward.

Bo shook his head, rubbing his bruised face and making no move to continue the fight. "I was just keeping an eye on her," he muttered, spitting blood onto the sand and wedging his finger into his mouth to check his teeth. "You're fucking lucky you didn't knock anything out."

He pressed on his ribs, wincing when he realized he'd re-broken two. "Sure you were," he panted, keeping one eye on his brother as he lay back to catch his breath. "More like aiming for another rubdown."

"You know I have a weakness for a good ear scratching," Bo said, angling himself to lie next to Alex. "Stop pressing on those fucking ribs. It hurts."

He grunted. "It was one easy request."

"And you were working while a Pirithous hunts around here," Bo countered. "You called her cell eighteen times during the drive north. Another nine on the way back. I figured maybe keeping an eye on her would be a good idea in case the bloodline decided to do a double-header."

"You broke my ribs again." He glanced over at his brother. "You weren't perving on her?"

Bo scoffed. "Of course I was. But in the most respectful way I could, given the circumstances."

The pair lay in silence for a few minutes.

"We need to get this guy before the cops do." Alex sighed. "It's kind of snowballed out of control, hasn't it?"

"We've dealt with this shit before," Bo murmured, tossing his arm over his eyes. "Maybe you're off your game because this may actually be it." He peered over at Alex. "Kind of overwhelming, being this close to home, isn't it?"

Home.

He thought back to his slip-up with Charlotte.

"Yeah. That's probably it."

Chapter Twenty-One

ALEX PRESSED HIS phone tighter to his ear, flipping his brother off as Charlotte's overtired, overexcited voice carried through the small trailer.

"What if one's a girl?" she exclaimed. "There might be puppies!"

Bo stood up, pushing his muscled stomach out as far as it could go and ducking when Alex tossed a pillow at him.

"There are no puppies." He groaned. "Forget about the damn dogs. Why are you calling me seven hours later than you were supposed to be off?"

"Oh. That." Her voice settled slightly, the frenetic pace lessening. "Becky and Jonas found an abandoned sedan hung up near Forty-Nine Palms. Max swears it's the same one that hit Butch a few months back, but who knows. Unfortunately, he went and opened his big mouth about it and he and I had to review all our reports and sit in with the head honchos to discuss everything we remembered about the guy."

He flopped back onto his bed and tossed his arm over his eyes, willing away his own exhaustion from staking out the Pirithous apartment for the past four hours. "Tell me you don't work today."

"I don't. I'm going to bed until Max drags me to the tavern at ten."

The tension that had settled in his shoulders during the long wait for her call released a fraction and he smiled. "I have to admit I like Max's idea tonight."

"Yeah, yeah." She laughed. "You say that now. But when I come in all cranky and demanding, you'll change your tune."

"I kind of like when you get bossy. Get some sleep and I'll see you at ten. Night, baby." Dropping his phone beside him, he lifted his arm and glared at Bo. "What?"

"Nothing," Bo said flatly, sprawling out on the small sofa. "I'm just wondering how rough the break-up is going to be for you."

"Neither of us are in a place for a relationship, so there won't be a break-up. Just a see-you-around," he muttered, refusing to think about it. "You driving in with me? Thomas cooks up a mean burger."

Bo stood up and walked to the small bathroom, examining his cheekbone and jaw in the mirror. "You're a fucking dick. You owe me a goddamn burger for this. And stop touching your sides."

He rolled out of bed carefully, holding his ribs in place until he was upright. "Next time I tell you to back off my woman, do it." He snatched up his wallet and keys and froze midstep.

"*A* woman," Bo corrected for him. "And there won't even be a next time."

✖

CHARLOTTE KEPT A pleasant smile on her face as she and Max approached Bo. "Max, this is Alex's brother, Bo. Bo, Max."

Bo gave a disinterested nod and polished off his drink.

"This really sucks," Max grumbled, his eyes moving to Alex while he approached. "Now that there's two of you, I'm never getting laid around here again, am I?"

"Bo will pass you his leftovers," Alex offered, grinning when Bo snatched the beer from his hand and held it up to Max in solidarity. He stepped closer to her before he hesitated and rocked back. "Everyone's over at the back booths." She bit her lip as she glanced over at the very memorable table her colleagues were now drinking at. Catching her eye, Alex smirked. "I'll be by after I run a couple orders out."

Max dragged her across the bar, muttering about fishes and ponds and sharks taking over his hunting grounds. He squeezed in beside the Montana mumbler, shrugging when Charlotte raised her brows a fraction. Eying the only seat left, she sank down beside Becky.

"You're passing one over to me," Becky stated without hesitation, looking over Charlotte's shoulder. "You don't get both."

Glaring at Max, she sat back in her seat. "Gladly." She watched Alex as he wove through the maze of chairs and people, nodding as requests came in and politely dodging the hands of women when he paused to collect their empty glasses.

When he finally made it over to them, he looked pointedly at the table before grinning at her. "Coffee, beer, or shots?"

"Beer and shots!" Max yelled over, tossing his credit card on the table. "Overtime's buying."

Alex noted everyone's request, leaning forward to whisper in her ear when he got to her. "You look tired. Want me to water your shots down?"

She nodded, biting her lip when he flicked his tongue against her earlobe before he straightened up to address the rest of the table. "Anything else before I grab the drinks?"

"You could send your doppelgänger over," Becky called out, crossing her legs and crowding Charlotte to the edge of the bench. "He looks lonely over there."

With a tight smile, Alex turned back to the bar. She watched him as he prepped their drinks, his movements slow and deliberate. He maintained a constant conversation with Bo, nodding toward Charlotte's table before shaking his head and turning toward the beer fridges. He passed two over to Bo, his expression unreadable as Bo made his way to their table and pulled a chair up tight to her side.

"You gonna introduce me?" he asked quietly, leaning in

uncomfortably close to her.

She scooted an inch closer to Becky, receiving an unimpressed sigh from the woman as she called out everyone's name, pausing long enough for each person to give a quick wave before moving on. "And this is Becky."

Becky reached behind her to give Bo a limp-wristed handshake. "So are you and Alex twins or brothers?"

Bo lifted one brow and sneered at her hand before he held both beers up. "Hands are full. Twins."

Becky smiled at him, turning sideways and bringing her knee up onto the bench, eliminating most of Charlotte's seat. "Are you the good twin or the bad one?"

He leaned forward, his eyes traveling down to her legs. "I'm the one who isn't drunk enough for that yet."

Charlotte's eyes widened and she locked her attention on Max, willing him to take his attention off the Montana mumbler's cleavage and intervene. Bo sat back in his seat and got comfortable, wedging his leg tight against her. When Becky dropped her knee in a huff and latched her focus back on to Jonas, Bo used his thigh to push Charlotte back into her spot.

"Drop-shots on the house," Alex announced from behind her, reaching between them to set a full tray on the table. He placed one shooter in front of her first, its slightly lighter color indistinguishable once it was separated from the other. "Gladiators for the gladiators," he stated, his eyes hard despite the upturn of his lips.

The group dove in, prepping their drinks as he walked back to the bar to grab another tray of their orders. Toasts were shouted out as Max attempted unsuccessfully to quiet the group long enough for a countdown.

Bo tapped her shoulder and lifted his shot to her. "To ticking clocks." He dropped the small glass into the larger one and tossed it back, downing it in one gulp and shaking his head as he swallowed. "Better drink up while you can."

✕

NINETEEN.

Charlotte mentally added the double-rye in Bo's hand to the total he'd had since she'd arrived at the bar.

He'd barely spoken in two hours, his blue and green eyes periodically scanning the patrons with disinterest before they'd stare blankly at the strobe lights on the ceiling. Becky had made several drunken attempts to gain his attention, going so far as to climb over Charlotte in her "rush" to the dance floor and falling into Bo's lap.

It had been mildly amusing when he merely lifted his drinks into the air wordlessly until she righted herself in a huff and walked off.

She leaned into Alex's hand as he brushed it across her cheek on his way by, arching her neck to watch him sweet-talk a table of tittering older women.

"Why didn't you push back?"

She looked over at Bo. "Excuse me?"

He hefted his chair forward. "With the knock-off ranger Barbie over there," he said, pointing his glass toward the dance floor. "Why didn't you push back? Reclaim your spot?"

She shrugged and took a sip of her coffee. "Not worth the fight." She leaned back and assessed him. "Speaking of fights, what happened to your face?"

"Your ugly-ass lay got in a cheap shot before I snapped a couple of his ribs." When her mouth dropped open, Bo smiled at her, his uncanny resemblance to Alex unnerving. "So do you have your break-up date circled on the calendar? Or are you two going to pick something stupid to argue over and make that the explosive end?"

Craning her neck to catch a glimpse of Alex as he knelt down slower than usual in front of the beer fridges, she pursed her lips. "Not that it's any of your business, but there's nothing to break up."

"I'd say anything that compromises my brother's concentration on the job is definitely my business," he countered, lifting his empty glass in Alex's direction until Alex saw it from across the room and nodded. "This little relationship experiment is a distraction for him. And distractions are dangerous."

She sat back and stared absently at the dance floor, giving Max a tight-lipped smile when he waved over at her. "And that," she said, rapping her finger on Bo's empty drink, "isn't a distraction?"

Bo chuckled and stretched his arms behind his chair. "No escaping it when Dionysus favors you." With an impatient glance in Alex's direction, he stared her down, smirking when she looked away.

Alex approached the pair, eying her warily. "Double rye, last call," he said, setting Bo's drink down. "Everything good?"

She nodded tersely as Bo swirled the ice in his drink and looked up at his twin. "Two more doubles, two shots of tequila. Don't forget the salt and lemon."

ALEX DROPPED OFF the last of his tabs and doubled back to Charlotte's table. The two tequila shots remained untouched as she and Bo sat in a silent standoff, Charlotte refusing to take the lemon from Bo's teeth and Bo refusing to back down.

Max waved his credit card in the air, his other hand inching toward Charlotte's tequila. "If no one wants that..."

"It's yours," Charlotte replied, pushing the salt at Max, a smile on her lips when Bo spat the lemon from his mouth and slammed back his own shot.

Alex pocketed Max's card and knelt beside Charlotte. "Dance?"

Her eyes lit up for a moment before they flicked to

Thomas standing at the till. "You're still working."

"I'm going to be here for another two hours clearing tables." He stood and held out his hand, ignoring Bo's hardened face and booting his chair when Charlotte tried to pass over him and Bo lifted his knee a fraction.

He led her onto the dance floor, the other couples awkwardly breaking apart as the song switched to a slower song he had seen on the upcoming playlist. Charlotte's arms wrapped around his neck loosely, her expressions shifting every few seconds.

Over.

He looked down. "There's enough room for a bible between us."

Charlotte smiled, holding position for a few beats before she stepped in closer to him and tightened her hold on his neck. "Do you want to come by after work for a bit?"

A bit?

He looked over Charlotte's head at Bo. "Should I?"

She went quiet, her fingers twirling his hair while she avoided answering him or meeting his eyes. He pulled her flush to him, rested his chin on her head, and stared his twin down until Bo looked down at his drinks and pounded them back.

THE LAST CUSTOMER opened the tavern door, stepping aside

to allow the sprite-like strawberry blonde to skip in, her hulking onyx-eyed protector stalking behind her. As Seph beelined it toward the end of the bar where Bo was slumped over, Hades stood stoically beside Alex, watching his wife.

"Boreus!"

Bo turned his head toward the familiar voice, grinning when Seph cupped his chin in her tiny hands and fussed over his bruises. "It was Alex," Bo ratted, wincing for show as Persephone ran her thumbs over the darkest one.

Lips pursed, she turned to him, her hands flying to her hips. "You damaged him!"

"He'll live," he muttered, snatching the last of the dirty rags from the counter and storming to the kitchen, Hades hot on his heels.

His master scanned the back room. "You two haven't fought since you were pups."

"We fight plenty," he called out, his spine prickling with Hades's proximity. "And we've got a lead. Ryan's been called in." He kept his eyes averted, pushing back through the swinging doors. "Hear that Seph? We'll be home soon."

Bo was on his feet, shirtless and swaying slightly as his mistress examined the various scratches and markings peppering his torso. She glanced up at Alex. "I should hope so. My pretty boys are getting all marred up here. Hades. Come take a look at this."

Obliging, Hades strode past him and bent down to scan Bo's healing injuries. "None of these are permanent," he stated, squeezing Seph's hand in reassurance before rising to face Alex. "If you have a lead, explain to me why you aren't tracking it right now."

He snorted, waving his hand toward his drunken twin, who was struggling to pull his shirt back over his head. "Someone has to babysit that."

Seph's blue eyes narrowed as she assisted Bo, running her hands over the tattoo that matched that of his brothers. "Aw, honey. You know it upsets me when you two fight."

Hades crossed his arms and regarded him for a moment before calling over to Bo. "Anything to report on this one's extracurricular activities?"

His twin flopped back down onto a bar stool and shrugged, yanking his phone out of his pocket. "Got a bunch of pics here." His unsteady hand held the cell out to Hades and he smirked at Seph. "Don't flip too far back. There's a few on there that aren't safe for work."

He watched as Hades swiped through the photos, mentally preparing himself for a grilling about Charlotte until the images flashed across the screen.

Aside from the shots from his drunken night at that Allison woman's apartment, Bo had several pictures of Alex at work.

Smiling down at a pretty blonde as she reached up to trace the outer ridges of his tattoo.

Leaning against the counter as another woman backed up tight against him.

Resting his hands on the hips of a brunette, her lips tilted up toward his.

What was missing from each picture was the context.

Alex, stepping away when the unwanted fingers grazed his skin.

The beer bottle that tipped off his tray moments after the customer bumped into him, her apologies profuse as she and her boyfriend pushed cash toward him to cover the accident.

His focused beeline through the crowd as Charlotte made her way out of the bar without a goodbye.

Hades passed the cell back to Bo and gave Alex a strange look. "We'll be seeing you soon, boys."

Waiting until the door slammed shut, he pulled out his phone and texted Charlotte. *"Won't be able to make it tonight."*

He finished a final wipe of the counter and rounded the bar, helping Bo to his feet and guiding him out of the lounge. "Nice pics."

Bo smirked, flopping into the passenger seat and sliding his phone across the dash. "I was gonna show those to your little whatever-you-call-her Charlotte chick. But I figured I'd cover your ass with the boss-man instead." He closed his eyes as Alex started the SUV. "I'm not too sure he or Seph would be too pleased knowing they were losing you to a human woman."

Easing onto the road, he gave his brother a quick smile. "No one's losing anyone."

Except me.

"Whatever," Bo grumbled, slinking into his seat in a futile attempt to get comfortable and reaching down to adjust the seat as he sprawled out. "Straight up. You aren't, like, in love with this chick, right?"

"Make yourself useful and pass out or something." He snorted, glancing at his silent phone.

Chapter Twenty-Two

ALEX HUNG UP the phone and turned to Bo, his arms crossed. "Ryan'll be here Sunday. He's driving down, leaving on Friday night." He tossed an outdated phonebook at his brother and began the hunt for his keys. "I might be back before you sober up enough to find a hotel for the two of you."

He flew through the back streets, slamming on his brakes when he almost passed the turnoff to Charlotte's apartment block.

He didn't want to be here.

Two days and nights of phone tag.

Shift work that didn't align.

Two early-morning stakeouts of the Pirithous.

He parked in a vacant corner of the lot and snatched his phone off the dash.

"We need to talk." Charlotte's last text, made at six that morning, sat at the top of his messages.

He'd never needed to talk. Never stuck around long enough to have to talk.

He buzzed Charlotte's apartment and waited until the

obnoxious system let him in the building, climbing the stairs slowly, his ribs still aching and his legs heavy.

He didn't want to talk.

She stood in her open doorway, her damp hair leaving wet streaks on the gray police training shirt she had on.

And his favorite jeans. Her ass looked great in those jeans.

Pausing at her door, he shoved his hands in his pockets. "Hey."

She was playing with the hem of her shirt, tugging the sleeves down over her thumbs as she stepped to the side to let him in. "Hey."

The warmth he'd felt every time he'd entered Charlotte's apartment was now uncomfortable and tense as she stepped into the kitchen and wrapped her arms around herself, examining the countertop with interest.

"I take it this is the talk," he finally said, leaning against the kitchen entrance.

She took a deep breath. "Pretty much. I know we both agreed this was temporary, so I don't know if we're supposed to have the talk to make it official or something, but..."

His jaw flexed, a strange tightness forming in his chest. "What did Bo say to you?"

"Nothing I didn't already know," she replied, her hands twisting inside the long sleeves of her shirt.

He nodded absently.

He already knew what Bo had said to her.

He'd beaten it out of his wasted brother the night before, and had the bruises on his chest to prove it.

"Oh, wow," Charlotte breathed out, shaking her arms out before she resumed her stance. "I suppose the park's fair game for you, since you might need to, uh, work there. But I'll steer clear of the tavern." She frowned. "I guess poor Thomas'll be shorthanded soon."

He shifted his weight. "I've been stashing resumes for him under the till." He took a step into the kitchen, freezing when she shook her head. "I'm not sorry we met."

"Me either."

He crossed the floor, pausing for a moment in front of her before he wrapped his arms around her and dropped his head into the crook of her neck, desperate to commit the scent of her shampoo to memory. "I'm really sorry for this though."

She took a shuddering breath that hit him harder than Bo ever had, her calm demeanor cracking. "Me too. See you around."

She kept her arms around herself, her head turning from him when he released her and backed into the hall without another word, the heavy click of a lock and the sound of Charlotte breaking down echoing in his head as he drove to work and began his shift.

✕

CHARLOTTE STRAIGHTENED HER hat and tilted her rearview mirror, assessing her red-rimmed eyes with resignation.

No amount of eyeliner or powder could hide how she'd spent the past three hours.

She rifled through her glovebox for her sunglasses, grateful the autumn sun was still strong enough to warrant them for a few more hours.

She didn't have it in her to answer any questions.

Walking into the station, she greeted everyone with a quick wave before hunching over the evening schedule and mapping her route.

"We're back to solo runs," Max called over to her, giving the small vending machine a shake until an aged chocolate bar fell out. "I'll take the Pass, you take the Keys, we'll meet up at the Garden on Pinto."

"Sounds good," she replied, her voice tighter and thinner than normal. "I'm heading out."

His mouth full, Max muttered something unintelligible as she grabbed a set of truck keys and left, fighting the urge to break into a run and get the hell away from anyone and everyone as quick as possible.

The park was quiet, most tourists having been scared off by the rash of deaths in the region. She tossed her sunglasses onto the empty passenger seat and dropped the truck to a crawl, scanning the terrain halfheartedly for any signs of dead bodies, killers, or dogs.

Anything to take her mind off Alex.

She turned off the air conditioner as the sun disappeared, the chill that had settled in her body when he walked out still sitting heavy in her bones.

Little relationship experiment.

She blinked rapidly, taking deep breaths as she pulled over and threw the truck into park.

Neither of us will be shocked when this goes to hell.

She jumped out of the vehicle and ran her hands over her face.

She missed him already.

She missed him waiting for her to call, to tell him she had made it home safe.

She missed knowing her silent phone would ping incessantly once she hit the highway, menial messages and funny anecdotes filling her alerts.

She hopped onto the hood of the truck and lay back on the windshield, her fingers ghosting her gun. The coyotes began to chatter, their voices crossing between the hills and mountains of the park and bouncing off the rock. When a husky, gravelly crooning broke in, she sat up and called into the darkness. "Hey, Not-Butch. Where are you, boy?"

The useless sliver of moonlight hid the enormous beast until he was almost in striking distance of her, his stalking gait more predatory than Butch's.

She slid off the truck and held her hand out, scratching under the dog's chin as he lay his muzzle in her palm. "Where's Butch? Hmm?" she cooed, smiling when the dog chuffed and nudged her fingers. "One of these days, I'm going to toss you two in the truck and take you home. I'll be picking up a pretty collar for you, too. Maybe blue?"

The dog retreated a few steps, snorting and pawing the sand.

"I'm heading back to the station," she said, standing straight and brushing her hands on her pants. "You coming?"

He padded up to her, using his head to herd her toward the truck and sitting back on his haunches when she relented and climbed in.

"Fine. I'll bring some steaks out tomorrow." She closed the door and rolled down her window. "Tell Butch I say hi."

✖

ALEX GAVE THE pretty brunette a smile and made a show of pocketing her number until she walked out, trashing it when the bar door closed.

"They can smell blood in the water," Bo stated, folding the number the brunette's friend had slipped him and tucking it into his phone case. He nodded toward a trio of women on the dance floor, their slinky moves in the deserted lounge a definite message to the brothers. "Two for you, one for me?"

Popping the cap off a beer, Alex pushed it across the counter to Bo. "Did you manage to book a hotel?"

Bo rolled his eyes and nodded, taking a swig. "Put it on

Ryan's credit card."

He printed off the last two bills and set them beside the till, his fingers brushing over the resumes piling up. "What about the Pirithous?"

"Swung by there, too," Bo replied, watching the dancing women with a mixture of interest and boredom. "No movement." He leaned forward on the bar. "We could be in the final countdown, Lex."

His shoulders tensed. "Don't call me that." He snatched the tabs up and hit the floor, dropping off one at a table of tourists before he strode across the dance floor and held the other out to the women. "Cashing out, ladies."

A heavily made-up blonde took the bill, motioning for him to follow her to the pile of purses sitting on a table in front of the till. "Put it through on this," she purred, passing him a Visa. She cocked her head toward Bo and smiled. "You two busy later?"

"Yup."

He ignored Bo's dead stare as he ran the card and passed the woman a pen. Her coy expression was gone, her eyes hard as she added a one dollar tip and signed off on the bill.

Bo held his tongue until the place emptied and Alex began counting out the till. "Get over one by getting under another," he stated, pushing himself off the bar. "Might as well take what you can get before we cross over."

He texted Thomas the total and tossed the cash into the bar's safe, spinning the dial. "I'm good."

He wasn't good.

He was numb.

On autopilot since he walked out of Charlotte's apartment hours earlier.

He grabbed his wallet and phone, not bothering to check the messages he knew weren't there. "Let's go."

Chapter Twenty-Three

MAX BROKE OFF a piece of stale chocolate from his bar and passed it Charlotte. "I don't care about what a nonissue you're calling it, you should've told me." He thumped his work boots onto her coffee table and snatched the remote from her. "You know, before I opened my stupid mouth."

She popped the chocolate in her mouth and tightened her blanket around her shoulders, every muscle aching from the double shifts she had pulled for the past two days. All she wanted to do was stare blankly at the TV and crash from exhaustion.

Until Max walked into her apartment, hollering about Alex.

"The guy outweighs me by, like, forty pounds," he grumbled, settling on an action film from the mid-80s. "And there I was, smacking him on the back and joking about you taking extra shifts so you could hook up with Jonas in the break room." He wrestled a bag of chips open, handing her the rest of the chocolate. "My life passed in front of my eyes. Thomas and his brother had to talk him down long enough for me to get out of there."

She continued to stare at the television.

"He looks like shit," Max offered after a moment. "I got a real good look at his face when he slammed me onto the bar." When she remained silent, he tapped her foot with his. "You don't look much better."

Inching her hand into the bag of chips, she shrugged. "Five shifts in three days'll do that."

Realizing she wasn't in the mood to talk, Max got comfortable and turned up the volume. She kept her eyes on the movie without watching it, her mind drifting between her upcoming shifts and her growing laundry pile before it would inevitably loop back to Alex. Working the extra hours had been counterproductive to her plan to eliminate him from her head. Instead of filling her days and nights, it had given her hours of solitary drive time to think and had exhausted her to the point where she was no longer able to actively pursue *not* thinking about him.

She sank further into the sofa, tucking her legs up. "So did he say anything about us?"

Max crumpled the empty chip bag and threw it onto the coffee table, ignoring it when it rolled off the edge. "Nope. His brother filled me in after Thomas dragged Alex into the kitchen."

✕

ALEX PASSED THOMAS the night's receipts and continued to stock the beer fridge under the bar owner's watchful eye. "I'm fine. All good."

The elderly man opened the till and began counting the bills. "I should probably fire you for that ridiculousness tonight," he stated, lifting the tray to pull the larger denominations out. "But it's Max, and I've had the urge to smack him around myself a few times."

He snorted and closed the fridge, using the counter to heft himself to his feet. "It won't happen again," he said as he stacked the coins. "I don't usually snap like that."

Writing down his count, Thomas folded the paper and slipped it into the bank deposit bag. "Can I ask?"

"Charlotte and I just decided our arrangement wasn't working out," he mumbled, the reality of it knocking him in the gut as he said it aloud.

Thomas eyed him, zipped up the deposit bag, and tucked it under his arm. "I assume from your mood it was her decision?"

"Mutual," he replied, staring at the stack of resumes under the till. "I'll finish up here and lock up." He gave Thomas a tight smile. "An hour or two of scrubbing down table legs should burn off any remaining aggression."

"I'll clock you out for three and leave your pay up beside the till."

Alex moved methodically through the bar, washing down every surface he could reach until his muscles ached and his feet were protesting. Collecting the soiled rags, he straightened up the last of the clean bar glasses and prepped the bar for the next morning.

Ice loaded.

Cutlery wrapped.

Billfolds and menus stacked.

He pulled the collection of resumes out from under the till, scrawling a quick note about his top choices as he added the wad of cash Thomas had left out for him to the pile. Scanning the stock of bottles under the counter, he selected four, tucking them under his arm before he walked out of the lounge and set the lock code for the last time.

CHARLOTTE PARKED HER car on the small gravel path and reached into the back seat to grab her stash of water bottles, bowls, and a small cooler. She balanced the items carefully under one arm while she tugged the hem of her shorts down and adjusted her shirt. Slipping her keys into her back pocket, she slipped a bright blue collar and leash over her wrist and began the hike to the top of the rocky ridge to the south.

"Where are you, boy?" she called, watching the scuffed path for the animals that were waking as the sun's peak waned. "I brought steaks and water."

Glancing back to ensure her vehicle remained in view,

she continued the climb, calling out every few minutes until she reached the end of the established pathway. She sat down on a rock, carefully filling the water bowl and opening the cooler to pull out the steaks she'd cooked up earlier in the day.

"Come on, puppies," she grumbled. "Not-Butch, I know you want this."

The desert was slowly coming to life, the ground scattered with small reptiles and snakes beginning the hunt for their nightly meals. She scanned the terrain, puncturing the quiet evening with intermittent whistles and calls until a low, clear howl carried across the land in reply.

She continued to whistle in response, smiling when the dog mimicked her tunes, his voice growing closer until she caught sight of him stalking over the rocks to her left, black collar hanging around his throat and his leash swinging from his jaws.

"There you are, boy," she said, lifting the bowl of steaks. "Where's your buddy?" Butch approached her tentatively, keeping just out of her reach. "Hungry?"

She lay the bowl down, nudging it toward the beast with her boot. He sniffed it and looked up at her, his eyes obscured by his long fur.

"Go on," she urged. "Where've you been hiding all week?"

Butch dropped his leash beside the bowl and tore at the meat as he watched the terrain, his ears up and twitching.

When he finally finished the last of the steak, he pushed the bowl back at her, his head bowed.

"I knew you'd be hungry," she cooed, exchanging the empty bowl with the water. "Max says I'm nuts for doing this. But you know what? Screw Max."

Butch snorted, lapping at the water.

"It's beautiful out here," she mused, looking around as the sun cast incredible shadows. "I forgot how stunning it can be. Too wrapped up in pretty boys and murder scenes, I guess."

The beast's ears flattened for a moment, a low growl rumbling through him.

She reached over to scratch his ears, pausing when Butch flinched away for a moment before relenting. "Is this your new hunting ground? You won't get many bunnies here, but the snake meat must be pretty plentiful." She took a quick look around, moving her hand under Butch's chin. "I could definitely come here more often. Would you like that, boy? Fresh steak and water every day?"

Butch backed out of her reach and tilted his head before he barked, knocking the water bowl over with his paw. She leaned over and picked up the bowl, looking toward him. "Is that a no?" she joked, stepping back when Butch flattened his ears and bared his teeth at her. "Don't you start."

She tucked the empty bowls into her cooler and zipped it up as Butch circled her, his hackles raised. Slowing her movements to avoid spooking him, she rose to her feet and began cooing platitudes at the dog, frowning when he became more agitated, his stance becoming defensive as he slapped the leash toward her with his enormous paw.

"It's okay, boy," she said softly, keeping her attention on him as she made her way down the path, Butch pacing behind her. "You know me. It's okay."

She jumped when he snarled in response, stalking closer to her until she resumed her trek to her car. Picking up her speed, she patted her hip where her work weapon usually sat, her fingers flexing when she remembered she was in civilian dress. Butch remained in sight on her left, growling at her every time her footsteps slowed.

"What's wrong, damn dog?" she muttered, scanning the darkening terrain for any sign of Not-Butch. "I'm not gonna hurt you."

Butch snapped at her, his teeth grazing her arm before he ducked his head and shoved the collar off his neck.

Her heart leapt into her throat and she drew her arms in tight to herself. She breathed deep to calm herself, her car almost within reach as Butch's growl followed her to the car door and she jumped in. Her hands shook as she started the vehicle, angling her rearview mirror so she could track Butch while he paced behind her, his enormous teeth on full display until she threw the car into drive and eased onto the road, her heart thumping in her ears.

By the time she hit the highway, her hands had stilled, the adrenaline in her system from Butch's strange behavior finally waning. She glanced down at her arm, breathing a sigh of relief to find he hadn't nicked her.

Damn dog.

✕

ALEX SAT ON the ridge, his eyes absently tracking a small snake as Bo padded up to him, nose wrinkling when he took in Alex's scent. Shaking his head, Bo took up position beside him and scanned the area, his ears twitching as he catalogued the sounds of the desert at night.

Rising to his feet, he wound his way through the harsh stone, ignoring Bo when he chuffed in annoyance and followed suit.

He shouldn't have approached her.

He should've continued his hunt for the missing Pirithous, continued on the path along the mountains where the abandoned rental had been located the night before.

He should've tracked her from a distance, stayed out of view until she gave up and went home.

He should've let her think Butch had moved on to greener pastures.

With her scent still clinging to him, he broke into a jog as the ground flattened, sand replacing the unstable rock beneath his feet. Bo came up tight beside him, nipping at his hindquarters until Alex relented and launched ahead full speed, his brother in pursuit.

They crossed the main road of the park, dodging the chollas until they made it to the small enclave where he had parked his SUV.

A road Charlotte didn't frequent during her shifts and hadn't sought out on her days off.

He prowled the area while Bo transformed and dressed, taking his turn once his brother stood at the ready. He tossed his bag into the back seat, rolling his eyes when Bo climbed in beside him and lit a cigarette.

"I thought you gave that shit up."

Bo snorted. "I thought you gave that woman up."

His jaw tensed. "Just wrapping up loose ends."

"With an ear scratching?"

His foot heavy on the gas, he kept his attention on the narrow road. "Hoping I gave her enough of a scare to keep her from coming out here alone and unarmed until we finish up business. We don't need her or anyone out here playing animal rescue."

Bo flicked his cigarette out the window, the cherry bursting behind the SUV in the darkness. "If we see her out here again, I'll drive the point home," he stated, putting his feet up on the dash. "Ryan'll be down Sunday, right?"

Nodding, he turned onto the highway and cranked the music.

All ties had been severed.

He was ready.

Chapter Twenty-Four

ALEX GROANED AND opened one eye, lifting his phone close to his face as he hit the replay button. Satisfied with his song choice, he sank back into the sofa, ignoring his brothers as they stood over him in the small trailer.

"And how long has he been like this?" Ryan finally asked, lifting up the empty bottle of rye tucked under Alex's arm and setting it on the kitchen table.

"Two nights." Bo's gravelly voice was clipped. "Change the fucking song already."

He grunted, pushing himself upright and reaching beside him for the bottle of vodka he had stashed. He held it up, squinting to get a good view of his audience. "It's not red. And it's not wine. But it's doing the same thing." He twisted the cap off and tossed it across the trailer. "Won't be needing that."

As he brought the bottle to his lips, Ryan snatched it from his hand, sending half the vodka onto his chest. He jumped up, stumbling against Bo for a moment until he braced himself on the table. "What the hell?" he snarled, swaying on his feet before he slumped onto the bench.

Ryan turned his back, dumping the remaining vodka down the sink. "Bo, you can head back to the motel. Call a cab and take forty from my wallet." He rifled around the sofa until he found another bottle with a few ounces left, pouring it down the drain and setting it neatly beside the others. "I'll be spending the night here."

Alex's head snapped back as he fought to keep himself conscious, glaring at the bills Bo was slipping into his back pocket. "He took sixty," he slurred, flinging one arm in Bo's direction and bouncing it off the small storage cabinet. "Goddammit."

Ryan's arm slipped behind him, hefting him to his feet. "I'll take the couch. One foot in front of the other, Lex."

"Don't call me that." He closed one eye and zeroed in on his bed, tripping forward and gripping Ryan's shoulder. "A mistake. Huge fucking mistake." He fell onto his bed and rolled onto his back. "Home sounds so awesome right now."

He flung his arm over his head and closed his eyes, shutting out the light and the quiet discussion Bo and Ryan were having steps away from him.

Huge fucking mistake.

Alex gripped his coffee mug, grunting in protest when Ryan attempted to open the kitchen curtains. "Not ready for that," he muttered, turning his head from the searing rays of the sun until Ryan fixed the blinds.

Topping up his own cup, Ryan sat at the small table, his expression unreadable. "I've been speaking with Bo about your condition. He'll be here shortly."

"Bender."

Ryan lifted a brow. "Excuse me?"

Downing the last of his coffee, he pushed his mug across the table and sat back, arms crossed. "Bo has a condition. I was on a bender." He looked over at the neat row of bottles on the counter and his stomach lurched. "A good one, too."

Glancing down at his watch, Ryan adjusted his position in the small dinette. "Bo suggested this was the result of an attachment to a local woman." He reached across to the coffeepot and topped up both mugs. "Is it out of your system now?"

"Treated with a strong dose of booze and self-loathing," he muttered, slouching down. "Yeah, she's out of my system."

Ryan continued to appraise him in the stoic way that drove Bo nuts, his brown and amber eyes unblinking as he waited for his victim to give something away. "So Bo embellished the seriousness of your attachment?"

Attachment.

The word sounded so clinical and impersonal, at odds with the intense craving that had coursed through him whenever she was near, the heated anticipation he had experienced when she would lick her lips and trail her fingers along his jaw, tangling them in his hair every time they kissed. It was a term that brought up images of favorite shirts and albums, not warm brown eyes that lit up when he made her laugh or slender fingers that tugged at shirts when she was nervous. It didn't come anywhere close to describing the staggering fear that had pulsed through him when she'd called from the station a lifetime ago, or the flood of relief he'd experienced every time she texted him after a shift.

He wasn't attached, and fuck anyone who thought he was.

Running his hand over his face, he shook his head in a futile attempt to clear his mind of the woman who torment-ed him day and night, drunk and sober. "Nope. Definitely no attachment. All ties are cut, and I'm totally ready for the hunt."

"You aren't in love with this woman then."

The L-word hung in the air for a moment, Alex staring at his coffee while images of the woman in question flew through his head. "Almost. Dammit, Ryan. We need to go home."

"THERE ARE TOO many cameras around to hop the fence," Bo stated, peering through the chain link fence at the Pirithous rental. "Probably no point in trying to break in, though. The cops would've wiped it clean and cleared it out already."

Ryan nodded, glancing around and stepping away from the security camera's reach. "I'll scent it out from here."

Bo and Alex stood back as Ryan stripped down quickly and transformed, chuffing when the scent of the Pirithous hit him. After a quick perusal of the grounds, he was back and dressing within minutes. "No missing that stench. The bloodline has definitely taken full hold."

While Ryan's words held no hint of accusation, his guilt rose. "I should've called you down earlier." He hesitated. "My head wasn't in the game."

"Your head was too busy being buried betw—"

Bo was cut short by Ryan's hand smacking him upside the head. "We've hunted them feral before, we can do it again."

He gave Ryan a grim nod.

Once a Pirithous bloodline went feral, they were harder to track, their movements and kill zones becoming less predictable. They abandoned all modern luxuries, their sole focus on the hunt and kill, their nutritional needs met by the bodies of their victims.

It was unpleasant and messy.

Bo opened the passenger door of the SUV, flipping Ryan off as he got in. "So what's the plan?"

Ryan folded himself into the back. "Since our window of opportunity to hunt in human form is gone, we'll need to work from within the park."

He tried to clear the sudden tightness from his throat. "They've reopened the campgrounds. If we pick up some camping supplies and food, we can establish a base inside and go from there."

✗

CHARLOTTE HIT THE brakes of her work truck, kicking up a plume of sand and dust. She craned her neck to get a better look at the campsite, her stomach sinking as she recognized the color and year of the SUV parked beside a small tent.

"You've got to be kidding me," she muttered, grabbing her CB. "Jonas? What's the name on site nine at White Tank?"

The radio crackled as Jonas looked up the information back at the station. "Ryan Echidna, paid for two weeks on a Visa," he replied. "Problem?"

Forcing her eyes off the small tent, she pulled back onto the road. "No. Just curious."

"Since you're in the area, could you confirm the vehicle plate and make sure the campers have the alert sheet?" Jonas called out. "Save me from driving out there after shift."

She took a deep breath. "Site looks empty right now. Have Max do it when he finishes the eastern loop."

"Waste of time," Jonas responded, his voice cracking on the poor connection. "Sun sets in an hour. Circle up to the northern entrance and hit them up on your way back."

Dropping her head onto the steering wheel for a moment, she kicked herself for calling it in. There was no way she was in any position to see him yet, no way she would be able to play it cool in his presence. Not when the heavy ache in her chest was still making itself known every time her mind drifted to his soft, skilled lips that moved every time he counted the bar till. Or his fascinating blue and hazel eyes that lit up when he'd caught sight of her from across the room. Or the way he always leaned forward in his seat whenever he was talking about some of his favorite movies, almost giddy whenever he realized it was one she had yet to see and they were *definitely going to have to watch it.*

She drove along the paved road, scanning the terrain as she linked up to Max's radio, cringing when his music crackled through the speaker. "I need a favor."

"Jonas already radioed in and told me to say no," Max answered. "What's the problem?"

She groaned. "I'm pretty sure it's Alex's SUV."

Max turned down his music. "Whoa."

"Pretty much my thought, too," she huffed, pulling off the road and squinting into the setting sunlight at a couple posing beside a large rock. "Advise me, king of unattachment."

ALEX HEFTED A jug of water from the back of his SUV and

set it beside the small camp stove. "Told you we should've grabbed a larger pan," he said as Bo flipped the two burger patties wedged side-by-side. "It'll be an hour before we eat at this rate."

Taking a long drink from his beer, Bo nodded in Ryan's direction. "Don't look at me. Blame the streamline junkie over there."

Ryan placed a lamp on the picnic table, pointedly ignoring Bo. "After we eat, you can lead us through the area the last kills were found," he said, opening the cooler and pulling out the cheese slices and condiments. "I grabbed a handful of maps at the visitor center that we can use to plot out our runs."

Setting a stack of paper plates beside Bo, Alex straddled the picnic table and opened a bottle of water. "Sheep's Pass is close. We'll start there and make our way to the Keys." He frowned as the lights of a vehicle turned onto the campsite road and passed over them and pulled into the site across from them. "Damn. I was hoping we'd be the only ones... Ah, hell." He gripped his water tighter as the door to the familiar truck opened.

Bo straightened up from the stove. "Is that—"

"Yup."

His throat tightened as Charlotte stood beside her truck, her shoulders squaring before she turned toward them and walked across the dirt path, stopping beside the SUV.

The need to run slammed through him, but whether it

was to run away from her or toward her, he didn't know.

She looked so goddamn beautiful in her uniform; it physically hurt to look at her.

"Welcome to Joshua Tree," she said, her voice stronger than his would be. She knelt down and locked her eyes on the back of the vehicle. "I'm just grabbing your plate number for our system and dropping off some information packages about the park."

Bo took a step closer to him as Ryan stood and approached her with his hand extended. "I can take those."

Charlotte rose to her feet and passed a handful of papers to Ryan, her face tilted away from Alex, hidden by the brim of her hat and the faint light of the lantern.

Not that it mattered.

He knew every curve of her face, every freckle, every expression.

Seeing it here, now, would only add to the plethora of images of her that cycled through his mind on a loop.

"You've probably heard we've had a string of murders in this area," she stated, stepping back out of the light and clasping her hands behind her back. "We're asking campers to remain vigilant to their surroundings, report anything suspicious to one of the stations listed on the back of the brochure, and to travel in groups of two or more at all times."

Alex looked over at the truck, his jaw tensing when he confirmed she was once again alone on the trails. Unguarded. He shrugged Bo's hand off as it settled on his shoulder. "Why isn't Max with you?"

Her breath hitched before she continued her spiel, her thumbs hooking into the cuffs of her shirt and tugging her sleeves down over her hands. "We're also reminding visitors to stick to established paths and to clean up all traces of activity prior to leaving the area. If there are no questions, have a great night and enjoy your stay at Joshua Tree."

He hopped off the table and took a step toward her. "Charlotte."

She pursed her lips, finally turning to look at him. "Question?"

He took another step, his stomach knotting when her eyes hardened and she retreated back. "Can I talk to you for a minute?"

Bo swore under his breath while Ryan watched Alex with a mixture of wariness and concern.

She stilled for a moment, her attention on the empty campsite beside him. "One minute." She turned her back to him and walked over to her truck, wrapping her arms around herself in a familiar defensive move that knocked him in the gut every time. "Go."

"You know why we're here," he said quietly, stopping a fraction closer to her than needed.

"Yeah, I figured as much when I saw the three of you together." She gave him a tight smile, her gaze averted. "Hopefully you'll have more luck than the FBI."

He reached to her instinctively, yanking his arm back at last minute and shoving his hands into his back pockets. "I don't want you out here alone until we catch the guy."

Her attention locked on something just past his shoulder and she yanked her keys from her pocket. "You don't really have a say in that, do you?" When he didn't respond, she exhaled and straightened her hat. "I'm turning a blind eye to you three. Clean up after yourselves, don't get yourselves killed while I'm on shift, and don't make me regret this."

She got into her truck and pulled the door closed, backing out of the site without another glance his way. He watched the taillights until they disappeared into the darkness, digging his knuckles into his chest in a futile attempt to relax that tension that had settled there, to relieve himself of the constant ache he'd endured since he'd walked out of her apartment.

Scanning the darkness with the faint hope she'd doubled back to him, he took a deep breath and returned to his campsite, silently accepting the burger Bo handed him.

Chapter Twenty-Five

"HOW MUCH FUCKING area can one guy cover?" Bo groaned, waving off the map Ryan was holding. "Skull, Chasm, Keys...why don't we start crossing off the places we haven't scented him and go from there?"

Alex spun his car keys on his finger and continued to stare out into the desert. "His stench is too strong around here. He has to be keeping a local base and traveling out to pick them off," he murmured, forcing his thoughts away from the ranger he knew was driving the trails alone. "What towns had bodies parts dumped this week?"

Ryan passed the map over, the three towns circled in bright red marker. "The FBI set up to the north," he said, tracing a line from their campsite. "Their focus on the cities will keep them out of our hair unless another body turns up around here."

Glancing around before he stripped down, he tossed his clothes into the tent and dropped to all fours to transform, recoiling when the overpowering odor of the Pirithous line hit him. He barked a warning to his brothers, stalking through the site until they joined him and latched on to the trail.

The bastard had been close. Too close. He fell back as Ryan took the lead, following the scent trail through the boulders and sand before he hit a stretch of flat terrain, the imprints of a motorbike marking the final leg of the path.

The brothers doubled back, fanning out to scour the area for any signs of where the Pirithous had holed up until they reached their campsite, taking turns transforming, dressing, and standing guard.

"Well, he knows we're here," Ryan stated. "Do we hunker down or move?"

Bo laced up his boots, knocking the sand off on the seat of the picnic table. "We hole up here and take him down the next time he comes around."

Alex nodded. "We're low on food and water. I say we go to town, fuel up, and prepare to lock down until he finds us."

✕

CHARLOTTE BLOCKED MAX'S hand as he reached for her fries, pulling her plate closer to herself and holding her fork out in defense. "Don't mess with me, boy," she growled. "I'm tired, I'm hungry, and in this state, I hold no responsibility for my actions if you try that again."

Max returned his attention to his own plate, poking at the baked potato he had insisted looked better on the menu.

"When can we go back to eating at the tavern?" he moaned, gripping his knife to slice through the tough steak. "I want real food."

"When hell freezes over?" she offered with a smile, passing him a pity fry. "Jonas mentioned there's a new bartender, so maybe we can hit the place up tomorrow."

Max scarfed down the fry and looked longingly at her plate. "The site was renewed for another two weeks under that Ryan guy." He chewed his steak, disgust crossing his face as he swallowed. "Don't know what they're doing every day. The campsite's deserted every time I go by."

She sighed and pushed her plate over to the partner who had taken over the northern loop of the park for her. In exchange for daily meals. "I don't want to know. Out of sight, out of mind, right?"

"Sure he is." Max snorted, diving into the fries and ignoring the half-eaten burger. "It's weird is what it is. Maybe Alex and his brothers are the ones dumping those body parts all over the Palms and Yucca."

"Unlikely!" She laughed. "The video footage from the gas station puts the guy well under six feet. And none of them could pass for that."

Released two nights prior, the FBI had finally had a break in the case. Security feed of a man depositing a bag into a gas station dumpster had provided the first visual of the killer. Enhanced imaging had provided a decent profile, one Charlotte shuddered to recollect.

The tourist in the sedan.

Max tossed his napkin on her plate and pushed away from the table. "I can't do this. Tomorrow, you feed me right or you take back the north run."

✖

CHARLOTTE CLOCKED OUT and headed to the back room to change out of her uniform before joining Max and the others at the tavern. Pulling the elastic from her ponytail, she shook out her hair, using her fingers to fan it out before deciding water was the only solution to the rigid line spanning her head. When her damp hair was flattened out enough, she nodded over at Becky as she entered. "You joining us?"

Becky gave her a once-over and smiled sadly. "You sure you're okay to go?" she asked with feigned concern. "It must be tough."

Reaching into her purse for her eyeliner, she glanced at her colleague in the mirror. "Why would it be? You should come."

"I would, but Jonas has me heading out on an animal sighting first." She sighed, squeezing beside her to check her lipstick. "Big dogs sighted around the Chasm. Tranquilize on sight are the standing orders."

Charlotte bit her lip, widening her eyes as she applied her mascara. "Probably Butch passing through again," she said, thinking back to the aggression the large animal had exhibited the last time she saw him. "I'll swing through the area on my way out. He knows me, and I know him. He was getting territorial the last time I saw him, so if I come across him, I'll call it in." She applied her lipstick carefully, using her pinky to smooth it out. "But don't tell Max."

Becky smiled at her, unbuttoning her work shirt and pulling a slinky silver tank top from her bag. "I won't."

ALEX LOADED THE last of the groceries into the back of the SUV and got in, rolling his eyes at the sound of a beer being cracked. "You can't wait an hour?"

Bo lifted the bottle into the sight line of the rearview mirror. "Curse of the gods." He grinned as he downed half the bottle, smacking his lips and wincing. "Too bad this swill ain't the nectar, right?" He stretched his arms across the back seat. "I only stocked up enough for a week, so you two fuckwads better lure the Pirithous in before my stash runs out."

Snapping a newspaper open, Ryan began perusing the most recent reports. "Amazing how much I've come to rely on internet service over the past few months," he mused, turning the large page awkwardly and pointing to a series of grainy photos. "The arch of the spine and bending of the legs is consistent with a late feral status."

Alex glanced over as he exited the parking lot and sped

up. "Barreling around on a moped and bagging the remains seems a lot more methodic than that of a full-on feral bloodline."

"This one may be on the cusp," Ryan said, closing the paper and folding it neatly into his lap. "I'm concerned that the populated campgrounds will become a slaughterhouse when he fully flips."

"And I'm concerned Alex is passing all the good bars," Bo chimed in, craning his neck back. "Pull into the Washout. We can have a half-decent meal, a drink, and then return to squatter's paradise for a night of scorpions and barking at the moon."

Ryan's brows lifted for a moment before he nodded. "I'm in."

Alex pulled into the parking lot, scanning the cars and letting out a breath. "Let's go."

CHARLOTTE SLIPPED ON her work boots and bent over to lace them, setting her flashlight on the passenger seat. The Chasm was deserted, the only sign of life the small brown snake watching her from a few yards off. She pushed her gun into her back pocket and began her trek toward the hidden entrance to the cavern, using her flashlight to scan the area for Butch.

Or Not-Butch.

"Here, boy," she called out, using the large stones to balance herself as she made her way into the opening. "You in here?"

Making her way through the first stretch of the Chasm, she continued to call out to Butch and Not-Butch, periodically tapping her gun in reassurance. She turned her shoulders sideways and squeezed through a tight formation, glancing behind her into the darkness as she wedged herself toward the pinnacle of the pass. Hefting herself to the shelf, she scanned the area with her flashlight, calling out for the damn dog.

"Stubborn little beast, aren't you," she muttered into the emptiness, looking around one last time before shining her light across her path and memorizing the descent into the chimney. Shoving her flashlight into her empty pocket, she steadied her footing and dropped into the darkness.

✕

ALEX STOOD AT the bar beside his brothers, tensing when gentle fingers ran across the back of his neck and the blonde woman he recognized from Tom's Tavern smiled up at him, a shot of tequila in her hand.

"I'm good, thanks," he said, waving off the drink and tossing an annoyed look at Bo. "We're heading out right away."

The woman pressed up against him, her perfectly lined

lips aligning with his ear. "We could sneak out back for a bit first."

Shaking his head, he leaned away from her and met Ryan's gaze. "Ready?"

"Am I ever." Ryan extricated himself from a gorgeous brunette and elbowed Bo in the ribs. "Now, Bo." He tossed his credit card on the bar counter and waved the bartender over. "I'll cover our tab and another round for the ladies."

His teeth clenched as the blonde continued to whisper offers in his ear while she traced her fingers down his spine, an inherent sense of wrongness washing over him as she pressed against his arm. He tracked the bartender's movements, cursing inwardly as the guy stopped to refill a water before swiping the card and handing the receipt to Ryan to sign.

Ryan hesitated, pen in hand. "What's the standard tip rate at bars?"

"Twenty percent," he muttered, frowning when he felt a strange bump under his feet. "What the hell was that?"

Chapter Twenty-Six

*C*HARLOTTE.

Alex hit the floor, bringing the blonde woman down underneath him and exposing his back to the bottles and glasses dropping off the counter. Her screams were drowned out by the clamor of liquor bottles rattling off the shelves, chairs upending across the hardwood floor, and wooden beams creaking under the strain of the quake.

Fighting against the instinctual need to transform in the wake of danger, he locked his eyes on Ryan to ground himself, his frantic thoughts funneling and channeling until they narrowed into a single stream.

Where the hell is Charlotte.

Bo lay crouched over another woman, snarling as his half-empty beer bottle bounced off the back of his head and shattered at his feet.

Who's with her.

Ryan crawled across the floor as it shook, making his way to assess the bleeding gash across Bo's head as the shaking came to an end.

Alex rose off the blonde woman screaming underneath

him and began the frantic search for his phone amid the overturned chairs and glass shards. Spotting it just out of reach, he scrambled forward and latched on to it, bracing himself as another wave rolled through the bar, the intense sound drowning out the screams of the patrons.

He wiped his phone on his shirt, snagging the fabric on the broken screen before he tapped his phone to life and hit Charlotte's number as he crawled toward Bo and Ryan, his cell tight to his ear and his pounding heart stuttering when it went straight to voice mail.

He dialed again.

And again.

Ryan reached over to him and ran his hand over his forehead. "Surface cut," he called over his shoulder to Bo, using his jeans to clean the blood from his fingers. "Fan out and start checking for injuries. Stay low to the ground."

He sat against the bar, staring at his phone as it went to Charlotte's voice mail for the fifth time. "I need to get to the park."

"Our site's fine," Ryan yelled back, easing a young guy to his feet.

Bracing himself on the counter as another aftershock rippled through the bar, he trained his attention on the exit. "I need to go."

Bo's hand gripped his arm. "You aren't going anywhere," he growled. "We're staying together, finishing off that bloodline, and getting the fuck out of this place tonight."

He looked down at his twin's bloodied hand before searching the room for Ryan, watching his brother calmly unbutton his shirt and press it against the neck of a man hunched on the floor. "I have to, Bo. I need to know she's okay before I'm done here."

Bo's fingers dug into his arm before he released him, cursing loudly as he stormed over to Ryan and knelt beside him. Ryan looked over at Alex for a moment, his expression unreadable before he turned his attention back to the chaos in the room.

Pushing through the heavy wooden doors, he tried Charlotte's number one more time.

Voice mail.

He jumped into the SUV and tore out of the lot, dodging a fallen power line as he turned onto the main drag.

Max.

Pulling up Max's cell, Alex veered to the shoulder of the street to allow an ambulance to rip past him.

"Hello, Alex?" Max answered, panting and frantic. "Where are you?"

"Just left the Washout," he replied, taking a deep breath to steady his shaking hands. "Where's Charlotte?"

Max swore and the SUV swayed on the road, another aftershock rippling through the area. "She was supposed to be here."

He smacked his fist off the steering wheel. "Where are you?"

"The tavern."

Running his hand through his hair, he took a sharp right and sped up. "I'm a minute away. Did she work tonight?"

"She was supposed to be off two hours ago. Her phone's going straight to voice mail."

He pulled into the lot, the mayhem of evacuating patrons forcing him to abandon his SUV along the fire lane before he took off toward the entrance and pushed through the horde pouring through the open doors. Catching sight of Max, he sidestepped the overturned stools and made his way to the rangers, kneeling alongside the group as Jonas assessed Thomas.

"Alex, boy," Thomas called over, lifting his hand toward the bar. "You walked out and the place fell apart."

Scanning the elderly man over, he gave him a grim smile. "You can bill me for it tomorrow." He turned to Max. "Where was she last seen?"

"The station," Max replied, his bloodshot eyes giving away just how drunk he was before the earthquake hit. "We're not getting an answer there either."

ALEX WATCHED HIS phone intently, pulling over once the Wi-Fi bars lit up. He threw his SUV into park and sat back.

The Keys.

The Mine.

The north entrance.

He'd run Charlotte's usual route twice, crawling through the park as he scoured the terrain for any sign of her or her car.

Wherever she was, she'd gone off course.

His phone vibrated as it filled with texts from Max.

He'd gone to her apartment.

The place was a wreck.

And empty.

He dropped his head to the steering wheel and swallowed in vain to rid himself of the lump that sat in his throat.

Where the hell are you?

He sped back to his campsite, kicking up a spray of sand as he braked. He turned off the engine and opened the door, yanking his boots off his feet and tossing them into the back seat. His clothes were next before he swung the large black collar around his neck and slammed the door shut, wedging the keys under a handful of sand behind the back tire.

Swinging his head to the sky to orient himself by the stars as he transformed, he tore southeast over the sand and rock with more agility and speed than he was capable of in human form. The silence of the desert in the aftermath of the quake amplified the scattering of stones under his paws as he ripped over the terrain hunting for any remnant of Charlotte's scent.

Where are you, baby?

He paused at the entrance of the Jumbo Rocks

campground, lowering his muzzle to the ground when a familiar stench hit him.

Pirithous.

His ears flattened back, his hackles rising as he skulked through the empty sites, the scent path strengthening as he moved closer to a cluster of smooth rocks stretching high into the black sky. Following the foul odor, he pawed his way over the formation, stopping once he breached the peak.

It had been there.

Within the hour.

He scanned the darkness for movement, bracing himself as another aftershock rippled under his feet, the stone ledge he stood on quivering.

He needed to find her.

He needed to track the bloodline.

He had a lead on one, and a shot in the dark for the other.

Lowering his nose to the rocks below him, he locked on to the Pirithous and descended the smooth stones until his paws hit the sand.

✗

CHARLOTTE TOOK A deep breath and contracted her shoulders, shrinking back into the cavern as the ground trembled under her boots again. She tucked her head down in anticipation of the shower of loose sand and stones that filtered through the rocks surrounding her, remaining motionless until the movement subsided.

Howling.

She froze, her heart jumping into her throat as a gravelly howl echoed through the rock, an unfamiliar voice joining in with punctuated growls.

"Not-Butch!" she yelled out, inching her feet along the narrow path, her fingers grazing the rock surrounding her. "I'm here! Here, boy!"

The dogs went silent, the complete stillness of the post-disaster desert stretched out as the seconds turned to minutes until a faint howl punctuated the silence in the distance.

About time, Butch.

Chapter Twenty-Seven

A LEX STILLED, THE fresh stench of the Pirithous coating his nostrils and tongue, overpowering every other scent in the desert. He lowered his muzzle to the ground, burrowing his nose into the sand in a desperate search for any hint Charlotte had passed through the area. Shaking the dust from his face, he arched his head back and scented the air for the only odor that could carry for miles in the still night.

Death.

Rot.

When nothing but the cursed bloodline filled his nose, he locked on to the scent and continued to prowl through the unchecked terrain, his ears perking up as Bo's coarse howl carried through the park, followed by Ryan's sharp yelps of warning. He barked back in spurts, allowing his brothers to track his location easier as he closed in on their howled replies.

Ryan's lithe form was first to appear over a ridge, his graceful stride almost regal against Bo's predatory skulk. He lowered his ears while he crossed the dirt road separating them, crouching down when he approached Ryan and sitting back as his brothers transformed.

He couldn't join them, couldn't risk them seeing the panic that was settling in his bones with every passing minute.

He needed to breathe. Needed to cool his head.

Needed their help.

Bo stretched his arms over his head, cracking his back. "I'm putting the Pirithous a mile south of here and moving slow. We can be done and drinking mead with Dionysus within the hour if we don't fuck around."

A peculiar look crossed Ryan's face before he looked into the desert. "We could bring him down and hold him," he said quietly, glancing down at Alex. "Give you ti—"

"Fuck no." Bo's eyes darkened. "We do this. Now."

Alex shifted into human form in a heartbeat, rising to his feet and watching Ryan. "We could find her," he said, unable and unwilling to hide the plea in his voice. "The three of us could cover the park easily. Once we do, we can pick up the trail here..." He trailed off when Ryan glanced in Bo's direction. "What?"

Ryan's mouth opened as Bo barreled into him, knocking him to the ground and pinning him down by the throat. "One mile from freedom," he snarled, grunting when Ryan flipped him over and shoved his face into the sand. "It's not fucking worth it!" he spat, bucking his head back and making contact with Ryan's jaw.

As Ryan's hold loosened, Alex knocked his older brother

off, jumping onto his twin. "Nothing's ever been worth it for me," he growled, panting to catch his breath when Bo's knee made contact with his gut. "I need one goddamn hour before I'm sucked back into hell to play show pony for gods who would sacrifice us to the sun if they thought it would gain them followers." Scrambling to hold Bo down, he shoved his forearm against his twin's face. "One. Goddamn. Hour."

Bo began to transform beneath him, his jaw locking on Alex's arm in a vise grip before Ryan dove in, the long canines tearing a chunk from Alex's skin as the jowls were pried open and Bo's face morphed back into human form. He booted Alex in the ribs, shaking off the echoes of his bite from his own arm. "I'm fucking dying up here," he hissed, doubling over as Alex's foot made contact with his gut. "It's not. Fucking. Worth it."

Alex jumped onto Bo, dropping him into the sand and grappling until Ryan leapt in. The eldest brother tossed his full strength into the fight, shoving Alex aside and keeping the upper hand until he finally subdued Bo enough to look over.

"Two miles southwest," Ryan growled, digging his knee into Bo's back. "Cluster of rounded rocks. We'll hold the Pirithous." He rose up off Bo as Alex took a step toward them. "Get her to safety and get your ass back here."

Pushing himself to his feet, Bo used the back of his hand to wipe the blood and sand from his mouth. "Not fucking worth it," he spat again, widening his stance as Alex closed in on him.

He stopped his advance.

The bloodshot eyes.

The almost imperceptible twitch of his nose.

The scars crisscrossing the length of his torso.

Bo was right. He was dying up here. His twin needed to get back to the underworld, back to the place where Diony- sus's hand channeled his most destructive urges, held him back from the ledge. Neither Alex nor Ryan had the power to control whatever it was in Bo that drove him in his search for the ultimate high, and the human world was a little more than a wasteland of temptation.

But Charlotte was in that wasteland, and he needed to find her. Needed to see for himself that she was okay before he joined his brothers.

Ryan continued to regard him with the stoicism that had earned him his place as their master's favored, his face showing the strain and pressure he'd carried throughout this last hunt. The weight of Bo's self-destruction and Alex's screw-ups had fallen to Ryan's shoulders as it always had whenever they were topside, out of the powerful control of Hades. The completion of the mission was more than a job to him, more than an order to be followed. Everything Ryan was was wrapped up in his service to his master and mistress, and failure was not an option Ryan could live with.

Bo took a step toward him, halted by Ryan's staying hand. "Don't fuck us over, Alex. We don't belong up here."

He looked over his shoulder to the southwest and his chest tightened. "I'm sorry, Bo. But I need to do this," he said quietly. "Find him and hold him. I swear on Charlotte's life I'll be back."

✕

CHARLOTTE SQUEEZED HER eyes shut and tucked her head down into her arms as another small tremor rippled under her feet and shook the rocks surrounding her, the ground too volatile to inch across the precarious pathways out. She released her breath and dropped her head back when the aftershock eased, unwilling to open her eyes and look at the freedom she was so close to.

Patting ridges she could reach, she assessed the positions of the rocks surrounding her and crouched low, sliding her feet over the smooth stone.

Butch's sharp bark cut through the silence of the park, growing steadily closer as she wound her way down a steep incline.

"Here, boy!" she yelled out, slipping her flashlight out of her pocket to do another scan of the caverns and to mark her route.

The barking morphed into a yelping natter, as though the beast was attempting to reassure her of his presence as his nails clicked against the narrow ledges of the Chasm. She shifted her weight on her legs, her muscles aching as she remained perched in preparation for another tremor.

"Watch your step, Butch," she warned, the relative normality of the statement releasing a fraction of the tension built up in her stomach. "The ground'll move again soon."

A chuffing sound drew nearer, Butch's enormous head peering through a sliver-sized opening above her position. He backed away and resumed his chatter while he paced the top of the stones, his paw or muzzle periodically dropping into the opening for a few seconds.

She slid her flashlight into her pocket. "I think I know the way out," she muttered, taking a final look up at the dog before she sat, scooting down the slope and cowering as another ripple shook the stones around her.

ALEX JUMPED BACK as the rocks trembled under his feet, the scent of Charlotte's fear permeating his senses and overwhelming his mind. He tore to the edge of the formation and scanned frantically for an opening, descending the rocks slowly for fear of causing a disturbance to the compromised structure.

Winding through the narrow passageways, he scoured for a way to her, maintaining a continual loop of barks and yelps so she could track his location. His footing stumbled as he closed in on a cavity, straddling two larger stones to peer into the darkness.

Bingo.

He dropped to his belly, inching toward the opening until he had enough room to sit back and push his head through, his shoulders catching.

Too fucking big.

He glanced up to the sky and assessed the stars.

It would be hours until sunrise. Hours more until her car was found, tucked tight against the Chasm and out of view of the main roads.

Checking his balance one last time, he leaned against a rock to brace himself as he transformed, shifting his weight to keep from falling forward and ducking down to squeeze into the narrow crevice. He shimmied between two large stones, shuffling one foot forward to test the stability of the pathway before he placed his weight down.

"Butch? Where'd you go, boy?"

Her breathing was more labored, her voice holding a hint of her rising distress.

He ran his hand over the smooth rock and let out a long breath. "Just me," he answered. "I'm coming at you from the side, so hold still."

There was a moment of silence before she whimpered. "Alex?"

His throat tightened at the hopeful relief in her voice. "Yeah, baby. Just me." He knelt down, contorting his shoulders to squeeze through a low pass. "I think I'm closing in on you, okay? We'll team it out of here."

She let out a shuddered breath. "My exit's blocked on this end. That last one shifted a boulder at the halfway mark."

He pushed through the opening and rose to his feet, stretching his hands overhead to get a sense of how much space he had. "We'll cross that bridge when we come to it. For now, I'm going to keep talking to you," he said, straightening up. "And if at any point my voice moves away from you, I want you to tell me. Okay?"

"Okay."

He crept forward, guiding his movements in the darkness with his bare hands and feet. "I don't know what to talk about," he muttered, running his fingers along a crack. "I suppose I could tell you about a Vietnam documentary I watched a couple weeks back, but it's pretty detailed and I'm aiming to have you out pretty quick."

She let out a small laugh, the shallowness of her breathing weighing heavy on his mind. "Tell me how you found me."

"Funny story," he called out, waving his arms out slowly and moving closer to her voice, the upper walls of the cavern dipping down and forcing him to crouch. "I made the lucky decision to celebrate my first earthquake with a midnight hike through the Chasm."

"Smart ass," she replied quietly. "And there's dozens of quakes a month around here, so it wouldn't be your first anyway."

"You're on the other side of this rock, aren't you?" he asked, feeling around the cavern to determine how much space he had. "Good news is it's loose. The bad news is I need you to listen real well, and move real fast."

Chapter Twenty-Eight

"STEP BACK FROM the rock," Alex ordered, tracing the boulder with his fingers. "When it moves, dive through and go. It's a pretty clear path from here." He could hear shuffling before a flicker of light radiated around the tiny cracks around the rock. "Steady that beam for a second."

"Good?" Charlotte asked, the ray holding still.

"Perfect," he replied. "I'll be opening it from the bottom, so drop, dive, and go," he amended, arching his neck back and rolling out his shoulders in preparation. "Don't wait for me, okay? I'll be good."

"But—"

"I'll leave right now," he growled, narrowing his eyes as the light disappeared. "Drop. Dive. Go."

He held his breath until she relented. "Drop, dive, go. Got it."

Stepping back, he fell to all fours and transformed, keeping to the middle of the small cavern to avoid inadvertently knocking any loose stones and worsening the situation. He wedged one paw under the large rock, bracing his front legs on one side of the opening and kicking his hindquarters up to the other.

Three. Two. One.

✕

WHAT THE HELL?

Charlotte's immediate confusion over the soft fur skimming over her back was overcome by the adrenaline that coursed through her while she propelled herself away from the shower of sand and pebbles falling onto her and Alex.

Drop. Dive. Go.

A low growl echoed in her ears as she shimmied through the dark cavern, away from the fallout of the heavy stones Alex was holding at bay. "I'm out!" She heaved, scrambling against a smooth surface and peering into her dusty prison. "Alex!"

The rumbling of stone collapsing in the cave reverberated through the Chasm, an animalistic snarl tearing across the air as she recoiled from the burst of debris barreling through the narrow opening. She squinted in the darkness, the faint light of her flashlight obscured by a fallen rock and a black mound. "Alex?"

The mound lifted its familiar head in her direction.

She flattened herself to the stone, eyes wide. "What the hell?" She pushed herself to her feet, crouching under the low overhang and taking a step toward the beast.

Butch arched his neck toward his hind legs, his huge

front paws twisting behind him to push against the boulder holding him down. Inching closer, she ran her thumb over his ears, grabbing her flashlight to look through the crevices. "Alex?" she called out, trailing the trapped legs of the dog with her fingers. "Alex?"

Butch's head lowered, his muzzle dropping against her hands as he yelped and nattered. A rising panic was building in her stomach as Alex remained silent and out of sight, her mind conjuring up gruesome images she needed to shake from her head. "Okay, boy," she whispered, forcing herself to remain steady while she scanned the stone. "Let's figure this out."

ALEX'S EARS LIFTED as the sounds of his brothers grew closer, their snarls and barks bouncing off the cavern walls while the scent of the Pirithous filled the enclosed space. He snapped his jaws at his trapped legs, narrowly avoiding Charlotte's hands as they pushed fruitlessly against the boulder crushing his hindquarters.

"Calm down, Butch," she crooned as she stroked his ears, oblivious to the faint stumbling gait drawing nearer. She turned her attention back to the stone. "Come on, Alex. Say something."

The shuffling feet of the approaching intruder competed with the clicking of paws over the rock path. He strained his eyes in the faint glow of the flashlight, scanning the small entrance for the Pirithous before howling out for his brothers. Bo's gravelly snarl answered back, his barked warnings closing in as he alerted Alex to the Pirithous's proximity.

Warnings that were unnecessary as the feral form of the bloodline crept into the cavern, its blackened eyes locking on to Charlotte.

CHARLOTTE FROZE, HER fingers wrapped tightly around her flashlight as Butch's howling morphed into a territorial growl. She could hear Not-Butch's raspy barks echoing through the Chasm, the combined sounds almost drowning out the gurgling panting at her back. She rose to her feet, turning to illuminate the intruder crouched in the entrance, his strange eyes squinting as the light bounced off them.

Butch snarled, his hackles rising as he pushed himself up on his front paws and drew the attention of the hunched man. She stepped closer to Butch, adjusting her hold on the flashlight. "I'm a US Park Ranger, sir. I'm going to need you to exit the area and return to your vehicle. The safety of the Chasm is compromised due to th—"

The man launched himself across the cave with inhuman speed, latching on to Butch's neck with his arms and teeth. Butch's enormous claws tore at his attacker's back, drawing a foul-smelling blood that watered her eyes and coated her tongue. Angling the blunt end of her light at the man, she brought it down on his head, earning a shriek of fury from him. He released Butch, his black eyes zeroing in on her as she stepped in front of the trapped dog and swung her makeshift weapon, Butch's bloodied paws attempting to nudge her aside.

The man leapt at her, the odd bend of his legs propelling him forward with enough force to knock her backward over Butch. She scrambled over the howling animal, her flashlight rocking against the corner of the cavern while the man's hands grasped for any part of her he could grip. As he took hold of her leg, she pummeled him with her fists, using her legs to boot out his malformed shins and keep him unbalanced enough to avoid gaining the upper hand.

"Don't even think about it," she growled as his attention returned to the injured beast in the corner. Hooking his ankles with her feet, she yanked the man to the ground, clambering over his warped body to place herself in front of Butch and holding her ground as the misshapen teeth closed in on her.

She brought her arms up to protect her face and throat, taking an involuntary step back as hands wrapped around her attacker's neck and jerked him backward into a snarling heap on the floor. Two men, naked as the day they were born, dropped onto his mangled body.

Two naked, familiar men.

"Al—"

"Bo," one barked back, the effort of restraining the feral man apparent in his gravelly voice. "Stay the fuck back."

Butch nudged her arm with his muzzle and she crouched beside him, assessing his trapped hind legs with her hands and watching as Alex's brothers twisted and contorted their bounty until he was immobile.

Ryan looked down at her, his arms wrapped tightly around the intruder's warped torso. "Is that your car on the road?"

She nodded, opening her mouth to respond before Bo cut her off, his eyes on Butch. "We're going to put this bastard in holding and we'll be back to get your sorry ass out of here." He held out his hand. "Keys."

Fumbling in her pocket, she found her car keys and passed them over. "Cell service won't work until you hit the highway," she warned.

"We'll be back in ten," Ryan replied, glancing beside her at the injured beast. "Hang tight."

ALEX'S HEART CONTINUED to pound in his chest, the stench of the Pirithous slathered on Charlotte's skin keeping his mind off his damaged hindquarters and the tremors rumbling underneath them.

She'd held her own against a feral Pirithous.

He nuzzled against her hand, scanning her over in the

dim light for injuries and growling low when he caught sight of the numerous bruises and cuts peppering her skin.

"Shhhhh," she whispered absently, her attention locked on the small crevices that led to the other side of the cavern. "You're okay, boy." She continued to tap on the boulder and talk quietly into the darkness. "Five more minutes, Alex. Between the three of us, we should be able to get to you." She smiled down at Butch and scratched his ears. "Too bad this old beast is hurt. He could've helped."

He lay his head on her lap and listened for his brothers, the clicking of their paws on the rock letting him know they were approaching the smaller caverns of the Chasm. He waited as the faint sounds of the shifting traveled into the cave, followed closely by human footsteps.

"All right, you useless sack. Let's do this."

Charlotte's arms tightened around his neck as Bo entered the cavern. She dropped her head into his fur, slightly disoriented by the tattoo on his chest that perfectly matched Alex's. And Ryan's. "Oh, god, you're still naked."

"Lucky you," Bo muttered, crouching beside him and assessing the boulder's position. "You're a fucking idiot."

Charlotte's eyes narrowed, her mouth opening to respond before Ryan jumped in. "The dog. The dog's an idiot." He kept his body angled away from her in a futile attempt at modesty. "We need you to take that flashlight and make your way to your car. It's an easy path from here."

Pressing her hand to the rock, she shook her head. "Alex

is behind this," she whimpered. "I think he's hurt."

Bo huffed and stood, completely owning his nudity and earning a growl from Alex. "Yeah, he's hurt. And the sooner you leave, the sooner we can get him out."

"I'm not leaving until I see him."

Ryan knelt down beside Alex. "Bo and I are going to try to push that rock off you enough to get you out. But we try once. Then we get you out of our way." He turned to Charlotte. "His tail is your job. If we manage to get this thing up, get that tail out of the way. Got it?"

She nodded, repositioning herself to be in reach as Bo and Ryan adjusted their stance beside the boulder and counted down. The stone rocked a fraction, easing the pressure on his hindquarters for a moment before it resettled on him, sending a jolt of pain through him and his brothers.

"This is fucking bullshit," Bo huffed, widening his stance. "I'm barely staying upright."

"Then push harder," Ryan grunted, throwing his weight against the boulder and cursing as it moved no more than their first attempt. "Goddammit. We have to do this another way." He looked down at Alex. "Bo, get Charlotte out of here."

CHARLOTTE ATTEMPTED TO shake her arm loose from Bo's grip, cringing when he tightened his hold.

"We're taking the path on the right," he ordered, balancing them on the narrow top of a smooth rock. "Fifty more yards."

She glanced back at the Chasm before she took her final steps out of the rocky formation, freezing as Butch howled and the sound of toppling rocks echoed in the dark night. "What's Ryan doing to him? He's not... Oh, god, he's not putting Butch down, is he?"

Bo continued to guide her forward, his vise grip at odds with his gentle lead of her down the path. "No, he's not putting Butch down," he replied, a peculiar tinge of humor in his voice. He paused, shaking out his left leg. "They'll be making their way out here soon. Alex, too." He kept his hold on her, loosening it slightly as they approached her car. "You're a tough little thing, aren't you?"

Her eyes averted from the naked man at her side, she locked her gaze on the trunk of her car, shrinking back when an animalistic shriek echoed in the park. "What's wrong with that guy?"

"Genetically defective," Bo muttered, shifting his weight from one foot to the next rhythmically and running his hand over the trunk. "When the others get here, we'll release him and you can go on your merry little way."

The seconds slowed as she watched the exit, her heart pounding in her ears until Ryan emerged, a nude Alex in tow. She exhaled loudly, running her hands through her hair and shrugging off Bo's hand from her shoulder. "Whoa," she breathed, the relief over seeing Alex overtaking the growing ache in her body. "So is the nudity a cultural thing for your, uh, hunting thing?"

Bo grinned, thumping on the trunk when the noises increased. "Pretty much."

Ryan and Alex made their way down the rocky path, Alex's arm draped over Ryan's shoulder as they maneuvered across the uneven landscape. Bo broke into a jog, meeting his brothers halfway and taking Alex's other arm, easing the weight Ryan was carrying.

A small tremor rippled through the park as the brothers crossed the sand and they hesitated, Alex unhooking his arms from Ryan and Bo as he found his footing and limped his way to the road.

Without thinking, she ran to him, wrapping her arms tightly around his waist, almost knocking him off balance as he embraced her, his chin resting on the top of her head. Her mind caught up with her actions and she released him, jumping out of reach.

He gave her a tight smile. "Hey."

Keeping her eyes averted, she shoved her hands into her back pockets to keep from embracing him again. "Hey yourself. Butch?"

"Ran off," Ryan called over, unlocking the trunk while Bo used his weight to keep it down. "Start your car and when we give the word, drive."

She paused and looked up at Alex. "What are you going

to do to him?"

"Nothing you want to see."

✕

THE PIRITHOUS WAS on the cusp when the trunk popped open and Ryan dove into it, yanking the feral creature out as Bo yelled at Charlotte to drive. Her car lurched forward, braking long enough for Alex to catch the uncertainty in her eyes before Bo slammed his hand down on the roof, startling her.

As the taillights disappeared around the bend, Bo and Ryan dropped to all fours and transformed, circling the shuddering body impatiently. Bo prowled toward him, nudging Alex's injured legs with his muzzle before he skulked back to Ryan, hackles raised and ready for the kill.

His steps faltered in the soft sand as he approached his brothers and he knelt down, ignoring the searing pain in his legs and tailbone as the transformation took place. He glanced down the empty road one last time and growled at the stench of the dying Pirithous, the stench that had overpowered Charlotte's sweet scent as the bloodline had tried to take her down.

Ryan cocked his head as Alex stumbled to him, lowering it when he let loose a low snarl.

He had a bloodline to eliminate.

✕

CHARLOTTE FLATTENED HERSELF along the stone ridge, covering her mouth with her hands, her eyes wide as they took in the transformation she was witnessing.

She had identified Not-Butch immediately, his gait that of a hunter, fluid and low. The larger dog stood guard, his head swinging toward her for a moment before it turned toward Alex.

Alex.

Alex, who morphed into Butch before her eyes.

Shaking her head quickly, she drew in a breath and held it while the three dogs aligned themselves, a distinctive limp in each of their hindquarters. Their bodies fused into one immense beast, the heads arching back as they howled into the night. Its shoulders were easily three feet across, a massive three-headed dog that would rival even the largest of the Wyoming grizzly bears she'd studied during her training. The long fur was almost blacker than Butch's, emitting a faint dark glow as it skulked toward its prey, the white of its claws and fangs brilliant in the dim starlight.

The thick tail swung, swiping a bush clean out of the earth and sending it skidding across the ground as the creature descended on the body of the man writhing in the sand, his gurgled gasps for air coming to an abrupt end as the middle dog's head thrashed violently.

A scream rippled through the park, tearing at her vocal

cords while one head swung her way, the enormous teeth bared until the beast froze, dropping his muzzle as the ground opened in a wave of fire, engulfing man and beast.

Chapter Twenty-Nine

A LEX SNARLED AS they plummeted onto the cold marble slab at Hades's feet, the sour blood of the Pirithous coating his tongue, the stench filling his nostrils. The collective segment of their minds worked in unity to move their singular body crouched protectively over its kill, Ryan snapping his jaws at Bo when the more obstinate brother raised his head to their master.

Hades rose from his ebony throne and grinned as he approached them, using his staff to prod the mutilated body of their prize. "I was starting to wonder if you'd found a new owner." He chuckled, hooking his staff under one motionless arm and allowing it to flop heavily onto the stone. "Release him."

They sat back on their haunches, bloodied paws dirtying the spotless floor.

Waving over his attendants to dispose of the corpse, Hades knelt before them, giving Ryan's ears a hard scratching. "Good work, Cerberus." He turned his attention to Bo and Alex and gave them the same treatment. "Dio's in the east wing," he mentioned, winking at Bo. "Swing by there and see him before you get yourselves cleaned up for dinner."

Alex kept his head down as they padded through the familiar ornate halls, pausing intermittently to be welcomed home by the lesser deities roaming the palace. Dionysus's roaring laughter echoed against the marble, Bo's mismatched eyes lighting up as they walked into a large receiving room and the god sauntered over to them.

"Cerberus, my boy!" he called out, bending to cup Bo's chin and running his thumb between Bo's eyes. "We weren't informed you were expected."

There was a shrill squeal of excitement behind them and Alex cringed. "You're back!"

Dio rolled his eyes and released Bo. "Let him settle in before you start spoiling him, Seph."

Persephone's long skirts billowed behind her as she scampered barefoot across the floor, wrapping her slender arms around Ryan's and Alex's necks. She burrowed her face in their fur, squeezing them tight. "You go freshen up and we'll see you get a decent meal." She glared back at Dionysus. "Poor thing's thin."

"He's not thin," Dio argued, offering his hand to assist her to her feet. "You've merely become accustomed to us burlier beasts, my dear." He lowered a bowl of mead to Bo's muzzle, patting his head when Bo dove into it.

Alex looked around the room, the luxurious tapestries and delicately carved pedestals adorned with statues and vases fashioned by the hands of favored artisans.

No pink.

No pilling blankets adorned with colorful cartoon characters.

No rows of photos hanging on the walls.

No intoxicating floral shampoo mingling with fruit-scented lotion.

No judgmental cat staring him down.

Home.

✖

ALEX SNORTED AS Bo squatted in his chiton to prove his point.

"Easy on, easy off," Bo stated, tossing his chlamys over his shoulder and needlessly demonstrating the speed of removal for him. "No buttons to fuck around with. No zippers slicing your junk. On. Off. Done."

Rolling his eyes, he sprawled out on the chaise, yanking at the fabric bunching under his leg as he called out to Ryan. "You ready yet? I'm pretty much done with the fashion lesson from Dior over here."

Ryan groaned from the bathing room. "Give me five. How's the knee?"

He straightened his leg, grimacing when the slightest shift in position shot fire through his nerves. "Not great."

"Shouldn't have gone in there," Bo snarked, booting the chaise. "Maybe your laid-up ass will luck out and Iris'll come by."

All levity disappeared from his head as his mind ripped through images of the only woman he wanted to see. He locked his attention on the flawless lines of the marbled tile, focusing his thoughts on the perfection of his surroundings.

The chaise molded to him, the cushioning remaining in place as he shifted and turned.

The bath temperature was always ideal, never turning cool with time.

There was no scorching heat of the sun, no overworked air conditioners humming in the background.

"Ready?"

Ryan extended his hand, assisting him to his feet and steadying him before they began their trek toward the banquet hall and the tempting aromas that were drifting through the palace.

✕

BO GRINNED AT Alex, a glass of wine in each hand and three of Dionysus's less dedicated servants lounging at his side. He raked his eyes over Iris's tiny form, licking his lips before smirking and lifting his glass to Alex.

Ryan and Hades sat at the end of the large banquet table, Persephone flitting around them as she refilled their plates with ripe berries and aged cheeses, stopping periodically to reprimand Hades on his perceived overindulgence in Dio's wine. Her hand would stroke Ryan's head absently as she passed him, a habit she'd acquired early during her time in the underworld when the brothers were confined to sharing a single body.

"May I?"

Alex blinked, returning his attention to Iris. "Excuse me?"

"Your wine." She smiled. "May I refill it for you?"

Shaking his head, he placed the empty glass at his feet. "No thanks." He glanced around the crowded hall. "Is it always this busy now?"

Iris drew her legs onto the chaise, carefully smoothing her skirt over her knees. "While Seph's here, yes," she replied, folding her hands demurely into her lap. "She brings quite an entourage with her. Hades and Demeter are in an open negotiation for the division of her time now, so I've become quite familiar with the place in between messages."

He craned his neck back at Persephone, chuckling when her hands flew to her hips and she stared down the fearsome Hades, his large form shrinking in his seat until he nodded and Seph smiled sweetly. "Who's driving the negotiations?"

"Seph, of course." Iris laughed, schooling herself quickly and tilting her head. "I'm sure you'll catch up on all the comings and goings soon. Have you resettled into your rooms?"

He nodded absently, keeping one eye on Dio's reaction to Bo nuzzling into the neck of an olive-skinned handmaiden. "Not much to settle," he muttered, pushing himself up a fraction on the cushions and cursing under his breath when his knee protested. "We pack light."

Another laugh quickly ended, Iris's practiced serenity returning with unnatural speed. She placed one hand on his leg, each of her manicured nails the precise length of the next as they trailed up his inner thigh. "Would you care to retire? I'm not expected anywhere until tomorrow evening."

He looked down at the pretty goddess, her delicate features accentuating her perfect nymph-like form. "Yeah, no. I'm taken."

✕

CHARLOTTE WATCHED MAX'S hardened expression through a haze, the injection from the medic having taken effect almost instantly. She blinked, losing the precarious focus she had before giving up and closing her eyes, shutting out the sterilized bags and syringes in sight and focusing on the rumble of the tires as the ambulance sped down the highway.

"She's even more out of it than she was when I found her," Max barked. "What the hell did you give her?"

She smiled, her veins warm and mind clouded with a heavy fog that blocked out the unpleasant thoughts lurking in the background.

Max's gruff voice grumbled incoherently for a moment, his hand pressing lightly on her elbow. "No, I don't know how she did it."

A cold hand pushed against her side. She turned her head and opened one eye, swatting a weighted arm at the invasion.

"He's just checking out those bruises, Chuck," Max reassured her, running his hand over her forehead. "We're gonna put that medical coverage to good use today."

✕

ALEX RESTED HIS weight against the wall and briefly debated how determined he was to make it to his quarters. When Dio's raucous laughter tore down the hall, he doubled his efforts to escape to the isolation of his room, not bothering to hide his limp as he sped up. Gritting his teeth, he crossed the threshold and collapsed on his bed.

He rolled onto his back and stared at the stunning mural on his ceiling, a piece commissioned for him by Hades centuries earlier after a particularly difficult hunt. All three of them had the same painting, their Cerberus form sitting regally at Hades's side, the shades of their kills standing faceless and nameless behind them.

It was a perfect replica of the tattoo that adorned their backs, the shades of the Pirithous stretching down their arms.

A morbid trophy case, updated by the artist with every successful Pirithous takedown.

He tossed his arm over his eyes.

Within the week, another figure would be added to the piece, leaving the wall of death distractingly lopsided. The transparent charcoal form would look like the others, void of life and expression, standing solely through the will of Hades. Ryan, Bo, and Alex would then sit stoically under Seph's watchful eye as the art on their bodies was adapted to reflect their skilled service to their master.

Ryan had posed proudly for the sketch, the hand of his master resting on his neck. Bo's head was slightly bowed, his eyes narrowed and hungry, the bowl of mead at the foot of the artist not making it into the artwork.

He lifted his arm and looked up. His own distinctive eyes held a glint of resignation, the scant cocking of one ear captured in the artist's mind as he completed the painting.

It was a duty. A job. An assignment no different than prowling the banks of the river for centuries.

While Ryan embraced it, Bo bucked against the restraints, his constant search for something he could control leading him by the nose.

And Alex accepted it, because it was what it was.

He lay in the darkness for hours as the revelry continued into the early morning hours, the absence of the rising sun wreaking havoc on his ability to track time.

This was home.

Chapter Thirty

ALEX STRETCHED HIS arms out across the cool marble of the bath, craning his neck to watch Hades as he approached, Ryan padding alongside.

His master grinned at him, tossing a towel within reach. "So this is where you've been hiding today." He chuckled. "Your twin is still facedown in a bowl of wine on the banquet hall floor."

Running his hands through his wet hair and sinking further into the warm water, he snorted. "I'll go by and drag his ass to his quarters after I finish up here."

Hades tested the temperature of the bath, wiping his hand on his chiton. "Overheard an interesting conversation between Seph and Iris after you retired to your room alone," he said casually as he rose up. "I was under the impression Iris was one of your preferred companions when you were down here."

"She's sweet," he muttered, slipping under the water to buy himself a few seconds.

Iris was sweet. Sweet and timid, and apparently still on hiatus from her millennia-old marriage.

Hades tracked him as Alex exited the bath and wrapped a towel around his hips, shaking his hair out and earning a chuff of amusement from Ryan. He put weight on his injured leg, bending it to test the amplified healing properties in the underworld water.

Not bad.

"What precisely does the term *taken* imply?" Hades pressed, his arms crossing.

He snatched his chiton off a chair. "Nothing," he replied. "Anything on the docket today or am I good to deal with Bo and hang out in the receiving rooms?"

His master remained motionless, dark eyes narrowing as he stared him down. "You're free for now," he said slowly, his hand dropping to scratch Ryan's ears. "I'll be holding court tomorrow. Your presence is required."

He waited until Hades walked out before he exited the bathing room and made his way down the hall to find Bo. His twin was sprawled out in the banquet hall, his muzzle resting on the edge of a bowl of wine, paws thrown over his eyes.

Maintaining a human body in the underworld required significantly more effort than it did topside, the weight of ancestry and blood bearing down on the brothers to return to their natural form. Alex often held out longer than the others, Ryan preferring his inborn state and Bo usually too drunk to uphold his human physique past the first few hours.

He knelt beside Bo, lifting the enormous paws from his face and easing the bowl from under his jowls. "Come on," he urged, meeting his twin's glassy, unfocused eyes. "Hades is gonna flip a nut if he comes back in here and you're heaving on his rugs."

Bo struggled to gain his footing, leaning against him for balance and nipping at his hand when Alex attempted to lead him by the scruff. They weaved through the halls, passing Dionysus's closed door and slowly making their way to Bo's quarters. Pushing the heavy wooden doors open, he waited for Bo to stumble into his bedroom and collapse on the floor, growling before he passed out.

Leaving his brother to sleep it off, he entered the receiving rooms, freezing at the entrance when a dark ponytail caught his eye.

"Alexandros!"

Snapping his attention to Persephone, he gave his mistress a quick smile and joined her at the elegant seating area Hades had put together for her, the pastel fabrics and rich rosewood furnishings at odds with the harsh ebony and marble palace decor. He accepted a heaping plate of smoked meats and breads from one of her many handmaidens, glancing back at the dark ponytail and letting out a breath when the woman turned around, her angular features bearing no resemblance to the woman plaguing his head.

Seph reached over to him, tucking a loose strand of hair behind his ear and scratching him under the chin. "Fill me in, honey," she ordered, nestling back in her seat, her blue eyes sparkling with curiosity.

He swallowed his first bite, shrugging. "You've seen what it's like up there. Same humans, same wars, same mistakes." He paused. "The air reeks."

Placing her cup down, Persephone leveled him with a blank stare. "Tell me about the woman. Charlotte, was it?"

His stomach knotted, the familiar tightness returning to his throat as he took another bite of the bread and chewed slowly to buy himself time.

Seph smirked at him, her time with Hades making her a master at identifying delay tactics. "You're stalling, and I have all day." She crossed her legs primly and cocked her head. "She was quite pretty."

"Gorgeous," he corrected, hunching over his plate. He looked over his shoulder to ensure no one was within listening distance.

"Still pining for her, I assume?" Seph posited, smiling sweetly at him when his eyes flicked to hers. "Your reaction to Dio's handmaiden over there gave it away. Is she bright?"

He poked at his food. "Smart, tough, and independent. Like Athena without the vengeance issues."

Persephone covered her mouth in feigned shock at his blasphemy, nudging his foot with hers as she hid her laughter. "That's how you end up cursed," she warned, waving off an approaching handmaiden. "How much did she know?"

"Nothing." He set his plate down and rose to his feet,

bowing quickly. "I better check on Bo."

She lifted a delicate brow and nodded. "Of course. Please let Boreus know his presence will be required for court tomorrow. And Alex?"

He hesitated, keeping his head slightly bowed.

"You're so much prettier when you smile, honey."

✕

CHARLOTTE STIRRED THE grainy mashed potatoes around on her plate, holding a forkful up to Max. "You're picking me up in the morning, right?"

Max nodded, angling his head away from the offensive food. "Yeah, yeah. I'll even bring you a change of clothes." He shuffled his chair closer to her. "You're lucky, Chuck. I thought for sure you had some serious damage, the way I found you..." He trailed off, clearing his throat. "We'll head over to the tavern tomorrow, okay? Thomas wants to see for himself that you're okay."

Swallowing the bland potatoes, she nodded. "How's the bar look?"

"A bunch of us pitched in with the cleanup this afternoon. The liquor stock took a hit, but it doesn't look like the place took any structural damage." Max popped the lid off a bottle of water and handed it to her. "You'll give me the rundown at lunch, right?"

She twirled her fork, keeping her eyes off the unappetizing bandages on her hand that held her IV needle in place. "I'm still piecing it together," she muttered. "I'm not sure what was real and what I imagined."

Pushing himself up, he gathered his wallet and keys and crossed his arms. "You freaked me out, Chuck. Don't do it again."

She watched him walk from the room and saunter over to the nurses' station, his sights locked on a pretty woman lining files across the counter. Reaching across the bed, she unplugged her phone and swiped it to life, surprised to see the number of notifications that up from well-wishers and coworkers. Scanning them over, she typed out a quick, generic update and copied it, sending it to every number before she opened her contacts.

Alex Echidna.

She hovered her thumb over his name, drawing a deep breath before she tapped the number and waited until the phone went to voice mail. Hanging up, she sank back in the uncomfortable bed and attempted to make sense of what she'd seen.

THOMAS RELEASED HER immediately, apologizing profusely when Charlotte jumped, her bruised ribs protesting the contact.

"It's okay." She laughed, grabbing his hand and smiling.

"I'm happy to see you, too." She scanned the bar halfheart-edly for a tall, muscled guy with long hair and a roguish smirk. "I can't think of anywhere else I'd rather have my first post-hospital-meal lunch."

"Take a seat and I'll send Daniel over right away," Thomas ordered, gripping her hand tightly in his. "You gave us all a scare."

Max hauled her over to a quiet corner and sat, his arms spread across the back of the booth. "Spill."

"There's not much to spill." She sighed, pulling an elastic from her purse and gathering her hair up. "The quake hit while I was coming down from the Chasm's peak and a rock dropped between me and the exit." She rubbed her elbow through the thick bandage. "Going back up was too risky with the tremors, so I just stayed put."

He frowned, lifting a finger to order their meals when Daniel approached them. "And Alex found you."

She pushed past Butch to the calming voice that carried through the caves. "Yeah, he did."

Waiting for her to elaborate, Max rolled his hand in the air. "And?"

"And I don't know," she replied absently. "He managed to move the rock enough for me to get under it. But Butch's legs got caught underneath and Alex... Yeah. I don't know."

He fixed her with a dead glare. "So Butch was there."

"No. Yes." She leaned back and stared at the table, squinting as though it would help her see the night clearer.

"He got me out and I left. I drove away."

"Alex and Butch left you alone in the park during the aftershocks of a quake."

She closed her eyes tight and groaned. "Dammit, Max. I don't know. He had somewhere to be. And Butch was... Can I just eat?"

"Eat and talk. So you made it under half a mile from the Chasm?" he demanded, eyes narrowed in disbelief. "Chuck. When we found you out there... Did Alex do something to you?"

She shook her head. "No. No, of course not. My head was just playing tricks on me. Spooking me."

"Your voice is still messed up," he stated, thanking the new bartender as he set down their coffees. "Fuck, Charlotte. You were so white and still, I thought rigor mortis had set in or some shit. Scared the hell outta me."

Taking her first sip of coffee in three days, she closed her eyes for a moment. "Did you see anything weird in the sand there?"

"Weird like how?" Max asked.

"Like a fire had been through there," she clarified, opening her eyes and glancing down at her phone as it buzzed. "Anything burnt?"

"Like a sand fire?" he snorted. "No, Chuck. No sand fires."

She smiled and stuck her tongue out at him, placing the memories she was dredging up squarely into the hallucination pile. "Cut me some slack," she whined, reaching across the table to grab his hand. "I was tired. Hungry. Injured. Without caffeine. It does stuff to your head."

"You get two days of me taking it easy on you," he relented, pouring half his coffee into her empty cup. "Only thing I saw out there were a ton of dog tracks and bear tracks. I put out the alert to the station already."

Chapter Thirty-One

A LEX PADDED ACROSS the marble tiles, the clicking of his claws alerting Hades to his presence. His master patted his thigh and held his hand out, waiting patiently for Alex to join him at the table and giving his shoulders a hearty rubdown as he continued to discuss the recent gossip about Hera with Dio.

It had only taken a week for him to fall back into the routine. Three more until he had it perfected once again.

Wake. Eat. Swim.

Eat. Wander down to the river. Swim.

Check in with Hades. Eat. Sleep.

Ryan was stretched out on his back in the corner of the room, one eye on Hades as he relaxed on the large pillow Seph had plumped and smoothed for him.

Bo's head lay on Dionysus's lap, his tail thumping off the floor as the god focused his attention on the sweet spot behind his ears.

Setting a paw on Hades's arm, he rose up and scanned the feast covering the table, sitting back when Hades began filling a plate for him and set it to the side. Climbing into the closest chair, he pulled the plate closer and dove in, pausing periodically to snort in amusement when Hades launched into a tirade about his sister.

Hera intimidated Alex, and he sure as hell wasn't embarrassed by it.

Persephone flitted into the room, Iris trailing behind her. Hades shifted his position, angling his legs out from under the table and wrapping his arms around his wife as she settled into his lap without a second thought.

Iris gave Alex a polite smile, sitting in the seat beside him and shuffling a fraction away as she continued to listen attentively to Seph.

He subtly placed his paw on her edge of the table, catching Dio's eye when Iris wrinkled her nose and crossed her legs away from him.

She hated dogs.

Dionysus smirked and made a production of scratching his ribs, earning a yelp of annoyance from Bo. Taking the hint, Alex lifted his hind leg and mimicked the movement, sending Iris halfway down the table with her chair.

Persephone delicately cleared her throat and gave him a pointed glare, appeased when he lowered his head to the table and looked up at her balefully.

Yeah, he knew the routine.

Just like Iris would be tracing her hand up his arm at the next banquet he attended in human form.

Just like Hades would be cursing the clock in five

minutes, annoyed when he realized it was time to hold court again.

Just like Seph's open smile would shift into cold appraisal as she took up her spot at Hades's side in the throne room.

"So I told her if she wo—Seph, honey. Is that clock right?"

Persephone nodded, rising from Hades's lap and reaching over to run her thumb over Bo's brow. "Only two new ones on the docket tonight," she replied, straightening her skirts and pursing her perfectly painted lips when her husband let out a string of curses. "Hades."

Ryan rose to his feet and joined his master, Bo reluctantly following suit alongside Alex. They trailed behind Seph and Hades, Iris veering off toward her rooms after flashing a look of disgust at him.

"The pomp of this is ridiculous," Hades muttered, snatching his staff from the corner of the hall. "Two shades. For this I have to stop everything I'm doing?"

As Seph stroked his ego, Alex, Ryan, and Bo united, blending into one body that moved under the collective will of three minds. The doors opened to the reception room, and Cerberus led his master to his throne.

HADES SLUMPED BACK in his chair and groaned as the last of the onlookers exited the room. "I'm too old to do this," he grumbled, placing his hand on Persephone's as she stroked his beard. He patted Cerberus on the back. "Up, boy."

The dog rose to its feet, Bo nipping at Alex behind Ryan's head and growling when Alex bared his teeth in response.

"Enough." Hades sighed, cupping Bo's chin to still him. "Time to get you three topside again. We'll feast tonight and send you back up in the morning."

Cerberus sat motionless on the marble as Hades and Seph exited, oblivious to the turmoil their beloved guard dog was unanimously experiencing. The large doors clanged shut and the beast disintegrated, the brothers rising to their feet.

"He's fucking joking, right?" Bo demanded, pacing the floor. "This is a fucking joke."

Ryan's eyes locked on to the throne, his shoulders hunched as his eyes hardened. "We must have missed one." His voice was void of emotion. "The Albany Pirithous."

"I fucking knew it!" Bo snarled, booting a marble pillar and watching as the vase sitting on top tumbled to the ground and shattered. "That kid'll be thirty by now. He could be anywhere. He could have his own fucking spawn."

Alex stood silent, his mind shredding through what-ifs as Ryan exited the room, his back rigid.

"I can't do it again," Bo muttered beside him before he dropped to all fours and padded across the floor, leaving Alex alone.

✕

THE BROTHERS ENTERED the banquet hall, chitons and chlamys neatly pressed.

"Orion, sweetheart," Persephone called over to them, waving Ryan over. "Come! I want you to settle an argument."

Ryan nodded tersely and strode across the room to join his mistress at the table, his left biceps flexing under the sting of his newest tattoo. Bo elbowed Alex in the ribs and pointed to a group of handmaidens eying them before he made his way over, snatching a jug of wine on his way.

"Orion is displeased."

He glanced over at Hades. "We were under the impression this was the last mission."

His master shrugged. "As was I, until my seer informed me otherwise. When I tossed the curse, I wasn't thinking past the immediate ramifications." He patted Alex on the back and joined his wife.

Ramifications.

Hades had faced none of the ramifications of his curse. It was his loyal guard dog that had been saddled with the weight of eliminating the prolific Pirithous line from the earth. It was Cerberus who was cast into the human realm when the gods shuttered themselves in their own, the last of their followers making them obsolete. It was Ryan who prowled across Europe in the early years, scenting out the bloodline of the man who dared take Persephone from Hades. It was Bo who tracked the line across the ocean into the new world. It was Alex who roamed the streets of the cities, following the stench of death and cursed blood.

Hades had no ramifications.

He sat on his throne, his wife tight to his side. He feasted with his brothers. Conversed with his sisters. For him, the Pirithous curse was a moment of anger.

For them, it was their existence for hundreds of years, bouncing between the underworld and the topside world.

He strode over to Bo, accepting the jug and taking a long swig of the sweet wine. Iris sidled up to him, her arm looping around his.

Passing the jug back to Bo, he disentangled himself from the tiny goddess. "Ah, no," he muttered, easing his arm out from under her hold. "Taken. Remember?"

CHARLOTTE TOSSED HER hat in the back seat as she wove through the side streets, unbuttoning her shirt and fighting the sleeves off her arms before she pulled into the tavern parking lot. Max tore in beside her, tossing his truck into park and hopping out before she had time to unbuckle her seat belt.

"Tonight," he announced, lifting his arms into the air, "we drink to freedom."

"Tonight," she corrected, "we drink to spending one of our two days off in hangover hell."

He linked his arm with hers. "You should wear that tank more often. You look badass."

"I am badass," she huffed. "So how awkward is it going to be with the mumbler?"

Cringing, Max opened the door for her. "Awkward enough for me to consider putting in for a transfer up north."

She rolled her eyes. "You aren't leaving me here alone. Suck it up, princess."

The new bartender waved at them as they entered, motioning toward the tequila bottle and receiving an enthusiastic nod from Max.

The new bartender.

Daniel had been at the tavern for over a month, his presence a constant in the old lounge. Frat-boy cute, he already had a dedicated following of high tipping, flirtatious women with expensive wedding rings adorning their hands.

She didn't care much for him and his vinegar-forgetting ways.

Becky rose from her chair as they arrived at the table, shuffling to the next available seat and bringing Charlotte into the conversation immediately.

No amount of reassurances had eased Becky's guilt since the earthquake, and the woman had gone above and beyond to make unnecessary amends.

Charlotte wasn't about to complain. Having a female ally who laid into Max on a frequent basis was kind of refreshing.

Becky leaned close to her, pointing her drink at a group of men a few tables over. "I'm thinking the one in the blue."

Looking them over, she shook her head. "They're cute, but—"

"No buts," Becky chastised. "Standalone, no comparisons. Those boys are cute, period."

"I'm not quite there."

Her coworker squeezed her hand and turned to get the Montana mumbler's opinion. She tossed her credit card on the table and smiled politely as Daniel set her drink in front of her and slipped her card into his pocket.

Max lifted his shot in the air. "To us, Chuck. May the gods of the hunt smile down on us tonight."

✖

ALEX STRODE INTO the reception room and slowed, eying Hades warily as he took in the scene.

Ryan and Bo sat beside the throne in hound form, Persephone's fingers absently stroking Ryan's ears as Bo shifted restlessly at his master's knee. Neither brother would look at him, their gazes locked on the marble floor.

Hades motioned to him. "Walk with me, Alexandros," he called across the room. "We were just discussing your return topside." When Alex remained motionless, Hades rose to his feet, his expression hardening. "I did not ask."

Bowing his head a fraction, he walked to the center of the receiving area, kneeling in deference. "Apologies."

Seph's expression was unreadable, her bright eyes shielded by the slight turn of her face toward Ryan as she continued to pet him. "Hades."

"I know, dear," Hades growled, nodding toward the banks of the river and leading Alex over, his voice growing quiet. "I'm facing quite the conundrum, sending you back into the belly of temptation." His eyes traveled the length of the river into the darkness of the distant entrance. "Cerberus belongs to me. You exist as three separate beings solely on your mistress's whim. Beautiful, golden perfection in this dark hell." He glanced back at his wife and smiled at her as she scratched under Bo's chin. "As you are, dear."

Persephone drew in a deep breath and nodded in acknowledgment.

Alex forced his clenched jaw to release, bowing his head in deference. "I know my place."

"Of course you do." Hades chuckled. "The problem lies in the disconnect between what your mind knows and what your heart accepts." He looked back at Seph. "I am well versed in that dilemma." When Alex didn't respond, he stepped in tightly to him. "I've lost my following. My strength. My position of power in the topside world. And selfish as it may be, I am not prepared to lose my guard dog. I'm sorry, Alexandros." Taking a step back, he straightened his back, his voice booming through the reception hall. "You are forbidden to seek the woman out, forbidden from seeking contact. Your mission takes priority, and disobedience will be met with swift consequences for you and your brothers. You are dismissed."

Chapter Thirty-Two

ALEX RAN HIS hands through his hair and looked up at the towering rocks of the Chasm.

"At least this time, our clothes are still in style," Bo grumbled, tearing his shirt off over his head and tossing it aside.

"I doubt any of our stuff is still at the campsite," Ryan murmured, looking at the sun's position in the sky. "We'll be best off dogging it to Alex's trailer."

"If it's still there," Alex stated, halfheartedly scanning the area for signs of a beautiful brunette park ranger before he snapped his attention back to the task at hand. "My SUV's probably been impounded. My wallet. Phone. It's been over a month." He glanced over at Ryan. "You think you still have a job?"

"Unlikely."

Bo snorted. "You'd think Hades would tuck a few gold coins into our pockets or something." He peeled his jeans off and flung them over his shoulder. "Let's go."

Ryan stripped down with deliberate slowness as Bo transformed, folding each item before placing them on a rock.

Alex followed suit, swatting at Bo when he nipped at his ankles.

The brothers tore over the sand, sticking far from the paved roads and dirt paths that peppered the park. Alex led the way, giving wide berth to Lost Horse Mine and skimming against the ridge and peaks until they reached the Keys. The sun was dropping fast, the cover it would provide within the hour eagerly anticipated by the brothers. Standing on a familiar ridge, he scanned the territory for signs of life.

Or white work trucks.

He stalked down the hill, Ryan and Bo holding back until they were given the all clear. Small lizards were making their evening rounds, scurrying between the chollas and taking refuge under the larger bushes. He paused, a familiar scent assaulting him.

Dog food.

Glancing back at his brothers, he shook his head quickly before descending the rest of the hill, stopping at the empty bowl, a few pieces of kibble still nestled at the bottom. He wrinkled his nose and looked toward the road, half expecting Charlotte to be crouched beside her car, hand extended.

Finding nothing but a delicious rabbit huddling motionless a hundred yards away, he doubled back to his brothers and led them across the deserted terrain.

✕

BO AND RYAN remained across the street, tucked tight in the shadows of the parked cars as Alex waited outside the trailer park gates, slipping in alongside a car and creeping along the fence until he came up on his site.

His site, and his SUV.

Checking the darkness for onlookers, he transformed and dropped to his knees, running his hands along the underside of his trailer, his fingers gripping the small plastic container and pushing it open. Key in hand, he scanned the area quickly and crept into his trailer, pulling the door closed and flicking on the light.

Power's still on.

He entered his bedroom and grabbed some clothes, tossing two sets onto the sofa and yanking his jeans over his hips before he threw on some shoes and jogged to the gates. He keyed in the code and motioned for his brothers to stick to the outer fence as they made their way to his trailer. Bo bounded in first, his tail bouncing off the tight quarters until he transformed.

Ryan held back, entering only after Bo moved out of the way to give him room.

"Your SUV made it here," Bo called out, his head ducked into the barren fridge while he fastened his jeans.

Alex opened his cupboard and set a few cans of soup onto the counter. "You start this, I'm going to check it out."

Grabbing his spare keys, he unlocked the vehicle and opened the passenger door, leaning in to hunt for any sign of how it got from the park to his site. Coming up empty, he eased the door closed and popped the hatch, brows rising as he took in the meticulously stacked piles.

Camp stove.

Backpacks.

Boots.

Hefting the first of the bags onto his shoulder, he scooped up the boots and opened his trailer door, dropping the items in before going back for the rest.

"Tell me Ryan's credit cards are in that pile," Bo pleaded, ripping open one of the backpacks. "This soup smells like shit and I want pizza."

Ryan held his hand out for his bag, rifling through it for a moment and producing the desired Visa.

Bo snatched it away. "Thank fuck. Alex. Call it in."

"We have three phones here," he muttered, setting them on the counter. "All dead, but all here. Ryan, could you plug these in?"

Spreading the phone chargers throughout the small trailer, Ryan frowned at the stack of clothes and camping gear. "Your little ranger?"

He shrugged, hoping he was projecting a much calmer response than the one that had a vise grip on his chest. "Maybe. I'd put my money on her partner, though."

Though Max didn't seem like the kind of guy to fold socks before packing them.

Ryan's phone buzzed to life, pulling the attention off

Alex as Bo launched into the onerous task of selecting pizza toppings and hot wing heat level.

✕

CHARLOTTE LAUGHED AS the little girl squealed, backing away from the small lizard Charlotte held gently in her hand. She placed it back into the sand and rose to her feet, adjusting her hat. "Have fun tonight! Remember to put your campfire out before you go to bed."

The little girl nodded solemnly and waved while she got back into the truck, Max giving the family a quick salute as he pulled back onto the road.

"Now we're clocking out late," he grumbled, his foot a little heavier on the gas than usual. "Bad enough we're even here."

She grinned. "Some of us were responsible with our consumption last night. Maybe others of us could learn something."

Flipping her off, Max pulled into the station, groaning as he opened his door and stepped into the heat. "Some of us shouldn't answer our phones on our day off. And some of us shouldn't volunteer others of us for extra shifts."

She linked her arm through his. "But then I'd be saving people from the great five-inch lizards alone, and you know you can't let that happen."

Max grunted, his eyes squinting behind his sunglasses.

The poor guy was hurting, painfully hungover from overindulging the night before.

She clocked out and led Max to her car. "I'm going to drop you off at home to shower and then I'm going to pick you up and take you out for dinner to make amends."

"Damn right you are," he muttered, putting his hat over his face until they pulled up to his apartment. "Gimme an hour."

She glanced down at her phone as she hit the main road, her breath catching when she caught the message that flashed across her screen.

"Thank you."

She turned her phone over and returned her attention to the road.

She hadn't actually expected Alex would return. When she was carefully packing the abandoned campsite up, she'd treated it as she had any other.

Respectful detachment.

As she'd brushed the sand off the small tent, rolling it tightly and wrestling it into its nylon bag, she'd talked cheerfully with a sweet retired couple from Canada, answering their questions about the wildlife and the best places for easy hikes.

While folding the discarded shirts and shorts, she'd snacked on a package of crackers and watched a small coyote watch her.

She'd even padded the deserted phones between the layers of clothes, resisting the urge to swipe the recognizable one to life and hunt for any information to justify, or negate, what she had seen.

She pulled into her apartment complex, slipping her cell into her purse before she headed upstairs to shower.

Max had been silent when he dropped her off at the site that evening, a wariness in his eyes as she'd packed the SUV up, tossing the tent into the back of Max's truck when the thought of spiders nestled in the folds of the fabric overtook any logic.

It had been his eagle vision that spotted the pile behind the back tire, a bottle-opener keychain poking through the sand. He'd followed her close as she drove the SUV through the park and hit the highway, her speed fluctuating with every unfamiliar sound the vehicle made.

She stepped out of the shower and dried off, glancing at the time.

Max.

He'd held his tongue when she quietly parked Alex's car beside his trailer, sliding his keys under the seat. He'd said nothing when she pulled their work truck up to the Keys the next night and set a bowl of kibble onto the sand. And he'd continued to hold back when she repeated the action every shift since.

All he knew about the night of quake was what she had told him.

He didn't need to know about the hallucinations she was

slowly starting to process.

She took her time getting dressed, giving her hair a chance to move from soaking wet to damp as she stood in front of her closet contemplating her choices, finally settling on an emerald green sundress she hadn't worn in ages. With a quick touch up of her makeup, she filled her purse, ready to treat her coworker to a meal he sorely deserved.

Picking her phone up off the counter, she swiped her thumb over the screen and reread Alex's short message before she deleted it, slipping the cell into her bag and heading out the door.

Chapter Thirty-Three

A LEX PASSED RYAN the release papers and followed him through the impound lot. "Think Bo will be up when we get back?"

"Doubtful," Ryan replied absently, beelining toward the row where his hatchback sat. "We'll hit the road tomorrow morning."

He inspected every inch of the exterior before unlocking it and getting in, repeating the intense scrutiny inside. Easing forward to give him room to open the passenger door, Ryan drove them out of yard, silent until they hit the main drag.

"Will you be pursuing the woman again?"

Alex stared out the window. "She saw us."

Checking his rearview mirror, Ryan adjusted the angle. "I know. She gave us the information packets."

"No," Alex said slowly. "She saw us. With the Pirithous. And me." He swallowed and exhaled loudly. "She saw me transform. Saw us end him."

Ryan went quiet, his brows knotting as he considered the complications a witness could bring about. "We'll check online to see if she said anything," he finally stated, pulling up to the trailer park and keying in the gate code. "This is a discussion for all of us."

He dragged his feet into the small trailer, inching past Ryan to wake Bo. "Get up, dickwad," he called, booting his twin's dangling arm. "Family meeting."

Hunched over his phone, Ryan scanned the area news from the past month, muttering updates about the stalled FBI investigation and the subsequent shrinking of its ground force in the valley. "Well, she didn't talk."

Bo rose up on his elbows, scratching at his bare stomach. "Who?"

"Charlotte," Alex replied as he sat at the kitchen table, her name feeling foreign on his lips. "She saw us."

Swinging his legs down, Bo shrugged. "Standard protocol then."

Ryan's hand shot out to Alex's shoulder, forcing him back into his seat. "I think this case warrants a little more consideration than a blanket doctrine," he stated, his fingers digging into the muscle. "Perhaps given Alex's past relationship with her, killing her should be pulled from the table."

Bo snorted. "Whatever. We're uprooting to Albany anyway, aren't we? Feel her out for any evidence she might have squealed and deal with it from there." He yawned and leaned over to the fridge to grab a beer. "What bar are we hitting up tonight?"

Ryan stared Alex down. "I think we need to discuss Hades's response to your attachment."

"There's no attachment," he growled, shaking Ryan's hand off his shoulder and rising to his feet. "Hades has every right to keep his junkyard dog leashed, right? Besides, we have a job to do."

"Perhaps Seph—"

"Seph won't intervene." He looked out the window at his SUV. "She loves her little show ponies. Sit. Smile. Shake a paw. We're trinkets to her, dolls she dresses up and parades around so everyone can compliment her on her pretty little pets."

Bo set his empty beer on the table. "It is what it is, man. Always has been, always will be. And you were fine with it until that chick came into the picture."

✖

MAX SET HIS phone down and dipped his last fry into the ketchup smeared across his plate. "The Washout?"

Charlotte leaned back in her seat and crossed her arms. "Aren't you getting a little old to do this every night?"

"Aren't you getting a little old to have a purse with hearts stamped all over it?" Max tossed back, grinning when her lips drew into a tight line. "Exactly. Everyone's already there. To the limo, Jeeves!"

Shutting her car door with more force than necessary, she reapplied her lipstick and backed out of the stall. "You're running defense," she warned. "Any drunk who comes near me is on you to fend off."

"Then you're running offense," Max countered, rifling through her purse and lifting her eyeliner out to examine it. "Any hot chick who comes near me, you talk me up."

She grinned, parking at the far end of the lot. "Deal."

The bar was packed, the music making even the loudest of conversation nearly impossible as they made their way toward the table of rangers seated by the dance floor. She waved to everyone before tapping Max on the arm and nodding to the bar to let him know she was covering his first round.

She swung her purse over her shoulder and squeezed through the crowd, her eyes locked on her destination. When she was within reach, she stuck her hand onto the bar to claim her spot, wedging into place against a beautiful blonde and the back of a tall guy leaning against the counter. The blonde smiled at her and slipped into the throng of people, giving her enough room to stake her spot, the bartender smirking when she angled her elbows out to increase her footprint.

"Two ryes and a water, please," she yelled over the din.

The bartender nodded and got to work, chuckling at something the tall man beside her said. She looked up as the man turned, dropping her head immediately when recognition set in, running a hand through her hair to create a veil to hide her face until she could leave, her heart pounding.

"Excuse me?"

Charlotte ignored him, burying her head in her purse as the bartender set her drinks down.

"I'll get those," the man said, setting a twenty down. When her head snapped up, her mouth opening to protest, he looked down at her, his dark brown and amber eyes worn. "Consider it a meager token for returning our things."

Fighting the urge to look around the bar for another tall blond, she gave him a tight smile. "Thank you. And you're welcome."

She gathered the drinks up and backed away, keeping her head down until she made it back to Max.

If he was here, she didn't want to know.

ALEX SLID THE shot of tequila to Bo, shaking his head. "Nope. No more. I'm out."

Bo shrugged and pounded back both shots, his blood-shot eyes closing for a moment before he turned his attention back to the women who had squeezed into their booth an hour earlier.

Alex shuffled over a fraction, subtly angling his legs away from the high-heeled foot sliding up his calf from across the table. Scanning the bar, he caught sight of Ryan beelining toward them, his hands loaded with bottles.

"We should head out after this," Ryan stated, handing out the drinks and thanking the redhead when she slid over to give him room to sit. "I want to be on the road early."

Bo waved him off, stretching his arm behind the brunette to play with the blonde's curls. "I'm sleeping the whole way, so…"

Ryan's eyes flicked around the room. "Alex and I'll meet you back at the trailer then."

Alex polished off the last of his beer and stood, happy for the graceful out. He snapped his fingers at Bo to get his attention. "Hey. Call when you're on your way."

"Yeah, yeah," Bo slurred, cocking a brow when the brunette whispered into his ear.

Ryan perused the bar again, stepping up tight to him and nudging him to the left. "Let's go."

Shaking his brother's arm off, Alex began jostling through the crowds, wincing when a piercing squeal echoed in the room, the intro to a song that brought back way too many memories blasting through the speakers. "We should grab a burger on the way home," he yelled over his shoulder, craning his head back when Ryan's response was drowned out by the frantic dance floor rush. "I sai—" He stopped in his tracks.

Charlotte was steps away from him, shaking her head and rolling her eyes as Becky dragged her toward the center of the room. Tugging her arm back, she turned, her smile freezing when she caught sight of him. Becky's eyes widened as she released her and she leaned into Charlotte's ear, backing up when Charlotte nodded.

"Hey."

He swallowed, vaguely aware of Ryan drawing up beside him. "Hey."

Her eyes moved to his brother and she gave him a tight smile. "Hey again."

Ryan nodded, elbowing him and tilting his head toward the exit. Taking the hint, Becky did the same to Charlotte, stepping between them and latching on to her arm.

He remained rooted on the spot as Charlotte disappeared into the crowd without glancing back, the rich green fabric of her dress fluttering around her thighs.

He didn't remember seeing that dress before.

Running his hand through his hair, he tore his gaze off her. "You knew she was here."

"I ran into her at the bar when I grabbed the last round," Ryan replied, following him as he pushed open the lounge doors and stalked toward the SUV. "I wasn't sure seeing her was something you wanted. Or needed."

Revving the engine, he ripped through the streets in silence, ignoring Ryan's subtle braking motions in the passenger seat.

Needed.

He attempted to rub out the knot forming at the back of his neck as he pulled up to the trailer. "Crash in the back with me," he muttered to his brother, flicking on the lights and tossing his keys on the counter. "I'll leave the door unlocked for Bo. But there's no way he's sleeping in my bed."

Opening the sofa bed, Ryan carefully moved his backpack to the dining table and checked it over. "You okay?"

He dropped onto his bed and tossed his arm over his eyes. "Nope."

The mattress shifted when Ryan sat down. "You can come with us tomorrow," he offered. "Once we track down the Pirithous online, we can set up shop in the area and deal with this once and for all."

"And then what?"

He lifted his arm as Ryan looked over at him. "What do you mean?"

"And then what?" Alex reiterated. "We return to the underworld to eat table scraps and listen to the gossip of a bunch of irrelevant gods while they scratch our ears and remind us of our place?" He rose up on his elbows. "What are we gunning for? It's not freedom. Or money. Just back to the junkyard until the boss sends us on another senseless errand."

Ryan's eyes hardened. "We have a duty."

"And you know I'll obey orders, so let's drop it." He fell back on his pillow. "It doesn't matter. I'm paid up here until the end of the month, so I'll jump ship once we figure out where the Pirithous is. Clean break, fresh starts, and all that."

Chapter Thirty-Four

ALEX TOSSED HIS dirty socks into his hamper, balancing his phone against his shoulder. "It's been a week. Do I bother paying another month's rent or do I put in my notice?"

Ryan went quiet for a moment as Bo grumbled from the background. "Stay put until we know where we're moving," he finally stated. "Bo's getting back to work here."

"And you?" he asked, knowing Ryan had been stressing about his own monetary situation in the wake of his absence.

"I'm on probation," he replied tersely. "Putting in over-time for the next little while. If we get a bead on the Pirithous, we'll regroup and examine the best location to set up shop." He paused as Bo muttered something behind him. "Would you feel better relocating now? I have a futon you can crash on for the time being."

Dumping his quarter collection out to count it, Alex grunted. "I might go grovel at Thomas's feet and try to score enough shifts to pay the bills."

"Are you sure that's wise?"

"Probably not, but a man's gotta eat. I won't go against

the decree, Ryan. I know our duty, and I know what's at stake." He gathered his coins up and tossed the container into the hamper. "I need to hit the laundromat, so call me in a few days and tell Bo he's a frog-fucker."

Adding his phone and wallet to the basket, he felt around the sofa cushions for his keys, huffing in annoyance when someone knocked on his door. "Gimme a sec," he called out, hooking his finger on the keyring and pocketing them before he misplaced them again.

He grabbed on to the frame and pushed his door open slowly to avoid thumping anyone, taking a reactive step back when Charlotte came into view. "Hey."

She tugged at the hem of her red tank, her thumbs digging into the fabric. "Hey."

With his brain firing in dozens of different directions, he clung to the frame, knowing he was staring at her but unable to stop.

She always looked so goddamn gorgeous in red.

"Could I come in?"

He blinked, backing into his trailer wordlessly as she gave him a tight smile and followed, pulling the door shut.

She glanced down at his laundry pile. "Is this a bad time?"

"It can wait," he replied, eying her cautiously. "What's up?"

She scanned his place intently, craning her neck slightly to peer past him into his bedroom. "Are your brothers still here?"

"Left last Sunday." He shoved his hands into his pockets and leaned against the counter, trying desperately to read her as she looked everywhere but at him. "Were you looking for me or them?"

She pursed her lips and stared at the floor for a few seconds. "I've gone over this a thousand times," she began slowly, tilting her head and finally looking at him. "Probably more than that. I've spent way more hours on Google than I should've, and I've watched some really weird homemade YouTube documentaries."

His muscles tensed, his head battling with his instinct to run.

But she'd sought him out, and he had to know what she knew, and what she'd said about the things she'd seen.

At least, that was the excuse he would be giving Hades and Ryan for his moment of weakness.

"None of the videos really fit with anything I saw," she mused, her brow knotting. "But some of the articles I read were interesting. I mean, there was a lot of crackpot to weed through, but at least I knew I wasn't losing my mind."

Easing his hands from his pockets, he crossed his arms over his chest, even the most veiled restraints on him feeling stifling. "Bounty hunter was a really loose explanation," he said quietly.

She exhaled, mimicking his position. "Can you do it at will?" When she was met with silence, she lifted a brow.

"Can you make it so Butch is right here, right now?"

Refusing to answer, he copied her expression, his mind replayed the various scenarios he'd been imagining for weeks.

Screaming.

Hysterics.

Disgust.

Fear.

She stared him down, her dark eyes clinical. "Alex."

"You've kind of got me by the balls," he finally stated, running his hand through his hair. "Either you're going nuts, or I'm hauled into some Area 51–level nightmare. I care for you too much to feed the first option, and I value my own ass too much for the second."

She nodded, her eyes narrowing as she considered his words.

The slight downturn of her lips didn't escape his notice. "Hypothetically," he said, digging his fingers into his ribs, "if we were to take insanity off the table, how likely would it be for me to find the FBI or wildlife officers pounding down my door at three a.m.?"

"Zero percent," she replied, rubbing her elbow.

He glared at her arm. "That still bothering you?"

Charlotte dropped her hand. "Show me I'm not losing it."

"Promise me you won't scream," he countered, his instincts howling in protest.

She crossed her heart. "I swear it."

He pushed off the counter, nudging the sofa bed with his foot to tuck in the final few inches. "This is probably a huge mistake," he said softly, turning his back to her as he pulled his shirt over his head. "If, *when*, you freak out and talk, I'm probably going to be hoofing it out of here empty-handed. End up sleeping on Ryan's couch for the next few months and delivering pizza for five bucks an hour." He chuckled humorlessly, unbuttoning his jeans and pushing them off his hips. "What the fuck am I doing?"

He kicked off his jeans and boxers as he transformed, internally preparing for the scream while Charlotte drew in a deep breath. When it didn't come, he placed his paws on the sofa, shuffling his hind legs awkwardly as he turned around in the tiny space before he dropped to all fours, his head bowed.

Time froze as he waited for her to react. He locked his eyes on the floor and inched back to give her room to run, her silence more terrifying for him than her screams. The longer the stillness stretched out, the tenser he became, his hackles rising when she took a step toward him and slowly lowered herself to the floor.

He risked a glance up at her, the scent of her lotion almost overwhelming him as her hand stretched out to him and she tentatively ran her thumb under his chin.

"Oh, wow," she whispered, one hand covering her mouth.

He remained motionless as she examined him, tilting his

head from side to side and lifting his ears.

"So this is why Butch never let me see his eyes," she murmured, holding his muzzle steady. "Sneaky thing, aren't you, boy?"

Ducking out of her grip, he sat back.

She squeezed her eyes shut, covering her face with her hands. "Not a dog," she whispered to herself, pushing her hair back. "Okay. I... Okay. I have questions. And you..." She gestured toward him. "You need to be you."

✕

ALEX EMERGED FROM his bedroom fully clothed, his eyes averted as Charlotte placed a filter into his coffeemaker and counted out the scoops.

"I suppose this is your way of saying you have a lot of questions," he muttered, standing as far from her as he could in the tiny trailer.

She bent down to glare at the machine, tapping buttons until he reached over and flipped a small switch on the side. "Thanks," she said, straightening up and sitting at the kitchen table. When he remained tucked tightly against his fridge, she sighed. "Does it hurt?"

He shook his head. "No."

"Can you control it?"

"Yeah."

Pursing her lips, she crossed her arms and sat back in her

seat. "Are you going to give me more than one-word answers?"

"Probably."

When he smirked, she rolled her eyes, the tension in her body releasing a little. "Are you going to sit?"

"Only if you command it."

Her eyes narrowed.

He gave her a tight smile and looked over to the coffee-pot. "Once that fills." He ran his hand through his hair and shifted his weight. "I should have said this earlier, but whatever I tell you doesn't leave here."

Her brows shot up. "Of course not."

"Not even Max."

She tilted her head and watched him as he opened a cupboard and pulled out two mugs. Every muscle was tense, the tendons in his neck taut. He had yet to really look at her, the usual fluidity of his movements abrupt while he poured the coffee, wetting a dishcloth to wipe the small spill before he picked up the cups and carried them over.

She inched her hand across the table to his, giving it a quick squeeze of reassurance. He glanced down at her fingers and drew his arm back. "Ask away."

Ignoring the ripple of hurt that hit her, she lifted her mug. "What are you?"

He grunted and stretched his arms across the back of his seat. "Might as well go big or go home, eh? We're the original junkyard dog."

Keeping her face as expressionless as possible, she waved her hand. "Go on."

He took a sip of his coffee and resumed his position. "Once upon a time, there was an old god named Hades. He oversaw the souls of the dead, broke up fights, assigned punishments, all that stuff." He paused, watching her reactions. "He had a dog named Cerberus that helped him monitor the perimeter to make sure no one got out. Or, in some cases, got in." He leaned his head back. "You'd be amazed at how many people inadvertently find themselves in realms they shouldn't be in."

She leaned forward. "You're kidding."

"Woof, baby."

She downed half her coffee, wincing when it burned down her throat. "Cerberus. The hellhound." Frowning to recall the image she'd spent sleepless nights erasing from memory, she pointed her pinky at him. "That's what I saw, isn't it?"

"Bo, Ryan, and I can exist separately, but the only way to transport ourselves and our kills back to Hades is to unite," he replied slowly, his attention drifting around the trailer. "And yeah, that's what you saw."

She nodded to buy herself time to think, her head struggling to reconcile the three-headed beast she'd seen with the man drinking coffee feet away from her. "Why are you here?"

"Glutton for punishment?" he grumbled. "Our master is

a little impulsive and vindictive when it comes to his wife. Some poor dumbass nabbed Seph a few thousand years ago." He lifted a brow when Charlotte opened her mouth to speak. "Persephone. She was back right away, totally fine, but thanks to Hades and his flippant curses, every male who carries the blood of the Pirithous line has to be eliminated before the job's done and the hex is satisfied."

Hunting for signs of deception in the tale he was spinning, she crossed her arms and narrowed her eyes. "How hard could that've been? I mean, thousands of years ago? There were, like, five developed civilizations."

He scoffed. "I made that very point when Hades booted us topside a few hundred years ago. Had he sent us up at the time, the three males carrying the Pirithous line would've been dead and gone within the year." Getting to his feet, he scooped up her mug and refilled it. "Instead, he kept us on the shoreline until the believers dried up and he didn't need the guard dog anymore. And Seph liked having her golden boys around to show off to her family. So, by the time we were sent topside, the line was all over Europe and Africa. One spinoff in India." He set her cup down for her. "That one was a real bitch to hunt down."

She tested the drink before taking a sip. "So this line is the guy who was in the park. The one who attacked me."

Alex's expression morphed, his eyes hardening. "I dropped the ball on that one."

"How so?"

He looked at her pointedly. "I was distracted." He bit his

lower lip and stared at the table. "The Pirithous males turn after their first run-in with one of us. Totally normal guys until we cross paths." He drummed his fingers along the back of the bench seat. "After the first time, they start to have violent thoughts. Controllable, but dark. They start to hunker down in their future kill zone without realizing what they're doing. The second run-in triggers the movement from thought to action." He reached down to rub his ribs. "The sedan hit was the second."

"Which is why the bodies began turning up," she mused. "He'd staked out his site."

He nodded. "I'd scented him in the area months earlier, but hadn't been able to track him. And by the time I did, the park was knee-deep in dead hikers and I was head over..." He paused. "I was slacking on the job."

Setting his fumbled words aside to think about later, she pressed on. "If you got him, why are you still here? I thought you were supposed to be gone once you got your target."

"Miscalculation."

She leveled him with a dead glare.

"Ryan and I believed we had the last one," he continued, lifting his hands in surrender. "Bo had been insisting the Pirithous in Albany thirty years ago had a kid, but nothing came up in our preliminary hunt, so we walked away." When she remained silent, he sighed. "With the last one, we'll return to our duties in the underworld. Prowling the grounds. Scaring the residents. Getting belly rubs." He patted his toned stomach. "Speaking of, I'm starving."

Chapter Thirty-Five

ALEX STAYED TIGHT to Charlotte's little coupe, following her to the empty lot of a restaurant off the main road.

We can eat, but I still have questions.

Of course she did.

The calculating dark eyes, the pursing lips, the way she tilted her head while she thought through his words.

Wary as it made him, her intelligence drew him in as much now as ever.

Pulling in beside her, he took his time getting out of the SUV. With the shock of her arrival at his door waning and the apprehension of her grilling wearing off, he was coming to terms with a truth he wasn't ready or equipped to deal with.

He missed her.

Missed her enough to recognize he'd been functioning through little more than routine for the past month. That the persistent apathy in his mind since he'd walked out of her apartment drew directly from her absence.

Missed her enough to expose everything he was.

Missed her and needed her.

"The dry ribs here are incredible, but stay away from the wings."

He grabbed his phone and got out, tightening his grip on it when his hand instinctively reached for hers as he scanned the deserted lot. "Are you sure this is the place?"

She led him to the unwelcoming metal door and heaved it open. "We have two hours before it fills. And I have a lot of questions."

"I don't know how much more you could want to know," he stated, following her to a small booth at the back of the restaurant. "I pretty well summed it all up."

She lifted a brow as she sat, accepting the menus from the waiter with a sweet smile and waiting until he walked away with their drink orders. "Are you still you in there? Like, do you think in words or, I don't know, barks?"

"You're kidding, right?" He snickered, schooling his expression when she folded her hands on the table. "Words. The physical change doesn't affect my head at all." He paused. "I'm more interested in rabbits, though. Lizards, too. Pretty much anything I can hunt and eat."

Her eyes widened as she unclasped her hands and lay them palms down. "Do you have any cool powers?"

"Aside from realm jumping?" he asked drily, grinning at her when she rolled her eyes and ignoring the guilt creeping through his mind over Hades's decree. "My senses are more refined, for sure. Faster, stronger. But no, no lasers shooting from my eyes or telekinetic powers or anything cool."

A hint of disappointment crossed her face.

And for a brief moment, he wished he was a hellhound with laser eyes.

He leaned back as the waiter placed their drinks down and took their order, resting his elbows on the table once they were alone again. "Anything else?"

"How old are you?"

He bit his lip as he did the math. "Three? Four thousand? Time was kind of irrelevant for most of my life, and I spent all but a few hundred years as a dog, so are we counting that differently?"

"I..." She shook her head. "Moving on. Where were you during the month you were gone?"

"Hades."

She drew in a deep breath. "Elaborate, please."

"Not much to say." He shrugged. "Good food, dark ambience, and a lot of ear scratching." When her eyes narrowed slightly, her expression shifting quickly to a feigned pleasantness, he slid his hand across the table. "I'm a pet down there. I spend most of my time on all fours snagging smoked meats from the banquet hall and sitting beside Hades, bored out of my head while he welcomes the one or two new arrivals that trickle in." He hooked his pinky around hers, his heart almost stopping when she didn't pull away. "I swam in the river a few times, but it has a weird smell to it I can't quite identify and it takes forever to get it out of my fur."

She hummed in acknowledgment, her gaze sliding to his

arm. "You added on to the tattoo."

"Hades did, yeah." The tilt of her chin was enough to loosen his tongue. He angled his shoulder toward her and rolled his sleeve up. "This is the Pirithous you fought off at the Chasm."

She reached across the table and traced the shade's form. "Pirithous," she echoed, snatching her hand back and placing it under her thigh. "He? It? It didn't look like that when he hit you in his car."

He shook his head and unrolled his shirt. "He went full-on feral quick. The physical metamorphosis makes the line harder to take down once you locate it." He exhaled loudly. "I knew you were tough, but damn, Charlotte. You held your own against that thing better than I could have. It took two hounds to subdue him in that cavern." A faint blush rose on her cheeks, and he pressed on. "If you'd run, he would've taken my head. So thank you."

CHARLOTTE UNTUCKED HER hands from under her legs as their meals were set down, anxious to turn the subject of conversation back onto Alex. "You realize you sound delusional, right?"

Diving into his ribs, he nodded. "That's the goal." He zeroed in on his food. "I'd rather be tossed off for that than for being what I am." With his attention on every bite he ate, he periodically glanced at her plate as she pushed her dry ribs around with her fork. "If you don't eat that, I will," he finally warned.

She pushed her plate toward him, plucking one rib for herself. "Are you allowed to tell me all this?"

"Mmm." He nodded, swallowing. "Technically, no. But my ass is covered under the myths-and-legends clause. And since I'm not revealing any of the post-Hellenic gossip from the hill, I'm in the clear."

"You aren't serious," she huffed, pulling her plate back.

He smirked. "Half-and-half. I'm in the clear with the gods, since most of them still hang out topside once in a while. And even if you did go to the press or online, you'd be dismissed as a nut bar, probably end up getting drug tested in the process. The second biggest risk is one of those crackpot conspiracy Bigfoot hunters getting it in his head that he's got a lead. But even that's easily dodged." Tugging her plate to the middle, he grabbed a rib. "Since pitchfork mobs are outdated, it's not much of a risk from a safety standpoint."

"What's the biggest risk?" she asked, eying her abandoned meal.

He examined a rib carefully. "Since we're sitting here, it's a nonissue."

He reached for another. She swatted his hand away, snatched a rib, licked it, and placed it triumphantly into the pile, mixing them around to claim her meal for herself.

Wow, did she miss this.

The glint in his eyes as he set his fork down in challenge.

The way he pursed his lips while he decided his next move.

Even the way he tucked his hair behind his ears before he made his choice.

Shoving the thought to the back of her mind, she wrinkled her nose as he shrugged and continued to plow through her food, knowing damn well it grossed her out. "Nasty."

He popped another rib into his mouth. "Hungry."

Admitting defeat, her appetite still waffling, she switched gears. "So the kibble…"

"Oh, god, no," he muttered as he took ownership of the plate. "Don't get me wrong. I appreciate the thought. It probably ties up there with one of the sweetest things anyone's done for me next to saving me from a feral Pirithous, but dog food is horrendous. It tastes exactly as it smells, and as a hound? That smell travels for miles." He hesitated, frowning. "Were you leaving it out there for me all month?"

She sat back in her seat and tugged at the hem of her shirt. "Not for the first two weeks," she replied hastily, suddenly second-guessing the action that had just seemed right at the time.

Sliding the empty plate aside, he tilted his head. "Thanks."

"It was the cheapest, foulest-smelling stuff I could find." She looked at his chest where his black shirt hid the tattoo underneath. "Hades marked you, didn't he?"

"Stamped me with his very own brand, yeah," he replied, clearing his throat. "So what have you been up to for the past month?"

She blinked. "I still have questions."

"Questions that can wait," he countered. "Tell me."

THIS WAS A *huge mistake.*

Alex held his coffee cup up for the waiter, thanking him absently as he listened to Charlotte describe a hiking tour she'd given to a group of seniors.

She was so animated, her facial expressions changing every few seconds while her hands augmented every statement. The self-conscious tugging at the hem of her shirt was long forgotten, her attention wholly focused on bringing him into the moment she was describing.

It was wasted effort.

The only moment he was in was this one.

Flopping back against her seat, she grinned. "I'm doing it again next week."

He sat there mute, memorizing how she looked in that instant until her smile fell. "Are you okay?"

Snapping back to attention, he nodded. "All good. So the park's busy as ever now? What shift are you working?"

"Evenings," she replied, wrinkling her nose. "I think I

actually prefer overnighters." She flipped her phone over and glanced at the time. "I guess reality's calling, isn't it?"

Waving the waiter over for the bill, he stood and held his hand out for her. "So what are the chances I'll talk to you again?" he asked as he passed the server a wad of cash.

She dropped his hand and fumbled around in her purse for her keys, her eyes obscured by her hair. "I don't know," she finally stated, tracking the waiter as he made change and walked toward them. "It's an awful lot to process, and I'm still trying to force my head to make the jump between real and imaginary."

Waving off the change, he followed her outside, his hands shoved deep in his pockets as he toed Hades's line a little too close. "You still have my number, right?" When she nodded, he pressed on. "Then how about I leave the ball in your court."

She leaned against her car and crossed her arms. "When do you take off for Albany?"

"I'm heading over to Thomas's tonight to grovel for my job back, so not anytime soon," he said, taking half a step closer to her. "We're not even sure Albany's the place anymore. And even if it is, I'm considering staying rooted here and just making business trips."

She looked up at him, lips pursed. "Business trips?" He smirked and she turned to open her door. "Good luck at the tavern," she said as she sat. "The guy who replaced you annoys the hell out of me."

He stepped away as she backed out of her spot and gave him a quick wave before she sped up and hit the road.

Enormous fucking mistake.

A strange ache was settling in his chest as he got into the SUV and started the engine, cranking the air-conditioning and glaring at it until the vents stopped blowing hot air into his face.

There was no way he could live in this town.

Seeing her out and about, making small talk with her at the grocery store, running into her at the bars while some halfwit bought her drinks and told stupid jokes.

He pulled into his site and hopped out, staying just long enough to toss his forgotten laundry in the back before he drove to the rental office to sign off on another month's rent.

Painful as seeing her was, the alternative would be borderline unbearable.

Chapter Thirty-Six

A LEX FOLDED THE last of his shirts and stretched over his bed to open his cupboard. "I've been putting it off, but I'm heading over to my old job after I finish up the laundry," he called toward his phone. "Hopefully I can pull enough shifts to cover bills until Ryan gets a bead on the guy." A loud rumble echoed through the speaker, drowning Bo's response out. "What the hell was that?"

"Hammer drill," Bo replied once the sound stopped. "Gimme a sec to get outside."

He moved his phone to the kitchen counter while he rinsed out his coffeepot.

"Way fucking better," Bo grunted, the clanging of metal and rumble of power tools no longer competing with his gravelly voice. "Ryan's barely had time to sleep with the extra shifts he's been pulling, so you might as well make yourself comfortable for a while."

Drying the pot out, he peeked through his window at the elderly lady passing by with her dog. "How's work going for you?"

"Shards of metal in my hair and grease in my ass crack,"

his brother replied, pausing to take a drag of a cigarette. "But most of the dealerships I hit up have hot receptionists, so it balances out."

He snorted and gathered up his phone and keys, slipping his wallet into his back pocket before he locked up the trailer. "Speaking of hot women, I saw Charlotte last week."

Bo exhaled loudly into the mic. "She buy you a squeaky toy?"

"Shut up." He laughed, backing out of his site and giving the elderly woman a wave. "I kind of told her everything."

Nothing but the long draw of smoke followed for a few seconds. "Were you drunk?"

Only on her eyes. "No. She showed up at my place and A led to B."

"So you got laid?"

"You're an animal," he muttered, turning into the Tavern lot. "I meant she showed up and asked and I answered."

Bo covered the mic and yelled over to someone, returning to the phone with a huff. "Goddamn tire busters," he grumbled. "Look, it sucks you didn't get laid, since Charlotte's probably the only woman around who can tolerate your ugly ass for more than a week. How'd she take it?"

Ignoring the insult, he ran his hands through his hair and let the SUV run in the heat. "Good, I guess. She didn't freak out or scream."

"Good sign," Bo replied, the flick of a lighter coming through the earpiece. "You going to hook up with her again?"

He turned the SUV off, unbuckling his seat belt. "This time, she sought me out. I don't think I can abuse that loophole again without ramifications, so..." He trailed off and cleared his throat. "Hell, if she ever calls me again, I'll be happy with that."

"I wouldn't if I was her," Bo stated. "You're one hideous bastard. And you smell like wet dog." When Alex snorted, he exhaled. "Smoke break's over. My advice? Go for it. Ryan and I already discussed this shit, and we'll go to bat for you with Seph and Hades once we catch this last asshole and return home for good." The noise of the shop returned to the background. "It would be weird to be down there without you, but we get it."

Refusing to allow himself to contemplate what Bo was suggesting, he leaned forward. "Cerberus is a package deal, brother."

"And I'm not spending the next nine centuries listening to your moping ass whining and whimpering over a chick," Bo yelled over the clanging. "Now go get a job, you useless fuckwad."

He tucked his phone into his back pocket and walked into the lounge, spotting the new bartender immediately. "Hey man, Thomas around?"

The guy gave him a once-over and nodded. "I'll go get him. Name?"

"Alex."

Taking a seat at the bar, he watched the man disappear into the back, returning moments later. "You can head on in."

He pushed through the familiar kitchen doors and waited for Thomas to emerge from the cooler, arms loaded with vegetables.

Thomas looked him over, dropping everything onto his prep counter. "Make yourself useful and pass me those bowls behind you." When Alex complied wordlessly, the elderly man handed him a knife and a bag of onions. "How's it going, boy?"

"It's going," he replied, washing his hands off in the sink. "The place looks good. Insurance cover the repairs?"

Grunting, Thomas reached over and corrected his hold on the knife. "Everything but a few bottles that hadn't been entered into the system yet." He stepped aside and appraised Alex's dicing skills. "Is this a social call or a business call?"

"Both." He scraped the first onion into the bowl. "I don't suppose you're hiring anyone under the table for a few shifts a week."

"Nope," Thomas replied, opening a bag of tomatoes up. "The last guy I brought in like that snuck out on me in the middle of the night and left me scrambling to fill his rotation."

He kept his attention on the blade in his hand. "I'm sorry," he grumbled, squinting at the uneven sizes of his onion pieces. "I had some family stuff come up."

Thomas leaned over and looked at the onion, wrinkling his nose for a moment before handing him another one. "That brother of yours is trouble," he stated. "Did he have anything to do with your disappearance?"

"Kind of." He widened his stance and bent closer to his cutting board. "I'm thinking of maybe staying around the area. Settling in and all that home-boy crap." He slapped the knife down. "Looks as good as yours."

"No, it doesn't," Thomas grumped. "If you consider getting some legal identification, I might consider hiring a dishwasher and prep guy."

He held his hand out for a tomato. "Not even my license is legal. I told you, man. I don't even have any birth records." He pushed the knife into the tomato, swearing when it crushed and sent juice onto his shirt. "This is probably a really dumb decision."

Thomas pointedly exaggerated his movements, angling his arms so Alex could watch his technique. "What's making you consider staying?" When he didn't reply, Thomas returned to his work. "Have you seen Charlotte since you got back?"

"Last week, actually," he muttered, going back to the onion.

"And how did that go?"

It's an awful lot to process.

"As well as expected, I guess." He sighed, glancing up as the new bartender came in and tossed an order onto the ring.

He waited until the door swung shut before continuing. "He's working out, I take it?"

"Daniel gets the job done," Thomas answered. "Customers seem to like him enough."

He walked over to the cooler and grabbed a stack of burger patties. "Charlotte doesn't like him."

"Charlotte hangs out with Max," the elderly man countered. "She's hardly the epitome of character judgment."

"Exactly." He grinned. "If she can identify the guy as a jerk, imagine how bad he must be."

Thomas fired up the grill. "I'll tell you what," he said, separating the patties and laying them on the metal. "Come back Sunday. If you're still determined to put down roots here, we'll talk. If not, I'll buy you a beer and wish you well. Sound good, son?"

He nodded and opened a bag of buns. "Mind if I hang around here tonight?"

"Start by bringing the liquor order over from the back."

✕

CHARLOTTE HUNG UP her radio and pulled onto the off-road path, slowing to a crawl until she reached her destination.

The ball was still in her court, sitting lifelessly on the sidelines.

Confident she had at least half an hour before Max

would be radioing in for her again, she turned off the engine, grabbed her flashlight, and gave the area a quick scan before she got out. Climbing onto the hood of the truck and leaning back against the windshield, she stared up at the expanse of the night sky.

"Who needs aliens when you have a hellhound sleeping in your backyard?" she muttered, rubbing her temples.

She liked order and facts and incredible animal adaptations that could be explained through Darwinism. She stuck to fiction books that existed in the realm of possibility, movies that held one foot firmly planted in reality.

In her opinion, myths were overly complicated stories bred from a civilization that hadn't the scientific evidence to explain their world.

They weren't the family history of some random guy working behind a bar.

Some random guy who made her heart pound. Or could keep her up for hours talking about everything and nothing.

That random guy who she'd been drawn to the moment she saw him, hiking boots haphazardly tied and a rakish grin on his face.

A low howl crossed the Keys, the high-pitched yelps of the coyotes joining in as the howl drew closer to her, coming up slow and steady on her right. She kept her eyes on the stars and ignored the hesitant approach of the beast in her peripheral vision.

"If you're looking for kibble, you're out of luck," she

called over, closing her eyes and folding her arms behind her head, a strange security settling over her with the dog's presence in the quiet desert. When Butch chuffed, she smiled and glanced over at him. "I dropped it off with a family on the east side. Some yappy little fur ball's eating it now."

Butch, Alex, held back a few yards, his ears perked up and head tilted.

"You put me in a tough position," she continued, turning her attention back to the sky. "I either have to rearrange my entire world view, or accept that both you and I are delusional and likely feeding off each other to create an alternate reality." She frowned. "Though I'm not sure what my head thinks it would gain by composing this."

She scooted over, dropping one arm over the side of the truck and tossing the other over her eyes. "If I go along with the delusional explanation, I have to accept that everything from the past few months wasn't real. Or at the very least, the parts of it involving you weren't." She rubbed her fingers together and waited until a soft muzzle bumped against her hand. "And frankly, that kind of sucks."

She grazed the beast's ears, lifting one at a time absently. "On the other hand, accepting that an entire society exists in another realm? That opens a whole other can of worms for me, doesn't it? I mean, one of the big questions is are you a dog that turns into a human or a human that turns into a dog? Because that's an important distinction."

The dog growled, nudging her hand.

"I'm going to go clock out," she said, giving him a quick pat before she sat up. "If I call you after I get home, and that's a big if, will you be home?"

She sighed as the dog took off across the sand, disappearing over the ridge. Swinging her legs over the edge of the hood, she hopped down and turned toward the driver's-side door.

"Such a pretty creature on four legs or two, isn't he?"

She spun around, her hand flying to the weapon on her hip as she took in the vaguely familiar woman gazing in the direction Alex had gone. She grazed her fingers over the snaps holding her gun in place and adjusted her stance.

"Persephone," the woman said, extending her hand in Charlotte's direction. "I don't believe we've been officially introduced." She took a step closer and shook her head. "I really need to work on those boys' manners."

She tentatively met the offered hand. "Charlotte."

Persephone smiled. "I know." She glanced back at the ridge for a moment before turning to face her. "He's a good boy. Well, he tries to be. He does have that snake gene running through his veins, after all." She flashed a brilliant smile. "But don't all men?"

Watching the woman warily, she released her hold on her weapon. "You're talking about Alex. You, uh, know him?"

"Know him? Oh, honey." Persephone laughed. "I own him."

She bristled at the flippant remark. "So you've come to, what, take him?"

Striding past her, Persephone opened the truck door. "I love the motion of these things. Take me for a drive and we'll talk, my dear."

Memories of high school history flew through her head. Mythological gods and goddesses and the callous games they played with humans for their amusement. "I—"

"I didn't ask," Persephone stated, buckling herself in and crossing her legs as she draped her long skirt over her thighs. "Come, Charlotte. I have to head home soon and I'd like to have a little chat with you." When her demand was met with stillness, she sighed heavily and gestured at the holster on Charlotte's hip. "If it would make you feel better, you can point that thing at me while we discuss my boy."

PERSEPHONE WAS QUIET for the first few minutes of their drive, her eyes flicking over the dark desert until she settled back in her seat, apparently unbothered by the gun resting in Charlotte's hand. "He's forbidden from seeking you out."

She remained silent, her attention bouncing between the road and her passenger.

"Hades fears you may be enough of a draw to keep Alexandros topside. And seeing as he lasted a week before coming to you, I believe my husband's fears may be justified."

"I tracked him down first," she muttered, turning off the main road onto a well-traveled loop.

Persephone played with the buttons on her door before finding the one that operated the window. "Hades won't be concerned about the details," she said, unrolling her window and sitting back in triumph. "Your mere presence places Alex in a precarious position. He, along with Orion and Boreus, do not have the freedoms of higher deities. Their choices are limited through both their station and their connection to each other."

Orion and Boreus.

Charlotte frowned. "Ryan and Bo?"

"Who else?" Persephone asked, playing with the reclining mechanism on her seat. "Alex is loyal to his brothers first, his master second. And his mistress third." She preened. "That's me."

"I figured as much."

Persephone faced her, her stunning features solemn. "He sought you out tonight. Knowing he was in direct violation of his master's decree, Alex came to you. Was drawn to you."

She slowed the truck to a stop. "This is insane," she muttered, sliding her gun back into the holster and snapping it in. "Look, Persephon—"

"Call me Seph, honey."

"Seph," Charlotte echoed in exasperation. "Whether you are who you say you are, or you're one of Alex's hookups that he convinced to back up his story, doesn't change the fact he and I knew we were short-term, whether we like it or not. *Liked* it or not."

The woman collected her long hair into her hands and draped it over her shoulder, patting it smooth as she opened her door. "Well, let's eliminate one of those uncertainties now, shall we? Come."

Rolling her eyes, she turned off the truck and followed her passenger, shining her flashlight on the sand as the woman ran her hand over it.

"Nothing grows in the darkness of Hades," Persephone said, digging her fingers into the ground. "Cerberus is a beast of darkness, an unchanging constant in the underworld. But in human form, my boys bring beauty into a place where beauty is hard to find, and even harder to hold." She tilted her head and looked up at Charlotte. "And sometimes we hold on to that beauty so tightly it loses that which we desire."

Charlotte kept one eye on Persephone's hands as they flitted through the sand.

"We lost Bo to Dionysus's call," she continued, lifting her fingers and watching the grains fall. "Orion's remained a loyal, unchanging force, but his eyes hold no spark. He lives to serve, and accepts his happiness through Hades's hand. And then there's Alex." She smiled. "I've always found his form of defiance fascinating. Total compliance, but on his own internal terms. And those terms have shifted recently, haven't they?"

Charlotte took a step back, steadying her light as Seph lifted one hand from the ground, a fragile vine wrapped around her fingers and inched its way along her delicate wrist.

Watching the vine while tiny buds began to form, Persephone eased more of it from the sand. "There was no spark in his eyes when he was home," she mused, flicking one bud open. "Complete detachment. Except for the brief moment he thought he saw you down there." Tiny pink flowers emerged along the growing vine and Persephone stood. "You're the only thing Alex has ever deemed worthy of raising above all else. Above my wishes. Above Hades's commands. Above his brothers."

"We were nothing more than tem—"

"Temporary? A fling?" Seph laughed, holding the vine out for Charlotte's inspection. "Honey, I'm the daughter of Zeus. I know a fling when I see one." She steadied her hand as Charlotte reached out to touch the delicate flowers. "That boy has had flings with more goddesses and women than even I care to think about. And I'm the goddess of fertility. But this? Honey, he's risking everything he is and everything he's known for nothing more than a kind word from you."

The vine continued to pile at their feet, stretching out across the sand. "Why are you here?"

Persephone knelt down, grasping the vine from the base and crushing it in her fist, staring at it as it browned and shriveled. "This is what we're doing to Alex. He'll be tied to us forever through his birthright, but it's time we lengthen his leash. And I can think of no better woman to pass him to than one who held her own against a feral Pirithous." She passed Charlotte the dead plant and brushed her hands on her skirt.

"Tell him I'll take care of Hades, but I expect frequent visits." She flipped her hair over her shoulder. "We're all that's holding him back. What's holding you?"

Charlotte's mouth opened to respond, snapping shut when the woman vanished, leaving her alone in the desert with a dead plant.

Chapter Thirty-Seven

A LEX SKIDDED TO a stop when he hit the top of the ridge, dust kicking up around him as he scanned the area for midnight hikers. Satisfied he was alone, he padded to his SUV, panting heavily from the exertion of his run but determined to make it home before Charlotte called.

If she called.

He hadn't intended to find her when he'd left the tavern. His plan had been simple—avoid thinking about her for a few hours by indulging in a little freedom. A quick run, a bit of exploring, maybe a rabbit for dessert.

The fact his preferred hunting grounds happened to co-incide with Charlotte's preferred route was purely coincidental.

He took another look around before he transformed, yanking the hatch of the SUV open and grabbing his clothes from his backpack.

As long as she was willing to talk to him, he had a shot.

His stomach rumbled as he drove through the park, a reminder of his failed mission to secure a bite to eat. Double-checking that his phone was charging, he tore onto the highway, watching for signs of a small coupe making its way back to town until he found a fast food drive-through on the main strip.

It wasn't rabbit, but the burger would have to do.

Tossing the food wrappers onto the floor, he punched in the gate code and inched through the trailer park to his site, one eye on his cell until he was inside.

Inside and staring at his silent phone.

Minutes passed, the first hour creeping by at a snail's pace.

Knowing he wouldn't be able to sleep as long as the possibility of her call hung over him, he stripped down and hopped into the shower, keeping his phone within reach.

The shampoo was circling the drain when it rang. Scrambling to dry his hands off, he tapped the green icon. "Hey," he called out over the din of the shower water.

The line was quiet for a moment before her voice came over the speaker. "You sound busy."

Slamming the tap off, he wrapped a towel around his hips and grabbed another off the hook for his hair. "Just washing the desert off," he replied, moving his phone to his bed so he could get dressed.

"Oh." She laughed, a strange nervousness in her voice. "I thought you were at the bar or something."

"Nope," he said, pulling his boxers on. "Just killing time around here pretending not to be staring at the clock on my cell." He hung up the towels and rifled around the bathroom for his brush. "I'm glad you called."

She hummed. "I didn't know I was going to until I did. How did it go at the tavern?"

"Not bad," he said, tugging on a knot and grimacing when the spine of a cholla ripped along his hair. "I hung around for a few hours and helped Thomas out in the kitchen. He wants me to swing by Sunday to let him know if I've decided to stay local or not before he considers hiring me back on."

"So you haven't decided?"

He set his brush down and turned the speaker off, bringing the phone to his ear and lying back on his bed. "Well, I'm kind of caught on that," he stated, deciding in the moment he had nothing to lose. "The only thing keeping me here is the possibility you and I might have another chance. If we do, I'll wash dishes for three bucks an hour if that's what Thomas is offering. If not, I'll head north and crash on Ryan's couch until we find that last guy and then set up shop wherever I need to."

When she didn't respond immediately, his shoulders tensed.

"That's a lot of pressure," she finally said softly. "I don't know how I'm supposed to reply to that."

"You're not." He sighed, turning off the lights. "I just want you to know where you stand with me. I miss you. I miss us. I don't really know if I'm supposed to be tiptoeing around it, or if I'm breaking some weird quasi-relationship rule, but there it is." He glared into the darkness. "And if it helps, hound form is secondary to this one up here. Different story in Hades, but I don't intend to be down there much if you and I... Yeah."

She exhaled. "We kind of walked into this on a timeline. What if things weren't the same without it?"

"And what if they're better?" he countered, sitting up and swinging his legs over the edge of the bed. "Maybe instead of being some random guy with a short shelf life, I could be, I don't know, the one or something." He cringed at the bitter tone of his voice and paced the small floor space. "You know what I mean."

"Oh, wow," she breathed. "I completely forgot how much I talked to Butch. You know what? That's a real dick move. Like eavesdropping."

He ran his hand over his face. "That's what you're focusing on? Dammit, Charlotte. If you're so determined to bring Butch into it, how about zooming in on the amount of time I spent riding around in the back of that truck to make sure you weren't offed by the goddamn Pirithous? Getting one or two hours of sleep a night? Or maybe you could zero in on every time my legs cramped up in the back seat so I could keep those FBI assholes in their place."

"Don't you go acting like you were protecting me from the big, bad, single cops for any reason other than irrational jealousy," she hissed back.

"Of course I was fucking jealous! That's not the point,"

he snarled, releasing the death grip he had on his phone before he crushed it. "I was guarding you. Always. Fucking. Guarding you. I'm a goddamn guard dog, Charlotte!"

She went silent.

He leaned against the kitchen counter, his anger and frustration combusting, leaving nothing but resignation in its wake. "I guess that's it, though, isn't it."

He squeezed his eyes shut as a shuddered breath came over the phone. "I don't know how to separate the two," she said, her voice trembling.

Separate the two.

Her words went straight to his core.

The blessing of his brothers. The faint hope Hades would lengthen his leash.

None of it mattered when he couldn't change what he was.

He sat down on his sofa, resting his elbows on his knees. "Me either. Night, baby."

"Chuck."

Charlotte jolted from her thoughts, blinking rapidly. "Sorry. What?"

Max sighed and tossed a sandwich onto her lap. "I said, we're heading out Saturday for dinner and drinks. You're coming."

She nodded absently, scanning the dark campground for movement. Or Persephone. "I hate these evening shifts."

"Preaching to the choir," he said through a mouthful of food. "Screws over your day and your night. Probably a lot like being married."

She peeked into her sandwich, content to find nothing but ham and cheese. "Easier on the bank account at least." She unbuckled her seat belt and pulled her legs up. "So I've been talking with Alex again." Max motioned for her to continue, barely able to chew the huge bite he'd taken. "Deal breakers are deal breakers, right? Like, if there's something really off about someone, that's it for a relationship, right?"

He swallowed, coughing for a moment. "Like his eyes?"

"What the hell?" she exclaimed. "No. His eyes are very cool. I mean something about him."

"His job?"

Giving Max a flat stare, she took a drink from her water bottle. "What's wrong with his job?"

"Nothing," he replied, shrugging. "I don't know what else. Is he a closet asshole? A drinker? Does he kill bunnies in his spare time?"

"I..." She paused, contemplating the bunny question. "Nothing like that. More like a family issue. A genetic family issue."

Max turned the truck back on, flipping on the headlights. "I thought you didn't want kids."

Buckling back in, she took a bite of her sandwich. "I

don't. Never mind."

"Is it his temper? His feet?"

She tossed her sandwich back into the cooler. "No. And what the hell is wrong with his feet?" When Max didn't respond, she crossed her arms and sat back. "You're just pointing out petty stuff because he's the big fish."

"Want my two cents?" he asked as he pulled onto the pavement. "If everything else about the guy works for you, and it sure as hell seemed to when you were together, why would you trash it over something he can't help? Whatever it is obviously isn't a big enough deal for anyone else to notice, so it can't be that embarrassing."

She turned back to her window, adjusting her hat. "It's not embarrassing. Jeez, Max. But it's something he can't separate from. Something that's ingrained in him."

He slowed to check out a pair of tourists loading their bikes onto their roof. "Then arguing about it is kind of pointless. And kind of vicious."

CHARLOTTE FLUNG HER blanket off, Max's words still haunting her.

Pointless.

Vicious.

With all her focus on her own confusion and uncertainty regarding Alex and everything he'd laid out for her, she hadn't once considered the brashness of her words, how cutting she'd been as she'd openly debated her ability to accept him for existing.

She swung her legs over the edge of her bed and switched on her lamp.

Separate the two.

Me either.

She winced as the resignation in Alex's voice echoed in her head.

It had been three nights since they'd spoken. She had taken to keeping her phone in the kitchen when she went to bed, eliminating the temptation to call him. Text him. Check to see if he'd texted her.

But he hadn't reached out to her. And with his defeated tone playing in her memory, she couldn't blame him.

She wandered into the kitchen, swiping her phone to life and pursing her lips when she saw the time.

Four a.m.

Pulling up Alex's number, she hovered her thumb over the delete button, hesitating as Persephone's words sank into her head.

We're all that's holding him back. What's holding you?

She set her phone down.

Chapter Thirty-Eight

A LEX TOSSED A cloth over his shoulder and held out his hand for the freshly sharpened knife. "I'm getting the hang of this prep work thing," he stated, slamming an onion down and slicing it in half. "Check out the evenness of this dice job."

Thomas glanced over, grunting when he saw Alex's handiwork. "Don't quit your day job."

"If I had a day job, I wouldn't be hanging out here for free on a Saturday night," he snorted, scraping his work into a bowl. "You still insisting I come by tomorrow? Or can we hash this out now?"

Slapping at the orders dangling on the line, Thomas returned to the grill. "Do I look like I have time tonight? No. I said Sunday, I meant Sunday." He squinted at an order and side-eyed him for a moment. "You're done here. Head on out."

Alex set the bowl of onions on the counter beside Thomas and shot the cloth into the hamper in the corner. "See you tomorrow."

He pushed through the kitchen doors, giving a nod to

Daniel as he passed the bar and freezing in his tracks when Max stepped into his path.

"Hey, man!" Max called over the music. "You just get here?"

His eyes darted around the room. "I was helping Thomas in the back. Everyone here?"

"Yeah, Chuck's here." Max grinned. "We're over by the dance floor if you want to come join."

Shaking his head, he locked his attention on the exit. "No thanks. Tell the crew I say hi."

Max planted his feet and flagged Daniel over. "Two tequilas, please." Shifting his focus back to Alex, he tilted his head back slightly and looked him over. "One drink and then you're free to go hide out in your trailer for the rest of the night." He smirked. "Unless you have a date."

"I don't have a date," he muttered. "I've got stuff to do in the morning."

With a shrug, Max passed a twenty to Daniel and handed Alex a shot of tequila. "Whether you join us or not, I'm telling Chuck I saw you. And if you leave without having a drink with us, I'll tell her you were on your way out on a date. Cheers."

He clenched his teeth as Max downed his shot. "Seriously?"

"Try me."

Tugging his wallet from his back pocket, he threw a ten onto the bar. "One vodka Coke, please." He turned to Max.

"I'm not buying your blackmailing ass a drink."

He followed Max through the Saturday crowd, fighting the urge to rub out the knots forming in his shoulders.

"Check out what I dragged over from the trenches," Max announced, grabbing two chairs from an adjoining table and flipping off the patrons when they protested. "Sit."

A chorus of hey-how-are-yous rose from the table, a few unrecognizable faces smiling politely as he gave everyone a quick nod, shaking his hair out of his eyes enough to see but not enough to unblock his view of the stunning brunette sitting beside him. Max immediately launched into a lengthy story about a wounded coyote he'd saved, showing off his bandaged arm to anyone who would look.

Five minutes into his embellished explanation, Charlotte finally chimed in. "Pull off the Band-Aids, you big suck. Show them how injured you really were."

Max reached across Alex and swatted the straw from her drink, sending a small spray into the air. "You're gonna be sorry you were mean to me when I'm foaming at the mouth and you have to put me down like a rabid dog."

Her hand dropped to Alex's leg, startling him. He risked a glance at her, his chest tightening when she squeezed his knee, her dark eyes narrowed at Max in a death glare until they widened and she snatched her hand away.

Max continued to rally sympathy for his cause as Charlotte kept her face angled away from Alex, her fingers tucked neatly under her thighs.

Taking a long sip of his drink, he leaned close to her ear, bracing himself for a hardened rejection. "Looks like I'm not the only guard dog on the premises."

She tensed and stared straight ahead, her lips barely moving as she replied. "Yeah? Well, it's not *that* hard a job, is it? Besides, that was an insulting species-ist statement he made."

Encouraged by the fact she responded at all, he shuffled his chair a fraction closer. "You have better instincts than Bo. More finesse, too."

She bit back a smile and leaned against her seat, nodding at Becky's long-winded story and rolling her eyes at Max. "You think I should consider a career change?"

"I think you should consider a dance," he offered, sitting back until she pushed out of her chair and walked wordlessly to the dance floor.

He scrambled after her, ignoring Max's barking laugh while he closed in on his target. She turned to face him, brows lifting as he put his arms around her waist. "It's not a slow dance."

"Who cares?" he muttered, nudging her arms with his elbows. "We can be that couple everyone rolls their eyes about but secretly wants to be." When her mouth opened to reply, he ducked down to whisper into her ear. "Just because we aren't one, doesn't mean we can't make 'em hate us."

Her arms rose to his neck as she relented. "Do you ever do something and just know it's a huge mistake, but you do it anyway?"

"You mean like every time I see you?" he muttered, tightening his hold when she tensed again. "I'm not kidding. Every step of the way, I've known I was going to regret going deeper in."

She relaxed slightly, her thumbs grazing the back of his neck. "So do you?"

"Regret it?" he asked, looking down at her. "I might in a few hours, but no. Not yet."

She nodded, her gaze locked on the lights behind his shoulder.

He adjusted his hold on her. "How about you? Wishing you weren't so damn good with animals yet?"

"You shouldn't be joking about it," she admonished, her eyes darting among the dancers. "Especially not in public."

"They aren't paying any attention to us." He chuckled. "Besides, I don't want to know the answer."

The song ended, a shrill guitar riff signaling the start of the next one. He released her, the loss of the warmth of her hands on his neck immediately noticeable as he followed her off the floor, grabbing her hand before they reached the table. "I'm going to head out."

She looked up at him in confusion. "Why?"

"Because right now, I'm in a good zone. The ball's still in your court, even if Max tried to force a serve." He glanced over at Max, grinning when Max gave him a crude gesture. "Have fun tonight and try to keep that Neanderthal out of trouble."

She tucked her hands into her back pockets. "'Night, Alex."

✕

CHARLOTTE TOWELED HER hair off and flopped onto the sofa, flicking on the television to keep her company in the darkness. It had been an ordeal, but she'd gotten Max safe and sound to his apartment, even going so far as to remove his shoes for him when he fell facedown onto his bed.

Her duty was done.

She fired off a quick text to Jonas to remind him Becky had his car keys before she settled back in the cushions and tapped on Alex's name. *"So is there an application process to get into the whole guard dog thing?"*

Forcing her attention to the TV, she held her phone in a death grip until it buzzed.

"Informal interview with an observation component. You interested?"

She hesitated for a moment. *"I have some questions."*

Little bubbles rippled across her messenger app as he took his time responding. *"Of course you do. Call?"*

Without thinking, she opened his contact info and placed the call, holding her breath until she heard his voice. "So are these questions numbered?"

"Hi to you, too," she grumbled. "Number one. What happens when you track down the last guy?"

He went quiet for a moment. "Technically, it means a return to the underworld for a reassignment. But I have it on good authority I may be granted a bit of a reprieve."

"So there's a good chance you'll just poof away," she stated, her voice flat despite the sinking in her stomach. "Which would pretty much nullify any other questions I have."

"There's a chance anyone could poof away," he argued. "Hell, you could be killed on the highway to wor—You know what? I can't go there. Yeah, there's a chance I could lose my request for release."

She pushed herself up against the armrest. "Okay. We'll leave that in the irrelevant pile." Alex grunted in response, his mood obviously souring from earlier in the night. "Question two. Do you age?"

"That's a tough one," he muttered, cursing quietly as something clattered in the background. "In the underworld, no. Here, yes, but at a reduced speed. And the longer I go between visits to hell, the faster I age topside. Make sense?"

"So in twenty years, you'll look like you're in your forties if you stay here," she clarified, unsure why it mattered so damn much.

He chuckled. "I suppose you looking ahead twenty years bodes okay for me. Yeah, I'll probably be graying. Maybe sporting a beer gut, too. Next question."

Staring blankly at the TV, she frowned. "Actually, I don't think I have another."

"Then it's my turn," he countered. "Come over."

Her brows shot up. "That's not a question."

"Fine. Come over, please?" he amended.

She paused.

The debate had been long over in her heart, but her head was struggling to keep up. "I need to think about it."

"Don't bother."

Chapter Thirty-Nine

ALEX TOSSED HIS phone onto his bed in frustration, swearing as it bounced off the mattress onto the floor. He hefted his bed up and snatched his duffel bags from the storage underneath. "I don't need this," he snarled, yanking open his closet and slamming his clothes into the first bag.

I need to think about it.

He emptied his drawers onto the pile and zipped the bag closed, sliding it across the floor toward the door and opening the next one, ignoring his buzzing phone beside the bed.

He'd been so certain they'd turned a corner, so convinced when he left the tavern that Charlotte had made up her mind.

I need to think about it.

Knocking everything from his medicine cabinet into the bag, he shoved his wet towels on top and stormed into the kitchen.

He could head north for a few months. Maybe work alongside Bo for a bit until they dealt with the Pirithous. Head down to Hades for a few years, maybe make the trek back to Olympus.

What he couldn't do was this.

It fucking hurt.

Scanning the kitchen, he packed all the sealed food into one cupboard for the next tenant, kneeling down to find a garbage bag for the rest when headlights lit up the trailer. He got to his feet, shoving the bags under the table to avoid tripping him up as he looked out the window.

Charlotte.

She was out of the car before the engine had a chance to shut off fully, one hand yanking the elastic from her ponytail while she knocked hard on his door.

He unlocked it, pushing the door open enough for her to fling it open as she stepped inside and pulled it closed.

"I don't need to think about it."

He crossed his arms and stepped back. "Not anymore you don't."

She tugged her phone from her back pocket, her chest heaving. "I've been calling nonstop for fifteen minutes."

He bent down to grab the abandoned garbage bag and snapped it open. "And I've been busy."

Her eyes darted around the trailer and she took another step in. "Alex."

"I know," he snarled, hurt and frustration overtaking his control. "You have questions. You want guarantees. You have reservations. Well, I have nothing more to hand over, Charlotte. You already have it all." He leaned against the fridge. "Just go, okay? Text me when you get home so I know you made it safe."

She held her ground, her dark eyes narrowing. "You're angry."

Running his hands over his face, he rolled his shoulders out. "I'm not angry," he groaned, her proximity destroying whatever rage had been building. "Dammit, Charlotte. Can we just not do this anymore? Maybe just shake hands, go our separate ways, and chalk the past few months up to bad astrological signs or something?"

"Is that real, too?"

He dropped his arms. "Seriously?"

She walked up to him and intertwined her fingers with his, tightening her hold when he recoiled. "I'm sorry." She reached up and pushed his hair behind his ear. "After you hung up, it hit me. All these questions I have? And trust me, there are a lot more than you can imagine. I want to ask them. But not like this." She waved her hand over the chaotic mess of the trailer. "I want to ask them when we're driving to the mall, or when we're picking up groceries, or when I'm kicking your ass at the gym."

She gave him a cheerful smile and scooped up his other hand, undeterred by his sullen silence. "Though no matter how many times I ask, I really don't want to know anything about your trail of goddesses."

He blinked. "What?"

"The goddesses notching your bedpost. I'll ask, but you

cannot tell."

He stared down at her, his mind firing in fifty directions, none of them involving goddesses. "Seriously?"

She stepped up flush to him and released his hands, wrapping her arms around his waist and dropping her forehead to his chest. "You aren't the only one with a jealous streak," she mumbled into his shirt, nudging his arms with her elbows.

The scent of her shampoo started to cloud his head. "Godde... So what are we doing here?"

"Getting together?"

He held his arms away from her, gripping the wall and the back of the dinette. "Not if you're still unsure, we're not," he stated, his voice stronger than his resolve.

She released her hold and leaned back, cupping his chin in her hands. "Absolutely certain on my end," she replied, rising up on her toes and tilting his head to the side.

When her lips hit his throat, his hands flexed. "And if I'm not certain?"

"Then I'll get a good dose of karma, won't I?" she whispered, trailing her lips to his ear. "I'll give you a few days to think about it."

Screw. That.

She had barely backed away when his arms locked around her and he dove for her lips. "If you're game, I'm game," he murmured before slipping his tongue into her mouth, his knees almost buckling when her fingers wove into his hair and she held him to her.

Any finesse he had was drowned out by an intense urgency to be closer to the woman who was roughly shoving his shirt up his stomach with one hand and yanking the neckline down with the other. The snapping of seams was drowned out by his own panting as her tongue moved across his collarbone and her fingers inched their way under the band of his boxers.

"Whoa," he gasped as she gripped him. "What's the rush?"

She released him long enough to pull her shirt over her head and toss it onto the sofa. "Time four," she breathed, biting her lip when he flung his own shirt onto the floor. "I'll never get bored of this view."

Backing her up, he gave the counter a quick shake to check how secure it was before he hooked his thumbs in her yoga pants and shoved them down her hips. "You plan on getting this view a lot?" he asked, his fingers grazing her bare skin and sending his lust into overdrive.

"Hell, yes," she panted, untangling her arms from the cage he'd placed around her and pushing his boxers down. Her foot slid up the back of his leg, her toes hooking into the band of his boxers and pulling them to the floor.

He lifted her onto the counter and glanced down, shaking his head. "Nope. Don't want to know where you practiced that." He ducked his head down to kiss her, his heart pounding as her knees parted. "You sure you're up for crossing into time four territory?" he murmured, kissing his way to her ear.

"We practiced enough for it during time three, didn't we?" she panted, her head falling back as he pushed inside her. "Oh. Yeah."

Her legs crossed over his hips, her heels digging into his ass as he pumped into her with excruciating slowness. He locked one hand on to the sink, the other slipping under the cup of her bra. "I have the control of a fucking teenager with you," he breathed into her ear, running his tongue along the shell when she whimpered in response. "We're going to need to practice for time five a lot to save my ego."

She laughed, her center tightening around him.

"Whoa," he gasped, pulling out of her warmth and sliding his fingers through her folds.

Her hips rocked against his hand while he worked her, his own body thrumming on the cusp as her nails dug into his shoulders.

He dropped his head into the crook of her neck. "You have no idea how often I've thought about this," he muttered, groaning when she trailed one hand up his spine and pulled lightly on his hair. "And that. Fuck."

Her core started to flutter around his fingers, her breath hitching as he sped up his movements. "Lex... I..." She wrapped one arm around his neck, her hips bucking as he pushed back into her heat.

He gripped her ass as she came, clenching his teeth while

he pounded into her.

No way was he going to miss out on this sensation by falling over the cliff himself.

When her thighs finally relaxed their hold on his hips, he released inside her, his own voice sounding miles away as he cursed with the intensity. He was vaguely aware of the sharp tugging of his hair, a move that sent his hips slamming into her as a second wave washed over him.

CHARLOTTE COMBED HER fingers through Alex's hair while his chest heaved, his head buried in her neck. "So you like that, do you?" she asked, grinning when he struggled to push himself up, his eyes glazed and unfocused.

"Uh, yeah." He looked around the trailer as he straightened, easing her off the counter and using the fridge to balance himself, smirking when he stumbled. "Definitely yes."

She tugged her yoga pants on and scoured the small living area for her phone.

"What are you doing?" he asked, frowning at her covered legs.

She snatched her cell off the floor, checking for cracks in the screen. "Finding the closest place that does takeout breakfasts," she stated, punching in her request on her browsing app. When he exhaled loudly, she looked over at him, admiring the view as he pulled his boxers over his slim hips. "Hungry?"

"Always." He flopped onto the sofa and ran his hands through his hair. "I thought you were taking off."

She froze midtype. "You want me to?"

"No!" He leaned forward and wrapped his arms around her, resting his forehead on her stomach. "No. I was just...yeah. Give me a second and I'll go with you to pick it up." He gave her a quick squeeze and stood. "We coming back here?"

Sifting through the restaurant options, she nodded. "I like your place better than mine," she said absently, flipping through a menu. When he didn't move, she glanced up at him and smiled. "Pass me my shirt?"

A strange look crossed his face before he reached across the dinette and handed Charlotte her shirt. "Find a good place?"

"Here," she said, setting her phone down and sighing as he pulled his own shirt over his head. "You need pants."

ALEX PROPPED HIS head up on his wrist and watched Charlotte as she slept, her face scrunching up every so often before she'd resettle with a huff.

Marry her.

The mantra had been playing in his head since they'd

eaten their lukewarm breakfast in bed, his heart having recovered from the spike of adrenaline that had coursed through him when she had started dressing.

He'd been so certain she was taking off, spooked by second thoughts. His stomach had sunk, the euphoria of minutes earlier replaced by a wave of nausea as he watched her casually flip through her phone, oblivious to how dark his thoughts were sinking.

But it had also been that moment that solidified exactly how he felt about her.

A soft knock on his door yanked him from the moment. He eased off the bed and padded to the door, opening it slowly and freezing as his mistress came into view.

She smiled as she pushed past him and arched her neck to look into his bedroom. "Oh, good. She smartened up."

"She what?"

Seph reached up and tucked a strand of hair behind his ear. "Did she give you my message?"

A chill ran through his veins. "You hunted her down."

"Appeared to her," Persephone corrected haughtily. "Hunted her down. I'm not Athena."

Stepping between his mistress and Charlotte, he eyed Seph as she ran her fingers over his counter. "We can barter," he said, unable to hide the plea in his voice. "Keep Ryan and Bo out of this, and I'll sign on for anything. Anything. Just give me a few decades, Seph."

"Silly girl," Persephone huffed. "Probably waiting for the

right time to talk or some ridiculousness." Lifting a perfect brow, she scanned the dinette bench and perched on the edge, arranging her skirt with excruciating slowness. "I expect visits alongside your brothers no more than two months apart to maintain your youthful appearance. Obviously, she can't join you yet, but absence can be good in small doses, as I can personally attest."

He stared at her.

"Your mission continues to take priority. That I couldn't negotiate. But I was able to eliminate any punishment on the condition Charlotte accepts the pantheon both here and in the afterlife."

His jaw dropped as he took in the enormity of Persephone's words. "You..."

"You're welcome. Talk it over with Charlotte and I'll check in on you two in a week." She rose to her feet and ran her hand over his chest. "You're so lucky you're pretty."

Chapter Forty

CHARLOTTE SMILED POLITELY at Daniel as he handed her a cup of coffee, sliding off her chair to join Alex and Thomas at the back booth. "Why don't I hang out over there while you two talk?" she offered.

"Stay, kid," Thomas grunted, moving over to give her room and watching with interest when Alex stood and she slid in on his side. "So I take it you're hanging around for a while."

Alex nodded, his hand resting on her knee, a move that didn't go unnoticed by the elderly bar owner. "Looks like it. How do I get hired back on here?"

Thomas leaned back in the booth and spread his arms across the back of the seat. "I have a full-time bartender and two part-timers coming on later this week," he stated, nodding at Daniel. "I'm also in the market for a cook." When Alex opened his mouth, Thomas grimaced. "Not you, obviously. You can't cook."

"Okay," Alex said slowly, glancing over at her. "You're saying you don't need any more staff."

"Nope." Thomas pulled his phone from his pocket and

set it down, swiping it to life and angling it to her. "See that? Cute little thing, isn't he?"

She grinned at the photo of an angry baby, sitting awkwardly in a car seat. "Oh, he's sweet! Grandson?"

"Yes, he is," Thomas stated proudly, showing Alex. "I showed you him before."

Alex nodded, looking over the picture. "He's getting big. Walking yet?"

Thomas set his phone down and clasped his hands. "That's the problem, Alex. He's not walking yet. Or talking. But he will be soon. And I'm aiming to be around when it happens." He settled back in his seat. "The problem we have here is I don't want to be working my fingers to the bone anymore. I need someone to oversee the place. Someone who knows what they're doing, knows the business enough to get by, and who needs the job."

Charlotte met Alex's eyes, the disappointment in them nearly breaking her heart.

Alex cleared his throat. "I suppose my documentation problem puts that out of my reach."

"Well, no," Thomas said, waving off Daniel when he walked by to check on them. "If we were to come to an arrangement, I could maybe see my way to paying you out of my personal accounts. Paying the taxes through my name. Of course, it would mean you'd have no social security benefits or medical coverage. May not mean much to you now, but it will when you're my age."

Alex glanced at her. "Yeah?"

"Definitely."

He squeezed her knee and looked at Thomas. "I'd love to. When can I start?"

"We're interviewing for the kitchen in three days," he stated. "Your job is to stand behind me and look threatening. Weed out the criers. Weaklings would never survive a Friday happy hour rush."

ALEX EASED OFF the highway into the park, pulling over before he lost connection. "Nothing? A whole month and nothing? How's that even possible in the age of the internet?"

Ryan sighed, muttering something under his breath about the grease stains on his walls. "Just dead end after dead end," he replied, exasperated. "No social media, no digital footprint at all. Unless he's operating under an alias, the guy has no online presence whatsoever," he grunted, a loud bang echoing through the phone. "I'm going to kill your brother one of these days."

"Do it." He laughed. "What now?"

"Boots. Overalls. Grease. Dirt. I can see the path he takes through here, because it's etched into the carpet." Ryan's voice became more muffled. "You should see this. I'll take pics and send them."

He glanced in his rearview mirror to ensure he wasn't blocking anyone's way. "At least he's still holding a job."

"He could be holding a job and living with you," Ryan countered.

"Ah, yeah, no," he muttered. "Charlotte's actually moving in with me until we find a place on the edge of town."

Ryan went silent for a moment. "A little quick, isn't it?"

Grabbing his phone from the passenger seat, he switched it off the speaker. "We've discussed that. A lot. Hell, even Seph's had her say. And it's not like we're eighteen-year-old kids."

"How's Charlotte dealing with the whole pantheon thing?" Ryan pressed.

He groaned and rolled his eyes. "Fine. Seph comes by every week for lessons, and to give her opinion on everything that doesn't involve her."

"That sucks."

"It's a small price to pay," he argued, the temptation to hang up becoming strong. "I'm pulling into the park now, so I better go."

Ryan exhaled loudly. "You two going to play fetch?"

He pulled his phone from his ear and looked down at the number for a moment. "Seriously?"

"She's not still trying to feed you bagged dog food, is she?" Ryan's voice had gone from mild annoyance to a hint of humor. "That smell was horrendous."

He closed his eyes and groaned. "Please tell me Bo

doesn't know about that."

"Of course not," Ryan said. "He'd just take it to the stupid level and it wouldn't be funny anymore. Did you tell her how demeaning that is?"

"Not in so many words," he muttered. "But, yeah, I told her. I'll do anything for that woman. But never that again."

Ryan chuckled. "When does she move in?"

"Thursday."

"You're in for a big change," Ryan warned. "Women don't live like we do. You've seen Seph's rooms."

He thought back to the opulent decor and rows of armoires packed to the brim with clothes and shoes and jewelry he wasn't sure he'd ever seen her wear. "It'll be fine."

Ryan's laugh barked over the phone. "I'm sure it will be. Good luck, brother. I'll call if I find out anything new."

Setting his phone down, he pulled back onto the road and followed the paved trail to a secluded path where he could pull over and transform. He got out of the SUV and scanned the area, sliding a large collar around his neck and checking the time.

More than enough time to hunt first.

CHARLOTTE HANDED THE cooler over to Max, smirking when he peeked inside. "That's cheating."

"I said I'd bring lunch," she stated. "I never said I'd make it."

Max lifted the takeout containers one by one and examined them, passing the grilled cheese over to Charlotte and hunching over the rest. "You sure Alex didn't spit in this?"

Thinking over the amount of ribbing Alex had endured from Max over the past month, she shrugged. "Possible. Does it matter?"

"It should," he replied, taking a bite of the BLT, "but it doesn't."

She wrinkled her nose and dove into her own meal. "Seems so quiet around here now, doesn't it?"

"Good riddance," he snorted, alternating between the containers. "FBI breathing down my neck for the past five months? No thanks. I'll take my chances with the serial killer. Besides, he's probably moved on."

She hummed in agreement. "Speaking of moving, you're helping me Thursday after work."

"Says you. I'm going drinking."

Knocking the fry from his hand, she narrowed her eyes and tilted her hat back. "It'll take three loads with your truck, a billion with my car."

He muttered under his breath, bending down to scoop the fry off the floor and inspecting it before popping it in his mouth. "Why isn't Alex doing it? He's the one getting laid on a regular basis. Let him haul your crap down those stairs."

"He's working," she replied, ignoring the rest of Max's complaint. "Two trips to the storage unit, one to the trailer.

That'll take an hour."

"You're buying me food after," he conceded. "And three drinks."

Satisfied with their arrangement, she eased back onto the road, setting the rest of her sandwich aside for later. "Keys or Skull Rock?"

"Better hit the Rock," he mumbled through a full mouth. "It's been stupid busy there this week."

They drove through the park slowly, pulling over periodically to pick up abandoned coffee cups and grocery bags. Skull Rock was crawling with tourists, their phones angled toward the unique structure from all sides as the braver people shimmied along the stone. Max waved her off when she got out of the truck, leaving him to digest in the air-conditioned vehicle.

She wandered the perimeter of the attraction, nodding at friendly sightseers and scooping discarded cigarette butts from the sand until a familiar beast jogged over to her, startling the young man crouched at her side to capture the perfect photo of the rock with his phone.

"He's friendly," she called to the poor kid as he backed away, eyes wide. She glanced down at Alex and looped the leash onto her wrist. "You have to stop doing that."

He nuzzled her hand, panting.

She smirked. "You aren't used to running that far anymore, are you? Stop eating out of the fry basket." She pulled her phone from her pocket and checked the time. "You have two hours before work. I hope you parked close."

Padding alongside her, he scanned the area, his ears twitching with the multitudes of voices.

He trotted up to the truck with her, sidling up to Max's side and rising up on his hind legs, barking once and dropping down to all fours when Max jumped, cursing a blue streak behind the muffled protection of the closed windows. Pleased with the reaction, he nudged her for a quick ear scratch before he took off back over across the desert, head down on the trail of a rabbit.

It was the one thing she was still trying to get over.

"I hate that dog," Max growled, throwing handfuls of fries from the floor into the empty takeout container. "And it hates me. You can see it. One of these days, it's going to rip my throat out."

She rolled her eyes and flipped on her turn signal. "He is not." She grinned at him. "Unless you piss me off."

ALEX GLANCED AT the time, pausing his beer count to start the coffee. "Hey, Dan. Did we have an influx of old guys in here this week?"

"Golf tournament," Daniel called out, loading his tray and heading onto the floor.

"Right," he muttered, adding another case of the lager to his order. He turned his attention to the hard liquor, eying the remnants of the open bottles until Charlotte arrived, Max's voice announcing their presence.

Penning in the last of the order, he turned to her, grinning as he took in her sullen face. "I take it I was right about how many pairs of shoes you could tuck into that cupboard?"

"Just give me a coffee and keep your rightness to yourself," she grumbled, slipping him a little tongue when he leaned over the counter to kiss her. "And I'm paying for whatever dumbass over here orders."

Max waved cheerfully. "She's all yours, man. Be warned, she's discovered the space limitations of RV bathrooms."

He passed Max a beer and slid the liquor order under the till for morning. "We've still got a week left in the month," he said, walking around the bar to stand beside Charlotte. "We could always flip everything to your apartment."

"There are two cabinet doors," she stated, resting her head against his arm. "Why have two when one is just plumbing? It's dishonest and deceitful."

"Both of those, eh?" he teased. "I'm serious. We can change our minds."

She took a sip of her coffee and shook her head. "No way. That new development on the edge of town will be listing soon and I don't want to be locked into another lease on that apartment. It would dip into our travel fund." She trailed her fingers up the inside of his arm, sending a shiver through him. "Oh, and I rearranged some of your stuff that didn't fit. Seph said you wouldn't mind."

Thinking through the short list of items he owned, he frowned. "Do I still live there?"

"Barely." She smiled. "When are you off?"

Looking around the room, he did a quick rundown of what was left to do for the night. "An hour or so. Are you waiting for me or heading home?"

When she bounced in her seat with a rare giddiness, it took him a moment to realize why.

Home.

He grinned. "You're waiting."

ALEX FOLLOWED CHARLOTTE into their trailer, scanning the place slowly as she talked a mile a minute about what she'd moved where to accommodate the influx of stuff in the small space. "All I need to know is where's my phone charger, where's the coffee, and where are my boots?"

She hopped over to him, opening a cupboard to reveal the coffee and a plethora of small appliances he didn't recognize and was certain she didn't know how to use. "Charger's by the bed," she replied, pointedly ignoring his last questions in favor of showing him a photo of a rolling storage unit she swore would tuck under the kitchen table.

"My boots?"

She stepped up tight to him and ran her hands through

his hair, a move he was becoming very accustomed to. "Well, my boots aren't as sturdy as yours, so mine are down there in the shoe cabinet. Yours are in the belly box outside."

He cocked a brow. "All right. Show me the rest."

Making her way through every possible hiding place, she revealed crammed cabinets and cupboards he hadn't even known he had. Marbles lay sprawled out on the sofa, opening one eye as he passed her and averting her gaze when he growled softly.

He was, after all, still the alpha. Even if his boots were relegated to the exterior of the trailer and the damn cat had a litter box in the cabinet where his stereo once sat.

Charlotte led him to the bathroom and paused. "Remember that right now we have doubles of some things."

She sat on the edge of the bed and bit her lip as he stuck his head into the bathroom, shrugging when he saw the cluttered counter. "We'll just move all that into the vanity and it's fine." He flicked open the mirrored door to prove his point, closing it without a word and checking the cabinet under the sink. "If you ever doubt my commitment to you, I want you to remember that you tucked the razor I put to my face under the drain trap."

"Promise," she said, her giddiness returning as he closed the bathroom door and looked around the bedroom. "I had to move a few of your shirts over there to get my work clothes in the closet, but I think I made it all fit."

She opened each door with a flourish, revealing stacks of

clothes he couldn't remember ever seeing before.

"Do you even wear those?" he asked, pointing at a pile of bright T-shirts neatly folded and stacked to the top of a cabinet.

"I might."

He licked his lips and scanned the room. "I'm impressed. You made it work."

She crawled across the bed and rose up on her knees, running her hands up his chest. "You sure you're good with this? We aren't moving too fast, are we? I'm not pushing you on this, am I? I mean, we're slowing down after this, so—"

"If anyone's pushing anything, it's Seph." He grinned, thinking back to the week prior when his mistress had stormed into the tavern demanding to know why a month had gone by without a wedding, completely aghast to learn human relationships didn't progress at the same speed those of the gods did.

"I dislike these self-imposed timelines, Alexandros. Love is love and I want an excuse to wear a new dress."

It had taken a lot of reassurances that her hard-fought negotiations with Hades hadn't been in vain.

Recalling the heated discussion, his eyes widened and they flicked to the small drawer beside his bed.

Charlotte followed his panicked gaze. "Oh, I didn't touch anything in there. I figured that was your personal space."

"Ah, yeah," he said, toeing off his shoes and kicking

them into the kitchen, smirking when her attention flashed away from the drawer toward his sneakers, her eyes narrowing. He bent down to kiss her, making a mental note to move the engagement ring from his bedside drawer to the safe at work for a few more months.

Epilogue

ALEX BIT BACK a groan as Seph straightened the hem of his sleeve and turned, continuing her appraisal of the grounds of his new home. "Perhaps I should have supplied you with a bust of myself to auction off instead of one of Dio's. Then you could have purchased a dwelling with brighter grass."

"It's a desert, Seph." He sighed, his mood lifting as Charlotte's coupe pulled into the driveway, Max's truck hot on her bumper. "Do you at least like the house?"

Looking up at him, she reached up and tucked his hair behind his ear. "You did well, honey. I'll be by another day to see what I can do with the grounds."

Charlotte skipped up alongside them, curtseying quickly before linking her arm in his and kissing his cheek. "So? Don't you love it? Did Alex show you the paint chips we were looking at?"

Persephone lifted a perfectly sculpted brow, stepping aside as Max jogged over to them and openly stared at the goddess. "He informed me pink was off the table," she stated, hands on her hips. "I recommend holding out on the gray palette he favors until he relents."

"I'm right here, Seph," he reminded her, wrapping his arm around Charlotte's waist and pulling her in tight.

"Then you understand you are both outnumbered and overpowered." When Max opened his mouth to speak, Seph tilted her head and gave him a devastating smile. "Young Max here agrees with me, don't you, dear?"

"Damn right, I do."

With a quick kiss on Max's cheek and a wink at Charlotte, Seph strode out of the yard.

"You have the hottest MILF in town, Alex," Max muttered, finally tearing his eyes of the gate the goddess had disappeared through. "I'm dropping your boxes onto the driveway and taking off." He cracked his knuckles with a sly grin. "I gotta date with the receptionist from the dealership doing my brakes."

Charlotte swatted at her partner's shoulder before she rose up on her toes and wrapped her arms around Alex's neck. "Thanks for the help, Max," she called out, her attention snapping back to Alex as she licked her lips and kissed his jawline. "I'm willing to give on the paint if you don't put up a fight about those pink throw cushions I want for the living room." Before he could respond, she pressed against him and wound her fingers through his hair. "And I get to pick the bedding."

Glancing over his shoulder to ensure Max was out of view, he slid his hands up her ribs, ghosting his fingers over the sides of her breasts. "Do I get to decide how we break in that new bedding?"

"Of course."

"Can we have a few practice sessions before it arrives?" he murmured as he nuzzled her throat, the brown fence of the property line catching his eye. "It wouldn't be too cheesy if we painted that fence white, would it?"

The End

If you enjoyed this book, please leave a review at your favorite online retailer! Even if it's just a sentence or two it makes all the difference.

Thanks for reading *Junkyard Dog* by Katja Desjarlais!

Discover your next romance at TulePublishing.com.

TULE
PUBLISHING

If you enjoyed *Junkyard Dog*,
you'll love these other paranormal Tule books!

Blood Bound by Traci Douglass

Animal Instincts by Patricia Rosemoor

What the Moon Saw by D.L. Koontz

Available now at your favorite online retailer!

About the Author

Katja Desjarlais is a music teacher by day and a paranormal romance writer by moonlight. She is an unapologetic music addict with an obsession for bad Bach puns despite her irrational aversion to Baroque. Her favorite words include 'plethora' and 'dapper', and she is physically repulsed by the word 'moist'. Katja's interest in the paranormal can be traced to her early childhood movie choices and to the collection of books she has stored on her phone for reading emergencies.

Desjarlais lives in northern Canada with her husband, three children, and polydactyl cat. Her summers are spent driving across North America with her family, while the long Canadian winters are made more bearable by attending heavy metal concerts.

Thank you for reading

Junkyard Dog

If you enjoyed this book, you can find more from all our great authors at TulePublishing.com, or from your favorite online retailer.

TULE
PUBLISHING